Where It All Lands

It All Lands

JENNIE WEXLER

WEDNESDAY BOOKS
NEW YORK

FOR J

AND FOR ANYONE WHO HAS EVER
WISHED FOR A DO-OVER

First published in the United States by Wednesday Books, an imprint of St. Martin's Publishing Group

www.wednesdaybooks.com

Library of Congress Cataloging-in-Publication Data

Names: Wexler, Jennie, author.
Title: Where it all lands / Jennie Wexler.
Description: First edition. | New York : Wednesday Books, 2021.
Identifiers: LCCN 2021005013 | ISBN 9781250750044 (hardcover) |
    ISBN 9781250750051 (ebook)
Subjects: CYAC: Friendship—Fiction. | Love—Fiction. | Choice—Fiction. |
    Fathers—Fiction.
Classification: LCC PZ7.1.W43755 Wh 2021 | DDC [Fic]—dc23
LC record available at https://lccn.loc.gov/2021005013

Our books may be purchased in bulk for promotional, educational, or business use. Please contact your local bookseller or the Macmillan Corporate and Premium Sales Department at 1-800-221-7945, extension 5442, or by email at MacmillanSpecialMarkets@macmillan.com.

First Edition: 2021

10 9 8 7 6 5 4 3 2 1

PART ONE

HEADS

CHAPTER 1

Stevie

DECEMBER

The entire high school fills the church, but he's not here. He's not anywhere. The football team shuffles in late and leans against the back wall. A low murmur hangs in the air, the sound of sadness. His family walks in and their faces are vacant, eyes hollow. The coffin is closed. I heard it was too gruesome for an open casket and I don't want to think about what that really means. Whispers from the row behind me are like hissing snakes, relentless and fraying my nerves. I try to tune it out, but bits and pieces worm through my ears.

The accident . . . So young . . . So unfair . . .

I close my eyes, squeezing the lids together to stop tears. When I open them, the church is blurry, like a dream, like maybe this isn't happening. If only it wasn't.

"Stevie," he says, his voice brittle. I grab hold of his hand, afraid if I let go, I won't be able to stay here. I need his hand, like an anchor to my seat. "Just breathe."

I inhale deeply, but my throat catches, and my vision blurs

again. One tear slides to my cheek, like a single raindrop before a storm, and then all at once it spills out of me. My chest heaves, the sobs escaping faster than I can catch them. My entire body screams, like I'm in a free fall, with no ground below.

I heard . . . A parent's worst nightmare . . . Pray for them . . . God, make them stop.

His hand squeezes mine as the priest walks in, and the room falls silent except for the crying, so much crying. I can't catch my breath. The stained-glass windows bend and distort as my mind struggles to make sense of this, my very first funeral. All the moments that led to this one flash before me as beads of sweat break out along my hairline. I squeeze his hand, holding on so I don't faint, wishing I could go back to the beginning.

CHAPTER 2

Drew

4 MONTHS EARLIER: AUGUST

I delete the voice mail without listening. Five total. One by one I delete the text messages, my fingers tapping furiously at the screen. An overwhelming urge to smash my phone on the kitchen tile crashes through me, but before I get the chance, Mom puts her hand on my shoulder. I shove my phone into the back pocket of my jeans and flip up my hood, hunching over the white marble countertop. She tugs the strings of my sweatshirt but won't look me in the eye.

"Your dad called for you."

"Tell him to go fuck himself," I say calmly. No reaction from Mom. It's like she doesn't have the energy.

"Said he couldn't reach you on your phone."

I don't respond. Mom opens the Sub-Zero and sighs, pulling a half-filled pitcher of orange juice off the barren shelf. The liquid splashes on the marble as she pours a glass. She rips a paper towel from the roll and wipes it up, a message flashing across the Apple Watch on her wrist.

"I'm going to be late," she says, pushing an oversize pair of sunglasses up her fake nose. She bends to kiss me on the cheek, but I turn away. I down the juice, grab my keys, and stand, a good head taller than Mom.

"Have a good day," she says as I head for the door, which makes me laugh because it's been exactly one hundred and eighty-three days since I've had a good day. If Mom ever asked, she'd know. But Mom never talks about the day Dad left. Since then, she hasn't talked much at all.

I back the Jeep down my driveway as Ed Sheeran croons on the radio about wanting to go home. It's all pointless, this longing for a place you once knew. You can't get it back. No matter how hard you try.

I turn down Sheeran and swerve into the driveway next door. Some guy walking a golden retriever shoots me a dirty look as I honk twice. Yeah, I know it's early. The huge iron gates swing open, revealing Shane jogging down the drive-way, a green backpack swinging from his shoulder. He turns, two drumsticks sticking out of his back pocket, and waves at Kathy. She stands in the bay window holding a cup of coffee. Our morning ritual started in elementary school, and it stuck. Except back then we boarded a big yellow bus, sporting matching light-up sneakers.

"You do realize it's August," Shane says, eyeing my sweatshirt as he settles into the passenger seat. He wedges his backpack and drumsticks between his feet.

"Didn't want my mom to see." Not that she would have noticed. She hasn't noticed anything in months.

"You actually did it?"

Shane grabs my arm and pushes up my sleeve, taking in the Roman numerals tattooed in black ink on the inside of my wrist—the number that represents a date. His eyes shift to the side, lost in our shared memory.

"That was a good day," he says, gazing out the window.

"A great fucking day."

"I wouldn't go that far. You almost . . ."

"But I didn't." I *didn't*. That's why it was a great day.

Shane unzips his backpack and pulls out a water bottle, taking a long sip. A blue stuffed animal peeks out from behind the zipper, a tuft of fuzzy hair at the top. He shoves it back in.

"What the hell is that?" I ask, gesturing at his bag.

"Nothing." Shane pulls down the brim of his blue EMT cap, almost covering his eyes. Ever since he started volunteering with the squad last year, that hat has become a permanent fixture on his head.

"Yeah, right." I elbow Shane and grab his bag, pulling out the stuffed toy, a powder blue Aladdin genie with a Cheshire cat grin. "Are you kidding me with this?"

"What? It's this season's theme," Shane says like it's normal to be carrying around a stuffed genie.

"I'm aware it's this season's theme. But c'mon. Might as well beg Brent Miller to kick your ass."

"I don't care about Brent Miller," Shane says, snatching the genie from me and shoving it in his bag, "I thought it would be cool if I attached him to my quads."

"Do not attach that thing to your quads." I cringe at the thought of Brent grabbing the genie and ripping into Shane. Brent's called Shane every name in the book, none of which I care to repeat.

Shane sighs, glancing at me. He smirks and grabs a penny from the middle console, flipping the coin over in his palm.

"Heads, the genie stays. Tails, the genie goes," Shane says. A familiar spark settles in his hazel eyes, reminding me of the day that started our heads or tails routine. We were little, probably six and seven, our skinny bodies squeezed together and balanced at the end of a high diving board. Blue pool water lapped below as we fought over who would get to jump first. I don't remember who initiated it, but we were both pushing, clawing at each other like rabid squirrels until we fell headfirst into the water, narrowly missing the cement edge of the pool. Freaked us out. From then on, whenever we disagreed, we flipped a coin.

"Leave it up to the universe," Shane says, tossing the coin, catching it, and flipping it on the back of his hand.

Fuck the universe. If Shane attaches a stuffed animal to his drum set it's an open invitation, the punch line to a joke Brent Miller is just gunning to tell.

"Heads," Shane says, a silly grin stretching to his ears as he reveals the penny. "Genie stays."

I shake my head as I turn up Sheeran who still *can't wait to go home.* Shane groans because he hates everything on the radio—but my car, my tunes. I back out of the driveway, and head down our street lined with oak trees, morning light slicing through the leaves.

As I drive through town, Shane's quiet, his fingers tapping a beat on the window. I know he's still thinking about the stuffed genie and wondering if I'm right, which I am. Deep down he knows I am. And he knows I'm still thinking about it too, even though we haven't said a word since Shane's driveway. That's one of the cool things about our friendship, the way we can read each other's minds. The way I don't have to talk if I don't want to. Except now I can't stay quiet, not with the beginning of school looming over us, stealing away our Brent-free summer.

"You know I got your back, no matter what," I say, my

eyes fixed on the road. Shane doesn't say anything at first, but he stops drumming his fingers on the window.

"I can take care of myself." His voice is soft, like he doubts his words.

"I know," I say. "But I'm also here, okay?"

Shane's quiet as he stares out the window. Without turning to me he holds out his fist and I tap his knuckles with mine.

"You talk to your dad yet?" Shane asks, and my empty stomach turns at his deliberate change of topic.

"Not talking about it," I say. "Stellar deflection, by the way."

"Fair enough. And thank you." Shane's fingers tap dance on the window again as I will myself to think of anything besides Brent and Dad, but I'm coming up short. I'm so caught up in this relentless mind loop that I almost miss the stop sign at the corner. My heart seizes in my chest as I slam on the brakes, nearly blowing through the intersection. Shane grabs the door handle, bracing himself as I skid to a stop. He turns to me with concern, but I rub my eyes, playing it off as a rough night of sleep.

"Sorry," I mutter as I continue through the intersection, wishing more than anything that I could quiet all the noise in my head.

When we get to school, I pull into my usual spot and throw the Jeep in park. Shane grabs his backpack and drumsticks, opening the door before I cut the engine.

"We're late," he says, hopping down from the Jeep. A mess of notes and chords floats through the air from the back field. I can't see them, but I can sure as hell hear them. I shrug my sweatshirt off and chuck it in the trunk.

"I'll meet you out there," Shane yells, booking it to practice. He can be such a kiss-ass sometimes but at least he's sincere about it. It's not like he's trying to get ahead—he genuinely likes being early, doing the right thing. I wish I had that kind of drive. Instead I reluctantly trail after him.

My pace slows as I spot an unfamiliar girl sitting on the curb, right in my path. A brown sax case rests next to her, like a piece of luggage. It's obvious she's new, her unsure eyes darting around the parking lot. Her eyes are dark, kind of like mine, but framed in long lashes. No doubt about it, she's pretty. So pretty, I wonder how Shane was able to jog right past her, oblivious. Rays of light weave through her long brown hair as she pushes it off her shoulders. My body relaxes for the first time all morning, thoughts of Dad and Brent Miller mercifully falling to the back of my mind. When she notices me, she straightens up, like she's been waiting for me. She reminds me of a mysterious character in a Bradbury novel. Her deep eyes grab hold of mine, a silent introduction instantly jolting me wide awake.

"Stevie," she says when I ask for her name, tucking a strand of thick hair behind her ear.

Like Stevie Nicks, I think, but don't say. I bet she gets that all the time. I bet it's really annoying.

A white BMW honks at me, followed by a random hand waving out the window. Football players and cheerleaders make their way to practice, everyone amped up for the new school year, even though we don't officially start until next week. They're all yelling my name and waving. I nod but they don't care about me. I used to think they did when we were little, but unless I'm talking about Dad, they stop paying attention. So now I don't pay much attention either.

"You here for band practice?" I ask, tapping Stevie's sax case with my foot.

"I went inside but no one was there." Her eyes shift from the school to the field to the parking lot. Everywhere but me.

"Just follow the painful music." I gesture at the back field and she laughs, the kind of airy laugh that makes me smile. Everyone in Millbrook knows marching band isn't the coolest gig going, but I couldn't care less. "C'mon. I'll show you where to go."

"You're in the band too?" she asks, finally making eye contact. Thank God she doesn't look at me like everyone else at this school, like I can hook her up with concert tickets or introduce her to some vapid celebrity. She has no idea who my father is. For once, someone doesn't know.

"Trumpet," I say with pride even though I suck. Being proud has nothing to do with ability, rather the experience, being part of something. "Left it here over the summer. You coming or what?"

"What's your name?" She squints as the sun catches her eyes.

"Drew Mason." I extend my hand and she places her palm in mine, small and smooth. As I pull her to her feet a thankful smile erupts from her mouth, hitting me in the pit of my stomach. Nerves flutter in my gut and I'm momentarily stunned by the unfamiliar sensation. Sure, I've felt uneasy before a class presentation or as I walk on stage to play a gig, but never like this, never in relation to a person. I take a deep breath and smile, silently telling my stomach to quit it as I lead Stevie to practice.

Mr. Abella shoves two fingers in his mouth and whistles, his too-big glasses slipping down the bridge of his nose. He clears his throat and steps on one of those green milk crates you would see at a 7-Eleven. He's stationed right at the edge of our practice field, but the band barely pays attention. A couple of guys from the horn section chuck a Frisbee over Mr. Abella's head.

"For the freshmen who don't know me, I'm Mr. Abella, the instructor for this band. Today we'll be learning 'Arabian Nights,' the crown jewel of *Aladdin,* this season's theme."

Not one member of the band glances up in acknowledgment. He tugs at the bottom of his sweater vest and drops his conducting sticks in the grass.

"We start in five."

Stevie's sax hangs from a red strap that hugs the back of her neck. Her fingers tap the keys, but she doesn't play a note. It's useless to compete with the chords, warm-up scales, and drumbeats—none of which make sense together, a sound assault. She scans the chaos and winces at a flutist's high-pitched, chalk-board-screeching, my-ears-may-actually-be-bleeding note.

"That's you." I point to the sax crew lazing in the field, all guys.

"Oh," she says, biting at her nail, her eyes hesitant. A Band-Aid covers her right thumb. "I guess I should head over there."

Stevie doesn't budge. The sun bounces off her flushed cheeks, and for a split second the noise goes quiet. The instruments, sheet music, and the dew-covered field disappear.

But then Shane steps between us.

"Are you new?" Shane asks Stevie, taking off his blue baseball hat, his hair a mess as usual. Stevie nods and introduces herself. The strap of her tank top falls down her tanned shoulder and she pulls it back in place with her thumb.

My eyes are fixed on her shoulder when Shane asks, "As in Nicks?"

I hold my breath, praying Stevie doesn't roll her eyes or react in a way that makes Shane feel small. I exhale when a laugh tumbles from Stevie's mouth instead.

"Yep," she says. "My parents just *had* to be creative when I was born. Now I'm destined to have this conversation on repeat."

Annoying. I knew it.

"Sorry. That must bother you," Shane says, kicking at the grass and voicing my thoughts. "Feeling like your name isn't your own."

"Only when people sing Fleetwood Mac to me." Stevie smirks and my eyes bounce between the two of them. Shane smirks too, then clears his throat dramatically.

"Don't you dare," Stevie says playfully, crossing her arms over her chest and stuffing down a smile.

"For you, the sun will be shining," Shane sings in a cracked falsetto, his arms outstretched to the blazing sun above. Stevie laughs into her hands, her obvious delight reaching all the way to her eyes. I want to jump in on whatever is going on here, to be the one making her smile, but I'm clueless when it comes to Fleetwood Mac.

"I'm surprised you know that one," Stevie says. "No one's ever sang it to me before. It's my favorite."

"Great tune," Shane says, tugging at the bottom of his blue polo, his eyes shifting back to the grass. "I'm going to grab a cup of water before we start practice. Want one?"

"Sure," she says, following him. I search my mind for something clever to say so she hangs back with me, but my mouth clamps shut. I've never had problems talking to girls but being around Stevie is tripping me up big time. I shake my head and tell myself to get it together, to jog over to them and try again. But Shane stops short, Stevie almost stumbling over his Adidas. Brent Miller stands right in front of the orange water jug, filling a cup, his football helmet suspended between his knees.

"That's for the band," Shane says, his voice strained. Brent grabs the helmet in one hand and the cup of water in the other, slowly swiveling his neck until his eyes are on Shane. I inch my way closer, close enough to hear, but not too close. Shane's words echo in my ear. *I can take care of myself.*

"Excuse me, Ringo?" A thin smile stretches across Brent's unamused face, his mouse eyes narrowing as his jaw clenches. My pulse accelerates knowing what's about to go down. I clench my hand into a fist, digging my nails into my palm.

"It's for the band," Shane repeats. I can't let this happen and inch closer, but Shane glares at me. I step back. The entire band gawks at them, but Mr. Abella's nose is buried in sheet music, oblivious.

"It's for the band," Brent mimics, like a toddler, then takes a long sip of water, his Adam's apple shifting as he chugs it down. He crushes the paper cup and throws it right at Shane, hitting him square in the chest. It feels like I got hit, the wind knocked straight out of me. Shane did nothing, literally nothing, and still Brent goes after him. I can't watch this for one more second but as I'm about to intervene, Stevie steps in front of Shane.

"Seriously?" Stevie says, her voice a whisper, a breeze. Her left hand is defiantly perched on her hip, but her right hand hangs by her side, trembling.

"This isn't your problem," Brent says, towering over her, like a bodyguard in reverse.

"My problem is football players who can't form complete sentences," she says, but this time her voice is thunder. Brent laughs, then spits on the grass. Stevie eyes his blue and gold jersey that hangs over white spandex football pants. "By the way, those tights don't hide your small penis."

Oh. Shit.

Shane stares at Stevie, his mouth hanging open.

"Who the hell are *you*?" Brent steps to her, breathing hard, a bull about to charge. His knuckles turn white as his grip tightens on the helmet's grill. I've seen him like this before, but his pointless rage was always targeted at Shane, never at a girl.

Fuck it. I'm done doing nothing.

"Brent," I say, walking fast now, straight up to his roided out shoulders.

"Hey man," he says, backing away from Stevie and Shane. "I didn't see you there."

"Well now you see me."

Brent kisses my ass for my connections, although he would never admit that. Frankly I don't give a shit why he likes me, as long as I'm able to stop him from messing with my best friend.

"Shouldn't you be getting to practice?" I nod at the football field and force a smile. A whistle beckons and like a dog, Brent snaps his head to the sound.

"Guess I should. I'll catch you later." He jams the helmet on his head and jogs away. My shoulders relax. The band returns to its usual cacophony of phlegm sliding through brass and conversation-halting flat notes. But Shane stares at me hard, hating that I intervened. But if I do nothing, Brent rags on him, gets a little too close to him. Last year during lunch Brent "accidentally" spilled soda down Shane's back just because Shane looked at him wrong. But if I step in, like I did today, Shane feels like a coward, like he can't handle his own problems. I mean, he's never said that to me. But every time I intervene his shoulders slump forward, his whole body folding in on itself.

"I had it under control," Shane says, his eyes burning into me, as he hooks the quads over his chest.

"I know," I say carefully, unsure how Shane wants me to respond. "I just wanted to help you out." He ignores me, instead turning to Stevie.

"Are you okay?" we ask Stevie in unison. I have the urge to jinx him like when we were little, but I doubt Shane would appreciate that right now.

"I'm good," she says, biting at that nail again. "Are you guys okay?"

"I'm good," we say in unison again and Shane finally cracks a smile in my direction. He holds my gaze, challenging me with his eyes and I know what he's about to say next. I can't help saying it with him.

"Jinx."

After practice, Stevie's back on the curb, stretching her legs. A late afternoon breeze cuts through the stale air, drying the sweat along my neck.

"Thanks for before," Stevie says when I reach her, the sun landing on her cheeks, a hint of pink rising from her skin.

"Drew, come on," Shane yells. He leans against my Jeep, arms crossed over his chest. Everything in me wants to sit next to her but Shane's waiting.

"That was cool," I say. "What you did."

"I've never done anything like that in my life," she says softly, picking at the Band-Aid on her thumb. Her silvery voice wraps around me, lifting my thoughts away from Brent's maddening sneer. Instead I focus on her hair, the sun bringing out strands of copper and gold. My eyes shift to her full mouth, nerves settling back in my stomach as she speaks. "I mean, I'm not usually like that."

"What are you usually like?" I fight the urge to step closer. She's looking at me like everyone else in this town, like she wants something. But then I remember—she doesn't know about Dad. She doesn't want anything from me. She wants to get to know me, plain and simple. It's the biggest relief in the world. Her dark questioning eyes roam my face as my heart bangs around my chest. Usually with girls it's cool if we hang out, but it's not something I *need* to happen. With Stevie, I can't keep cool, and even though it's impossible, I want to know everything about her in one shot. Because piece by piece isn't fast enough.

"I'm . . . I don't know . . . careful," she says, her chestnut eyes locking with mine. I can't look away. It's like I've known those eyes forever, even though that makes no sense. She's a stranger. "But I couldn't watch that guy be such a jerk."

"I know what you mean." I've watched Brent Miller be a jerk to Shane for years. If Shane wasn't so adamant about me staying out of his business, I would have decked Brent a long time ago.

"Who is he anyway?" Stevie asks.

"Brent Miller. Junior like me. Horrible human."

"Yeah I got the horrible human part," she says, and I laugh.

"This century," Shane yells, and I hold one finger in the air.

"I should go." I can't help myself and steal another glance before stepping off the curb. Her mouth curves into a sweet smile, her eyes crinkling at the corners. I need to know the careful girl who also has the balls to stand up to Brent Miller. The thoughtful girl who doesn't see Dad when she looks at me. She yells bye and even the way her sneakers kick at the gravel intrigues me, like she's thinking with her whole body. Shane curls the brim of his baseball hat in one hand and waves at Stevie with the other. She doesn't see him, instead her eyes are still on me.

"Don't rush or anything," Shane yells, and I deliberately slow my pace.

"You're more than welcome to walk home."

"Then who would you torture with your cheesy music?" he jokes when I reach him.

"Get in already," I say, unlocking the Jeep. I have impeccable taste in music.

I don't say anything else because I'm too busy eyeing a silver Lexus that pulls to the curb. Stevie gets in and I squint to get one last look as the car drives past us.

"What are you looking at?" Shane asks as he pulls himself into the passenger side, throwing his backpack and drumsticks on the floor by his feet. "Oh," he says when he spots Stevie.

"Must be her mom," I mumble, as the Lexus drives out of the parking lot.

"She—" We say in unison but this time no one yells jinx. We both stop short and stare at each other.

"I'm gonna ask her out," I say fast as I turn on the ignition, praying Shane doesn't have the same plan.

"You can have any girl you want, anyone. Her?" His eyes get wide as he shifts in his seat and my heart sinks. I can almost always guess what Shane's thinking and right now, I bet his thoughts are exactly the same as mine. My hand reaches for the ignition and I turn it off.

"She's just . . . I don't know . . ." I don't have the right words to describe how Stevie made me feel today. Real? Whole? And then it hits me. Alive. For the first time since Dad left, I feel alive.

"You don't even know her," Shane says quietly, putting his hat back on so it casts a shadow over his eyes.

"*You* don't even know her," I say. "We *both* just met her."

Shane sighs, his shoulders tensing.

"Well *I'm* asking her out," Shane says with a bit of an edge to his voice. Shane's never asked out a girl in his life.

"Not if I do it first," I say, serious.

"Not if *I* do it first." Shane's face flushes and we stare at each other, deadlocked.

"This is stupid, Shane," I say, shaking the hair out of my eyes. "I say we flip for it."

Shane's mouth falls open and his eyebrows knit in confusion.

"Flip for it? This isn't like choosing top bunk at sleepovers."

"I didn't mean it like that," I say. Shane should know me better. Hell, sometimes he knows me better than I know myself. I would never think of Stevie as a bet or a game. But there's no easy way to navigate out of this inescapable hole. If we both ask her out, it'll get messy and one of us will inevitably resent the other. What if we stop talking altogether? I can't risk it. Shane's too important to me. "It's just . . . flipping a coin is what we do. How we've always made choices. It's the only fair way to decide. I don't want to fight with you. I *can't* fight with you."

Shane narrows his eyes, trying to decipher my next move. After twelve years he should be able to predict what I'm about to do.

"You do realize that Stevie can still say no, regardless of who asks her out," Shane says. Of course she can say no. Hell, she probably *will* say no. But we can't both ask her out. And I can't fight with my best friend.

"Get out," I say, gesturing at the door.

"Huh?"

"Just get out." I grab a penny from the middle console and fling the door open.

"This is ridiculous," Shane says under his breath, jumping out and marching to the front of the Jeep.

"Have a better idea?" I toss the penny in the air. I agree that this is completely ridiculous. Probably one of the worst ideas I've ever had. Worse than the time I decided to race Dad, me on a bike with training wheels and him in his black Porsche. After one block, I wiped out and broke my arm. Dad never even realized I was behind him.

"For the record, this isn't cool," Shane says, but his eyebrows soften, like he's about to give in. He sighs and kicks at the Jeep's tire. "And odds are, you're the one she's going to choose, regardless of where that penny lands."

"You can't back down," I say, certain of how this will play out if Shane steps aside. "If you back down, you're going to resent me. If I back down, I'm going to resent you. This is the only way. And you know it." I grab the penny with one hand, kissing my closed fist.

"Heads," I shout.

"You're an idiot," Shane says, which is probably true.

I flick the penny high into the air, the sun catching on the copper and sending a sliver of blinding light into my eyes.

"Tails," Shane mumbles, glaring at me.

"Shit." I look away as the penny falls to the ground next to the tire. It bounces and clinks against the asphalt until my boot slams down on the coin, sealing fate.

CHAPTER 3

Stevie

Everyone says the first day is the worst, fraught with uncertainty and nerves. But if you ask me, the second day sucks harder than the first. On the first day it's blissful ignorance, all rainbows and sunshine. A perfect image of what could be, not yet tainted by reality. But by the end of the first day, reality crashes down.

I should know better by now. I've repeated this new girl routine five times in five different towns. And even so, I followed Drew Mason like a little lost puppy yesterday, picturing my school's band back in Seattle. A place where I could lose myself in notes and chords, where I could play songs that mean something, where I could dream about NYU's music program, a way out of my exhausting nomadic life. But that's not the Millbrook Marching Mustangs. I heard they're not even invited to play the town's Memorial Day parade. Back in Seattle I fought for my spot in the school band, earning first chair. But here, I didn't have to audition. They don't have a first, second, or third chair. That should've been my first clue. And now, without a top-notch music program, there's no way I'll get into NYU.

So today, on the second day, my thumb throbs as I close the car door to Mom's silver Lexus. The high school casts a shadow on the concrete, shielding me from the just-woken-up sun. Different wings connect together in an intimidating brick maze, and I have no idea how I'll find my way around when I start for real next week.

Bright red blood seeps from my cuticle, pulsing through my finger. I wave at Mom as she drives away and place my sax case on the curb, fishing for a Band-Aid in my backpack. Enough with this disgusting habit. The thing is, I don't even know I'm doing it until it's too late. It started in seventh grade after we moved from Indianapolis to Seattle and I haven't been able to stop. I cover my thumb with a Band-Aid, throwing the wrapper in a trash bin by the curb. It reeks of curdled milk. Out of nowhere a can of Diet Coke sails through the air and smacks right into my hand. Sticky soda sprays up at my face as the can plummets into the garbage. My wrist throbs along with my thumb as I clutch my hand to my chest.

"Shit, I'm so sorry!"

A girl wearing a Mustangs jersey and gray leggings runs to me, waving a napkin in the air.

"Good shot," I say when she reaches me. I take the napkin and blot my face dry. She stands too close to me, her hazel eyes wide.

"I'm so sorry," she says again. "Are you new here?"

"Is it that obvious?" I use this line at every new school. It makes me sound confident and cool. But of course it's obvious. Millbrook High is a quarter of the size of my last school, the kind of place where everyone knows everyone.

"Kind of," she says. "I'm Ray Stone, sophomore."

"Same. I'm Stevie Rosenstein." I chuck the napkin into

the garbage, my face still sticky from the soda. I wonder why this girl is here before the official start of school. Maybe she's a cheerleader. That jersey probably belongs to her boyfriend, number twenty-three. She looks like someone who would date the quarterback with her movie star blond hair and teeth that for sure benefitted from years of braces. I bet she still wears a retainer.

"Rosenstein?" Ray echoes me.

My arms fold across my chest, my defenses kicking in, honed from my time as one of only a few Jewish kids in our Indianapolis suburb. But Millbrook has three temples within a ten-mile radius. I'm not a novelty here.

"As in Caleb Rosenstein?"

There it is. I take a step back as Ray's funhouse mirror grin almost reaches her ears. The way she stares at me, like I'm suddenly someone worth knowing, makes me long for Sarah. Sarah couldn't care less about my family. My stomach knots like one of those ropes in gym class and I brace myself for the interrogation.

"Yeah," I say, eyeing the practice field, a steady drum beat rat tat tatting through the air. I'm going to be late.

"No way. They're saying on ESPN that he could make a huge difference for the Jets this season."

So what? Dad's the quarterback coach for the Jets. It's not like he won a Nobel Prize or cured cancer. He tells a bunch of overgrown boys how to throw an oddly shaped ball across a field. I don't get it. I never have. What's worse is because of Dad's job, I never know if people want to become friends with me for real, and I never get to stay in one place long enough to find out.

The thing is, it's usually the guys who react this way. At my last school, Martin Ross followed me around every Monday during the season begging me for inside information. It's not like he actually wanted to hang out with me. And forget about when Dad's team loses. When the Colts were down when I was in sixth grade, a few kids spray painted *loser* on my locker, complete with a black swastika. It took a whole week for the school to scrub it clean.

I mess with the Band-Aid on my thumb, almost tearing it off before I realize and stick it back in place. A steady stream of cars head into the lot, dispensing football players, cheerleaders, and people I recognize from band.

"Ray!" Brent Miller yells as he jumps out of a black Range Rover, holding his helmet in the air like a trophy. Ray waves and I pray Brent isn't number twenty-three.

There's a Brent Miller at every school. Same square jaw and same inane jokes directed at that one kid who doesn't deserve it. In Indianapolis it was Scott Barrett and his anti-Semitic jabs were directed at me. When you're always the new kid, you're an easy target. Fresh blood. It starts young, probably around fourth or fifth grade. I'm sure there's a reason the Scotts and Brents of the world are the way they are, but that reason doesn't particularly interest me. Sometimes the reason doesn't matter.

I've never had the guts to talk back. Not until yesterday, and even as the words vomited up my throat, I couldn't believe I was actually, finally saying them. Maybe I'm sick of the same old story at every school. Maybe it's because I felt the humiliation on Shane Murphy's face in the pit of my stomach. And even though my heart hammered against my chest, it wasn't enough to stop the words. If only that momentary surge of confidence stuck with me, permeated through my skin and settled in my core. But if I had to rewind the clock, there's no way I could repeat that convincing performance.

"Ray, c'mon!" Brent yells, and I want to shrink down and hide between the blades of grass lining the sidewalk. Thank God he ignores me.

"Are you guys . . ." I nod at Ray's jersey. "Is he your boy-friend?"

Ray throws her head back laughing, blond hair swishing across her back, revealing brown roots by her hairline.

"God no." She bends to my ear and her words are like tiny puffs of bubblegum. "Brent Miller's the worst."

I exhale, and even though Ray's in awe of Dad, I won-der if maybe I made my first Millbrook friend. It's a known fact that location dictates friendship. It's called the prox-imity principle—the depressing idea that my entire social circle is predetermined by the town I happen to live in. The truth is I don't need a theory to tell me I would still be best friends with Sarah if we had stayed in Seattle. Before Sarah, there was Krystal from Indianapolis, and before Krystal there was Emily from Chicago, and before Emily there was Nicole from Miami. Nothing in my life has been a choice. Not the big things at least. And it's the big things, like where you live, that determine the little things. I've moved enough times to know. I've been forced to leave the friends I chose over and over, my entire life demolished and rebuilt with each new town. My chest tightens as words like *leaving, loner, loser* come at me like rubber balls in a dodge-ball game. I rub my eyes, tired from another fitful night of sleep.

"So who's number twenty-three?" I ask, gesturing at Ray's jersey. She kicks the curb with her sneaker and smiles.

"Me."

"For real?"

"Coach finally agreed to let me kick for the Mustangs. He even helped me coordinate football with soccer."

"That's really . . ." My thoughts trip over themselves as they struggle to get out of my mouth. Even though I don't care about football, I care about this. A girl actually playing right alongside the boys. A girl tough enough to keep up, to be the star. "That's really cool."

"I'm scared shitless," she says, gazing at the practice field. "Don't tell anyone."

"I won't," I say, but Ray doesn't seem scared. Just the opposite and I wish I could have a fraction of her confidence.

"I should get to practice, but let's hang out, okay? Everyone is heading to Dino's Saturday night if you want to come."

"Dino's?"

"This diner everyone goes to. I know, most boring town ever," Ray says with a shrug. "Later." She starts to jog backward, waves, then turns and books it to the field.

I shake off the thought that's permanently lodged in the back of my mind. Does she want to be friends with me, or friends with Caleb Rosenstein's daughter? I tie my hair up with a black and gold silk ponytail holder. Sarah and I each bought one at Anthropologie's sale rack last year, right before the winter concert. After I left, she claimed my spot as first chair. I had tried out three times before I finally made it, but that same day I came home to a family meeting and news we were moving again. Frustrated tears spilled from my eyes when I stepped down, years of practice straight out the window. But if anyone was going to take over, I'm glad it was Sarah. My phone vibrates from within my backpack and I pull it out, smiling at the text.

Sarah
How much do you miss me?

Me
So much you have no idea. Why are you up so early? Isn't it 5 AM in Seattle?

Sarah

Set my alarm to catch you. Rumor has
it there's a talented freshman coming
in, trying out for my spot.

Me

Don't let the new kid steal it.

Sarah

Never. Verbal Disturbance are playing
The Paramount tonight. Wish you
could come.

Me

That'll be a great show.

Sarah

So come back.

Me

I wish.

Sarah

Don't replace me, k?

Me

Same.

Sarah

You okay? I miss you.

Me

Yeah. I'll text you later. Miss you too.

I shove my phone back in my bag as I make my way out to practice.

Once I'm out on the field I instinctively reach for my neck strap, but my collar is bare.

Sweat breaks out on the back of my neck and my pulse quickens. My vision turns fuzzy as a quiet panic zips through me. I kneel and set my sax on the ground, my eyes skimming the grass. It must be here somewhere. I can't play without it. Mr. Abella straightens sheet music at the edge of the field and I pray I find it before he starts practice.

"You dropped this."

My red neck strap dangles in front of my nose. Clouds start to break, the sun demanding to be seen, the glare temporarily blinding me. Drew steps in front of the light, and I take the neck strap from him. When I picked it out six years ago, I thought the color was so cool. Dad took me to the music store, one of our rare father/daughter outings. He convinced me to pick something bold, pride beaming from his face as he grabbed the red material. But even after all these years, Dad's never seen me play. And now this neck strap seems bright and obvious, like something a little kid would choose. Even so, the second I place it around my neck, my body recalibrates and steadies.

"Thanks," I say. Drew extends his hand to help me up, leather cuffs and ropes covering his wrist. As I place my palm in his, a cuff shifts on his arm, revealing a small tattoo. Roman numerals maybe, but I can't make out the exact symbols. His hand is warm and so big it practically swallows mine. As he pulls me to my feet a toned bicep peeks out from under his black T-shirt. Everything about him is dark, intense even, down to his beat-up black army boots. The laces are untied and hang in the grass.

"When did you start playing?" He gestures at my sax, as I clip it to the neck strap.

"Around nine."

The first time I played a note, in the middle of fourth grade music class, I was hooked. There was a raw quality to the sound, like playing was an extension of how I was feeling. Still is. Notes take up the space in my mind that's usually reserved for nerves and over-analysis. As soon as I play, my shoulders relax, dominoes of tension falling down my back.

"What about you?"

"Last year." He laughs, his voice hoarse like he just woke up from a long nap. An orange Frisbee sails my way and Drew grabs it, then chucks it to one of the horn players. "I kind of suck. And between you and me, I hate the trumpet."

"So why do you play?"

"Long story." Drew fidgets with one of the leather ropes around his wrist. He glances at Mr. Abella, who's now adjusting a music stand, a stack of papers tucked under his arm. "You just moved here, right? Why Jersey?"

I consider lying to him, fabricating a story about being a military kid. The truth will get out though, it always does. And considering Ray knows, I'm sure the entire football team is already up to speed on my bloodline. It's only a matter of time before Drew finds out, so he might as well hear it from me.

"My dad's a football coach,"' I say casually. "He's the new quarterback coach for the Jets."

The team name hangs in the air as I wait for the reaction,

but nothing registers on Drew's tanned face. He doesn't seem impressed. In fact, he doesn't seem to care at all.

"I'm more of a basketball guy," he says, shrugging. "I bet people are annoying as hell about your dad." His dark hair falls in waves around his face. He rakes it back with his fingers.

Drew's words are filled with such certainty, like he actually does understand. The sun catches on his brown eyes, revealing a thin amber ring hugging his iris. I'm about to ask him more when Mr. Abella's whistle pierces the air. He steps on a green milk crate stationed at the edge of the field, tugging at the bottom of his sweater vest.

"Places, everyone." Mr. Abella holds a conducting stick in the air. No one snaps to attention like we did in Seattle. In fact, no one glances up, except Shane, who silences a cymbal crash and folds his arms over his chest, still holding drumsticks. My heart clenches as I picture Brent pitching a Dixie cup at Shane, like he's a garbage disposal.

"Catch you after practice," Drew says, falling in line with the trumpets. I hurry to my spot with the saxophones, almost slipping on the wet grass. When I reach them I smile, but no one smiles back. I lick the wooden reed which is still gross no matter how many times I do it. My fingers press the keys of my sax one by one. No sound, just tapping out a song in my head. Even in the most unfamiliar of places, the rhythm of these keys is like Mom's hot chocolate. Warm, sweet, and instantly calming.

"A quick announcement before we begin," Mr. Abella says. Drew dangles a trumpet by his thigh, like he couldn't care less about this practice. He checks his phone, gives it a dirty look, and shoves it into his pocket. "All-State auditions are in December. As most of you know, only the best musicians in New Jersey will qualify."

My fingers freeze, holding down the G note, still no sound. Mr. Abella searches the band with hopeful eyes, but the horns are still busy chucking a Frisbee back and forth. The clarinets and flutes whisper to each other. Mr. Abella sighs, his face a defeated Eeyore. But when his gaze meets mine, his mouth stretches into a smile.

"Stevie, are you interested?"

Of course I'm interested. With All-State on my resume, I have a chance at NYU's music program. A chance to live in one place for four whole years. I nod at Mr. Abella, almost giving myself whiplash from the excitement coursing through my veins.

"Great! Shane can help you." Mr. Abella points his conducting stick at Shane, a stuffed Aladdin genie perched on top of his quads. Shane kind of looks like the genie, especially his broad smile, and the way his stomach puffs out a little, like he ate one too many slices of pizza.

He smiles, adjusting a blue baseball hat with the letters EMT stitched in white on the front.

"All-State typically doesn't accept freshmen, but they made an exception for Shane."

Shane smiles again and shrugs, his drumstick tapping the snare. How in the world did he get in as a freshman? I have to talk to him.

"Okay, percussion up," Mr. Abella says and the guys scramble to their feet, hooking drums over their shoulders. "Today we begin with 'A Whole New World.' And one, two, three, four!" he shouts at the mess of us on the field as Shane starts a beat. Before I know it, we're marching while butchering "A Whole New World," all while forming the image of the genie's lamp, which unfortunately can't grant my wish of making this band better. Sweat beads down my back from underneath my neck strap. Shane attacks the quads, each drum stroke purposeful and precise. No doubt about it, he's good. Easily the best musician in this band. Which isn't an achievement, but still.

The afternoon sun stings my eyes as I head for the parking lot, practically running to catch up with Shane. He leans against a black Jeep at the far end of the lot, one foot propped against the tire. Before I can reach him, Drew falls in step with me, pulling car keys attached to a mini carabiner out of his pocket.

"Hungry?" Drew stops walking, right at the edge of the curb. I put my sax down, flexing my fingers.

"Starving," I say. There's a hole in his T-shirt, right by the collar, and his eyes are so dark, so never-ending, it's hard to tell where the pupil stops and the iris begins. He tucks a loose strand of hair behind his ear, a small smile playing on his lips.

"I'm going to grab a burger at the diner. Best in town. You should definitely come," Drew says raising his eyebrows in anticipation.

Of course I want to go, but why should I? So I can be a blip in Drew's life? So I can move away and he can forget I ever existed? But maybe this time'll be different. Maybe Dad's contract will get renewed here and I can finish out high school in New Jersey. Maybe this could be something for real. Yes. Say *yes*.

"I can't," I lie. "I have a thing."

A thing? Is that the best you can come up with? Heat rushes to my face and I pick at the Band-Aid. I don't have a thing. In fact, I have nothing. No friends, no boyfriend thanks to my smooth moves, no first chair, nothing. And why should I have anything? I'll just have to leave it all behind.

Drew's phone dings and his expression morphs from hopeful to annoyed. When he pulls the phone out of his pocket his nostrils flare as he reads the message. He shoves the phone back in his pocket, his brown eyes tired. They remind me of my own. I want to know what the tattoo on his wrist means and who keeps texting him. But most of all, I want to know why my pulse double times it when he comes near me, my body demanding I stop and pay attention. My mouth falls open to say *Yes, I'll go with you,* but before any sound comes out Drew steps back, his fingers curling around the keys.

"Another time," he says as he turns and heads for his Jeep.

I throw my phone on my comforter and head to the kitchen. No phones allowed at dinner. I sidestep the moving boxes that line the hallway, the sides labeled in marker. Mom swears she's going to finish unpacking this week, but she said that last week, and the week before, and well, I'm not holding my breath. It's like she doesn't see the point, like leaving a rumpled blanket on top of your bed in the morning. Why make something perfect and pretty just to mess it all up at night?

My hand instinctively reaches for the banister, the shiny wood smooth under my skin. The fourth and fifth step creak under my feet, no matter how gingerly I tread, announcing my presence. I eye the front door, more boxes piled in the entryway, illuminated by a hanging chandelier. This is the biggest house we've ever lived in, a consolation prize for moving across the country. It's almost obnoxious, the way the ceiling stretches two stories high. The sheer excess of our homes embarrasses me, especially in some of the towns we've lived in, where it's not the norm. No one needs this much. I'm grateful for it, don't get me wrong, but I'd also trade it for a chance at stability.

Drew's probably at that diner by now. Saying yes to his invitation would have been like unpacking these boxes, and settling into a new place, new routine, a new person. Part of me understands why Mom procrastinates. It's easier when we have to pack it all up again, fewer memories to box away. But then again, this big house feels empty with its soaring ceilings and naked fireplace mantel. The air is cold with nothing to curl around and sink into. Even though the furniture is unpacked, pieces of us still sit in boxes begging to be displayed. The walls are bare, Mom's favorite paintings buried beneath her winter wardrobe. It's like our lives are on hold, trapped in cardboard.

When I slide into the kitchen chair across from Joey, he half smiles, but his eyes are fixed on something off in the distance. I turn around, but as usual nothing's there. My hand reaches for the side of his chipmunk cheek, like his therapist taught me, and I gently adjust his gaze to meet mine.

"Hey, buddy," I say. His eyes, like the sea after a storm, register my face.

"Stevie!"

Joey pronounces the *v* in my name as an *f* as he jumps from his seat and throws his arms around my neck. I nuzzle into him, his hair like fresh farm-picked apples. Mom scoops meatballs into a serving dish, my stomach gurgling at the smell. Her hair is up in a hurried bun, loose curls falling around her face. A couple of dots of green paint freckle her forehead. She must've been in the basement. The art studio is the one room Mom prioritized, lining paints and brushes on an otherwise bare shelf, her easel positioned beneath one of the high hats for optimal light.

"He was upset he didn't get to see you when we got home

from speech therapy." Mom smiles at Joey like he's her only child as she pours a pot of pasta into a strainer. I'm used to it by now, the constant attention Joey needs. The kind I don't need, but still want.

"Andrea says he's almost all set for kindergarten." Mom beams at him, and she should. A couple years ago we were all so worried about him, especially Mom. She freaked out before this last move knowing she had to find him a new therapist and change his entire routine. But as soon as we moved here in the beginning of the summer, she found Andrea. Mom calls her a miracle worker.

"Mama, balls," Joey says, pointing to his empty plate, the plastic one with a train painted in the middle.

"Please," Mom says, scooping him two with extra sauce, just how he likes it.

"Peas." Joey forks a piece and takes a huge bite. "Stevie, you like see, uh. Um. Stevie?"

"Yeah, buddy?" I smile because I know where this is going. I wait for him to find his words, never completing his sentence for him. Andrea said to be patient and give him time.

"Uh. Do you . . . uh . . . you like seafood?" Joey's already giggling, his shaggy curls bouncing around his head.

"I do."

Here comes the punch line. Joey opens his mouth wide, laughing, gross bits of meatball chewed up inside.

"See." He almost spits a chunk at me, he's laughing so hard. I can't help laughing with him. "Food!"

"Gross!" I scream like I always do and he erupts into hysterics, sending a piece of meatball onto his favorite dinosaur T-shirt, the one with the velociraptor playing basketball.

"Joey, eat your food," Mom says sternly, but even she's smiling. I stand, reaching for the serving spoon, helping myself. "Oh, I'm sorry, Stevie." Mom shakes her head, taking the spoon from me and placing meatballs and pasta on my plate.

"Where's Dad?" I ask, eyeing the empty chair across from Mom, no silverware or plate on his placemat.

"Practice ran long tonight," Mom says, "Should be home soon."

"I think I'm going to try out for All-State," I start to say, even though no one asked me how my practice was today.

Before Mom can answer, the front door swings open and Joey jumps from his chair, the wooden legs scraping against the tile. He runs full speed to the foyer screaming, "Daddy!"

Mom places a fork, knife, and plate at Dad's end of the table. He walks into the kitchen, Joey clutching his ankle like a koala bear. Joey attempts to climb Dad's leg, but he's too slow. Dad picks him up and throws him in the air, Joey's machine gun laughter bouncing around the room.

"How's my little man?" Dad says, a whistle swinging from his neck as he puts Joey down on the tile and squats so he's eye level with him.

"Good!" Joey yells, grabbing for Dad's Jets hat. Dad secures it over Joey's curls, making it a few notches tighter. He has those same curls but they're thinning. As Dad straightens up, he smiles at Mom like he hasn't seen her in years. It's the way he always looks at her, like they're in on a big secret together. I would give anything for someone to look at me like that. To *know* me like that.

Joey runs full speed to his playroom. A whistle toots from the train table, followed by the annoying Thomas song and Joey's tiny voice yelling, "Choo choo!"

Dad takes off his green windbreaker and hangs it on the back of the chair. He sets a clipboard on the kitchen island and Mom kisses him. It's like I don't exist.

"Hey, Dad?"

He finally wraps both arms around my neck and kisses me on the cheek, his stubble scratching my skin. He stinks like locker room and sweaty socks, but I breathe him in. He's barely around anymore, especially since we moved here. Says he has to prove himself, being the new hire. But we all know it doesn't matter. Like most coaches he'll likely be let go after a few years and transferred to another team.

"Stevie girl, how was your day?" he asks as he sits next to me.

"Good. There's All-State Band tryouts in a few months, and . . ."

Dad inhales long and slow, like it's an effort to breathe. He forks a meatball and shoves the whole thing in his mouth. I fidget with a napkin, which is better than ripping apart my cuticle. Dad swallows and sets down his fork. His hair is still slick with sweat.

"What's All-State?"

"It's a really big deal. One band that represents all of New Jersey, and they only take the best players in the state."

"That sounds great, Stevie, but . . ."

"It'll help me get into NYU. The music program is supposed to be—"

"Stevie," Dad says, the crease between his eyes deepening like a tiny mountain ridge. "You're a talented musician. But there are so many programs that offer a general education degree. Don't pigeonhole yourself."

If I had a dollar for every time Dad said *pigeonhole,* I'd be a millionaire. What does that even mean anyway? To go after what you want and love and can't stop thinking about? When Joey was two it was music that came first. He sang before he could talk, his little voice singing *lellow* to "Yellow Submarine."

Ever since I witnessed the way music could reach him and pull him out from under himself, my mind was made up.

"Caleb," Mom says, putting a hand on his shoulder.

"Naomi, she needs to be practical," Dad says, putting his hand over Mom's, and seriously it's like I'm not even here.

"I *am* practical," I say, my voice rising. "You're the one who isn't practical, choosing a career that moves us every couple of years."

Dad's pale blue eyes fall to the table. He can't look at me when we start talking about our lifestyle. I know he hates disappointing us. The night he announced our move from Seattle, I couldn't sleep and snuck downstairs for a glass of water. Before I reached the kitchen, I heard him crying softly in our living room, my heart clenching at the sound. But it wasn't enough to erase my anger. I crept back upstairs, still thirsty, never mentioning what I saw.

"Exactly. I turned my passion into a career, but you don't have to. You can choose a stable career and follow your passion on the side. You're always complaining about our lifestyle. Well, it's my love of football that got us here," Dad says, forking another meatball, his eyes fixed on his plate.

His words give me pause because he's right—I never want to duplicate this life for myself. Even though music is an unconventional field, I know I could find something that keeps me grounded in one state. I'm not trying to be a rock star.

"Music isn't football," I say, my eyes narrowing at him. "Football is a game. A pointless game."

Dad's face winces, like I sucker punched him. Mom crosses the room and stands in front of me, taking both of my hands in hers. Green paint is dried on her knuckles, but her palms are warm, forgiving.

"Stevie," she says, glancing at Dad then returning her gaze to me. Her brown eyes are full of compassion for both of us.

"Football is music to your father. The thing that inspires him. You of all people should understand what that feels like."

"I know." I swallow my pride, my eyes apologizing to Dad. "I'm sorry. Even though I don't get it, I'm sorry. But why does it have to be at our expense?" I ask, because that's the real question. Can't Dad have his precious football without ruining our lives?

"I don't have a choice." Dad sighs, like he's exhausted from explaining something I should have accepted long ago. "I have to go where the opportunities are."

I have absolutely no say in how my life unfolds because my father's job uproots us over and over. Maybe when I was younger I could handle it, but now I'm not sleeping, and I'm terrified to make new friends just to have them yanked away.

"You *do* have a choice." My voice rises, my throat constricting. "You can do something else. Get another job. One that keeps us in the same state."

"It's not that simple," he says, like I'm a kid who doesn't get it. But I do get it and it is that simple. A local high school in Seattle offered Dad a job last year, just as he got the offer from the Jets. I begged him to take it, but he fed me the same line he's feeding me now. *It's complicated. You don't understand.* Well I understand perfectly. We could've stayed, but Dad chose for us. "Stevie, if I could change things, I would."

Yeah, right. Hypocrite. I tear at my cuticle, a sharp pain shooting from my thumb and blood spilling onto my nail. I jam it against my jeans.

"Don't you realize we all have to start over. I have to make new friends *again*."

"You're great at making new friends," Dad says, but he has no idea. This is high school. It's not like starting over in fifth grade. The people in this town have been here forever, with deep histories and friendships. How can I even begin to compete with that?

"You don't get it," I say. "I left first chair and Sarah and a city I loved. And now I'm here and I don't know anyone and it's so overwhelming that I can't even fall asleep at night. Every decision you make screws it all up for me."

"Stevie." Dad glances at me, and I know what he's about to say. It's something he always reminds me of when the world feels unsteady.

"You can't be certain that one decision will mess everything up. Each new decision takes us on a different path, that's all."

But this time I don't believe him. I want one path, one set of friends, one school. I can't figure out who I'm supposed to be until I get the chance to stand still.

CHAPTER 4

Drew

I park in front of the intimidating metal gates that guard Shane's house. Those gates won't open without the code, which is Shane's August birth date, same week as mine. He grabs his backpack and hoists it onto his lap, but he won't look at me. I stare at the penny in the middle console, worried I made a huge mistake. Shane hasn't looked at me square in the eyes since we flipped that coin, and he only acts like this when he's pissed.

"We cool?" I ask, trying to diffuse the thick cloud of tension filling the car.

"Whatever," he says reaching for the door handle. "You get what you want, like always."

Shane flings open the car door and I reach across him, pulling it shut. He breathes a heavy sigh.

"I don't *always* get what I want, and you know it."

"I know," he says, finally looking me in the eye. Of course he knows. He was there the afternoon Dad left, sitting with me on the living room couch in stunned silence. Mom screamed obscenities at Dad as he quickly shoved clothes into a duffel bag. He didn't even say goodbye to me—just got in his Porsche and sped off, down our street and away from our lives. Overdramatic and embarrassing. I hated him for it. Still do. Mom's hand shook as she grabbed her keys, promising to be home in an hour. She didn't come home until the next morning. It unnerved me that she didn't cry but looking back I bet she was holding it all in for my benefit. After Mom bailed, it was only me and Shane, the silence of my house swallowing me whole. I struggled to catch my breath, gripping the arm of the sectional. But then Shane put his hand on my shoulder and simply said, *Wanna play basketball?* I couldn't help but laugh. But that's Shane—even when he says the wrong words, they somehow feel right.

"And anyway, Stevie turned me down," I say, picking up the penny and flipping it over in my palm. "Said she was busy."

"When has a girl ever turned you down?" Shane shoves a water bottle in his backpack and reaches for the door handle again. "Maybe she really *was* busy."

"Think so?"

Shane glares at me.

I drop the penny back into the console. I don't want him to resent me and hold one of his epic grudges. Not that it's the same thing, but when I was seven, I swiped his favorite Hot Wheels car, the silver one with the red lightning bolt on the side. I was going to give it back, but Shane found out before I had the chance to return it to his collection. He didn't talk to me for a whole week, the longest we've gone without speaking.

"Seriously, are you mad?" I ask.

Shane sighs, then shakes his head, smiling his real smile, the one that reveals a dimple in his left cheek.

"I'm cool," he says. "For real." I exhale as I realize he's not angry, relief flooding my body. "And anyway, if she's meant to be with you, she will be. If she's meant to be with me, she will be. And maybe she's meant to be with someone else entirely. No penny would change any of that."

Shane's always riffing on some philosophical bullshit, but I love him for it. His unwavering faith in the universe makes me believe everything with my fucked up family will work out, even as it crumbles down around me. *"You'll be okay,"* he said the day Dad left, and even though I didn't believe him, the certainty in his voice gave me hope.

"You coming by for basketball?" I stick my head out the window as Shane jumps out of the Jeep.

"Give me five," he says over his shoulder, punching the code into the keypad. The gates swing open and Shane jogs down the long winding driveway.

When I walk inside my house, no one's home, as usual. Mom's still at the nonprofit she started when I went to elementary school and she got bored with all the free time. At least she used Dad's money for something good, creating music programs in inner-city high schools. But lately she's been coming home later and later. If it wasn't shitty enough that Dad left, Mom had to freak out too. Even though she's still physically here, it's like the mom part of her disappeared with him when he left six months ago. Last week I caught her rearranging candles in the bathroom with this space cadet look on her face. She stood with her hands on her hips, head tilted to the side. Big candle, then little candle, then medium-size candle. She re-ordered them and tilted her head to the other side. She never even noticed me standing in the doorway.

My house feels bigger now that Dad's gone, our antique grandfather clock ticking away silent seconds. My fingers graze a couple keys on the baby grand in the foyer, the notes lonely and hollow. It needs a tune-up. Once I'm in the kitchen, I set my wallet next to a bowl of fake apples and pears, the only thing on the counter. I open the Sub-Zero like there might actually be food in there besides leftover take-out and random condiments. It's been this way since Dad left. I reach for a Chinese food container, and lean against the dishwasher, forking day-old General Tso's chicken. It's too fucking quiet in here.

After a couple bites, I toss it and head down the hall, glaring at the framed silver, gold, and platinum records. The legendary Don Mason smiles at me from an enlarged photo, his arm around a very young Bruce Springsteen. They're in the studio, probably late seventies, right after Bruce wrapped *Darkness*. Loving Springsteen is a Jersey state requirement and all my friends gawk at this one. I used to gawk right along with them. But that was before.

The door to his office is open and it's exactly how he left it six months ago. More records line the walls, ostentatious and screaming Dad's accomplishments. He's such a show-off. Electric and acoustic guitars are propped on stands by the bay windows, sunlight bouncing off the strings. Papers cover the huge mahogany desk and the flash drive is still where I left it over a year ago. I was so naïve to think he would actually listen to it. A thin layer of dust coats my finger when I pick it up and read the label.

Dark Carnival, Summer Garage Sessions

Dad flipped the demo over in his hands that night, squinting at the label. He leaned back in his chair and propped his feet on the desk. White Hanes socks stuck out of his sweatpants.

"What's the sound?" he asked, like I was an aspiring rock star hoping to sign with him, not his son.

"Rock. Kinda alternative," I said. "Like the Black Keys."

"You shouldn't sound like anyone else." He took off his glasses, the ones that make him look like Elvis Costello. I wished we sounded like the Black Keys. "You sing on it?"

"Yeah." Dad hadn't heard me sing for real yet. He'd heard me mess around in the car, and once he walked in on me screaming above a Kings of Leon song. I couldn't wait for him to hear the demo. Him liking it would've convinced me I actually did have the chops to front a band. That I wasn't some hack, a guy who gets up on stage not realizing he sucks.

"If you want to be a real musician, you need to learn an instrument." He pinched the bridge of his nose and inhaled deeply.

"Will you listen to it?" I asked—no, I begged. My eyes shifted to a photo of him, Paul McCartney, and me at seven years old, the same year I swiped the Hot Wheels car.

"Learn an instrument, any instrument. Join the marching band like I did."

"Done," I said. Back then I would do anything Dad told me to. Plus, maybe Dad had a point. Maybe learning an instrument would help me be a better singer. But after Dad left, I hated the trumpet right along with him.

"I'll take a listen, Andrew," he said, sliding the glasses back on his face and checking his Rolex. "I have to get back to work."

"Let me know what you think, okay?" I said, rocking back and forth on the balls of my feet.

"Absolutely."

Every day when he left for the city, I checked his office. Every. Damn. Day. And every day, the demo was still on his desk where I left it—where it still is today.

"Dude, where are you?" Shane yells from down the hall.

He bounces a basketball in the foyer, the rhythm echoing through the house.

"Be right there." I throw the flash drive on the desk. "Let's get out of here," I say when I reach him.

Once we're outside, Shane pegs me in the chest with the ball and I dunk it into the basket at the top of the driveway. The sun hides behind the trees, sinking lower toward the horizon. It's still warm out, the air holding tight to summer.

"You looking at the demo again?" he asks and I pass to him. He bounces the ball between his legs and misses. It rolls down the driveway and he runs to grab it, laughing to himself.

"Whatever," I say when he bounces the ball back to me. "I don't want to talk about him." Since Dad left, Shane comes over every day after school, sometimes without me asking. Sometimes he even brings me leftovers from whatever his mom cooked the night before. Every time I thank him for the handouts, equally humbled and grateful.

"You're lucky you still have him, you know," Shane says, and of course he's right, even if it doesn't feel that way. But Shane's dad was nothing like mine. He was caring and present and losing him sucked. For Shane *and* me. Shane was twelve and I was thirteen the day his dad took his last breath, after the weeks and months of uncertainty. Both of us too fucking young to deal with something so heavy. I promised Shane's dad I'd always look out for him, but now it sometimes feels like it's the other way around. I have no one except Shane. "Maybe you should give him a chance."

"Maybe you don't know what you're talking about." I take a shot and sink a basket. Shane grabs the ball.

"I've known Don my entire life. He screwed up, no doubt about it. But what he did has nothing to do with you."

I wish I could view the world through Shane's eyes, always hopeful and determined to see the good in everyone. But the fact is, Dad screwed his personal assistant, which is the most cliché thing ever. She's not much older than I am. Not only did he screw her in our Manhattan townhouse, he screwed her so much that he decided to leave Mom and me, like we didn't need him anymore. In my opinion, what Dad did had *everything* to do with me.

"Just be on my side, okay?" I grab the ball from Shane and sink another basket. Dad always liked Shane better and we both know it. And why wouldn't he? Shane's the talented one, the smart one, the real musician. The EMT for fuck's sake. The one who never messes up.

"I'm always on your side," Shane says. "But you can't run away from this."

"Why not? You dodge Brent Miller."

"I don't *dodge* him. And besides, you're always there, stepping in. You never give me the chance to deal with him myself."

"I'm your best friend. I have to step in. I can't let him do that shit to you."

"Well I can't sit back and watch you sabotage your relationship with Don, just to prove a point. I know he screwed up big time this year but he's your *dad*. It's not the same as me ignoring a jerk who doesn't know how to spell his own name."

"Fair enough," I say. "But I'm still not ready to talk to him."

"Fair enough," Shane says, dribbling the basketball. The rubber bounce echoes between us and it's obvious we're both done talking about the things we hate talking about.

"You still having that party Saturday night?"

"Yeah," he says, chucking the ball at me. "Just band people."

"Cool," I say. "Let's just play." I dunk the ball, the net swishing as it falls through. My back pocket vibrates, and I swear if Dad's texting me again, I'm changing my number. I pull out the phone as Shane dribbles the ball in circles around me.

Ray

We need to talk.

"Your dad?" Shane asks, knowing he's been texting me nonstop. "I know you're not ready to talk, but maybe start with a text? There's no time like the present."

"It's not him." I stare at the text, the bouncing making my head pound. "Enough with the basketball."

Shane catches the ball midair and asks, "Who is it?"

"Ray."

"I thought you guys weren't talking." Shane sits on the basketball like a little kid. Saying Ray's name reminds me of the way she used to look at me last year, her eyes locked into mine. But then Dad left, and she stopped coming around, stopped answering texts, which was almost worse than Dad leaving because Ray never gave me a reason. After a couple weeks of radio silence, I decided I was over being left and broke it off completely. I glance at the text again, then erase it and shove the phone into my pocket. I don't see the point in responding to a girl who bailed when I needed her most.

"We're not," I say, but Shane's not listening. He's staring at his own phone, his eyes fixed on the screen, like John Bonham rose straight out of his grave and asked him to take his place behind the drums on a Zeppelin reunion tour.

"What?"

"Nothing." Shane stands, shielding his phone against his chest.

"Who's texting you?"

Shane turns his back to me, but I reach around him and grab his phone, reading the screen.

Stevie

Hi Shane, it's Stevie. Any chance you can help me with All-State?

Shane

Hey Stevie Nicks

Stevie

Don't start

Shane

Don't stop . . . thinking about tomorrow

Stevie

Groan. Eye Roll

Shane

Okay. Okay. I'm officially done with the Fleetwood Mac references, promise. And I can help with All-State. You just need the right audition piece.

Stevie

Thank you. Done eye rolling. Is All-State that easy?

Shane

Easier

Stevie

Maybe for you. How'd you get in
freshman year anyway?

Shane

Jedi mind tricks

Stevie

Never seen Star Wars

Shane

Forget it, not helping you

Stevie

For real?

Shane

Kidding! But it's gotta be on
Wednesday. On the days we don't
have band practice I volunteer with
the EMT squad after school.

Stevie

Wednesday it is!

Heat rises to my face, like the time Dad asked Shane to head backstage with him at the Foo Fighters show instead of me. Even though I was psyched for Shane, it still sucked. Dad and Shane disappeared behind a black curtain, Shane getting to meet one of his idols, while I was stuck with Mom waiting on the other side. Dad could only bring one person backstage and he chose Shane.

"How does she have your number?" I ask, handing Shane his phone.

"I don't know. Band list? Everyone has everyone's number." Shane shoves the phone in his pocket without texting Stevie back.

"Ask her to come to your party." I pick up the ball and pass it to Shane. He wraps his arms around it like a bag of groceries, narrowing his eyes.

"You don't have the guts to ask her out again yourself?" He takes a shot and misses, the iron hoop vibrating.

"Of course I do." I grab the ball and throw it at him.

"Uh huh," Shane says, dribbling a steady rhythm, seeing right through my bullshit.

"But you're the one throwing the party. Can you just invite her?" I ask, my voice pathetic.

"I'll text her now," Shane says, biting away a smile as he taps out a message. I steal a peek over his shoulder.

Shane

I'm having a party at my house Saturday night. Only people from band. You in?

Shane and I watch three little dots appear on the screen. I elbow him and he elbows me back until another message appears.

Stevie

In. See you then.

"Happy?" Shane asks, shoving his phone back in his pocket.

"Thanks," I say as Shane sinks a basket. I know that penny landed on heads, but I also know Shane's putting aside his own feelings for me. Regardless of how this plays out, Shane's legit, the one person who always has my back. "I owe you one."

CHAPTER 5

Stevie

A willow tree presides over our front lawn, branches bending toward the earth. I'm underneath the green dome, fading sunlight cutting through the leaves, like the inside of a kaleidoscope. Of all the places I've lived, underneath this willow is the best spot in the world. Ever since we moved here in the beginning of the summer, I've sought refuge under this tree. Tonight is no different. I pull my headphones on, blocking out the birds chirping their goodnights. My favorite album, the one Sarah calls old-people music, slides through the tiny speakers and into my ears. My parents think I'm already at Shane's party, but I needed to come here first to slow the somersaults in my brain. I stretch my legs as the first track of *Ten* calms my body, Eddie Vedder's low growl replacing my racing thoughts, the driving chords somehow relaxing my muscles.

Sarah always convinced me to go to parties, pulling a cut up concert T-shirt over my head, the kind she made look cool with a pair of scissors and beads, and practically pushed me out the door promising a night to remember. *It's going to be epic,* she would always say, even if it was only a few people from the band playing Fortnite in someone's basement. With her by my side, I wasn't the kind of girl who hides under trees.

But I haven't heard from Sarah since the first day of practice, my last video chat request sitting unanswered in my phone for three days. I begin to doubt if I was ever best friends with Sarah, Krystal, Emily, or Nicole. Maybe I was a filler, a pit stop, a girl they played Barbies with when they were little. Even so, I long for the way Sarah's able to transform me, temporarily fearless and carefree, so I text her again.

> Me
>
> How's Seattle? I'm heading to a party. Wish you were with me.

A tidal wave of relief washes over me when three dots appear on the screen, a lifeline to my past life.

> Sarah
>
> Party? Do tell. Sorry I've been MIA.
> My mom's been on my case.

I'm not sure her mom is a good enough excuse for slacking on texts. But I push past my annoyance because I'd rather have a fading best friend than no friend at all.

> Me
>
> A band party. What's going on with
> your mom?

Sarah

It's too much for text. I'm sorry I
haven't called you back. The time
difference sucks.

Me

Yeah

The time difference sucks. The distance sucks. Being far
away plain sucks.

Sarah

Why are you being weird?

Me

I'm not being weird. And anyway,
you can't read tone over text.

Sarah

I can with you. Is there a guy?

Me

No

Sarah

There is! Who is he?

I stare at the screen, shaking my head. Night falls
around me, the remaining light slowly dimming into darkness, as Eddie sings about his whole world turning to
black.

Me
This guy Drew.

Sarah
He sounds hot.

The thought of Drew makes me feel off balance, like standing in an elevator that shoots up fast. Drew on the curb outside of school, the light falling around his shoulders, his eyes boring into me, my stomach in a back handspring, definitely not sticking the landing. Excitement bubbles in my gut, a can of soda cracked wide open. I inhale the humid air, then breathe it all out, trying to be the kind of girl who doesn't get nervous for high school parties.

Me
You're impossible.

Sarah
You love me. But seriously why are you texting with me right now? Get to that party! You're not having a Stevie moment, are you?

Me
No. I'm fine.

Sarah
Turn off Pearl Jam and GO TO THE PARTY!!

Me
How do you know I'm listening to Pearl Jam?

Sarah

**Because you're always listening to
Pearl Jam. JUST GO.**

I stand and slide the headphones off, stuffing them in my bag. I pull apart the branches and step into the moonlight. The air is thick, like the clouds are about to burst open and unleash a downpour.

Me

Going.

Sarah

It's gonna be epic. Text me later. xoxo

I shove the phone in my bag and head over to Shane's. My eyelids are heavy, an unwelcome side effect of the insomnia that's plagued me since we moved to Seattle. It only intensified after we settled here in New Jersey. I pray the eyeliner and mascara hide the dark circles that make me look older than I am. It's not that I don't want to sleep. I want nothing more than to get a solid eight hours, but my head hits the pillow and my thoughts are like a thoroughbred gunning for the finish line. Thoughts of never getting what I want before we have to move and start over again.

Before I know it, I reach Shane's house, only a few blocks over from mine, surrounded by manicured hedges. The *Aladdin* genie sits between two grooves at the top of an intimidating gate, his silly smile welcoming me. I press a button on a call box and a fuzzy voice asks for my name. When I reply the gate slowly swings open, revealing a long, winding driveway, lined with purple and pink hydrangeas. My flip-flops smack the asphalt, bringing me closer to Shane's house. But this isn't a house. The structure that looms before me is an estate, a castle even. Something you would see in a Disney movie with gray stone covering the entire façade. My heart jackhammers against my chest as I pick at my thumb. I smooth down my hair and urge myself to continue walking instead of bolting. *It's gonna be epic.*

Before I reach the front door, a Ray LaMontagne song and the steady bounce of a basketball catch my attention. "Be Here Now" floats through the air, soft like a breeze. I follow the music back through the gate, across the front yard, and to the driveway next door. Drew sinks a basket, grabs the ball, positions it against the night sky, and launches it at the net. I stop short, almost tripping over my flops. He misses, the ball banking off the side of the backboard, crashing to the ground, and knocking over a stack of red Solo cups like a set of bowling pins. Drew takes another shot, humming softly to the song playing from a phone balanced on the hood of his Jeep. He sings a line as he dribbles the ball, a beat to his melody. My breath catches. He sounds like Ray LaMontagne, or maybe like James Bay. I'm starting to feel like a creeper, so I step closer to him and clear my throat. The basketball drops from his hands and rolls down the driveway, slamming into the mailbox.

"What are you doing out here?" I ask, but really what am *I* doing out here, stalking him on his driveway?

"I live here." He gestures at his house, which is surrounded by a never-ending wraparound porch, all white posts and wooden rocking chairs. The lights are off, like his entire family went away on vacation. "What are *you* doing here?"

"Shane's party." I state the obvious. "But I heard your music. I didn't peg you for a Ray LaMontagne fan."

Drew hops on his car, his boots banging against the

metal. He turns the music off and pats a section of the hood, scooting over for me.

"His voice is cool." He shoves his phone in his sweatshirt pocket. I climb up and lean back on the windshield, dropping my bag next to the tire. The clouds move fast, revealing stars, then hiding them again. "He never sounds like he's trying too hard, and yet his voice is so stripped down and real. It almost feels like you know him."

"You sound like him," I say, and Drew's eyes shift to the sky as he tucks his hair behind his ears.

"I wish." His eyes, dark like the night, meet mine. "But thanks."

"Why aren't you inside?"

"I was for a while. Shane needed more cups." Drew gestures at the plastic cups, still toppled over at the edge of the driveway. He leans on the windshield, so close to me our shoulders touch. "Was about to head back. But I needed a break. Do you ever feel like that? Like all the people, some party, is just, I don't know, tiring?"

All the time. And it's not only at parties. At school, in class, at lunch, wherever I am, it's always like I'm trying, like I'm a cheesy fluorescent billboard begging for someone to see me. I always blamed it on the impermanence of my life, but maybe it's an excuse I give myself for never belonging. Someone like Ray wouldn't care about moving. She'd fit right in wherever she landed.

"Yeah," I say, glancing at Shane's house, music spilling from the windows. I don't want to go inside. Drew clasps his hands over his stomach and sighs, flashing me the Roman numerals tattooed on his wrist, the symbols clear.

"Eighteen?" I ask, my finger almost grazing his skin. At first he says nothing, his eyes fixed on the clouds. I never have the right words, especially in moments like this one.

Sometimes it's like my mind is a blank piece of paper, but I don't have a pen. "Sorry, I shouldn't have asked."

"It's for October eighteenth." Drew shifts his gaze to me, a hint of gratitude playing in his deep eyes, a prelude to the story he launches into.

"It was the start of eighth grade, the first real fall day. Shane and I were super into skateboarding back then." Drew shakes his head and laughs a little. "Wannabe punks I guess. Anyway, we were at the skate park in town, messing around, trying to one up each other. A bunch of the guys from my grade were there. I was showing off, trying to copy this Shaun White double mctwist trick, which was stupid. I didn't think it through." Drew fidgets with the ropes on his wrist. He won't look at me.

"I never made it one full twist around and flew completely off the ramp, crashing to the ground. That was the last thing I remembered, the sound of my body crunching against the pavement. When I woke up in the hospital, Shane was the only one there. My parents hadn't even gotten there yet. The doctors said Shane called the ambulance and knew enough not to move my body. I shattered a few bones in my back and a couple in my neck. They said I was lucky. A few more inches and I might have been in a wheelchair or . . . you know."

Drew finally looks at me, his eyes ablaze. He sits up, leaning to me, the strings of his sweatshirt grazing the hood of the car. His lower lip juts out slightly and curves into a disbelieving smile.

"It was the best day."

"The best day?" I tilt my head, trying to fathom how almost dying could be the best day. If I almost died, I'd want to erase the entire day from my history and pretend like it never happened. At sleepaway camp one summer I fell out of a canoe, right in the middle of river rapids. I hadn't yet learned to swim, but a counselor dragged me out of the water. I remember thinking it. *You could die.* And the thought alone, even though I was safely in my counselor's arms, sent the shakes down my entire body.

"A few inches saved my life. And Shane knew enough to know what to do. So yeah, it was the best day. The luckiest day. Even if I don't act like it most of the time, I try to remind myself of that feeling—the euphoria of a second chance. Easier said than done though," Drew says, raising his eyebrows.

Maybe Drew's way is better. To think of the most terrifying moments of our lives as the best ones. To realize you *didn't* die that day. That you're still here.

"Eighteen is the numerical equivalent to the Hebrew word *chai*," I say. "It means life."

"I didn't know that," Drew says. Chills fly across my skin as our eyes connect. He glances at the tattoo. "Life. That's exactly what that day means to me."

"Do you still skateboard?"

"Nah, I lost interest after that day. I know, get back on the horse and all that. But really, some horses aren't worth riding. Shane stopped skating too."

"Is that when he started volunteering with the EMT squad?"

"Yeah, it's his thing. Besides drums. Smart as hell too. It's kind of annoying," he says with fondness. "I bet you're smart too. Shane says you share some honors classes."

"Honors English, history, and chem," I say, smiling. "But there are a lot of different ways of being smart."

"That's what Shane says." Drew glances over his shoulder. "Speaking of Shane . . ."

"I guess we should head over," I say with absolutely no conviction, because I would much rather stay here than make pointless conversation with people I hardly know.

"What I really feel like doing is heading down to the shore. Perfect night for it," Drew says, gesturing at the sky.

"I've never been."

"The beach at night is . . ." Drew says, gazing out at the neighborhood. He clears his throat. "The world, my world at least, always feels like a series of random events. But when I look at the ocean, especially at night, it feels like there's a synchronicity to things, like maybe the answers are out there somewhere."

Drew shakes his head, smiles to himself, then turns to me and says, "Kind of corny, huh?"

"No," I say, my voice a whisper, wanting more than anything to see the ocean through Drew's eyes. "It sounds perfect."

"When's your curfew?"

"Way too early." I probably have a couple hours, but the shore is far.

"Another time."

"Let's go," I say, the words surprising me as they tumble from my mouth and hang in the air. Crickets chirp around us, almost like a tiny chorus chanting *go, go, go.*

"You sure you won't get in trouble?" Drew hops down from the hood and unlocks the door.

"Nah, my parents are probably busy with my little brother," I lie, and for this split second in time, I don't feel remorse. "They won't even notice if I'm late."

I'm going to get in so much trouble. My nails dig into the upholstery as my heart pounds against my chest. I've never missed curfew. Not once. Drew turns on the ignition, and the Jeep roars to life, vibrating beneath me. One wrist rests casually on the steering wheel, and his jeans are so ripped it looks like the bottom half might fall off. He turns to me, shaking hair out of his face.

"You sure this is okay?" he asks, pulling out of the driveway.

I nod, but it's so *not* okay. My parents are going to murder me. But he looks at me like he never wants to stop looking at me and there's no way I'm getting out of this car. I'm sick of missing things and nodding along to each move and rule my parents declare. A strand of purple and green beads dangles from the rearview mirror and I flick it with my finger.

"Mardi Gras?" I ask. His melodic laugh, like a song, puts me at ease. He flicks the beads too.

"Went a couple years back, with my dad." His foot hits the accelerator and he rolls the windows down. My hair flies back as he drives fast, weaving in and out of lanes. I try to smooth it down but it's no use, as strands tornado around my head. Both of his hands drop off the steering wheel and my nails dig deeper into my seat. The car sways into the next lane and he shifts the wheel back with his knee. He reaches into the middle console for one of those Adidas headbands tennis players wear, and pulls it over his head, securing his hair out of his eyes. Both hands grip the steering wheel again.

"Faster," I yell above the rush of air as trees, houses, and the entire world blur by us. The speedometer needle quivers higher as we hit seventy, eighty, and hover close to ninety. "Okay, too fast." My hand grabs the door.

Drew takes his foot off the accelerator and we slow. He reaches out and tucks a strand of my wild hair behind my ear before flipping on the radio.

"Nice," he says as "We Will Rock You" booms through the speakers. His thumb taps the steering wheel in sync with the song. I reach for the volume and turn it up. Drew turns it up even louder, raising his eyebrows. The car shakes with each stomp and clap of the beat. He starts to sing over the radio, and I was wrong. He doesn't sound like Ray LaMontagne or James Bay. My mouth falls open as he rips through the verses, his deep baritone soaring into a rich tenor at the chorus. He's not as good as Freddie Mercury. I mean, no one is, but still. He kind of sounds like Scott Weiland who tried too hard to sound like Eddie Vedder who sounds a little like Layne Staley, but that's not the point. The point is, he's incredible, his voice cutting through me. It's pure, unfiltered, and raw, the person behind that voice praying to be known.

"You have a great voice," I say as the song fades out. "You should front a band."

"I'm in a band with some of the guys from my grade." Drew smiles, a memory tugging at the corners of his mouth. "We play local shows. Nothing fancy."

"What's it called?" is all I ask. But I really want to know what's it like to play in front of people. To have an audience dancing to music you wrote, maybe even singing your words. To make a connection with an entire room. It must be the greatest feeling in the world.

"Dark Carnival," he says. "I got the name from a Ray Bradbury short story collection. You know it?" The air turns salty and I know we're getting close to the shore, more than twenty minutes from home. I pray my parents don't wait up tonight.

"Science fiction, right?" I think back to a Bradbury story we had to read in middle school English class. It's pretty out there, dark and mysterious, kind of like Drew.

"Yep. I read all his stuff. Anyway, the name is an oxymoron of course." Drew turns down a small side street. "Carnivals are supposed to be colorful and cheerful. But a dark carnival—that's something else entirely. It's all about the unexpected—kind of like the stuff Bradbury writes. It's a name that confuses you and makes you think. And that's what I want people to feel at our shows—confused and thinking about what they saw, but in a great way, you know?"

"Does the audience feel that way?"

"I hope so." A faraway look settles in Drew's eyes and I know he's back in a moment I wish I could be a part of. "Anyway, we're here."

Drew puts the car in park by a beat-up set of wooden stairs. He pulls the headband out of his hair, strands flopping around his face like a curtain call. When I hop out, the salty air sticks to my skin and I can almost taste it. I hug my arms around my body as Drew shrugs off his hoodie, a gray T-shirt clinging to his chest.

"Here," he says handing me the sweatshirt, which is still warm as I wrap myself in it. "Come on."

I take off my flip-flops once we hit the sand and the soft beach is one big beanbag squishing through my toes. Drew kicks off his boots and balls up his socks, stuffing them inside. This stretch of beach is deserted, silent except for the waves rising and crashing.

"Isn't the Inkwell somewhere around here?" I ask, referring to the famous coffee shop that Springsteen used to frequent.

"A bit up the road," Drew says, sitting on the sand. I sit next to him and he scoots closer to me, resting his arms on his knees. His phone vibrates from inside his sweatshirt pocket. I pull it out and catch a glimpse of the message on the screen.

Tom

Can you hook me up with Gotham
Fest tickets?

I hand Drew the phone. He glances at the text and shakes his head, tucking the phone into his jeans pocket. He pinches the bridge of his nose and lets out a long sigh.

"Tom Walker. Our quarterback," Drew says as if he owes me an explanation, which of course he doesn't. A wave crashes at the end of the beach, pushing a soft breeze across my face. Drew draws a circle in the sand, tracing the shape, hesitating.

"Why is he asking you for concert tickets?" All the biggest acts are playing Central Park tomorrow and the festival is completely sold out. There's no way Drew can pull off those tickets.

Drew stops playing with the sand, dusting his fingers off on his jeans. He gazes at the sky and pulls his hair off his face.

"My dad's a music producer. People ask me for stuff," he says softly. "A lot."

I snap my head to him as it hits me—Drew *Mason*. Drew's dad is Don Mason. The guy who discovered Springsteen. The visionary who's shaped countless careers. I watched a Netflix documentary on him a few years back. He's one of the most powerful men in music, if not *the* most powerful. My jaw drops, but I close it fast as I notice the way Drew's face falls, the way he starts to shut down. He shifts from me slightly and I recognize this move. It's the same way I act when someone finds out about my own dad, especially someone I care about. Once someone knows, all bets are off. My judgment blurs, and I can't tell if their intentions are genuine. Drew needs to know I'm here for him and nothing more.

"I know what that's like," I say, making sure our eyes connect so he knows I mean every word. The moon reflects in his dark irises as he holds my gaze. "It's hard to trust people, to know the real reason someone is hanging out with you."

"When I was younger, I thought Tom and his football crew were my friends. This was before Brent started messing with Shane and before I realized they were always using me for something. They were at the skate park the day I wiped out. They didn't even bother coming to the hospital or even stopping by as I recovered at home. That's when I realized they weren't worth my time."

My heart squeezes, beating faster. I understand every word that comes out of Drew's mouth, not only because I sympathize with what he's saying, but because I've lived it. The excitement of a new friend, a connection, followed by the crash of realization—the new friend is a fake, a pretender. I say the one thing I longed to hear growing up with a larger-than-life father.

"Drew, I don't want concert tickets. I'm not here because of who your dad is." Drew's eyes flick to mine and they're less heavy, like a veil has been lifted. "I'm here because of you."

Drew shifts closer, his eyes on me. Heat from his body settles on my skin and all at once it's hard to breathe. His knees poke through the holes in his jeans as his hair falls in front of his eyes.

"Same," he says, a slow smile stretching across his face. "I'm here because of you too. And only you." He wraps his arm around my shoulder, and I lean into him, the waves crashing ahead, a symphony of ocean water against the sand. We sit like this, listening to the tide, understanding each other. For the first time, someone understands. Every second of tonight feels like the best type of beginning, a guitar riff that's destined to build into a gorgeous melody.

"You think it's cold?" Drew asks, nodding at the waves.

I'm not sure if it's the salty air, or being close to Drew, but I say, "Let's find out." And before I can think, I wiggle out of my shorts and peel Drew's hoodie off, giggling, my heart racing, and it's like I'm not even in my own body. It's like I'm watching an alternate version of myself, someone who breaks all the rules. Drew freezes, his mouth parting open, eyeing my pink heart underwear and red tank top.

"What? It's like a bathing suit." I don't recognize my voice either, bold and confident. "You coming?"

I take off for the water, not even looking back.

"Hold up," he yells after me, but I head for the ocean, laughing the entire way. I gaze over my shoulder and he's down to his dark blue boxers. All at once the sight of him brings me straight back into my body. I stop short right in front of the tide, crossing my arms over my tank top. I'm in my underwear in front of Drew Mason. I've never even kissed a guy unless you count that one game of spin the bottle, and I honestly wouldn't know what to do if a guy actually liked me. In middle school, an eighth grader sent me a rose on Valentine's Day and I pretended I never got it. He never asked, and I never brought it up.

What in the world am I doing?

"What are you waiting for?" He jumps into the water, disappearing beneath the surface. It's quiet, the water almost black. I stare into the darkness as the waves lap on the shore.

"Drew?"

His head reappears, and he spits out a mouthful of salt water before floating on his back.

"It's warm. Come on!" He backstrokes through the water, but I can't move, suddenly acutely aware that I'm half naked. "Fine, then I'm coming for you."

He jumps out of the water, soaking wet. His hair hangs limp, grazing his shoulders. The boxer shorts stick to him and I can't look. But I can't *not* look. He comes for me and I run backwards, my feet making divots in the sand.

"Oh, no way," I say, laughing and stopping dead in my tracks, giving him time to catch up. "You're soaked."

Drew wraps both arms around my waist and pulls me toward the dark sky. I let out a yelp, and then I can't stop laughing, uncontrollable breathless laughs. Drops of water run down my stomach to my legs and all the way to my toes.

All of a sudden, a bright light shines on the sand and Drew puts me down, almost dropping me.

"Shhh," he says, holding a finger to his lips. He eyes the boardwalk and quickly crouches in the sand, guiding me down with him. "Shit. Cop."

My breath is short and fast, right in time with my heart. If a cop busts me, my parents will murder me, resurrect me, and then murder me again.

"What are you two doing down there? Beach is closed," echoes a voice from the boardwalk.

"Sorry, sir. We're heading out," Drew shouts back, his voice tentative and polite. We rush to our clothes and scramble to get dressed.

"You have three minutes," he warns, and I silently thank the starless sky.

"Yes, sir." Drew grabs my hand and looks me in the eye. "Let's get out of here."

"That was close." Drew turns to me, unconcerned about the road ahead. He tucks his damp hair behind both ears. "What do you wanna hear?"

"Whatever's on," I say. Sand falls from my toes as I take

off my flip-flops and put them back on. The bold and sponta-
neous version of myself from the beach has completely disappeared. I'm brought back down to reality as the seductive
crash of the ocean waves is replaced by the quiet hum of the
Jeep's engine. My confidence drains away and instead I'm
shaking like I stepped out of a swimming pool.

"You cold?"

"Yeah," I lie to cover up my nerves. Drew glances at my
trembling fingers as my mind searches for something, anything to say. "So, why did you join the band?"

"Why did you?" he fires back at me, his eyes focusing on
the road.

"Because I love to play," I say. A simple answer, but the
truth. The truest thing I've ever known.

"I can tell," he says, expertly turning the steering wheel
with his palm only, the Mardi Gras beads swaying as we
merge onto the shoulder of the highway. The beach disappears in the side mirror.

"I joined band because he asked me to." Drew karate chops
the blinker before jerking the car into the left lane. "My dad,
he wanted me to expand my musical horizons, or whatever.
That was right before he left us for his personal assistant. So I
probably shouldn't have taken advice from him."

"I'm sorry," I say, but I'm not surprised. The split was all
over music blogs and gossip magazines. I want to ask Drew
more, but pain settles in his eyes, so I change the subject.
"You don't seem like a Marching Mustang," I say, pulling at a
thread from my shorts as a green highway sign passes overhead.

"Oh yeah? What exactly defines a Marching Mustang?"

"Someone a bit more . . . someone . . . not you," I say, my
cheeks flushing. Drew laughs and shakes his head.

"I'm not a *type,* you know. No one is. I can be in the marching band and sing in a rock band and like sci fi and be obsessed with basketball. Not one thing defines anyone, you know?"

"I know," I say, wishing he wasn't driving so I could meet his gaze. "I guess I've never been in one place long enough to really know someone."

To really know myself, I think, but don't say.

"Have you ever tried?" He glances at me again, his eyes narrowing, like he's trying to decode me. "I don't know what it's like—packing up and moving around. But if you ask me, you don't need to stay put to figure all that out."

Drew toggles through the radio stations and settles on one. It so quiet in the car, that I'm thankful when the DJ breaks the silence and introduces an old Taylor Swift song. Drew groans and I laugh. Her stuff is always on—it's like you can't ever escape it.

"What does this even mean? Go to lonely Starbucks lovers?" Drew asks shaking his head at the radio.

"Try, *got a long list of ex-lovers,*" I say and Drew laughs.

"I like it my way better," he says, turning up the radio, and when he starts singing I can't help joining. I sing even louder than Drew, and we're like two over-dramatic chorus kids. He's laughing now, so hard that little lines form by the corners of his eyes. We end the song in unison as Drew pulls onto my street. When he approaches my house, the porch light is mercifully off, the windows dark and still.

"That song sucks," he says, wiping laugh tears from his eyes.

"Terrible. Although many other people think otherwise," I say, as Drew shifts into park in front of my house.

"Maybe we're not other people," he says, turning the engine off, and maybe he's right. The car goes so quiet and still, I'm almost afraid to breathe. Drew shifts, exposing a small rip in his hoodie, right by the elbow. A couple loose strings fray down his arm. He steals a glance at my lips and I watch his eyes carefully, trying to uncover their secrets. Those eyes are like an abyss—never-ending and impossible to understand. Outside, the moon bounces off the hood of his car and everything—the car, the headlights, the dark sky—is fuzzy, and it almost looks like I'm in a dream. Part of me wonders if I am.

His hand grazes over mine and for a split second my heart forgets how to beat. His touch, almost like a feather, sends a chill through my body.

"Still cold?"

"Maybe," I say, and I don't even know what I'm saying anymore. I look out the window, willing myself to stay calm.

"Stevie?"

I turn to him as he takes my hand, threading his fingers through mine. My hand squeezes back, almost like an invitation, and just like that, his lips meet mine. And it's nothing like I imagined. His perfect mouth is soft and hard, wanting yet tentative. Fingers slowly comb through my hair and his other hand lightly touches the side of my face. His thumb traces along my chin as he softly takes my lower lip between both of his. He pulls back and leans into me again, his mouth dancing with mine. A sprinkler sputters outside, but I barely notice. My eyes peek for a second as his hair falls in front of his face, and I see him, lost in a moment with me. I don't want him to stop, but he pulls away, his mouth still parted, breathless. I'm stunned.

"Night," he whispers.

"Night." I'm so shaky and buzzy from that kiss that I can barely get the car door open. I climb down to the curb and I have never felt so completely alive. Not even the time when I stayed up all night with Sarah to watch the sunrise—pinks, purples, and oranges splashing across the six a.m. sky. This isn't like watching the sunrise.

This is like *being* the sunrise.

CHAPTER 6

Drew

"Night," Stevie says as she jumps down from the Jeep, her brown eyes alive. She heads for her house, gazing back at me. I'm sure I have some shit-eating grin plastered on my face, but I don't care. Because now, Stevie's not only the intriguing girl I noticed on the first day of band practice. She's thoughtful and smart as hell and sincere. In one night, Stevie made me feel like myself, not the guy with the famous father and not the guy who can hook up tickets—just me. Stevie doesn't want anything from me. Nothing. And just knowing that is everything.

"Let me walk you to the door," I say, hopping down from the Jeep and catching up with her on the stone walkway to her house. But before we reach the door, the porch light flicks on, like a jailhouse spotlight. Stevie freezes and shout-whispers, "Go!"

She pulls away from me and runs up the steps as the front door swings wide open. Stevie's dad steps onto the porch in a Jets T-shirt and drawstring pajama pants, his face pure stone. His chin and cheeks are hidden behind an aggressive five o'clock shadow. A dog from across the street barks like mad, fraying my nerves.

"It's midnight, Stevie." His voice is steady, stating a fact. He's too calm and it's freaking me the fuck out.

Stevie's mom steps onto the porch, pulling an oversize Jets sweatshirt over her head. She rubs her eyes, makeup smudged underneath. Even though sweat breaks out on my palms, it's cool her parents actually waited up. My parents have never waited up for me, claiming they trust my judgment, when in fact they're probably lazy. But that's only on the infrequent nights they don't have an industry party or social engagement. They always *have* to make an appearance, like it's not a choice. But of course it's a choice—it's their choice to leave me home alone. When I was little it was a rotating door of nannies and now—well, it's only me.

"I lost track of time. I'm so sorry," Stevie says, picking at her finger. That dog's paws are pressed against the window, each maddening bark echoing through the quiet street like he's announcing to the neighborhood how badly I fucked up. "This is Drew Mason. He's in the band with me."

I step forward and extend a hand. Stevie's dad glances at me, but he doesn't smile. He doesn't take my hand either.

"It's my fault," I say, burying my hand in the front pocket of my hoodie.

"Stevie can make her own decisions," her dad says. "You should head on home."

No way am I heading home. I'm not stepping off this porch until he understands it was my idea to go to the beach, not Stevie's.

"Caleb." Stevie's mom puts her hand on his shoulder, but he doesn't relent. "Give them a minute to explain."

"Come inside, Stevie," Caleb says calmly. Too calmly. He gestures at the entryway, which is completely bare—not even a coatrack or photo on the wall. He glances across the street at the dog, which is about to hurl itself through the glass window. "You're going to wake the whole neighborhood."

"I don't *care* about the neighborhood. Since when can I make my own decisions?" Stevie's voice rises. "Nothing in my life is my decision. Your job dictates everything."

Caleb's expression stays frozen, undecipherable, which is worse than him screaming at us. Dad's a yeller. Mostly at his clients or at his staff, never at me. When I was little, I hated the yelling, but then it became normal, a barometer of how pissed he was. At least if Caleb yelled I'd know where we stand. My heart rams into my chest and part of me wants to get the hell out of here.

"It really was my fault," I say. Stevie bites down on her bottom lip, like she's stuffing in tears. She glances at me and says under her breath, "I'm sorry."

"You need to leave," Caleb says, his eyes serious and holding my gaze. He's not fucking around. I back down the porch steps, my hand slick on the railing.

"I'm sorry," I say again to all of them, stumbling backwards. They don't respond and head inside the house, the front door slamming shut. I'm not sure if it was Stevie or her dad, but my bet's on Stevie. Once I'm back in my car, it's quiet. The dog stops barking, and the porch light flicks off, this whole night gone to shit.

When I pull the Jeep into our driveway there's no spotlight waiting for me. The house is dark and quiet. Mom must still be out with the finance guy she met last week. He donated a ton of money to her charity and Mom says he's *nice*. But I think her standards should be much higher than nice.

Once I'm inside, I peel off my hoodie and throw it on the baby grand. I consider texting Stevie to make sure she's okay but then think better of it. Her parents are probably still up lecturing her or, worse, grounding her. Me and my impulsive ideas. I never should have brought her to the beach, so far away from home. I hope her parents can forgive me and most of all I hope Stevie's not mad.

The light in Dad's office is on, taunting me. It reminds me of being little and getting up in the middle of the night scared of some dream. Dad loved to work weird hours and would always be in there, obsessing over a contract, on the phone, or sometimes playing one of the guitars softly. I would scamper in, rubbing my worried eyes and rambling about the nightmare. Dad would smile and say *I got you* with outstretched arms. Once I was safe, wrapped in his embrace, the monsters didn't seem as big. They didn't seem real at all. He would show me what he was working on and talk to me like a grown-up. I couldn't wait to grow up and be just like him—successful, confident, a person who makes his dreams a reality. But last year I realized it was all smoke and mirrors. He's cocky, not confident. He's careless with his success and his family. I see him clearly now—he's a man who pissed all over me and Mom, the two people who unconditionally had his back.

I push the door open to flick off the light and jump back when I spot Dad, his feet propped on the desk.

"Andrew," he says, standing. He slides his glasses onto his face and steps toward me. I don't smile. "It's late," he says, like he's actually trying to parent me.

"Since when do you care how late I stay out?" I inhale deeply but this anger, this pure hatred for the one person I loved the most bubbles up inside me. I'm afraid if I keep talking it'll boil over and I'll never be able to take it back. "Why are you here?"

"Where's Mom?"

"I don't know."

He scratches the back of his head and pulls on his gray hoodie. Dad's the only sixty-eight-year-old I know who can get away with wearing a hoodie.

"You still in your band?" he asks, leaning against the desk and crossing his legs at the ankles. His salt and pepper hair is thinner and shorter, a physical reminder that I haven't seen him in months.

I kick at the carpet, but when I look up my demo is in his hand. "You never listened to it," I say flatly.

"Andrew, it's good. It's really good."

"What?" I say, a few bricks falling from my fortress of hate. "When did you . . ."

"Just now. I was supposed to meet Mom, and well, she's not here. It got late, and I was about to head back when I saw your demo. You can really sing."

"Thanks," I say, stepping closer to him, thinking of the Dark Carnival show booked for next week. My heart double times it, a woodpecker knocking against my chest. A small voice from inside my head whispers *just ask him.* "You know, we're playing a show after the first football game. Old Silver Tavern. You should stop by."

I try to sound casual but hope soars from my mouth into my words.

"I'd love to," Dad says, like he's been waiting for this invitation. For a brief moment I catch a glimpse of the man I knew before the cheating and the leaving, and my heart lurches in my chest. "I've been trying to get in touch with you for a while now."

"I know." Maybe Shane's right and all I have to do is give him a chance. "I'll pick up next time."

"I'm glad I saw you, Andrew. You really shouldn't be out so late though." There he goes trying to parent me again. I can't say I mind it. "Tell Mom I left something for her." He pats a manila folder on the desk.

The next thing I know he envelops me in a hug, tight and long, and for these few seconds I'm safe again. But after he's gone I sit in his huge leather chair and flip open the manila folder. Divorce papers. They're not signed, a blank box full of hope. But deep down I know better. Fuck it. My hands grab for my phone and I tap out a message fast.

> Me
>
> **Hey Stevie. It's Drew. I hope you're okay.**

But she doesn't respond.

CHAPTER 7

Stevie

SEPTEMBER

I reread the text from Drew for the hundredth time. *I hope you're okay.* I'm not okay. I'm rattled, thrown completely off balance, my mind consumed by thoughts of the beach, Drew's hands through my hair, inhaling his scent, like getting lost on a trail in the middle of the woods. After that night, everything changed. For the first time since moving to this New Jersey suburb I'm ready to start over again, excited even. Being near Drew shifts this black-and-white town into color. But once I saw the look on Dad's face, the way he eyed Drew's Jeep like it had cast an evil spell over me, I knew I was done for. Dad would never flip out in front of Drew, but seconds after Drew's Jeep sped away from our street, he stormed into our kitchen, pacing between the island and fridge.

"What were you thinking?" Dad's voice rumbled low and serious. He braced his hands on the corner of the kitchen island, glaring at me. The wall clock ticked away each second, grating my nerves. "Why didn't you text us? You're over an hour late."

"I lost track of time," I said, picking at my cuticle. My thumb and pointer finger pulsed in pain. "I guess I wasn't thinking."

"Exactly, you weren't thinking," Dad said, his voice rising.

"Listen to her," Mom said, putting her hand on his shoulder. For a split second Dad's expression softened, but then his nostrils flared in the way they do when his quarterback throws an incomplete pass.

"You're too easy on her, Naomi," Dad said, which isn't true at all. Mom remembers what it's like to be young, unlike Dad, who always seems tired.

"C'mon, Cal," Mom said, her doe eyes apologizing to me. But her protests won't matter. In the end it's Dad's call. It's been that way as long as I can remember—Mom the jury, always eager to hear every side of the story, and Dad the unfair judge, slamming down a gavel without really listening.

"He's not good for her."

"How do you know that?" I yelled, stepping in front of Dad so he had to look at me. "You're barely around. How can you possibly know who or what is good for me?"

Dad flinched, like he felt my words in the pit of his stomach. We stood in silence for a moment, a standoff. My phone dinged with a new text message, but I didn't dare check it. Dad paced back and forth in front of the kitchen island, then stopped abruptly.

"I know I'm not around," he said softly, shaking his head. "You don't know how much I wish I could be here every time you need me." His shifted his gaze from me to Mom then back to me again. "It's because I'm not around that I try so hard to protect you. And trust me, I've heard enough locker room talk to know when a guy is up to no good."

If Dad wanted to overcompensate, he could spend more time with me instead of obsessing over old games and re-writing old plays. Even when he is around, when I try to talk to him it's like he's far away—physically in the same room but mentally somewhere else entirely. There's no way my overly distracted father could've judged Drew's character in those five minutes on our porch.

"You don't have to protect me," I said, trying to sound older and self-assured, like someone who has it all figured out, but my voice stumbled on the way out of my mouth. "He's a good guy, I promise."

"Let's at least meet Drew properly," Mom said, and I held my breath, my eyes darting between them.

"Please, Dad." My voice caught again, and I swallowed it back.

"Okay," he sighed. "Bring him over to the house so I can talk to him. But you're grounded for the week, and no seeing Drew outside of school until I meet him."

I didn't say anything else, too afraid to ruin the momen-tary reprieve from Dad. If only he would put half the amount of energy into our family that he does into football. Maybe then he would trust me to make the right choices. But the truth is he doesn't know Drew and sometimes I wonder if he even knows me.

A sea of nameless faces blurs past me as I make my way down the hall. It's always like this in the beginning, a barrage of new people, fast introductions, and overwhelming first im-pressions that are almost never correct. I prepare myself for the inevitable, fully knowing that I'm never going to remember the names of all the people I'll meet in the next few hours. The thing is, there's only one face I want to see in this crowded hallway, my eyes desperately searching for a glimpse of Drew's dark waves, his ripped jeans. Sneakers squeak on the linoleum floor and a couple guys high five each other over my head. I duck, my fingers curling around the strap of my backpack. When I reach my locker I click through the numbers like a pro and yank the door open, the metal vibrating against my hand. I've already memorized the combination, a personal record for me. I check my phone, but nothing from Sarah. I texted her right after the beach, my excitement an overfilled helium balloon about to pop. I haven't told anyone about that night and I'm starting to wonder if it even happened. Some things in life feel more real when you share them with someone.

Shane heads down the hall, drumsticks peeking out of the top of his backpack. His face brightens as he spots me, his hand shooting up in an enthusiastic wave. Tension releases from my skin at the sight of a familiar face, a friend among strangers. I wave back, about to make my way over to him, but suddenly his arm drops and his face falls. I follow his gaze until my eyes land on Brent Miller hulking down the hall. Shane ducks around the corner, disappearing from sight.

"Jets suck," Brent yells in my direction, walking in sync with another football player. It's only the first week and I'm already the coach's daughter. I should expect this, but every time, in every new school, I'm caught off guard. Brent pumps his fist in the air like a belligerent fan. A Mustangs hat sits backwards on his big head, making his forehead protrude. There's a Band-Aid above his right eye, probably an injury from practice. My stomach clenches.

"Fuck off, Brent," Ray says, appearing at my locker. She flips him the finger and Brent laughs, like they've been through this routine before. Ray rolls her eyes at me and says, "Welcome to Millbrook High."

I laugh as Ray pulls a stick of gum from her bag and pops it in her mouth.

"Sorry about him," says the other football player, the name *Walker* written on the back of his jersey. He must be Tom Walker, the quarterback who texted Drew about the concert tickets. He doesn't walk over to us, he swaggers, like he owns this school. Brent trails him until they're standing beside us.

"What happened to your eye?" Ray asks, squinting at Brent's face. When she reaches up and touches the bandage he flinches.

"It's nothing," he says quietly, staring at his sneakers, his bravado stripped away by one innocent question.

"It doesn't look like nothing," Ray presses, examining the wound.

"Drop it, okay?" Tom says, stepping in front of Brent. Ray eyes Tom and Tom holds her gaze, serious. No one looks at me. It's obvious that Band-Aid isn't hiding a football injury. Like I said, first impressions never tell the full story.

"Guys, this is Stevie," Ray says, cutting through the silence. She gestures at me like I'm a shiny diamond in a display case. "She's the one I was telling you about. Stevie, you've met Brent," she says, her eyes skimming over the bandage. "And this is Tom Walker, our quarterback."

My hand shoots up in a small wave as my stomach knots, my mouth going dry. I repeat the names in my head, trying to keep everyone straight. Three sets of eyes all on me. When people know about you before actually knowing you, they have a certain expectation of what kind of person you should be, when in fact you're nothing like they imagined.

"Nice to meet you," I say, as my hand self-consciously runs through my hair.

"That's so cool about your dad," says Tom, as he adjusts a gym bag on his shoulder. "What's he saying about the season?"

"I don't know," I say, picking my cuticle. "We don't really talk about football."

"He must tell you something," says Tom, twisting the cap off a water bottle and taking a long sip.

"Jets are a lost cause." Brent leans against the row of lockers, his hand grazing the bandage.

"Cool it, guys." Ray steps in front of me. "She doesn't want to talk about her dad. Leave her alone."

A petite girl with auburn curls breaks free from the hallway crowd and sidles up to Tom, putting her arms around his waist. Her wrists are covered in bangles and rings hug half her fingers. She stands on her toes, kissing him on the cheek, her crop top riding up and exposing a toned stomach.

"Hey, baby," Tom says, nuzzling into her neck.

"Jenna Reed," Ray whispers in my ear, nodding at Jenna, whose hand is now buried in the back pocket of Tom's track pants. Another person. I do my best to smile but she doesn't notice me. "Cheerleader. Junior. Tom's girlfriend."

"Gotta go," Tom says, and I exhale an overwhelmed breath of air. "See you on the field, Ray. Nice meeting you, Stevie."

I yell bye as the guys head down the hall, Jenna's arm curled around Tom's bicep. Ray's eyes are still on them as she says, "God, our quarterback looks like Michael B. Jordan, don't you think? Ugh but completely off limits. He's been with Jenna since they were freshmen."

She sighs, still eyeing Tom, before snapping her head back to me. Ray's words barely register as I try to commit the new names, people, and stories to memory. With each new school it gets harder. Maybe it's because I know this place, these people, aren't permanent.

"What happened to you Saturday night?" Ray asks, fiddling with a stack of beaded bracelets that dangles from her wrist. She chews on the piece of gum like it's a steak, mouth slightly open, her lips shimmering with gloss. I grab books from my locker and shut it. "Where were you? I thought you were going to stop by Dino's?"

"I had another party," I say, even though I never made it there. The hallway begins to thin out as a warning bell sounds for first period. Ray doesn't budge. I'm dying to tell someone about the beach and the waves and the almost-but-not-quite skinny dipping. Ray narrows her eyes at me.

"Who is it?"

"Huh?"

"That look on your face." Ray clutches her heart and swoons dramatically, swaying back and forth, until she stops and looks me square in the eyes. "Who is it?"

Every image from Saturday night bursts from my brain, demanding to be let out. Ray crosses her arms over her stomach and taps her right foot impatiently.

"Wait, let me guess . . ." Ray's pointer finger touches her chin as her eyes shift to the ceiling. Drew rounds the corner, a beat-up notebook stuffed in the back pocket of his ripped jeans. All at once sand squishes through my toes and salty air dances on my tongue.

"Drew!" yells a guy in black skinny jeans, and Drew joins him in the corner of the hallway. He doesn't see me standing here, my heart a plane taking off from a runway, the ground disappearing from sight.

"Oh," Ray says sharply, her voice deep diving into a low baritone. I snap my head to her, but she steps back, her eyes growing wide. "Is that him?"

Ray gestures at Drew and I nod, everything inside me churning, as the color drains from her face. She flips her hair off her shoulders, then ties it up in a loose ponytail, her eyes still on Drew. I don't want her to say what I think she's about to say, but I ask anyway.

"Did you guys..." The air is vacuumed out of my lungs, and I can't complete the sentence. I like Ray and I could really use a girlfriend right about now, especially one who defends me against Brent Miller, and part of me hopes that the obvious isn't true.

"It was last year," Ray says, and my heart crashes through my feet. She fidgets with the bracelets, her strawberry shampoo wafting through the air. "We weren't together that long. He ended it right around the time his dad moved out. I was super focused on making the team and he... well he was... he shut me out. We weren't good together. And now, I'm much more interested in football."

"You sure?" I ask because I don't want to be that girl—the one who doesn't know girl code.

A nervous laugh falls from Ray's mouth as she forces a smile, her eyes darting from me to Drew. "Sorry, this is kind of weird. We've been over for a while though. Anyway, I should get to class. I'll see you later, okay?"

But she doesn't say it like she means it. As she pivots on her sneakers and heads for class, I can't shake the feeling that this fledgling friendship is crashing before it got off the ground. Maybe if I'd gone to Dino's, I'd already have a friend by my side, helping me learn the ropes at this new school. But maybe I don't need someone to show me the ropes. I've lived in enough towns and trust me, it's all the same. Maybe it's time to forget about what I should be doing in favor of everything I want, even if it scares me, even if it could be ripped away.

When I glance over my shoulder, Drew's eyes flick to mine, but only for a second. A small tremor of panic settles over my body. He's freaked out by my family, he must be. Who wouldn't be? I bet Ray's dad never intercepted the end of one of their dates. As I try to calm my racing nerves, I wonder if Drew's avoiding me. My heart sinks deeper with every second he doesn't glance my way. But then he slowly raises his gaze to mine and this time his lips curve into an unsure smile. He motions for me to join him, cocking his head to the side. I take a deep breath and walk over to him and his friend, landing smack in the middle of their conversation.

"So set list? We play Old Silver on Saturday," says the skinny-jeans guy.

"Hey," Drew says, shoving his hands in his pockets. "This is Gabe. He plays with me in the band I was telling you about."

"This is Stevie," he says to Gabe, shifting closer to me. More people. More names. But this time, with Drew by my side, it doesn't feel so overwhelming. It feels like a beginning. "She just started here."

"Cool. Welcome," Gabe says, shaking surfer hair out of his face.

"So set list," Drew says. "I wanna try some of the stuff I've been writing."

I'd love to see some of the stuff Drew's writing. I wonder if anyone's seen it, if Ray's seen it.

"Let's stick to the covers," Gabe says, struggling to pull a phone out of those impossibly skinny jeans. Once he frees it, he taps out a text.

"Oh crap, forgot to tell you, Trevor can't come on Saturday," Gabe says. "He has a family reunion or something."

"I'll ask Shane," Drew says, then he leans to my ear so

Gabe can't hear. "Shane's a better drummer than Trevor anyway."

"I can *hear* you," Gabe says, barely glancing up from his phone. "So we'll start with 'One Night Only'?"

Drew sighs like playing that Struts song is a punishment. The second bell rings and Drew says, "Sure."

Gabe slaps him on his back and heads down the hall. But Drew leans against the white subway-tiled wall, defeat settling on his face.

"Hi," he says, shifting his brown eyes to me.

"Hey," I say, waiting for Gabe to be out of earshot. "Do you like playing with that guy?" I ask because Drew doesn't seem excited to go on stage with him. In fact, he doesn't even seem to like him.

"He's okay," Drew says, shaking his head. "But if he cared about me at all, he'd know I'm stressed as hell about my dad showing up on Saturday. But Gabe is badass on the guitar and his boy Kevin holds it down on bass. I wish they'd let me replace Trevor with Shane, but they're all tight with Trevor. And when it comes down to a vote, it's three against one. The thing is, I love singing in this band, even if I don't love the guys in it."

"Saturday? Your dad?"

"We're playing a show, at Old Silver Tavern. Wanna come? It looks like my dad may actually make an appearance." Skepticism drips from Drew's voice yet his eyes crinkle at the corners as a hopeful smile breaks free on his face. I want more than anything to go to the show, to watch Drew's expression when his dad takes a seat opposite the stage.

"I wish I could, but I'm grounded," I say, and Drew's smile disappears. He steps closer to me, his eyes locked into mine.

"I'm so sorry. Is that why you haven't texted me back? I thought maybe you were pissed at me from the other night." He scratches the back of his head and paces in front of me, then abruptly stops. When he speaks, his words are soft, almost a whisper. "I thought maybe you didn't want to talk to me again."

"What? No," I spit out fast. "I didn't know how to explain it all over text." I'm desperate to make him understand how much he already means to me and how afraid I am that in one moment Dad yanked it all away. "I thought that maybe you didn't want to deal with my dad."

"He's not that scary," Drew says, reaching for my hand and intertwining his fingers with mine. For a split second I wonder if he held hands like this with Ray, but shake the thought off. The hallway is empty now, except for a couple gum wrappers and loose paper that litter the linoleum. He pulls me to him, wrapping his arms around my waist, his T-shirt collar stretched and hanging from his neck. "I'm not going anywhere. You can explain it to me."

His brown eyes gaze at me with such sincerity that I stop stressing about how he'll react. Instead I start talking without planning and thinking through each word.

"I'm technically not allowed to see you until you officially meet my dad."

"I guess I didn't make the best impression," he says, regret swirling around his eyes, but he shouldn't feel guilty. I decided to go with him to the shore, not the other way around.

"My parents . . ." At home there's no room for mistakes and maybe that's my fault. I strive for good grades and honors classes to get Dad's attention during our limited family time. All the rule-following is just to hear Dad say he's proud. The thing is when I bring home those report cards and follow the rules, Dad's not even there to congratulate me, so what's the point?

"I've never missed curfew before." My fingers curl around Drew's hand as his deep eyes stare into mine.

"So why'd you do it with me?" Drew softly squeezes my hand as the answer dances on my tongue.

"I didn't want to get out of your car," I say simply as he pulls me closer, our lips inches apart, our eyes trusting each other.

"I'm glad you didn't," he says, closing the gap between us, kissing me, right here, in the middle of the hall. The final bell rings, and he pulls away, then kisses the tip of my nose.

"I'll apologize to them, make them understand." Drew says as he untangles himself from me. "I'll come by tomorrow night."

"Shane's coming by to help me with All-State tomorrow night."

Drew's eyebrows furrow slightly, so slightly I might be imagining it.

"I thought you were grounded," he says, tucking his hair behind his ears.

"Academic stuff doesn't count," I say. "Anyway, my dad won't be around until Saturday."

"Saturday then, after the game. I'll stop by on my way to the show. Maybe even convince them to let you come with me."

Classroom doors close and echo through the empty hallway, signaling the start of first period. We part ways, holding hands until the very last second, when we have to let go.

Shane steps inside my bedroom, his eyes taking in my world. Suddenly I'm acutely aware that the yellow fabric duck hanging above my bed is childish, embarrassing even. I held on to it all these years, needing at least one thing in my life to stay the same. It's adorned every bedroom wall since my nursery, and I can't seem to leave it behind. Even so, heat rushes to my cheeks as Shane examines the yellow duck complete with blue suspenders.

"I need to replace that," I say.

"I like it," Shane says, kicking off his sneakers and making himself comfortable smack in the middle of my yellow rug. He drops a green backpack next to my wooden nightstand, two drumsticks peeking out of its front pocket. "Is that Pearl Jam?" My computer shuffles through a playlist, *Porch* barely audible through the tiny speakers.

"I can turn it off," I say, standing.

"No way." Shane reaches for his drumsticks and taps along to the song, smiling. "Greatest band ever. Dave Krusen plays on *Ten*," Shane says, referring to Pearl Jam's original drummer. "But then Matt Chamberlain took over. Then came Abbruzzese. His first name is Dave too. But he only played on *Vs.* and *Vitalogy*. Then Jack Irons came on the scene." I know all this, but I let Shane explain it to me anyway. "And now they've got Matt Cameron, who—"

"Was Soundgarden's drummer." I can't help finishing his sentence. I've always been drawn to the music I feel in my gut, lyrics with meaning, the stuff that makes me feel less alone.

"Impressed," Shane says, and he looks it.

"So impressed that you'll tell me how you got into All-State?" I ask. He's still tapping along to Pearl Jam. "It's obvious you can play. But how did you get in as a freshman?"

"I nailed the audition," he says simply, not missing a beat. "I played something that I cared about, not something I thought they wanted to hear. 'Moby Dick' by Zeppelin—killer solo."

I'm not sure if Shane realizes it but he switches the beat

to Zeppelin as he's talking, his hands moving precisely to a rhythm in his head, so precisely I can almost hear the kick of the bass and the metallic pop of the snare drum.

"How do you do that without sheet music?" Shane's not simply tapping the rug, he's playing intricate beats, one song morphing into the next. I wonder how I will ever get in. I'm not in the same league as Shane, nowhere close.

"I don't need it." He shrugs like it's normal, like everyone has music flowing through their body and out through their fingertips.

"What do you mean you don't need it? You've had it out every day at practice." I glance at my music stand, covered in white pieces of paper dotted with black notes.

"I play by ear. I can't even read sheet music. Don't tell Mr. Abella. He'd probably make me take a torturous music theory class if he knew." My playlist switches to "Rearview-mirror" and Shane seamlessly changes up the beat, all while continuing our conversation. "Best song."

"So let me get this straight. If you hear something, you can play it? Just like that?"

"Just like that," Shane says softly, a modest smile playing on his lips as he continues to use my rug as his own personal drum pad. "I can't not play, you know what I mean?" I do know what he means. Music, playing the sax, it's more than a hobby—it's my sanity. "So what's the big deal about All-State anyway? It's a cool honor, but most people don't go for it until junior or senior year. I would have waited but Mr. Abella convinced me to try out."

Suddenly, the door flings open, bouncing off the door stop. Joey runs into my room and plops in my lap, shoving a *Pete the Cat* book in my face, my nose barely avoiding a paper cut. It's Joey's favorite, the one where Pete takes a train ride to visit Grandma. I spent hours reading him this book, praying he would repeat one of the words, my stomach clenching when he sat there silent.

"Stevie, read, please." His curls tickle my chin and it's still such a relief to hear him speaking even if the cadence isn't perfect and even if the inflection goes up and down like a see-saw. I'm about to shoo him out of my room when Shane holds out his fist.

"Hey, little man, I'm Shane."

Joey doesn't look up, so I nudge him on the shoulder.

"Hi," Joey says softly.

"His name's Joey," I say, but Shane doesn't focus on me. Instead he scoots forward, making sure his eyes meet Joey's gaze.

"What's that book about?" His finger points to the train on the cover. "That's a cool train."

Joey bounces in my lap, first staring up at me, then looking straight at Shane.

"Um . . . it's . . . a train . . . and a cat."

"Very cool," Shane says. "Nice to meet you."

He holds out his fist again and this time, Joey bumps it with his own fist, a smile erupting on his face.

"Hey buddy," I say, wrapping my arms around his waist. "Can I read this to you later? We're doing some high school stuff."

"Okay, Stevie," he says, flinging his arms around my neck and attacking my cheek with a kiss before releasing me, jumping up, and running full speed out of my room. Shane holds his drumsticks in one hand. I didn't even realize he stopped playing. I can practically hear the question dancing on his lips, the question people are too afraid to ask. *What's wrong with him?* The answer is nothing. Joey's just Joey.

"That's why I want to get into All-State," I say. "When

Joey was two and all the other kids were talking, he was having trouble. Like, a lot of trouble. But music got through to him. It was incredible. The Beatles actually. And ever since he was able to sing along, the words came slowly. So yeah, I want to be able to help kids with music like that. To reach them, like 'Yellow Submarine' reached Joey. All-State will give me an edge with college and I have my heart set on NYU. It'll be the first time I get to live in one place for a big chunk of time. I don't know how long my family will stay in New Jersey and I want to grab this chance before it's gone. So yeah, I have to get in."

Shane smiles at this, a dimple appearing in his left cheek. I never noticed it before and it's like his entire face changes, pure joy spilling from that dimple. And he doesn't ask me about Joey. Instead he looks at me with eyes that seem to understand. Up close his eyes are the color of honey, and even though we've spent hours at band practice together, today is the first time I've really looked at him.

"I didn't talk until I was three. Not one word. Then all of a sudden, I was speaking in sentences. That's what my mom tells me at least," Shane says, softly tapping the carpet again with his drumsticks.

"Really?"

"Yeah. Your brother's cool." His eyes shift to me fast, like a flash of lightning, then dart back down to the rug. "And you'll get in."

"I'm thinking a Coltrane piece for the audition," I say, stretching my legs, pins and needles zapping at my feet.

"Do you like Coltrane?"

"He's a legend," I say.

"I know, but do you *like* him? Do you listen to him? Does he make you feel the way Pearl Jam does?" Shane asks, still drumming, playing along to "Why Go" as Eddie Vedder screams from my laptop. God, I wish I could play like Shane. He's not even thinking about it, the sticks moving so fast and effortlessly.

"I guess not," I say.

"Pick something you feel. A song you can't get out of your head."

"Springsteen," I say. "A Clarence solo. Maybe 'Born to Run'?"

"Play it."

"What, like now?"

Shane grabs my sax and hands it to me. I stand, securing my red neck strap and shuffling through the sheet music until I find "Born to Run." Shane clasps his hands together and sits cross-legged on the rug, gazing at me like I'm a famous musician playing Madison Square Garden, not a high school girl in a yellow bedroom. Even though I tell myself this is just Shane, a hummingbird flutters somewhere inside my chest. I take a deep breath and shift my focus from Shane's gaze to the notes, black dots and lines that make up a melody, that tell a story.

The piece is two minutes of pure bliss and I launch into it. I pretend Shane's not watching, that he's not a mere three feet away. My mind slows down as I concentrate on striking the keys in the right way at the right time. The tempo grows faster, and it's like I'm soaring, flying out my window, high above my house and into the clouds that paint the sky. I need this feeling, this break from myself. It's a way of being that's hard to explain, but when I'm playing and listening to music it doesn't matter what town I live in. For a few minutes I forget that I'm the new girl. I forget someone is watching. When I play, I'm fully and completely in the moment, and every worry disappears. The last note trails off and my eyes shift to Shane.

"Now you're talking." That dimple is back in Shane's cheek. I unhook my sax and place it on the stand, excitement growing inside me. I might actually have a chance at this. "I have a studio in my house if you want to come over next week and practice. We can record it, so you can hear which parts you want to work on."

"That would be . . ." I start to say but I can't even finish my thought I'm so pumped at the idea of actually recording. "Yes, thank you!"

"Anyway, I should get going. You heading to the Dark Carnival show Saturday night?"

"Can't. I'm grounded."

Shane reaches for his backpack.

"If you're grounded, why am I here?"

"You're not Drew," I say quietly, my nerves igniting at the mention of his name. I look down and realize I'm picking at my cuticle.

"I heard about the beach," Shane says, avoiding my gaze. All at once I'm desperate to know more. Being with Drew is like being on the best vacation, one with vast ocean views and beaming sunshine. Because when I'm with Drew it feels like everything could change for me. I don't think about my family's lifestyle, in fact I don't think about the future at all. I want the moment to stretch out forever, to live my whole life on that deserted beach, or beside him in his car. But at the same time, I know how much it hurts to leave. And in this case, I wouldn't recover like I usually do. I couldn't pack away all my feelings about Drew, even if I tried.

"What did he say?" My heart rams into my chest, like a bull attacking a red cape.

"Well it's Drew, so he didn't say much. But he's happy. Happiest I've seen him in a while."

I could spontaneously combust right here in front of Shane, little Stevie pieces flying around my room. I could scream at the top of my lungs out my window. But I don't do any of that.

"Cool," I say instead. One word, because if I say any more I won't be able to hold it in.

"Anyway," Shane says, standing and shoving his feet in his sneakers. He slings his backpack over his shoulder, still avoiding my eyes. "I should get going. I'll see you at the game tomorrow."

We do this awkward back and forth dance where I think he's going to hug me, but then he backs off, instead patting me on the arm.

"Thanks again for all your help," I say as he fumbles with the zipper on his backpack.

"You're welcome." He shoves the drumsticks inside the zipper, but they fall out, crashing to the floor. "Sorry," he says, grabbing the sticks and putting them in his pocket. "So yeah . . . I'll see you tomorrow."

"You said that already." I smile at him and he smiles back, and we stand here for a beat until he cracks his knuckles. It's like he doesn't know what to do with his hands when he's not holding drumsticks.

"Okay so I'm really going to go now." Shane backs out of my room until he reaches the doorway. He taps the door-frame before saying, "Um, okay . . . yeah . . . later."

"Bye," I shout to him as he heads down the stairs and out the front door. All at once I'm desperate to talk to my old friend Sarah about my new friend Shane, to tell her about Drew and the beach, to get her advice on all the exciting things happening for me in this town. I grab my phone, texting Sarah, hoping this time she'll respond, even though I know she's three hours behind and still in class.

Me
**How was the first week of school?
Are you okay? Haven't heard from
you.**

But my phone stays silent, my past life slowly slipping into a memory.

CHAPTER 8

Drew

I grab a bouquet of pink carnations from the passenger side of my Jeep, my eyes landing on a penny in the middle console. The penny. I freeze, my grip tightening on the flowers. I tell myself it's not a big deal, that it has nothing to do with my feelings for Stevie. Even so, guilt courses through my veins and I think about fessing up. Maybe she would understand. Would she? I shake it off and hop out of the Jeep. My button-down hangs over my jeans and I hastily tuck it in as I make my way to Stevie's front porch. The outdoor lights are on even though the sun is still shimmering low in the sky. I wipe my feet on a black and brown mat that says *Welcome*. I feel anything but. My heart shakes the rest of my organs with its incessant pounding. The doorbell chimes as I push it, followed by footsteps and the door swinging wide open, revealing Stevie. Gray sweatpants hang on her hips, a tight blue tank top hugging her body. I breathe through my nerves and hold out the flowers.

"Hey," she says, taking the carnations from me and pressing her nose to the petals. Then she smirks. "These aren't for me, are they?"

"For your mom," I say. "Does she like carnations?" I glance over Stevie's shoulder expecting to see her parents right behind her, but the hall is empty.

"Couldn't hurt," she says, waving me inside. The house is quiet, kind of like mine, but with less stuff. "But they're not home. My mom's out with my little brother. My dad just called and said he got stuck at practice . . . again."

"Oh I guess I should—"

"No, stay."

"But aren't you—"

"They won't know." Her lips curl up on one side and I'm done for. I know I'm doing the wrong thing, but no way am I turning around and heading home. She sets the flowers down on a table by the front door and reaches for my hand, pulling me into a living room. A laptop is open on the coffee table, a screen frozen on a YouTube video. One quick glance and it's obvious what Stevie's been watching. It's what our entire school has been watching ever since the afternoon football game. Stevie's eyes shift to the computer screen, then back to me.

"I think it's gone viral," she says, and I don't doubt it. When Ray took the field and got into position with seconds on the clock the crowd lost it, screaming and waving blue and gold banners. Her blond ponytail peeked out from underneath her helmet as she charged the ball like a complete badass, punting it straight through the goalposts, clinching our first win of the season. She ripped off her helmet, curtseyed, and blew a kiss. Typical Ray. I have to admit, I was happy for her. But I'm not about Ray anymore, not even close. The only girl I want to talk about, the only girl I even want to *think* about, is Stevie.

"I was more interested in watching another girl during the game," I say as I close the laptop.

"You were watching me?" Stevie's left eyebrow raises in the most adorable way.

"Couldn't help it," I say.

"Maybe I was watching you too," she says as we settle into a plush couch directly across from a TV that's playing a cartoon with talking dogs. Stevie points the remote at it and zaps the screen to black.

"Joey's favorite show," Stevie says, tucking her legs underneath her. "I can't wait for you to meet him."

"Me too," I say, knowing how important Joey is to Stevie. The other day at practice she pulled a blue Thomas train from her bag as we were setting up. She placed it in my palm and told me Joey hides his favorite toys in her bag so she doesn't forget about him during the day. Yesterday a plastic Paw Patrol figure hitched a ride with Stevie's books. Her entire face lit up as she explained the dalmatian's name is Marshall and he's a firefighter. I wonder what it would be like to have toys hidden somewhere for me, tiny reminders that someone's always in my corner.

When I was younger I pretended a stuffed elephant was my brother, even called him Brother E and carried him around everywhere. I wished for a sibling, especially when Dad and Mom argued or Dad was away for work. But as I got older I learned wanting something doesn't mean you get it. So I stopped dreaming of the day my family would make some *you're gonna be a big brother* announcement. I don't even know what happened to Brother E.

"Do you ever wish you had a sibling?" Stevie asks, reading my mind, knowing me in this moment almost better than I know myself.

"When I was younger," I say, then remember the real reason I stopped thinking about a sibling and smile. "But in kindergarten Shane moved next door and I didn't need a sibling. Shane's better than a sibling."

"Because you chose each other," she says, picking at a beige Band-Aid on her thumb. I cover her hand with mine and her cheeks flush. "Sorry, worst habit."

"Why do you do it?" I ask, thinking if I knew her reasoning I could somehow help her stop.

"Half the time I don't realize I'm doing it," she says. "But I guess it's kind of like a release. It usually happens when I'm nervous."

"Are you nervous now?" I ask, as I fidget on the couch, my body sinking into the cushions. I tuck my hand under my leg as my breath becomes shallow. I'm the one who's nervous. So fucking nervous.

"Yeah, but good nervous," she says softly. "Are you?"

"Yeah." I barely get out the words. "Good nervous."

Stevie's eyes are like molasses, and before I realize I'm doing it, I reach out and put my hand through her hair. I can't stop myself for another second and lean in and . . . my phone dings, snapping me out of the moment. It dings again. I sigh, pulling it out of my jeans.

Dad

Something came up. Not going to make it to your show tonight.

My body folds in on itself, a tire deflating. That's it. That's the whole text. No *I'm sorry.* No *I love you.* No *I'll make it up to you.* Just *Something came up.* Dad making an appearance tonight was like a door opening, a possibility to have him back in my life. It was never about him thinking we're a quality band or wanting to sign us. I never cared about all that. I wanted Dad to see what he's missing out on by running around the city with his assistant. I wanted him to realize he messed up and that I'm worth coming back for. Well, fuck him and fuck me for believing he would show.

"What is it?" Stevie says, her hand on my shoulder. I flip the phone so she can read the text because I can't tell her. A golf ball lodges itself in the back of my throat and my eyes burn with tears demanding to be let out, but there's no way in hell I'm crying right now. Now way is Dad getting the best of me.

"I'm so sorry."

Stevie says the words I've been longing to hear from Dad. I can't look at her. She cups my face in her hands and pulls my gaze to meet hers. I close my eyes and swallow all the bullshit down so it doesn't seep out. "Drew." She runs her hands through my hair, her lips landing on my forehead.

I force my eyes open and take in a deep breath before I say, "I never want to be like him."

"You're nothing like him," she says. "At least the guy I see. The guy I'm starting to know. You're nothing like your dad."

My mind shifts back to the penny taunting me from inside the Jeep. For the first time, I feel like I'm lying to her, even though that coin toss isn't technically a lie. But it feels like a secret now, and it feels wrong. My mouth falls open to tell her as I rub my sweaty palms on my jeans, but no sound comes out. She deserves to know the truth, but if I tell her, she'll end this, or worse, she'll hate me.

She kisses me, and I kiss her back to make all the noise in my head disappear. Everything about her is soft and real and the more I kiss her, the more I want her. My hand slides down her back as she pushes herself closer to me, undoing the buttons on my shirt one by one. I'm losing all sense of control.

"Is this okay?" I ask, out of breath.

"God yes," she says, laughing and pushing the hair out of my eyes. We're a tangled mess of limbs sinking deeper into the couch. Laughing and kissing, then kissing and laughing.

"Stevie!" booms a voice from across the room.

I jump, rolling off the couch and smack onto the floor. I stand, straightening out my jeans, and come face-to-face with Stevie's dad. His hands are on his hips and he glares at me from under a Jets baseball hat. Beads of sweat drip down his temples and his face drains of color as he eyes my chest.

"You need to button your shirt and leave," he says, his eyes still on me, burning holes into my skin. My shaking hands fumble with the buttons and I can't get this damn shirt closed fast enough.

"Dad!" Stevie stands, her face flushing as her fingers comb through her wild hair.

"Now."

"No," she says, stepping closer to me.

"I don't want you seeing him anymore." He's got a few inches on me easily, plus a lot more muscle than my skinny frame has to offer. I back up, bumping into the coffee table.

"Sir, please," I croak out, my heart annihilating my chest. "My intention was to come here and meet you—"

"I was the one who told him he could stay. He wanted to leave when I told him you weren't home, I swear." Stevie's voice trembles even though she's yelling. "If you would let him explain. Let *me* explain."

"I don't want to hear it," Caleb says, the tips of his ears flushing red, his eyes searing into me. "Drew, go home," he says with a finality that makes my heart shrivel up and drop through my feet. I can't let Caleb take us away from each other, and yet, I'm under his roof totally disrespecting his home. The only decent thing to do in this moment is leave.

"I should go." My voice is hoarse. I trip over the corner of the rug, then steady myself. Caleb signals at the door. "I'm sorry. I'm really sorry," I say, but he doesn't respond.

"It's not your fault," Stevie says, but she's wrong. I head for the door and say *I'm sorry* one last time before I find myself alone on her front porch. Always alone.

CHAPTER 9

Stevie

OCTOBER

A long yawn escapes my mouth, the kind that stretches your lips wide. Racing thoughts flood my mind, making it impossible to power down. It's been a few weeks since that afternoon with Drew and Dad won't look at me, like I'm a stranger living in his house. It's just as well because he'd see straight through my lying eyes. He'd realize I'm not his perfect daughter, that I'm sneaking over to Drew's house every week when he thinks I'm practicing for All-State with Shane. Instead of running through my audition piece in Shane's studio, I'm in Drew's bedroom, his arms around my waist, his lips on my neck.

Around midnight, my eyes burn, refusing to close. I finally let my insomnia win and head downstairs. The house is dark and still, except for colors flashing from the flatscreen in the den. Dad points the remote at the TV, rewinding a play from practice and jotting down notes on a legal pad balanced on his lap. He wears the plaid pajama bottoms I gifted him for

Chanukah last year, the ones he dubbed his *house pants, the most comfortable pants in the known universe.* Dad watches the play again, shaking his head. I try to suppress it, but another yawn falls from my mouth, making Dad jump.

"Stevie girl, you scared me," Dad says, pausing the video, greens and blues falling on his face. "What are you doing up? It's late."

"Can't sleep," I say, desperate to talk to Dad like I used to.

When I was little, I would tell him everything, even the bad stuff, like when kids made fun of me for wearing a Jewish star necklace. Baba got it for me and it was all gold, with tiny diamonds at each of the six points. The numbers tattooed on Baba's forearm had fascinated and scared me when I was small. But as I grew I came to understand all they symbolized, and what that meant for my family. Her strength is the reason we're all here, and when she gave me that necklace I couldn't wait to show it off at school. Except the other kids didn't get it. It was foreign and weird and by the end of the day I took it off and stuffed it in my bag. That night I told Dad everything and sheepishly pulled the necklace out of my bag, the star dangling from my finger. He hugged me tight and fastened the gold chain around my neck.

"We're stronger than them," he said, looking me straight in the eye. "*You're* stronger than them."

I wore that necklace the entire year, ignoring hurtful comments, and Dad was right. I was stronger than their meaningless words. Just like Baba.

But tonight, in our den, with the Jets' football practice on pause, I wonder if Dad still thinks I'm strong, or if he thinks of me at all.

"Want me to make you tea?" he asks, his eyes fixed on the screen. He doesn't ask me why I'm not sleeping or what's wrong. It's like he's afraid of the answer.

"I'm sorry about everything," I say, stepping between him and the TV. More words dance on the tip of my tongue but remain tucked safely inside my mouth. *I'm sorry I've been lying to you. I'm sorry I've been sneaking around. You think you know me, but you don't.* He fiddles with the remote, staring at my bare feet. "But Dad, if you got to know Drew, you would see he's not the reckless guy you think he is."

"You know how I feel about him," Dad says, clicking the practice back on. "It's late. Get some rest, okay?"

As I creep back upstairs I feel so far from the strong girl who proudly wore a Jewish star in a school full of ignorant kids. Each move depleted my *chutzpah,* as Baba called it, all the best parts of me left behind, scattered in towns across the country. And now, I'm sneaking around behind my parents' backs and lying to them like a coward.

Last night's conversation with Dad sits heavy in the folds of my brain, taking up space. Shane flicks on the mixing board as I throw my black bubble vest on one of the chairs, feigning interest in this practice session. I unfasten the buckles of my sax case as Shane clicks on his Mac, pulling up my audition piece, the one I can't seem to get right. Every time I sit down to play, my fingers don't listen to my mind and then my mind gives up and wanders to that afternoon with Drew, and every afternoon with him since. Gray soundproof foam covers the walls, and when Shane speaks, his voice sits suspended in the air.

"How long do you and Drew plan to keep this up?" he asks, not in an accusatory way, just questioning my intentions.

"I don't know," I say as I fit together the pieces of my sax. "Thanks for covering for me . . . for us."

Worry seeps from Shane's hazel eyes as he paces the recording studio, sidestepping his drum set and pulling out my sheet music. He pinches the bridge of his nose, something Drew does when he's tired, and I wonder which one of them started that mannerism and which one copied it. Shane tugs on the brim of his EMT hat and merely says, "He's my best friend."

Shane continues pacing and throwing empty soda cans into a garbage bin under the mixing console. He takes off his hat and Frisbees it onto one of the cymbals. His hair sticks up in every direction.

"It's been a few weeks of this," he says, turning to me. "Do you really think you should be lying to your parents?"

Shane thinks it's wrong to sneak around, a cheapened version of what Drew and I could be. He thinks I should come clean and talk it through with Dad, to really talk, not the poor excuse for a conversation we had last night. Shane's urged me to be truthful every time we sit down to practice and every time, I give him the same answer.

"I hate that I'm lying to my parents," I say, my throat constricting. "But this thing with Drew, I can't walk away from it either. You know what I mean?"

"Yeah." Shane's eyes shift to the expensive-looking Persian rug beneath the drum set. The bass bears his initials. Shane drew the cartoonish font himself and had the letters silk-screened on the front. His eyes flick back to me as he wipes his palms on his gray track pants. "I mean . . . I can imagine what that feeling is like . . . you know . . . not being able to walk away."

Shane blows out a heavy breath of air and I hate that he's part of my lie. I hate that stress settles in his eyes and that he grows increasingly flustered each time we talk about Drew. But I can't figure out a way to unravel it all. So for now I tread water, hands and feet moving in fast, desperate circles.

But I know it's only a matter of time before I gasp for air and my head disappears beneath the surface.

"Anyway, audition's in two months," Shane says, and I'm grateful for the change in topic. He grabs a drumstick from a metal bin next to his set. I swear there are probably a hundred wooden sticks in there.

"I break 'em a lot," Shane said the first time I came over, my jaw dropping at the sight of all the equipment. When Shane started playing drums, Drew's dad worked out the design for the studio and Shane's dad built it for him, just like that. Like having a recording studio in your house is no big deal. But that was before Shane's dad got sick. He told me about him the first time I came over, his eyes igniting at the mere mention of his father. I wonder if he feels his dad's presence in here, if he thinks about him every time he turns on the mixing board.

"Can we play back the part I worked on last week?" I ask and Shane presses play on the Mac. My rendition of "Born to Run" spills out of floor-to-ceiling speakers and I cringe at the missed notes. Shane rewinds it and plays it again, nodding at the computer.

"There," he says. "You hear that?"

It starts off okay, the notes all where they should be and the tempo increasing, but then it's like I can't keep up with the song.

"It sucks."

"It doesn't suck. It just needs work."

"What about you?" I ask, hoping to shift Shane's focus. He hasn't rehearsed at all, at least not when I'm here. "Are you going to try out again this year?"

"Definitely," Shane says, effortlessly twirling the drumstick between two fingers. "Problem is, I can't play the Zeppelin song again, the one that got me in last year. And I'm having trouble picking something else."

"Can you make something up?" I ask. Shane cocks his head at me, a smile curling the ends of his mouth.

"I don't see why not. Do you think I could pull that off?"

"Absolutely," I say. "Make it into whatever you want."

Shane sits on a stool in front of the drum set, grabbing his hat from the cymbal and chucking it on the mixing board. A kick at the bass drum pierces through the air, one lone beat that shouts *listen up*. Then, all at once, Shane launches into it. The intense rhythm is so loud and contained in the room, hammering at my ears, escalating. Shane drums fast and precise, almost like the drumsticks are extensions of his hands. Every muscle flexes in his arms and his hair becomes messier as he goes. I can't see his feet, but the kick of the bass drum vibrates through my chest. He closes out the beat and grabs hold of the cymbal, silencing the crash. Shane isn't good. He's exceptional.

"Think that'll work?" he asks.

"Absolutely. A hundred percent in the bag."

"Your turn," he smiles and moves from the stool to the chair behind the mixing board.

"No way am I following that." I rub my eyes, Shane turning blurry. Fatigue grabs hold of my body, squeezing out every last ounce of energy. "I don't have it in me today."

"Stevie?" Shane scoots closer to me and examines my tired eyes. "You're not okay, are you?"

"Not really." It's a relief to admit that to someone. Sarah barely texts me back, and when we do finally connect, it's mostly about which new bands we're listening to or tough teachers we have. It's never about anything real. Each time I try to tell her about something that matters we get cut off. It's either the time difference or a bad FaceTime connection, and after a while I stopped trying. I guess she stopped trying too. She has no clue what happened with Dad or that my insomnia has gotten worse or that I'm falling for Drew. She has no clue I'm worried it might all disappear. She doesn't even know I'm trying out for All-State, or that I'm using these practice sessions as an excuse to sneak out. The physical space between us created this awkward rift in our friendship that neither of us wants to admit. "I can't sleep."

"You're talking to the right guy." Shane stands and zips his navy hoodie. "I can help. What's the one thing you love to think about?"

"Music," I say without hesitation, not sure where Shane's going with this.

"Favorite band?"

"Pearl Jam." This conversation is like one of Shane's rhythms and I don't miss a beat.

"Should've guessed that," Shane says. "Okay, get up."

He leads me into a soundproof booth with a microphone hanging from the ceiling. This room is a vacuum. No air conditioner clicking on, or hum of a lawnmower outside, or his mom's footsteps upstairs. Shane holds his finger to his lips and smiles.

"This is what your mind should feel like, right before you fall asleep," he says, his voice cutting through the silence. "This quiet in here, this stillness, it's the only way to turn everything off. And you can't do that if your mind is dialed up to eleven."

"Okay, so how do I dial my mind down?"

"Top five Pearl Jam songs on *Ten*," he says, his eyes sparking. "Go."

"In no particular order," I say, playing along. "That would be too hard."

"Of course," he says, nodding at me.

"'Porch.'"

"Good call," Shane interjects.

"'Black.'"

"Obviously."

"'Jeremy.'"

Shane groans loudly and I laugh.

"I was hoping you weren't going to say that. So commercial."

"I'm *kidding,*" I say. Only posers would rank "Jeremy" in their top five. "'Even Flow,' 'Why Go.'"

"Phew." Shane exhales.

"'Release,'" I say. "Best song on the album, in my opinion."

Shane smiles but his mouth is tinged with sadness, the kind of smile that breaks your heart. And without asking him I know why, the lyrics of the song running through my head.

"I listened to that one on repeat when my dad died," Shane says. "You know he wrote it about his own dad, about missing him after he was gone?"

I nod and step closer to Shane.

"Did it help?"

"Yeah, more than anything else at the time," Shane says, and I know exactly what he means—the songs we need to make sense of what we don't understand.

"You would think 'Release' would be my favorite on the album," Shane says quietly. "But if you're gonna pick a slow one, I'd go with 'Oceans.' Great lyrics. *Hold on to the thread. The currents will shift. Glide me towards you.*"

"Great song," I say, a soft flutter beating in my chest, a sensation so slight that I almost miss it. "How do you know these lists will help?"

"I like to think a lot at night too," he says. "For me, it's usually if Brent gets in my face at school. I replay it over and over changing how I reacted, making up a different script in my head."

"Is that really what keeps you up?" I ask because Shane's

not looking at me. He's messing with the zipper on his sweat-shirt.

"It's not only that," he says, meeting my eyes. "I think about my dad, almost every night. Some nights I swear I can hear his key in the door coming home from a late night at the office. He was an architect. Did I tell you that?"

I nod. He told me last week, but I let him tell me again.

"He didn't just build this studio. He built my house and most of the houses in this town." Shane shifts his eyes back to his zipper. "Am I talking about him too much?"

"Of course not," I say, and before I realize I'm doing it, I reach out and touch his arm. Shane flinches ever so slightly, then clears his throat and steps back. The warmth of his arm stays with me, fusing with the palm of my hand.

"Anyway, it was a long time ago," he says, even though it's only been a few years. "What keeps you up?"

"I'm scared everything's going to get taken from me. I've had to leave behind every friend I've ever made. I want one thing to last, to be forever."

"It doesn't work that way," Shane says, leaning against the foam wall, his eyes tethered to mine. "Nothing lasts. It's about living it all while it's happening, not stressing about when it's going to end. And trust me, the right people will stick with you, no matter what."

It's so quiet in the recording booth, the air listening to our breathing. Two people locked together in a moment, Shane's words resonating. Maybe it's time to stop thinking about endings. My heart palpitates from inside my chest, alive and ready. Shane's dimple appears and it dawns on me that I *did* make my first Millbrook friend. And he's nothing like Sarah, Krystal, Emily, or Nicole. He might be the kind of friend who stays even after I leave.

Through the glass walls of the recording booth, I catch

the time on a digital clock displayed on the mixing board. All at once my stomach jumps and I'm jolted from this conversation.

"I should probably get going," I say quietly, my eyes fixed on the floor, my heart clenching.

"You're meeting him now, aren't you?" Shane says.

"Yeah." My answer sounds louder than I intended, magnified by the still air of the recording booth.

But this time Shane doesn't urge me to fess up to my parents. He doesn't lecture me.

"If you ever need to talk . . ."

He offers me a half smile and it feels so good to have someone on my side. I throw my arms around Shane's neck, hugging him and saying, "Thank you," in his ear. When I step away, for a split second his eyes are different, like they're hugging me back.

The moon is low and full, casting a bright halo into the dark night sky. An acorn drops from a branch landing in a pile of red and yellow leaves. I pull my bubble vest in close as Drew's Jeep swerves into his driveway, a beat thumping from his stereo, stopping me in my tracks. The music goes quiet and Drew hops out of the car, wearing a leather jacket slung over a gray hoodie. A smile takes over his face as he jogs to me, wrapping his arms around my waist.

"Hey, you," he says, kissing me, my body relaxing into him. "Just got done with band practice. How's the Springsteen piece coming?"

"I can't get it right," I say. "I don't know if this All-State thing is happening this year."

"You'll get in," he says, tugging at the bottom of my hair. "So listen, there's a homecoming party Saturday night at

Tom's. I was hoping we could *bump* into each other there. For once you don't have to lie to your parents. I wish you didn't have to lie," he says, his eyes apologetic. At first Drew wanted to come back over, to try again with Dad. But I thought it would only make things worse. Lying seemed like the easier option, but now guilt creeps in every time I'm with my parents.

"I heard the whole school goes to Tom's party," I say, thinking that Drew's right. If I meet him there, I won't have to lie about where I'm headed, and that part would be a relief. But the mention of homecoming makes me think of Ray and the cardboard signs plastered all over school covered in little yellow suns and bubble letters—*Catch Some Rays. Vote for Ray for Homecoming Queen.* The other day she handed me a flyer, the first time she'd spoken to me since I told her about Drew.

"Hey, Stevie," she said, as I looked at the piece of paper in my hand. She fished through a shopping bag and pulled out a small cellophane pouch filled with multicolored Starburst, handing it to me. "Vote for me?"

"Sure," I said, missing a friendship that never was. As much as I love hanging out with Shane and Drew, I need girlfriends. "Are you around after practice today? Maybe we could meet up?"

"Can't," she said, her eyes darting around the hallway. She waved to a group of girls walking past us. "Super busy with this homecoming stuff. And doing both football and soccer is kicking my ass."

"Oh," I said, not entirely believing her. The bell for first period rang and she said a quick goodbye, disappearing into the crowded hallway.

And now I need to know what happened between Drew and Ray, to know if lying to my entire family has been worth it. If giving up a friendship with Ray has been worth it. I need to be able to trust that this thing with Drew is real and not going to disappear.

"I heard Ray's nominated," I say carefully, searching Drew's face for a clue to his past. "Is she going?"

"I don't know. Probably." He scratches the back of his head and stares out into the night sky. It's obvious he doesn't want to talk about her, but I need to know.

"What happened with her?" I ask, hating the sound of my voice, small and desperate. "I mean, I heard you guys used to . . ."

"We were a thing, and then we weren't," Drew says, his dark eyes taking hold of mine. "I cared about her, of course. But it's over. It's been over for a while."

We stand there for a beat, Drew fidgeting with the sleeve of his jacket and me picking at my cuticle. In a year from now, will Drew say the same thing about me? That I was a girl who moved away. A random girl he used to know.

"Why are you with me?"

"What do you mean?" His hand reaches for me, his fingers lacing with mine. My first instinct is to pull away, shield myself from getting too close. But his brown eyes are vulnerable, not cocky. I curl my fingers around his, and take a deep breath, about to spill all the insecurities that keep me up at night.

"You could be with any girl in Millbrook. Why me? Why a girl who has to sneak around her parents to see you? Why a girl who could pack up and leave at any moment?"

He gives my hand a little squeeze, pulling me closer, touching the tip of my nose with his finger.

"There's a million reasons." He rakes the hair out of his midnight eyes and smiles. "Like when I talk to you, I know you're listening, not pretending to listen. And when you sing along to the radio, it's like you're up on a stage. And you don't want anything from me but *me*." He brushes the hair out of my face and looks at me, really looks at me. "And I don't care about you *maybe* leaving. You need to let all that go and realize that what we have going on right now is what matters."

My chest pounds, like a typewriter permanently imprinting each one of Drew's words on my heart. I squeeze his hand and decide in this moment that I'm going to forget about it all, my parents' rules and Ray and leaving, always leaving. Because Drew's right, I'm *not* leaving right now, and if I don't start living the moments I have, I'm going to miss it all.

"Why me?" he asks, his voice soft, like he's unsure of my answer, which is so simple and true it should be obvious.

"Because you feel like freedom."

"Freedom?"

"It's a feeling I have, when I'm with you. Like everything else disappears."

Drew kisses me, slowly pushing me against the Jeep, the metal cold on my back. The leather from his jacket brushes against my face as he tucks my hair behind my ear. I pull him to me, but for the first time it's not enough. My hand reaches for the door handle and I yank it open, guiding Drew into the back seat. I scoot back, and he lingers at the door, his eyes roaming my body, his mouth parting like that night at the beach.

"C'mon," I say, laughing. Drew slides over me, the scent of his lemon shampoo filling the back seat as his hair grazes my face. I pull his hips to me, feeling him beneath his jeans, my heart racing. He kisses me over and over as his hand slides under my shirt, undoing the top button of my jeans.

"You're shaking," he says in my ear. "Are you okay?"

He pulls away from me and gazes right into my eyes, kissing the tip of my nose.

"It's just . . ." I stammer, my whole body in flames. "I've never . . ."

Drew kisses the tip of my nose again and says, "It's okay. We can go as slow as you want."

"Can we just stay where we are?"

"Absolutely," Drew says kissing me again, his nose touching mine and his hair tickling my cheeks. He speaks softly between kisses.

"I love . . ." His thumb traces the bottom of my chin. ". . . where . . ." His deep eyes connect with mine, holding me tight, assuring me. ". . . we are."

CHAPTER 10

Drew

Shane lies on my living room couch, throwing a Nerf football at the ceiling. He's in track pants and his dad's worn Princeton sweatshirt. When Shane's dad died, he wore that sweatshirt for a week straight. And now Shane wants to go there too. But he hates the idea of the whole legacy thing. If you ask me, he doesn't need his dad's clout. I'll bet when the time comes he'll have his choice of any school that would be lucky enough to have him. The ball hits the ceiling and plummets into Shane's hands. He chucks it up again, his eyes fixed on the ball, not saying a word. I wonder if Brent got in his way this week, but I don't ask. Shane prefers to work that shit out on his own.

Mom's out with that finance guy again. When he came to the door earlier, my stomach turned at the sight of his Sperry loafers and blazer. He's nice enough, opening the door for Mom, asking me about my day—trying. And Mom seems to be doing a little better, even hugging me on the way out. Or maybe it's me. Stevie and I laid in the back seat of my Jeep for a while the other night, Stevie nuzzling into my shoulder as I stroked her hair. Even though right now my family is complete shit, being with Stevie makes me feel the way I did when I was little, tucked in tight beneath a cozy blanket.

Shane banks the football off the side of the fireplace mantel and it flies into the coffee table, knocking over a glass candy bowl. At least the rug cushions the fall.

"Dude, be careful," I say, searching the room for my wallet. Tom's party is starting and I'm ready to get out of here. "You sure you don't want to come tonight?"

"Nah," Shane says, picking up the bowl and setting it back on the coffee table. "I have an EMT shift, and besides it's not my scene. Is Stevie going?"

"She might have to watch Joey. Her mom has an art show."

Even though I still haven't met Joey, I feel like I know him. I get why Stevie would drop everything for him, but still, I hope her mom gets home early and she can come for a bit. For once she doesn't have to lie—just get the okay to go to Tom's party, which is much easier than making up a practice session at Shane's house. The chance to see Stevie is the only reason I'm making an appearance tonight.

"She's still sneaking over to your house," Shane says, his eyes fixed on the candy bowl. I don't look at him either, instead rummaging through our magazine bin, hunting for my wallet. "How long do you expect me to keep up this routine?"

"Just for a little while longer," I say, even though Shane's right. He shouldn't have to cover for us, and we shouldn't have to sneak around. But I don't see another solution. Not yet, at least. I throw a magazine on the floor and dig through the bin. "I'm still trying to figure it all out."

"You need to tell her," Shane says, putting the magazine back in its place. "She's sneaking around, breaking her parents' trust. C'mon."

"Tell her what?"

"You *know* what." Shane glares at me. I know he means the coin toss, but I can't bring myself to tell her. She'll think she was a bet or a game and it was nothing like that. It was a split-second decision, one of my irresponsible ideas. And now, she's everything and I can't mess with that.

"I can't tell her," I say quietly.

"You're making a mistake." Shane stands and gestures at the mantel. "Your wallet's right there, by the way."

I grab my wallet and stuff it in my pocket. Shane's right. He always is. But I can't take his advice on this one.

I squeeze past a crowd by the keg as a heavy bass line pulses through Tom's house. I stuff my hands into the pockets of my military jacket, scanning every face for Stevie. I've suffered through this party for an hour and I'm about to call it quits.

"Drew man," Brent yells over the music. I pretend I don't hear him. He jumps wildly with the football team, in sync with the music, like drunk pogo sticks. But soon enough he bounces over to me, beer sloshing over his cup and onto my jacket.

"Sorry, man. Party foul," Brent slurs. I can't stand him. I peel off the jacket and search the room.

"Is Stevie here?" I ask.

"Who?"

He's such an oblivious jerk.

"Stevie. My girlfriend."

The girl you're a dick to for no reason.

"Haven't seen her," Brent says as Tom yells for him. "Gonna hit the keg. You want?"

"I'm good."

I snake through the party, past a game of beer pong. A

ping-pong ball splashes into a red Solo cup and everyone cheers as one of the football players chugs it, beer spilling out the sides of his mouth. The Dark Carnival guys chill in the living room so I head in the opposite direction. Still no sign of Stevie.

Cold air bites at my skin as I step onto the back porch. The quiet feels good, like letting a long breath out of my lungs, the pounding music fading into a muffled heartbeat. I pull my jacket back on and rub my hands together to stay warm. The screen door slides open and Ray steps onto the wooden deck, plopping down on the outdoor couch. She pulls a joint from her bag and lights it, taking a long drag. She holds it out for me, but I shake my head and say, "Sorry about homecoming queen."

Ray smiled through the entire ceremony, even when Principal Davis announced Jenna's name and placed a plastic crown on top of her head.

"Jenna had it locked down. I don't know why I thought I could win." Ray takes another drag and pulls her knees to her chest.

"Sorry," I say, reaching for the screen door, my stomach on edge. "I should head back inside."

"Drew?" Her voice hangs in the air and stops me. I glance over my shoulder and she stands, killing the joint in an empty Solo cup and shoving the lighter in the back pocket of her jeans. They're tight and ripped, the ones she bought with me that day in the mall when a security guard busted her for bringing Toast inside. She rescued Toast from a local animal shelter, dragging me there saying she only wanted to look. But once she laid eyes on Toast's brown fur and even browner eyes, she was sold. The shelter had no idea what breed he was, but he had floppy ears and feet that were too big for his little body.

"I'm not leaving him here," she said, grabbing my arm, and dialing her mom's number to get consent. Toast was on death row, and the shelter was eager to give him away. And once Ray got Toast home, he wouldn't leave her side, even following her into the bathroom. So naturally, when we went to the mall, she brought him. "No one will notice," she said, pulling a big overnight bag from her closet and placing Toast inside.

I wonder how that little guy is doing as Ray steps closer to me.

"I've been trying to talk to you." She corners me against the screen door. I sidestep her and make my way to the patio table, but she follows me. "Why haven't you answered any of my texts?"

"I've been busy," I lie. But the truth is when everything went down with Dad, Ray wasn't there. She bailed right when I needed her. So now, I don't see the point in answering texts or being around when she needs me.

"I miss you," she says, touching my shoulder, her flowery perfume floating through the air. I shrug her hand off me.

"You left me," I say, a cold breeze making the hair stick up on the back of my neck. "You're not allowed to miss me."

"*You* broke up with *me*."

"You bailed. The second things got shitty, you bailed." I'm transported back to last year, to the month after Dad left, when Mom wouldn't come out of bed. It was like someone sucked the air out of my room, the walls closing in on me. My stuff, all the stuff Dad gave me, mocking me from shelves *he* bought. I grabbed the signed LeBron James basketball off its stand and threw it at my bookshelf, a couple Bradbury books falling to the carpet. And then I couldn't stop, ripping all my books down, chucking them all over my room, denting the door. I texted Ray over and over that night, crawling out of my skin. She never wrote back, so I trashed it all.

"You were so angry," Ray says, her eyes getting wet, and she'd better not cry. I only saw Ray cry once the entire time we were together, and it was out of frustration after Coach told her to stick to soccer. I waited for her after football try-outs, watching her nail kick after kick, and even so, Coach still said she wasn't ready. She kept a stiff upper lip, but as soon as Coach walked away she said, "Fucking boys club." And then she lost it, sobbing into my shoulder. But Ray didn't want me to intervene. It took every ounce of restraint to keep me from going after Coach and begging him to reconsider. Instead we stood there, on the side of the field, Ray crying and me holding her, urging her to keep trying.

"You shut me out. Don't you realize that? Every time I tried to talk to you . . . Jesus, Drew, you wouldn't even look at me."

"You were busy with football."

"I was busy with football because it was easier than admitting I was losing you. That we were imploding. And then you broke up with me. That's how it went down, Drew. Not the other way around."

I stare at Ray, scenes from last year flashing at me like a movie montage. Ray avoiding me at school, ducking into the crowded hallway instead of waiting for me before first period. Me, idling by Ray's locker, desperate to talk to her, and Ray flashing me a fake smile as she walked past, not bothering to stop. And finally, me giving up and telling her I'm done for good.

"Maybe I broke up with you, but you stopped trying," I say, avoiding her eyes.

"You didn't let me try," Ray says, her voice breaking. My eyes shift to her as she tucks a strand of blond hair behind her ear. All at once a different montage plays in my head. Ray skipping soccer practice and showing up at my house, and me too upset to answer her texts or open the door. Me telling Ray to *leave me the hell alone* after she pressed me about Dad, trying to understand. I cringe at the memory. It's funny what the mind chooses to remember, what stories we tell ourselves.

All this time, I thought it was Ray. Maybe it was easier to blame it on her. So I didn't have one more thing to blame myself for.

"I couldn't deal with him leaving," I say quietly. "I'm sorry I didn't let you help me. I was just . . . it was just messed up."

Tears line the bottom of Ray's eyes, threatening to spill over. She blinks them away and says, "I'm sorry I wasn't the one to help you. Stevie seems really great."

"She is," I say, longing for Stevie's voice, her hair between my fingers, the way her smile makes everything seem okay. "So why were you texting me?"

"We had to put Toast down," she says, her voice catching. "He was old when I got him, remember? Well, his little heart couldn't hold on anymore."

Ray's tears finally fall, streaking down her cheeks. She steps to me, like she did that day with Coach, and wraps her arms around my neck, burying her face in my shoulder. This is so familiar that I could fall back into it, hold on to the back of Ray's head and let her cry.

"I miss you," she whispers again, but it's all wrong. She lifts her head off my shoulder, her watery eyes looking straight into mine. I know this look, her eyes ablaze, roaming from my eyes to my lips. The same look she always gave me, right before she would kiss me.

CHAPTER 11

Stevie

Joey jumps on the couch and drops into my lap, pulling the cord to my headphones straight out of my iPhone. He leans back into me, kicking his legs.

"Play with me," he whines into my ear and I sigh, pulling the headphones off.

"Buddy, I thought you were watching your show?" I gesture at the TV, which is showing the tail end of *Paw Patrol*. Joey points the remote at the TV and clicks it off.

"It's boring," he says, grabbing my headphones and putting them on his head, still kicking his feet like two little clock pendulums. The headphones are big on him and the band sticks up above his wild curls. "Can I listen?"

He grabs my phone and plugs the headphones back in, scrolling through playlists. I know which one he's looking for and I know it'll take him moments to find it. Even though Joey can't read yet he has a few sight words—*Beatles* is one of them. He cues up my all-time favorite, "A Day in the Life," and closes his eyes, his long lashes resting on his milky skin. I wrap my arms around him, listening as the song comes through the headphones. His whole body relaxes the same way mine does, and he stops kicking, his legs dangling limp off the couch.

I peek at my phone and it's nine o'clock already. If Mom doesn't get home soon, I won't be able to go to Tom's party. A text comes through my phone and I smile when I see it's from Sarah.

Sarah
Heading to Muse

Me
Forgot that's tonight. Jealous.

Sarah
Wish you were coming with me. What are you doing?

Me
Babysitting Joey.

Sarah
Typical.

Me
There's a party tonight. I told Drew I'd meet him, but my mom's not home yet and it's getting late. His ex is going to be there. Is that weird?

Sarah
His ex? You never mentioned an ex.

I never mentioned it because we barely talk anymore. A burning sensation swirls around my gut and I consider not responding. Why should I tell Sarah anything when she barely qualifies as a friend? But then I picture her jet-black hair, dyed silver streaks framing her face, and the way she would grab my shoulders at a concert, her ice blue eyes igniting as the band broke out into a perfect jam.

> **Me**
>
> Her name's Ray and she's the kicker for the football team and they were together last year.

Sarah

What kind of name is Ray? She's on the football team? That's badass.

> **Me**
>
> It's short for Rachel, I think. I don't know, she kind of avoids me.

Sarah

What do you mean avoids you?

> **Me**
>
> She was cool before she knew about me and Drew. Now she avoids me.

Sarah

You have to go to that party. I don't trust this situation with Ray. Why don't I know any of this?

The garage door opens, sending vibrations through the living room. I crane my neck and check the door, waiting for Mom to walk through.

> Me
>
> She's pretty cool actually. And you don't know any of this because you haven't been around.

I'm surprised as I hit send, my true feelings about our friendship exposed. Three dots appear as Sarah types a response, and maybe this is the beginning of us getting back what we had. Maybe Sarah misses us too.

> Sarah
>
> I'm sorry. It's hard with the time difference and school and band.

Another weak excuse I don't want to hear.

> Me
>
> Sure.

> Sarah
>
> Don't be like that.

> Me
>
> Whatever, my mom's walking in. I gotta go.

> Sarah
>
> Stevie wait.

I throw my phone on the couch as Joey rips the headphones off and runs to Mom. She picks him up and kisses him on the cheek, then eyes me.

"Joey, why are you still up?" she asks as he pulls on one of her curls and laughs.

"Mama, I was listening to the Beatles!"

"Sorry," I say, but Mom smiles at us with so much happiness on her face, like nothing could bring her down from whatever high she's on. "How was the show?"

"I sold it!" Mom puts Joey down and covers her mouth with her hands. She practically runs over to the couch and plops down next to me. Joey follows her and wedges himself between us. "I actually sold a painting. Can you believe it?"

"The one with the little girl being carried away by the yellow balloon?"

Mom nods and puts her hands over her mouth again. I love that painting and secretly hoped she wouldn't sell it so I could hang it in my room. But this look on Mom's face, it's the way I feel when I play the sax and I'd rather stare at the joy exploding from her eyes than a painting. Besides, she can always make me another one.

"Congrats, Mom," I say, and she kisses me on the cheek, just like she did when I was little.

"Okay, mister," Mom fakes sternness, putting one hand on her hip, then pulling Joey to his feet. "Time for bed."

I flip over my phone and read Sarah's last text.

Sarah

Fine, be mad at me. But go to that
party, trust me.

"Hey, Mom, do you think I can go to that party for a bit? It's down the street so I can walk."

"Joey, head up to bed. I'll be right there to tuck you in," Mom says, her eyes on me. Joey runs upstairs, clutching a black-and-white stuffed dog he named Pizza. Mom pulls her curls up into a messy bun, holding it all together with a small clip. If I didn't straighten my hair, I'd have those same curls, and for a moment I think about letting it air dry. But there's something wild and free about Mom's hair that I could never pull off.

"Is Drew going to be there? You know how Dad feels about him." Mom's brown eyes narrow like she's trying to uncover the truth from my expression.

"I don't know if he's going," I say. Not exactly a lie, but not the truth either. The thing is, Dad's at an away game in Miami until Tuesday. And when it comes to dating and guys, Mom's a sucker, a true romantic, and I'm hoping she won't press me for more information.

"Be back at eleven," she says, raising an eyebrow. "And if Dad asks, you went to Shane's tonight."

"Thank you!" I wrap my arms around her neck, breathing in her musky perfume.

"Mama, come onnnn!" Joey yells from upstairs.

"Stevie, I'm glad you're making friends here and going to parties. Have fun, okay? Love you."

"Love you too," I say, then yell upstairs to Joey. "Good-night, bud!"

I sidestep a guy getting sick on Tom's front lawn as I head up a cobblestone walkway to the front door. Music pounds from the house, spilling into the night air. When I step inside, there's a thin haze of smoke coming from a bong stationed on the living room coffee table. There are people every-where, people I don't know. I squeeze through the crowd, hoping to find Drew. Tom's by the dining room table, point-ing a ping-pong ball at a row of red cups, then expertly sink-ing it in. I push past a group of girls laughing loudly and force a smile once I reach Tom.

"Have you seen Drew?"

"Hey, Stevie!" He throws an arm around me. "Jets better beat the Dolphins tomorrow. What's your dad saying about the game?"

"I haven't talked to him about it. So, have you seen Drew?"

"Jets should start Simmons. Tell your dad." A ping-pong ball sails across the table and splashes into one of Tom's cups.

"Chug, asshole!" Brent yells, and Tom grabs the cup and downs the beer in one gulp.

"So where's Drew?"

"Oh, sorry. I think I saw him go out back."

"Thanks," I say, heading for the screen door. I stop short as the cool night air slips into the house and sends a chill down my spine. The hairs on the back of my neck stand up as I peek through the tiny pinholes of the screen and see Drew. He's not alone. My stomach spins and I hold my breath, care-ful not to make a sound. Ray's head rests on Drew's shoulder and she's crying, wet tears landing on his military jacket. His hand cradles the back of her head and she's saying something into his ear. Something short and soft. She picks her head up from his shoulder and they're looking at each other. Staring at each other. My heart is pounding in my head, a relentless drum banging my thoughts together. She's going to kiss him. He's going to *let* her. I can't watch this. I *have* to watch this. I have to know.

She touches the side of his face and he flinches, pulling back and for a second relief floods my body. But then, she leans in and her lips are on his, her blond hair waterfalling around them. I gasp and Drew snaps back from Ray, rubbing his mouth on his jacket sleeve. He turns to the screen and notices me watching.

"Stevie," he says, coming for me. I hear Dad's voice warning me about Drew, and a wave of nausea hits me knowing he was right. Drew messes with the lock on the screen door, fumbling with a flimsy piece of plastic to get to me, but it's stuck. I push my way out of the party, the screen door screeching as it's thrust open.

"Stevie . . . It's not what it . . ." Drew sounds panicked but I don't hear the rest because I'm out the front door and on the lawn. Bile rises up to my throat. I stop for a moment at the end of the driveway and crouch down, certain I'm about to get sick. The image of them flashes at me. Did he kiss her back? I couldn't see with her hair everywhere.

I slowly stand and walk down the block, hugging my arms against my body. Wind picks up and bites at my face, stinging my eyes. I squeeze my lids against the cold air, but I'm already crying. Trees sway, their branches bending low, away from the cloud-filled sky. A sob escapes my mouth as I walk through the empty street.

Drew's Jeep slows behind me, and I want to scream until I can't scream anymore. I walk faster.

"Stevie, wait," he shouts at me, but I pick up my pace. He stops in the middle of the street and slams the door, metal echoing through the stillness.

"Stevie, come on." His voice is strained. His boots thud against the pavement and I know he's jogging, maybe even running.

"Leave me alone," I choke out.

He touches my elbow and I spin around. He's pale, like he's running a fever, and his eyes are wild, darting across every inch of me. I want to slap him right across his perfect face.

"It's not what you think it is."

I stare at him and wipe tears off my cheek. Our shadows reflect in a puddle on the street, blurry and faceless.

"I was caught so off guard, Stevie. I was about to pull away when I heard you at the door," he says, and I want so badly to believe him. "I'm so sorry. You have to believe me. I want nothing to do with her."

"Well, I want nothing to do with you right now," I scream at him in the puddle. I can't look into his eyes. Drew's hand trembles as he reaches for me. I back away as tiny drops of rain begin to fall from the sky.

"Let me drive you home."

"No, I'll walk." The drizzle explodes into a downpour, soaking us both. Drew pushes wet strands of hair off his face as I stubbornly stand there, my entire outfit drenched through.

"You don't have to talk to me. You don't have to look at me," he pleads. "But I can't leave you out here alone."

Drew's car is the last place I want to be. But a bolt of lightning flashes overhead, and my jeans are sticking to my thighs. My hair is sopping wet, water sliding down my arms and legs, my insides beginning to shake.

"Fine," I practically spit at him and get in the Jeep.

CHAPTER 12

Stevie

I stare into space, and my room goes fuzzy, flashes of last night's party playing in my mind like an evil highlight reel. Morning light cuts through the blinds burning my eyes. The closet door blends into the dresser, which blends into the wood floor. One giant blob of a mess. I get up fast and slam my big toe into my antique yellow desk. It rattles, and my old shoe box falls to the ground. Postcards, key chains, and all sorts of junk I've collected over the years scatter across my wood floor. I sink down, my hands curling around my throbbing toe.

"Stevie?" Mom yells, the buttery smell of pancake batter wafting up from the kitchen.

"I'm fine," I yell back through gritted teeth. My toe has a pulse.

I fill my lungs with air and breathe out the pain. A friendship bracelet, the one with neon lanyard stitched in box pattern, sits on top of an Indianapolis postcard. I pick it up and run my fingers over the uneven stitches. Krystal made it for me right before my family packed up and moved, promising to stay in touch. And we did, for a little while at least. That's how it always goes. A few texts exchanged until a month goes by, then two, then a full year, until all I have left are memories and friendship bracelets that mean nothing.

I text Sarah, hoping she responds because I need to talk to her about last night. She always has a way of fixing things.

> Me
>
> **Something happened. I need to talk to you.**

But it's six a.m. Seattle time and my phone stays silent as I pull the black and gold ponytail holder out of my hair. My throat catches, and I bet Sarah doesn't wear hers anymore. It's only a matter of time before this hair tie lands in the shoebox.

I get in the shower, and the water is so hot my skin turns pink. I make it even hotter, hoping to feel something other than the burning in my stomach. My hair is soapy with my favorite vanilla and lavender shampoo. I scrub and scrub, the suds dripping down my shoulders. Maybe I can wash last night away. There's so much steam that it's hard to breathe, but I don't care. I can barely breathe anyway.

My hair hangs wet, strands coiling down my neck. I don't have the energy to flat-iron it. A depressing playlist comes through my computer speakers, a soundtrack to my mood. Soft pajamas, the ones with the drawstring pants, hang from my hips, but they don't help. I make my way back to my bed, but I trip over my bag and silently curse myself for leaving it in the middle of the floor. Books spill out and I crouch down to put them back. My hand touches something soft and smushy like a pillow. The genie. Shane gave him to me at the homecoming game yesterday, when I told him I could sew the loose stitching by his arm. I pull it out and grab for my phone.

> Me
>
> **Are you there?**

> Shane
>
> **Always. Just messing around in the studio.**

> Me
>
> **I ended up going to Tom's**

> Shane
>
> **Boring? Worst party ever?**

> Me
>
> **I saw Drew kissing Ray**

The words make me sick all over again, written proof of what I wish was a lie. The light of my phone burns into my eyes and I need more than typed words. I need Shane's voice, his steady timbre that always calms me down. But he's still typing.

> Shane
>
> **. . .**

> Me
>
> **Shane?**

My phone rings and I fumble it before picking up and putting it on speaker. I rest it on my nightstand, falling back against my pillow and staring at the string of white lights that hang from my ceiling.

"What happened?" Shane asks.

"It's good to hear your voice," I say, my body relaxing for the first time since last night.

"Stevie," he says, and then waits, the silence stretching out between our phones.

"They were kissing," is all I can manage to get out before crying again, then choking out the details word by word, completely unloading on Shane. But he doesn't say anything.

"Shane?" I wipe my face on my sweatshirt sleeve and breathe out the last of my tears.

"He's such an idiot," he practically whispers and I'm not sure if he's talking to me or to himself. But before I can respond Shane says, "I'll be right there," and hangs up.

Three songs later, the doorbell rings. I shut off my music as Mom answers the door, her voice going up an octave. Shane's hurried footsteps climb the staircase and he doesn't even knock. My door flings open and Shane stands there, his eyes moving from my face, which is probably all red and splotchy, to my hair, which likely resembles a bird's nest by now.

"Curly."

"Yep," I say, reaching for a hair tie.

"Pretty."

I put the hair tie back on my nightstand as Shane taps on the doorframe and walks over to my bed.

"Can I sit?"

I hug my knees to my chest making room for him next to me. When he sits down the bed moves a little, and the box spring makes an embarrassing creaking sound. He puts down his bag and folds his hands in his lap. He's not wearing his EMT hat today and his hair is messy, like he forgot he owns a comb.

"He really is an idiot." Shane leans back against the wall,

never taking his eyes off me. "But he's not an asshole. He would never be with another girl while he's with you. That much I know."

"Well, that's not what it looked like." I'm picking at the stitching of my comforter when Shane puts his hand over mine. His hand is warm and comforting, and for a second, I feel like this might all be okay.

"Here." Shane reaches into his bag and pulls out six roses that are so red they look like they're painted. I detach a small card from the bouquet and place the flowers on my nightstand. "They were on your front porch."

Stevie, I'm so sorry. You're right. She kissed me. But I didn't kiss her back. The only girl I want to kiss is you. The only girl I can think about is you. The only girl I could ever picture myself with is you.

I crumple up the paper and chuck it next to the flowers. Shane watches me carefully. "Did you read it?"

"No," Shane says quietly as he bites his bottom lip. "What is it about him? I mean he's my best friend. But why are *you* into him?"

The truth is I don't have an answer. Not a real answer, anyway. Drew is everything at once, and sometimes I think it might be too much.

"I," is all I can manage to say.

"So then why . . ."

"Am I with him?" I look at Shane and he leans forward a little. Part of me wants to reach out and ruffle his messy hair. "It's almost like being with him . . . is less like a choice and more like a bigger force propelling us together."

Shane flinches at my words. His eyes shift to the stuffed genie, resting beside me on the bed.

"Glad to see you're taking care of him."

I smile and pull Genie in for a hug.

"Do you think you can stay a little?"

Shane kicks off his sneakers and they land across the room, right next to my shelf of old DVDs. Shane's eyes flicker and he gets up and grabs one of the movies, holding it in front of my face.

"*This* is what we should do."

"*The Wizard of Oz*?" I haven't watched Dorothy since I was seven. I look at him skeptically.

"Wait for it . . ." He hurries around my room, opening my Mac.

"Um, Shane?"

"I bet you have it." Shane's finger glides over the mouse, scrolling through my music collection. "Got it!" He swivels my laptop and I see the familiar rainbow prism.

"Pink Floyd?"

"How do you *not* know about the *Dark Side of the Moon/ Wizard of Oz* mashup? My parents were so into this in the nineties."

Shane paces my room, holding *The Wizard of Oz*.

"Legend has it that if you play *Dark Side* while watching *The Wizard of Oz* on mute, the music and lyrics are exactly in sync with the movie. It's supposed to be trippy. We're doing this."

He kneels in front of the old DVD player Dad gave me when he no longer needed it for work. Shane queues up the movie, like a wild maestro trying to get it just right.

"You're supposed to press play after the third roar of the MGM lion," he says to himself on the first roar. "Wait for it . . . and go!" He presses play on my computer and quickly jumps up to turn off the light. The opening credits flash across my TV as the first few notes of "Speak to

Me" fill the room. Shane settles in next to me on the bed, and we both stare at the screen waiting for the magic to happen.

"You know, to really do this right we should've gotten high."

My head snaps in his direction. "You smoke?"

"Not really. Sometimes with my sister. But for occasions such as this, I've been known to dabble," he whispers. Shane always manages to surprise me. "Okay now, shhh. No talking."

Shane's right. The album is eerily in sync with the movie. He grabs my elbow every time the music lines up with an image. "On the Run" starts exactly as Dorothy falls off the fence. "Brain Damage" plays as the Scarecrow sings "If I Only Had a Brain." When the heartbeat at the end of the album coincides with Dorothy listening to the Tin Man's chest, I'm officially freaked out.

Shane's closer to me now, my legs draped over his. We got into this position as my feet started to fall asleep about halfway through, but neither of us moved. And neither of us moves now, not even to turn on the lights. Yellows, greens, and blues from the movie credits light up Shane's face.

"Well that was super cool," he says, and it feels like we shared a big secret. Like we're in on something that the rest of the world knows nothing about.

"Do you think Waters and Gilmour planned to do it?" I ask.

"You think they wrote *Dark Side of The Moon,* one of the most thematic, brilliant, and cohesive albums of all time, and synced it up with *The Wizard of Oz* intentionally?"

"Maybe?" I say, shrugging.

"No way. Not even remotely possible. It's just random."

"Yeah but it's perfectly in sync, how is that all random?"

"The best things in life are," Shane says. "That's the good stuff."

"I know," I say. I lift my legs off his and scoot back toward the headboard, bringing my knees to my chest. "Like when you get a text just as you're thinking about that person."

"Like when the perfect song comes on the radio right when you need to hear it."

"Like falling in love," I say, rolling my eyes and sighing dramatically. "Not like I would know."

Shane sits straight up and laughs.

"I'm hopeless in that department," Shane says. He picks up the stuffed genie and tosses him around a little. He stops and looks him square in the face. "Maybe if this guy were real and could grant me three wishes, I would get a clue."

"Oh yeah? What would you wish for?"

"First wish . . . to look a little more like a ripped super-hero and a little less like Shane Murphy."

"Superheroes are overrated. Plus they're not real," I say. Shane stuffs down a smile.

"Second wish . . . Ferrari."

"These are the most shallow wishes ever."

Shane holds up his index finger, smirking.

"Third wish . . . Unlimited wishes, obviously. So I can ask for world peace and all that."

"Shane, you don't need the wishes," I say.

Shane opens his mouth to say something, but quickly closes it and smiles instead. I feel a yawn coming on and swallow it back, but Shane notices. He stands up, stretching his arms high above his head.

"Are you going to be okay?" He shoves his feet into his sneakers, not bothering to undo the laces.

"I think so," I say.

"You know how you said Drew doesn't feel like a choice?"

I nod as Shane takes a few steps to the door and opens it, letting in light from the hallway. His hair is really such a mess.

He taps his fingers on the door frame like he did when he got here. Like a punctuation at the end of a sentence.

"You always have a choice, Stevie."

CHAPTER 13

Drew

NOVEMBER

The basketball banks off the rim and into my hands. I take another shot, this time sinking the ball through the net. I've been out here for at least an hour and it's getting dark. But I can't stop playing, even as my fingertips go numb. I flip the hood of my sweatshirt up to block out the cold. Should've worn a jacket. Then again, I didn't think I'd be out here for this long.

I take another shot and dribble to stay warm, glancing at Shane's front door. Not that I'm keeping track, but they've been practicing for All-State multiple times a week. And not that I'm counting, but Stevie's been hanging out at Shane's house for hours. Maybe I'm wasting my time. It's been a few weeks since Homecoming and Stevie still won't talk to me. Maybe she never will. If I sink this next shot, I'm heading inside. But as the ball swishes through the net, the door swings open.

"Night, Stevie. Talk to you later," Shane says as he hugs

her. I blow hot air into my hands and rub them together. Fallen leaves rustle under light footsteps as I take another shot at the net. I miss and the ball rolls to the bottom of the driveway.

"Nice shot," Stevie says with an edge to her voice as the ball bumps into her shin. She puts down her sax case and picks up the ball, chucking it at me. I quickly shift out of the way, narrowly missing a basketball to the gut. She picks up her sax case and starts down the sidewalk, a purple winter hat covering her ears and her hair falling over a black puffy coat.

"I deserved that," I say, shoving my hands into the pocket of my hoodie and trailing after her. She doesn't slow down.

"Can I talk to you?" I fall in step with her, but she keeps going, her eyes fixed on the sidewalk. "Stevie, please?" My voice cracks on her name, all of me breaking as she walks farther away from me.

Suddenly, Stevie stops and huffs out a sigh, her breath making a tiny cloud in the air. Her sax case dangles from her hand, her knuckles turning red. She places it on the sidewalk and fishes out two purple gloves from her coat pocket, sliding them on. Only then does she finally look at me.

"What?" she says, in a pissed-off way that makes me lose my train of thought and forget the speech I had planned.

"Um. How was your Thanksgiving?"

"Seriously?" She crosses her arms over her chest, then rolls her eyes. "It was nice. You?"

"It was good," I say.

I should've gone to Dino's after the Thanksgiving game. Anything to avoid what went down at home. When I got there, Mom was in the kitchen, a fresh turkey glistening, the whole house smelling like stuffing. She darted around the dining room table, setting three places, using our best china. Her pointless hope gave me hope, even when I knew better. And sure enough, as the sun set, the house got quiet anticipating a guest who was never arriving. Mom kept checking the time and shaking her head at her phone. I knew Dad wasn't coming, and if I'm being completely honest, I knew he wasn't coming even when I told everyone at the game that he was. Finally, after the turkey got cold, our phones buzzed at the same time. He didn't even have the decency to call.

Dad

Got caught up. See you guys soon.

Mom pushed her phone so hard, it slid across the kitchen island and onto the floor. I didn't say anything. I couldn't. So I crashed in my room and didn't come out. Mom didn't check on me all weekend.

But I don't tell Stevie any of it. That's not why I waited out here in the freezing cold all afternoon.

"I should get going," she says, picking up her sax case. That fireplace smell wafts through the air and I bet some family is sitting down to dinner, all happy and cozy. The only person who ever made me feel like that was Stevie. She starts heading down the sidewalk again, but I can't let her walk away.

"You know when you walk into a room, it's all you?" I shout after her. This isn't the exact speech I had planned, but it's close enough. She stops abruptly but doesn't turn around.

"You're the only one I see. I could be lost in a room full of people, but when I see you, it's like no one else matters."

I pause, staring at the back of her coat.

"I'm listening," she says, her back still to me. I take a deep breath and keep talking.

"Ray kissed me, not the other way around. I didn't want it to happen. I'm so sorry it happened. Please, you have to believe me."

Stevie turns, the tip of her nose pink and her cheeks flushed. She opens her mouth, then closes it again.

"I really need to go," she says softly, before turning and walking away from me.

I head inside and rip the hood off my head. Mom's in the kitchen polishing off a glass of chardonnay. She places the glass in the sink and checks her phone, shaking her head.

"Mom?"

She finally looks at me and sighs.

"You must be freezing," she says, enveloping me in a hug and rubbing my shoulders. "What were you doing out there for so long?"

"Nothing." I wipe my nose on my sleeve, longing to be upstairs in my room. "I'm gonna head up."

"I made dinner reservations." Mom's smile is too wide, all teeth, but her eyes don't crinkle at the corners. I trail her to the mudroom, unease hitting my stomach as she rummages through the closet. "Albert's going to be here any minute."

She grabs a long fur coat and my North Face, pushing the jacket at me. I rush to the living room window and pull the curtains back. Sure enough, a black SUV slows to a stop in front of the curb.

"Your dad's waiting at Keens." She fastens her coat and heads for the foyer.

"He sent Albert?" I ask, referring to Dad's driver, as Mom grabs her bag and opens the front door. I follow her to the car and as we get in Al tips his hat to me. As much as Al is the man, it feels wrong to be driven around like royalty when some kids in my school don't even have a car. Sometimes I get so overwhelmed by what we have, acutely aware of my advantages and the pressure to do something great with it all. I sink down in my seat, the weight of responsibility pushing hard against my chest, making it difficult to breathe.

"My man," Al says, and all at once I'm ten years old, riding with Dad to a Knicks game, or headed to see one of his clients backstage, or on my way to meet him for one of our weekly dinners, which were always at Keens.

"Only the best for the best," he would tell me.

The leather seats are cold against my body. I lean my head against the window, staring at the sidewalk, wishing I was still freezing my ass off outside with Stevie. Mom sits next to me and fishes through her bag, the one that cost more than a piece of furniture.

"What's this about?" I ask, as we merge onto the turnpike, cars whizzing by, everyone rushing somewhere.

"Your dad wanted to see you," Mom says carefully, and it's bullshit, I can tell. I don't ask her anything else because, frankly, I'm afraid of the answer.

When we walk inside Keens, the maître d' nods as we step into the mahogany-paneled room. Tiny candles centered on white tablecloths light our way through the restaurant, and a plate carrying a fifty-dollar steak glides past us, precariously balanced on a waiter's hand. We head for Dad's table, the one in the back away from the main dining room. He's about halfway through a glass of scotch when we reach him. He stands as we sit, patting me on the back and pulling out Mom's chair. I have no patience for his theatrics tonight.

"Where's what's-her-face?" I can't stand to say her name.

She's not that much older than me, which is disgusting. And before her, Dad was actually, you know, my dad. Once he started seeing her, he stopped caring about Mom and me.

"Vicky's back at the apartment," Dad says carefully.

"Where were you?" I demand, leaning across the table.

"What are you talking about?" he asks, looking at Mom for answers, but Mom stares at the napkin folded in her lap.

"My show. Old Silver. Thanksgiving dinner. Where were you?"

"Oh." Dad takes a slow sip of scotch. "Got tied up with stuff. You know how it is. I'll catch the next one, promise." He flashes me a smile but doesn't say sorry. He doesn't even *look* sorry. Mom eyes him.

"Listen, Andrew, we wanted to talk to you."

"Your father and I . . ." Mom starts to say.

"We've come to a mutual decision."

"Well it wasn't exactly mutual," Mom says under her breath and Dad puts his hand over her wrist, the light reflecting off her gumball-size diamond engagement ring. It kills me that she still wears that thing.

"We've decided to get a divorce."

"Well that's the fucking shocker of the century." I stand.

"Andrew, sit." Dad glares at me and I plop down in the chair. A waiter appears and sets down three steaks, with an assortment of side dishes. I spoon mashed potatoes and creamed spinach onto my plate, but I have no intention of eating. "Vicky and I are having a baby. You're going to be a big brother."

It's the sentence I longed to hear as a little kid, the promise of a built-in best friend. But this news is all wrong, stinging like rubbing alcohol in an open wound.

"You're replacing us." My voice catches and the spoon

shakes in my hand. I drop it on the tablecloth, creamed spin-ach staining the pristine fabric.

"Andrew, no," Dad says, but I don't want to hear it. I can't even look at him.

"That's not what this is," Mom says, a futile attempt. It's obvious even she doesn't believe it.

"How much is he paying you?" A rage builds in me, a vol-cano that's about to rip wide open. I need to know the price tag for keeping Mom so calm. No amount of money could keep me from going off right now.

"Andrew, enough." Dad takes off his glasses and stares at me. "You're seventeen. You're not a little kid anymore. Man up."

When he says those words, I feel like a little kid. I feel like a little kid so much that my throat burns. My nostrils flare and I swallow it back.

"What does that even mean? Man up? To be like you? Well, fuck that, Dad." I stand again.

"Drew, sit," Mom says, but I don't listen. She looks at my father and sighs, fiddling with a diamond necklace that sits above her collar bone. "We never intended to hurt you like this."

"We?" I yell way too loud for this fancy restaurant. "Like you had a choice. Face it, Mom, Dad traded us in for a newer model." My stomach twists as those vile words shoot from my mouth. I expect to see hurt on Mom's face, but instead she narrows her eyes and glares at Dad.

"You sit down right now," Dad hisses at me, his eyes dart-ing around the restaurant. I don't give a shit if anyone hears me. Mom shifts away from Dad and pushes her plate across the table.

"He's right, Don," she says softly.

"Mom, let's go," I extend my hand to her and she hesitates,

looking at me, then at Dad. Dad won't meet her eyes, so she stands, taking my hand. We leave him, surrounded by steak and money.

It's been a few days since the Keens dinner and my plan is to play basketball until I forget about Dad. I stand outside after school, throwing shot after shot, hoping Shane comes by, but he doesn't make an appearance. He hasn't been by in a few weeks. As night falls around me and my fingers begin to cramp, thoughts of Dad still torture my mind. Even though Shane never showed, I head for his house because the fact is, he's my best friend, the one I need right now.

Shane opens his front door and stares at me. He takes in my matted hair as a chilly gust of November air cuts through my sweatshirt. I march past him and sit on the leather sectional in his living room. There's a fire going in the stone fireplace that extends all the way to the ceiling. Even though the heat warms my cheeks I shudder into myself.

"Are you okay? You don't seem like . . . you."

I sigh, pulling my hair back then letting it fall around my face. I really need a shower.

"It's official. My parents are getting divorced." I grab one of the couch pillows and hug it against my chest. Ever since I saw those unsigned divorce papers, I expected it. But expecting isn't experiencing. Expecting still has a sliver of hope attached. Experiencing is definite, no rewinding, no last-minute script change.

"I'm sorry," he says, sitting next to me. "When did this happen?" he asks, as he tries to piece it all together, his eyes concerned. Shane should already know about my parents. At first I wasn't ready to talk, hoping to stuff it all down, ignore it until it went away. But it didn't go away. Instead this disgust I have for my father keeps growing inside me, an unstoppable weed squeezing out all the love I ever held for him. And now I'm afraid if I don't talk, it'll consume me.

"A few days ago. My dad's having a baby with his girlfriend. I'm going to be a big brother." I chuck the pillow at the couch.

"I take it you're not happy," Shane says, meeting my eyes.

I shake my head, afraid to speak the words out loud. But I can't pretend in front of the one person who sees right through me. "I'm jealous of a kid I'm supposed to love. A kid that's not even born yet. What kind of person does that make me?"

"It doesn't make you anything. You can't help how you feel." Shane shifts his gaze to the floor. "I really thought your parents would work it out."

"Well, shit doesn't always work out."

"Maybe not now, maybe not a year from now. But one day, you'll be okay."

"How can you be so sure of that?"

"Because you're you. There's a reason you're my best friend, even if you drive me nuts most of the time. You don't see it, but you're a survivor, the kind of guy who gets through stuff and is better on the other side. Take the day at the skate park. You turned that around into the best day of your life. And now, you're the guy who lives for the moment, instead of planning everything out. Not everyone can do that. Plus, you stick up for me, even though I hate it. You rise above every bad situation and find a way to go on, to really live. And you help everyone around you do the same. This is no different."

"I wish that's how I saw myself," I say, because it sure as hell doesn't feel that way.

"Well I do," Shane says, smirking. "And I'm smarter than you, so . . ."

He is smarter than me and kinder and a better musician. Even though the coin landed on heads, Shane's the obvious choice. I'm quicksand, losing it all with nothing to grab hold of. And yeah, maybe I'm a guy who wants to make it right. But it's not enough. Because I'm also the guy Stevie's dad hates, the guy who kissed his ex, the guy whose dad left him to start another family. *I'm* not enough. And then all at once, it hits me—the reason Shane hasn't been by for basketball. But I ask him anyway, because I need to hear him say it.

"Why haven't you been over for basketball?"

Shane stammers then collects himself.

"Stevie's been here. We've been practicing for All-State."

Even though I don't have the right, I flinch at his words, a slight twinge eating at my stomach.

"I thought you only practice once a week?" I ask carefully.

"We've been practicing a bit more lately." Shane won't look at me, and I wonder if he feels it too—the crack between us that's threatening to split wide open. "I think I'm going to tell her."

"Please, Shane," I beg him. I need a little more time, another chance to ask for forgiveness. If Shane tells Stevie about the coin toss, she'll never forgive me. No more chances.

"Just tell her, okay?" Shane's eyes are serious, but I don't nod in agreement. He sighs and throws a basketball game up on his flatscreen. We sit here in silence, the crooked crack extending a bit further, two halves of a lifelong friendship barely holding on.

CHAPTER 14

Stevie

I'm on my way to second period when Drew rounds the corner, his hair hanging limp like he hasn't showered all week. His eyes are bloodshot, the sight of him making something within me break. He doesn't know it yet, but I've already forgiven him. Last week, as he stood outside his house, remorse pouring from his eyes, I knew he was telling the truth. But even though I've forgiven him, I haven't told him. The thing is, the past few weeks have been, I don't know, *easier*. My audition piece is almost ready, and my parents have been pretty chill. Dad took me to a fancy sushi place in the city on his day off. Just me and him. And even though he still hasn't warmed to the idea of music school, he pointed out some of the NYU dorms as we drove past, a small flame of excitement flickering in his eyes.

So now when Drew approaches me, I freeze. Part of me wants to talk to him and make everything right. But another part of me wants to avoid it all. So that's what I do, ducking into the girls' bathroom.

I pull gloss from my bag and smear it on my lips. The

mirror is cloudy, my reflection only partly visible. A lighter clicks from behind one of the stall doors and a small exhale sends a puff of smoke through the air.

"Shit," says a hushed voice.

I crouch down and Converse shuffle back and forth against the tile as the toilet flushes. The door squeaks open revealing Ray, her eyes sunken and her blond hair hanging over a gray sweatshirt covered in tiny white hearts.

"Don't tell anyone." She pulls her hair into a neat pony-tail. "I'd get kicked off the team if I was caught smoking in school. Maybe I should get kicked off." She steps next to me and we stare at each other in the mirror as she dabs concealer under her eyes.

"Why would you say that?"

"I'm sure you saw the way I completely screwed up our last game."

I saw it. Everyone saw it. Fans stomped their feet, shaking the metal bleachers as Ray geared up for the game-winning field goal. It was hard to tell from way up in the stands, but she seemed unsure of herself as she charged the ball, running at half speed. And when her cleat launched it into the air, it sailed to the right just outside of the goal. Ray ripped off her helmet and threw it on the sidelines, storming off the field.

"I saw it," I say as she turns on the sink. She punches at the soap dispenser, then lets water rush over her hands. When she's done, she grabs for a paper towel but there are none left.

"Now I have to work extra hard to keep my spot on the team." Ray dries her hands on her ripped jeans. She pulls her sweatshirt to her nose and inhales. "Do I smell like smoke?"

"No," I say, heading for the door, desperate to get away from her.

"I fucked up," she says again, as my hand touches the handle.

"I told you I saw it." I'm losing patience and she doesn't deserve my sympathy. "I gotta go."

"No, at Tom's party," she says quietly, and I glance over my shoulder.

Ray stares at the soap dispenser, her eyes glassy. "I'm sorry. Like, really sorry. I don't know why I did it. I shouldn't have done it."

"You told me you were cool with everything," I say, echoing her words from September. "Were you lying?"

"I didn't think so," she says quietly, shaking her head. "But maybe I was. Maybe I was lying to myself, trying to forget about him, you know?"

"What you did was so—"

"Shitty, I know. I've been hating myself for it ever since."

Ray's not the confident girl I thought she was. Nowhere close. Even in this dirty mirror, I see her clearly now. She sits on the radiator and tightens the laces on her sneakers. Dirt cakes the bottoms. "You should know he didn't kiss me back," she says, looping one lace over the other. "He's a solid guy and it's obvious he's fallen for you."

As much as I want to hate Ray for what she did, I can't. She's a girl like me, trying to figure it all out but messing up along the way.

"You know," I say, our eyes meeting in the mirror. "If it weren't for this Drew stuff, I think we would have been friends."

Ray pops a piece of gum in her mouth and smiles, turning to me.

"We definitely would have been friends." She extends a stick of gum at me. "Maybe we still can be?"

Forgiveness is easy. It's the forgetting part I'm not so sure about. Friends without trust is a tall order.

"I'll think about it," I say, taking the gum.

Shane powers down the mixing board and throws his drumsticks into the bin. He sits next to me on the Persian rug, right in front of his drum set. A drawing pad rests on his lap and he starts to doodle on the white pages.

"Audition's in two weeks. How do you feel?" His eyes are warm as he glances at me, then back to his drawing, a night sky.

"Ready," I say with confidence.

"You sleeping?"

"Define sleep," I say. Shane puts down his charcoal pencil and shakes his head. I check out his drawing and now there's a girl with long brown hair soaring among the stars.

"That thing where you get into your bed and dream about cool stuff like playing drums for The Who and then you wake up eight hours later." Shane smiles.

"You have great dreams," I say. "As for me, it's more like dinosaurs chasing me through New York City."

"Jeez, you're messed up."

I shove Shane in the shoulder, and he fakes an injury, clutching his arm dramatically. He picks up the charcoal pencil and scratches it against the paper.

"But I've been there. Trying to run away from the things you can't control. But sometimes you can't run. You have to stand still and face it."

"How do you do that?" I ask, as Shane scribbles a menacing T. rex in the sky, hovering above the girl.

"Well first, you need a solid eight hours before the audition. Promise me you'll do a top five list before you go to bed."

"Promise, but all I really need that day is this." I hold up my red neck strap. Without it my sax feels foreign and the notes don't flow. Shane scribbles something on his sketch pad, then flips it in my direction. Now there's a saxophone in the girl's hand shooting fire at the T. rex. My breath catches as I read what he wrote.

You're super talented and you don't need anything but yourself.

It's not true and Shane doesn't even realize it. For three months, he's been the one to push me to keep practicing, to believe I can make the cut. Without him, I wouldn't be ready. In fact, I probably would've made up an obvious excuse to skip the audition, promising myself I would go for it next year, knowing that next year I could be living in an entirely new state.

"I need you," I say quietly. "I never would've been ready without you."

Shane scribbles something else on the notepad.

You're very welcome.

I laugh and say, "Thank you."

Shane clears his throat and stands, chucking the sketch pad on the snare. He heads for his computer, pulling up one of his obscure playlists. "Wanna hang for a bit?"

For the past few weeks our practice sessions have been extending later and later. I tell myself it's because the audition is so soon, but after a certain point, we put down our instruments and talk. And it's not only during practice. We've been talking at night on the phone, marathon conversations that stretch on for hours, the kind you wish would never end. It started with that first call, the day we watched *The Wizard of Oz*, and it hasn't stopped since. Shane usually obsesses over a random band or what he learned that week during his EMT shift. Sometimes he tells me about the stuff Brent

Miller pulled with him, swearing me to secrecy. Like I would ever tell. I ramble about all the cool spots in Seattle and how moving sucks and how Dad doesn't know me. *I know you,* he said last night, and we both fell silent as something shifted, slight, like tectonic plates rearranging the world.

"I love Peter Gabriel," I say as "Solsbury Hill" comes through the speakers.

"Great song," Shane says, sitting next to me, sketchbook in hand, right as Peter Gabriel sings *I'm never where I want to be.*

"I disagree with that," he says as he grabs the charcoal pencil and scribbles words on the sketch paper. *Sometimes I'm right where I want to be.*

Shane's eyes are different, softer. Flecks of gold swim in a sea of honey. His mouth plays with a small smile, revealing that dimple in his left cheek. This is right where *I* want to be.

Being with Shane isn't like being with Drew. Drew is the opening song on my favorite album. He's the song that everyone loves, the song that draws me in and makes me want to listen to the whole album without stopping. He's the catchy song with the great hook, fancy guitar solo, and soaring vocals. But Shane . . . Shane's the hidden track. He's the song I don't listen to until I've devoured the whole album. He's that quiet song with the unbelievable melody. The song that makes me understand myself a bit better. Once I discover a truly special hidden track, I never get sick of it.

Shane cranks the volume on the playlist and lies on the rug, music filling the room. I settle in next to him as he air drums along, both of us staring at the gray egg crates on the ceiling. Every few songs he says, "This one is great" or "Good tune." As I lay close to him, his chest moves with his breath, and to my surprise, I long to kiss him. Being with Shane is easy, effortless, and in this moment, I can't help comparing him to Drew and wonder *What if?* I consider looking at him to see if this feeling is real, but I don't move, afraid to find out the answer. Every feeling swims around my body at once—the wanting with Drew, the ease with Shane, and the plain confusion at not knowing which one is right.

"Top five favorite songs of all time," he says quietly.

"In no particular order because that would be too hard."

"Of course," he says like he always does.

"'Imagine,' John Lennon."

"Absolutely," Shane says.

"'Songbird,' Fleetwood Mac."

"I knew you would say that."

"'A Day in the Life,' Beatles."

"Wow, two Beatles tunes."

"One is Lennon, one is the Beatles," I correct him.

"Semantics. Lennon is a Beatle."

"Not semantics. We wouldn't have 'A Day in the Life' without Paul, George, and Ringo," I counter.

"Fair enough. Go on."

"'Black,' Pearl Jam."

"Predictable."

"And this one," I say nodding toward his laptop, which is now playing "Fields of Gold" by Sting.

"Really?" He's surprised by my choice.

"The melody is sad, happy, and beautiful all at once," I say. The notes are longing, missing someone. But the words are gratitude, the experience of love, real love before it disappears. "It's a perfect song."

"What do you think it means . . . a field of gold?" he says, staring at the ceiling.

"Maybe a wheat field? Or I don't know . . . heaven?"

"Do you believe in all that?" he asks, his voice almost a whisper.

"I don't know. Do you?"

"I do. I'd rather believe in something than *not* believe, you know?" he says, his eyes still fixed on the ceiling. I know I shouldn't, but I snuggle into Shane's side. He doesn't move.

"But there's no proof," I say. "How can you be so sure?"

"I'm not. That's the whole point," Shane says, and I smile.

"I can't *not* question it."

"I know." Shane's body shifts, and for a second his pinky finger hooks over mine, like a promise of something that could be.

As the song trails off my eyelids get heavy with sleep. I can't help it. I feel so completely safe, like nothing bad could ever happen. Lying next to Shane, my unstable life feels balanced, steady. With his voice in my ear, I don't pick at my cuticles. With Drew I don't think about what comes next, but with Shane I don't fear what comes next. I fall asleep with ease, my head quiet and secure in the crook of his arm.

CHAPTER 15

Drew

DECEMBER

A moving truck idles in our driveway, a giant fuck-you. A short guy with jacked arms pushes Dad's baby grand up the ramp to the truck. His ass crack hangs out of his jeans. Mom gets to keep the house today, but Dad's taking all his things, the things that make it a home.

"We'll get new stuff," Mom says, watching with me from the window. "Fresh start." She closes one of the curtains, though, like she can't watch it all disappear.

"How can you say that?" I put my hand on the cold window, my fingers leaving smudge marks on the glass. Mom smooths back my hair.

"What else is there to say? Sometimes we don't choose what happens to us, baby. Sometimes life hands us a new plan." The moving guy is carrying Dad's mahogany desk with another taller man who stops for a moment, takes a deep breath, and picks up his corner again.

"What if I don't want a new plan?"

"I don't either. But here we are, right?" Mom cups my chin in her hands and kisses me on the forehead. "We'll figure it out together. You and me."

Even though Mom's been MIA for months, thank God she's here now. I couldn't handle this one alone. I put on my brave face, faking a smile and tucking my hair behind my ears. Mom kisses me again on the forehead and says, "I'm going to see if the guys want anything to drink."

"I'll come with you," I say, following her out the front door. Mom chats with the movers, pulling her sweater tight around her body. It's fucking freezing out here. I step around the maze of Dad's things, my hand lingering on the leather couch from his office. I picture him playing a James Taylor tune on his guitar, me ten years old and snuggled up against his shoulder. He would sing a line and I would sing a line, back and forth until we were singing together. Even then, I wanted to bottle the moment, so I could replay it when I needed Dad. Right about now I could use a replay.

"I'll grab you boys some hot coffee," Mom says before turning to me. "Come inside, you're going to freeze."

"In a minute."

The tall guy hoists a wardrobe of Dad's clothes up the ramp to the truck. But I don't see a box. I see me at four, drowning in Dad's suit, his Hermès tie hanging loose around my neck. I hear my tiny voice saying, "I'm going to work," and Dad scooping me up high, laughing and blowing a raspberry on my belly.

I head down the driveway, no clue where I'm going as long as it's not here. The endless blue sky is too blue, too beautiful for this shit day. When I reach the mailbox, I can't decide if I should turn left or right. Shane's not even home. He left with Stevie for All-State auditions before the truck arrived. As they hopped in an Uber bound for Rutgers, I wished them good luck, certain they'd both get in. Stevie smiled at me, her real smile, and she's been on my mind ever since. But she still hasn't spoken to me, even after I tried to apologize and explain it all. I'm starting to think she's never going to forgive me, so what else could I say except good luck? I'm about to go for a walk to clear my head, when a splash of red catches my eye, something sticking out of the bush by the sidewalk. When I get closer I know where I'm headed and it's straight to Rutgers because that splash of red is Stevie's neck strap. And she can't audition without it.

I swerve the Jeep into a parking spot and say a quick thank-you to the traffic gods. Ninety on the parkway and no ticket. I grab the neck strap and bolt to the student union. A girl with a nose ring directs me to the audition room and I take two stairs at a time, following the music. The hallway is lined with black folding chairs and clogged with musicians. I stop short when my eyes land on Shane and Stevie, but they don't notice me. They are standing inches from each other and Stevie's shaking her head.

"I'm not doing it," she says, pieces of her dark hair falling out of her ponytail and grazing her cheeks. Her sax is propped against the wall. She straightens out her black skirt and shifts on her heels, like it hurts to stand. A girl carrying a flute maneuvers through the crowded hall and opens the door to the audition room, the golden bleat of a trumpet spilling into the air.

"You don't need it, Stevie," Shane says as she picks at a Band-Aid on her pointer finger. He holds up a black neck strap and says, "Use this one. Remember, you just need you."

"Let's go. You already auditioned. It's fine, I didn't want All-State that badly anyway." Liar.

"You need a top five," Shane says, like some secret code they have with each other. My stomach churns. Even though I know they're friends, seeing them like this somehow feels like a betrayal. "Top five best voices in rock and roll."

Stevie crosses her arms over her chest and smiles, her real smile. The smile I thought was reserved only for me.

"Dead or alive?" she asks, not missing a beat.

"Both."

"Freddie Mercury." She sticks her thumb out like she's hailing a taxi. "Robert Plant." She adds her pointer finger, the one with the Band-Aid.

"Obviously," Shane interjects. The way he says it makes my mouth go dry, like they've been through this routine before.

"Ann Wilson, Chris Cornell, and . . . Bono." Stevie flashes her palm at Shane, all five fingers extended.

"You're giving your last spot to Bono?"

"That I am." Stevie smirks.

"That's it. We're not friends anymore."

Stevie playfully shoves Shane and he laughs, and I can't watch this anymore, so I take my chance and head for them.

They both see me at the same time, confusion settling on their faces. The slightest hint of disappointment takes hold in the corner of Shane's mouth. But Stevie's brown eyes come alive, turning a lighter shade.

"What are you doing here?" she asks.

I hold up her red neck strap. "I found this on my front lawn. Figured you might need it."

Stevie might have said thank you, but I don't hear a thing. Her arms fling around my neck and her body presses against mine. She's shaking and squeezing the hell out of me but then as quickly as she pulled me close, she lets go.

"Thank you," she says, putting the neck strap on and clipping it to her sax. "I'm up next."

"I'm sorry," I say. "For everything that went down. You have to know . . ."

"I know," she says. Shane's eyes ping-pong between us. "Ray told me. I believe you. I'm sorry it took me so long to believe you."

And I don't know if that means we're okay or we're starting from someplace entirely new. I don't care as long as there's the chance.

"Stevie Rosenstein," a voice calls from the audition room.

Stevie smiles and heads inside, leaving Shane and me in the hallway. The door to the audition room closes and I eye Shane, who leans against the concrete wall.

"Shane?" I rake my hair back, waffling over whether to ask him the question tiptoeing on my tongue. For the first time in weeks, I have a real opening with Stevie. But at the same time, what I witnessed before wasn't just two friends prepping for an audition. "What's going on with you and Stevie?"

"What do you mean?"

"Are you guys like . . ."

"We're friends," Shane says, staring at the linoleum floor.

"Look at me and say that."

He picks his head up, looks me straight in the eyes, and says slowly, "We're just friends."

"Bullshit."

"I'm allowed to be friends with her." Shane's eyes fall back to the floor and I know he's full of it. He can't even say her name without blushing.

"We talked about this," I say. "I thought you were cool."

"That was before."

"Before what?"

"Before I knew her," Shane says quietly. I want to punch him.

"What makes you think you know her like I do?" I ask. "Don't go behind my back, man. In fact, don't go there at all."

"We talk."

"Huh?"

"Every night. We talk on the phone. Sometimes for hours. She's never told you, right?"

"No," I say, my pulse accelerating. "So what?"

"Maybe you don't know her as well as you think," Shane says under his breath.

"She might talk to you on the phone, she might be friends with you, but you're *just* friends. At the beginning of the year she chose to be with *me*."

Shane tightens his grip on a drumstick, like he's about to stab me with it. His eyes slice right through me.

"That's not how it went down, and you know it," he says, serious, and I take a step back.

"Regardless of what went down, she still chose to be with me. I know I screwed up, but now I think I have a shot at making things right," I counter, my insides on fire. I don't know if I believe it. Even though the coin landed in my favor, maybe it's Shane Stevie wants.

"Tell her," Shane says, and I know he's talking about the coin toss.

"I can't," I say softly.

"If you don't tell her, I will," he says, his eyes challenging me.

"This isn't your secret to tell," I say, stepping to him. "Stay out of it."

He shakes his head slowly and even though I'm terrified to tell her, part of me knows he's right. In the beginning, flipping that coin was a way to make it fair, so we wouldn't fight. But now we're fighting anyway, and instead of it being fair, that coin toss is wrong. It's a lie.

"So you admit it's a secret. It's not right, and you know it.

You need to tell her we flipped a coin in the beginning of the year. That the coin landed on heads and you're the one who got to ask her out," Shane says, his eyes softening like he's on my side. But telling her could destroy everything. Maybe that's exactly what he wants.

"What?" Stevie's voice snaps my head to the audition room. She stands in the doorway, her brown eyes darting between me and Shane, her mouth parted open. Her face contorts as she computes everything she heard. God, how much did she hear? Shane and I stare at her, speechless. My heart begins to pound as a million apologies flood my brain, none of which leave my mouth.

"Stevie—" Shane starts to say.

"Forgot my sheet music." Stevie's voice is barely audible. She gestures at a pile of papers with a shaking hand. Her chest rises and falls and so much pain settles in her eyes that a wave of nausea hits my stomach. She holds my gaze, then turns to Shane. My heart drops through the floor when she speaks again, her voice trembling.

"You flipped a coin for me?"

"It wasn't like that," Shane and I say in unison, desperate. We both step to her, but she holds out her hand. The distance between us is a mere few feet, but it's like a canyon opened up in the hallway. One false step and I'll plummet to the rocks below.

"Don't," is all Stevie says, her voice breaking. She pushes past us, her hand over her mouth as she runs down the hall and out the door.

Shane and I stare at each other in stunned silence for a beat, frozen. I can't catch my breath, my mind circling for a solution, a way out of the colossal mess we created.

"Fuck," I whisper, and Shane glares at me, his eyes two weapons ready to destroy me.

"Stevie Rosenstein?" one of the judges calls out. "We only have ten more minutes for your audition slot."

Shane runs over to her, begging for an extension.

"Stevie had to run out for a bit. She'll be back. Please wait for her?" Shane asks the judge. She raises an eyebrow.

"We're here until five p.m. If she comes back before then, she can still try out," she says before disappearing into the audition room.

I furiously tap out a text to Stevie.

Me

Don't throw away this audition.
Please let us explain.

Shane's texting too until both our phones ding with an incoming message.

Stevie

Got in an Uber. Not auditioning. Leave
me alone.

"She has to try out," Shane says, throwing his drumsticks in his backpack, already heading for the exit. I follow and put my hand on his shoulder as we reach the top of the stairs. Shane turns, but this time all the anger and resentment over the coin toss drains from his eyes. He needs me and I need him. The only way we can fix this is together. "Let's go find her. Get her to audition. Make her understand all of it. It's the only way."

"My car's right outside," I say, and we book it down the stairs.

CHAPTER 16

Stevie

I'm not in an Uber. I'm alone in a bathroom in the student center lobby. It smells like pee and Lysol, and I swear I'm about to be sick. My hands shake as I reread the text I sent to Drew and Shane.

Me

Got in an Uber. Not auditioning.
Leave me alone.

A lie.

I turn my phone off. My sax dangles from the red strap hugging my neck. The weight strains my back as I close my eyes. My fingers tap the keys of my sax one by one. I worked too hard for this to walk away now. Tears soak my lashes and seep through my lids, warming my cheeks. A cavalier coin toss, a kid's game. How could they view me like that? How could they not tell me, after all this time? An audible sob escapes my mouth, echoing against the cement walls. I cup my hand over my face as if I could stuff it back in. My heart pounds as I glance at my phone—only a few more minutes left of my audition slot. I don't have time to process what this all means, my mind spinning at each possibility. I'm a bet. I'm a joke. I was never in control. They left me up to chance. Like Dad, they puppeteered the strings of my life.

Not this time. No one is messing this up for me. I'm not a chance. I'm someone worth fighting for. I am in control and I *am* auditioning. I breathe in deep to quiet my pounding heart. I lied so they wouldn't wait for me, so they would leave this building, so I could concentrate without the two of them lurking outside the audition room. My tears dry on my cheeks as I smooth down my shirt. When I open the door to the bathroom, I peek around the corner to make sure the hallway is empty. Once I'm upstairs, more tension releases from my shoulders as I confirm Drew and Shane are nowhere in sight. I snatch the sheet music off the chair and head into the audition room. The judges look at me with concern, but I calmly adjust the music stand, arranging my papers in order.

"I'm ready," I say with conviction. The judges nod in unison and my fingers hover over the keys. My mind flips from Drew to Shane one last time. Maybe it wasn't a game. Maybe everything was as real as it felt. Despite what I learned, I care about them both, I know I do. I also know who I would choose if I had to pick. But now I'm unsure if I ever really knew either of them. I'm unsure if I *want* to choose. But when you fall for someone is it ever really a choice?

And then I shut it all off. I am in control here, not Drew, not Shane—me. And I am going to kill this audition. The reed vibrates against my tongue as I push out the first note of "Born to Run," brassy and unapologetic. Music fills the audition room, the notes building on each other, the tempo increasing. I rip through the bars, jamming into the solo, the melody pumping through my veins. This song is pure magic. And when I get to the last note, it doesn't peter out. It crosses the finish line loud and triumphant. I let out an exhausted breath of air and shift my eyes to the judges. They stare at me for a heart-stopping beat, then a judge wearing cat-eye glasses nods, the corner of her mouth curving up ever so slightly in approval. An unstoppable smile takes over my face, and for once nothing else matters except me, nailing this audition.

CHAPTER 17

Drew

Snow begins to fall from the sky, dusting the road. I turn on my high beams as the windshield wipers scrape at the glass. It's like I'm inside a snow globe, flakes flying up, down, and sideways, the world slowly drifting to sleep beneath a white blanket. Shane and I didn't speak the entire time we were on the highway. But when we finally get into town, the silence is so heavy I can't stand it a second longer.

"Shane?" I ask quietly. He grunts in response, still pissed about everything that went down outside the audition room. Shane doesn't think I notice the way he steals glances at Stevie in class, but it's impossible to ignore. Hell, just the way he talks about her, it's obvious. But the part I don't want to admit, the part I've pushed deep down into the pit of my stomach, is the way Stevie looks at him. But like I said, I'd rather not think about it.

"Think we'll get a snow day tomorrow?" Shane says, clearly not ready to talk about whatever is going on with him and Stevie.

"Hope so," I say, double-timing the wipers, snow flying off the windshield.

"Maybe we can hit Mountain Creek," Shane says, pulling his blue baseball hat from his backpack and securing it on his head. The thought of hitting the creek sends a smile across my face. Just me and Shane again, losing ourselves on the slopes.

"We need to apologize to her," Shane says.

I snap my head to him before returning my gaze to the snow-covered road. I'm losing her. I know I am. Maybe I stole a chance from my best friend when we flipped that coin. God, his face when he says her name, all giddy like a little boy. So fucking happy, the way I was when I first kissed her, before I made a mess of it all.

"Admit it," I say as I turn onto Ridge Road, all curves surrounded by woods on both sides. Snow-covered branches arch to the ground. I take my foot off the accelerator, slowing around the twists and turns.

"Admit what?" Shane unbuckles his seatbelt and takes off his jacket, wiping perspiration from his forehead. I turn down the heat, but something tells me it's not the heat making him sweat.

"C'mon. Don't make me say it."

"Then I don't need to tell you," Shane says softly.

"I messed it all up," I choke out. I messed it all up and I don't know how to fix it. To get back to the beginning, when it was right and good. When Stevie made all the bad disappear.

"Fine, I admit it," he whispers, leaning his head on the window. "I care about her, okay. A lot. And we need to explain everything to her. She needs to know that the way I feel is real."

"It's real for me too," I say, hating that there's no easy way out of this. Even though she finally forgave me for everything that happened with Ray, we're barely hanging on. But what if I've already lost her? What if she was meant to be with Shane all along? And what if I lose him too?

"I wrote her a note," he says, twisting one of the buttons on his shirt. "I told her everything about the beginning of the year, about the way I feel. I couldn't take the lies and stuffed it in her locker yesterday. I wasn't thinking. I shouldn't have done it."

"You what?" My hands clench the steering wheel, my knuckles turning white.

"I didn't mean to go behind your back," Shane says, shifting in his seat, his voice strained, reaching for any excuse.

"That's exactly what you did. How could you do that to me?"

"I was just trying to do what's right."

"Who are you to say what is right and what is wrong?" I'm yelling now, Shane's betrayal coursing through me, hurting worse than any type of physical pain. "How is keeping a secret from me any different than keeping a secret from Stevie? Same fucking thing in my opinion."

"Would you listen to yourself? You're so focused on her forgiveness that you're not even thinking about *her*. Don't you get it?"

I slam my fist on the steering wheel because of course I get it and of course Shane was right to tell Stevie. I hate myself for not telling her sooner. I hate myself for flipping that coin in the first place.

"Of course I get it," I say, but I'm having trouble breathing, sharp pains shooting through my chest.

"I'll fish it out of her locker first thing Monday morning," Shane says, a peace offering.

None of it matters because she heard every last detail back at the audition. My foot hits the accelerator. I'm desperate to get out of this car, to find a solution to an unsolvable problem.

"Dude, slow down," Shane says. I turn to him, my foot still pressed against the accelerator, and his eyes go wide.

"Deer!" Shane yells as he points at a shell-shocked animal in the middle of the road, huge flakes of snow plummeting to the earth.

It happens fast. I jam the brake with everything I have, but Shane reaches out and grabs at the wheel, yanking it hard to the right.

"No!" I yell, but it's too late. The Jeep skids through the snow and flies off the road, smashing through branches and trees. And then we're falling, my hands still braced on the steering wheel, as metal crunches, the sound stabbing my ears. Shane screams as glass shatters around us, until all at once everything stops. Snow-covered leaves and branches are inside the car. A blast of cold air smacks me in the face and runs down my spine. Shards of glass cover my lap. My heart speeds, pumping so hard it might break through my chest or seize up completely. Shane's blue baseball hat is on the dashboard behind the steering wheel. The car smells like smoke, gunpowder, I don't know. Fuck, where's Shane? I need to get to Shane. I try to turn my head, but everything blurs. Warm liquid spills from my forehead and drips down my cheek. My eyelids are heavy, closing and opening like flicking a light switch, until it all goes dark.

PART TWO

TAILS

CHAPTER 1

Shane

AUGUST

"I'm gonna ask her out," Drew announces after practice, once we're settled in the Jeep. My heart stops. Not Stevie. Any girl but Stevie. I've never seen someone stand up to Brent Miller the way she did at practice today. The way I wish I could. It's like she landed here, in our town, for the sole purpose of cutting Brent down to size. And she actually did. He looked like he was about to pee himself, it was so perfect. Word on the street is Stevie's from Seattle, just about the coolest music city in the world, which figures. She's beyond good on sax and of course she's not just talented, she's beautiful. The kind of beautiful that keeps you up at night. Although I'm always up at night.

"You can have any girl you want, anyone. Her?" I shift to face him, so he knows I'm serious.

"She's just . . . I don't know . . ." Drew says, shaking the hair out of his eyes. He shuts off the ignition, a strand of Mardi Gras beads swaying from the rearview mirror. It's obvious

Drew's hooked, like me, reeled in before we even knew a line had been cast. He can barely get the words out of his mouth, flustered like I've never seen him before.

"You don't even know her," I say, trying to downplay it all. Maybe if Drew thinks about this logically, he'll step aside.

"*You* don't even know her," Drew says, both hands gripping the steering wheel. "We *both* just met her."

"Well *I'm* asking her out," I say, because screw logic. Nothing about my feelings for Stevie is logical. Not the way my breath catches when I try to talk to her. Not the way her laugh sends my heart into a full-on spasm. And certainly not the way her dark eyes all but paralyze me, my hands fumbling drumsticks like an amateur.

I refuse to back down.

"Not if I do it first," Drew says, his eyes ablaze.

"Not if *I* do it first." I stare at him and he stares back, sighing. His eyes dart to the loose change in the center console and my pulse escalates. His mind seriously can't be going there—not about this. For as long as I can remember we've flipped a coin to settle disputes. But this isn't some childish disagreement. This is a person with thoughts and feelings, and there's no way Drew can be thinking this is okay.

"This is stupid, Shane." Drew glances at me, then at the coins. "I say we flip for it."

My mouth falls open, disbelief pouring from my eyes.

"Flip for it? This isn't like choosing top bunk at sleepovers."

"I didn't mean it like that," Drew says, raking his hair back with one hand. "It's just . . . flipping a coin is what we do. How we've always made choices. It's the only fair way to decide. I don't want to fight with you. I *can't* fight with you."

He's out of his mind. Stevie isn't a coin toss.

"You do realize that Stevie can still say no, regardless of

who asks her out," I say, hoping he will forget about this awful idea and let whatever's supposed to happen, happen.

"Get out," Drew says, nodding at the door.

"Huh?"

"Just get out." He grabs a penny from the middle console and flings the door open.

"This is ridiculous," I say, following him to the front of the Jeep.

"Have a better idea?" He tosses the penny in the air. I wish I had a better idea. The obvious solution is to call it off and give in to Drew. Except a girl has never talked to me the way Stevie did this afternoon—like she actually cares about getting to know me, like I'm not some nobody drummer in the marching band.

"For the record, this isn't cool," I say, one last Hail Mary pass, but it's too late. Drew's mind is made up and there's no stopping him. Once when we were little Drew decided to swing a full three-sixty around the swing set in his back yard. He pumped his legs so hard and went so high, his sneakers kicking at the clouds. Even though he never made it all the way around, he was out there until dusk trying. It was amazing he didn't kill himself.

I sigh as it hits me—the realization of how this will play out.

"And odds are, you're the one she's going to choose, regardless of where that penny lands," I say, wondering if Drew is aware of this inevitable truth. It doesn't matter if it's heads or tails. This penny won't change anything. Even if it lands on tails, Stevie will fall for Drew. They all do.

"You can't back down," he says. "If you back down, you're going to resent me. If I back down, I'm going to resent you. This is the only way. And you know it."

My mouth opens, but my intended counterargument

doesn't make it past my throat. Even though I'm against this, part of me agrees with him. If I back down, I would be so pissed, but not at Drew—at myself.

"Heads," he announces. This is happening whether I like it or not. He grabs the penny with one hand, kissing his closed fist.

"You're an idiot," I say.

He flicks the penny high into the air, the sun catching on the copper.

"Tails." I barely get the word out.

"Shit," Drew says, squinting at the sun as he misses the penny completely. It falls next to the tire, and his boot slams down on the coin. I drop to the ground and pull hard on Drew's boot, trying to pry it up. He won't budge.

"Come on, man, let's have it," I say, my patience waning, because even though I don't agree with this, I'm holding my breath, praying it landed on tails. I know it's wrong, but now that we've gone through with it, I'm desperate for this chance.

"Hold on." Drew shifts a little, careful to keep the coin concealed. "You're cool either way?"

"I'm cool. Are you? Either way?"

"Always." Drew shakes his hair out of his face.

"So what are you waiting for?"

Drew slowly lifts his boot off the ground and crouches next to me. We examine the tiny coin. Our eyes go wide as we stare at the penny and then at each other.

I never catch a break. When I was little it used to bother me, like when I would strike out during baseball or get smoked in a running race. I was never the kid everyone would cheer for, always the kid that pulled the short straw. As I got older, it happened so often that I expected to lose. That's why yesterday, when that penny landed on tails, I was sure Drew was messing with me. Because Drew's the one who gets picked first in gym class while I wait on the sidelines, the team captains avoiding my eyes until I'm the only one left. And Drew's the guy whose name'll be drawn out of a hat at random. Drew's the one who gets all the girls without even trying.

But yesterday, that penny landed on tails. It really did. Maybe that penny is some sort of sign that things are starting to change for me. Maybe Brent Miller will finally leave me alone. Maybe *I'll* get the girl.

The shiny coin swims in my pocket as I head to the band room, even earlier than usual. The lights are out, the instruments all still waking up. I punch my elbow against the switch and head straight for my set. The stool wobbles a bit when I sit, but I steady it and grab the drumsticks. I need to think and the only way I can think clearly is to hit these skins. First the snare, then a kick at the bass, then the snare, high hat, snare, and around again. I need a plan, a way to talk to Stevie so she'll see me instead of Drew. Because, I'm not oblivious. She looks at Drew the way I want her to look at me. The way *I* look at *her*. Round and around again, the beat speeding, my thoughts slowing.

"You're good," a voice says from the doorway, and I grab the cymbal to silence it. Stevie holds her sax case with two hands, right in front of her ripped shorts. I'm staring at her tanned legs and I have to force myself to look away. I lock into her deep brown eyes and I'm frozen.

"How long have you been standing there?" I ask, hoping I'm not visibly sweating.

"Long enough to know you're good," she says, taking a step inside. Her voice knocks the wind out of me. There's a softness and kindness that other girls lost sometime in middle school. Other girls do that thing where their voice goes up an octave at the end, like they're asking a question, when in fact they're not asking anything. Not that I would know. Girls at this school don't know I'm alive unless I'm standing next to Drew. Even then they just use me to get to him. But right now, Stevie's talking *to me*.

"Thanks" is all I say because my mind is melting, one big brain mush.

"EMT?" she asks, gesturing at my hat, which I forgot is on my head. My fingers adjust the brim a touch lower. She sounds like poetry in motion, her words falling into an easy rhythm.

"I volunteer with the squad. I try to ride with them a few days a week after school. It can get pretty intense," I say, hoping I don't sound like a complete loser. But I can't help it. Volunteering with the EMT squad is an adrenaline rush. Not the same high I get when I'm wailing on my drum set, but pretty close. When I'm out on a run, and we're racing to a call, it's like every minute, every action we take, not only makes a difference in someone's life—it makes *the* difference in someone's life.

"Wow," Stevie says, her brown eyes roaming my face. Her mouth parts like she's actually impressed and sweat collects on my palms. I wipe my hands on my shorts.

"It's not that big of a deal. Just something I do. And the guys are pretty cool. Last month the lead guy, Mack, did CPR on an infant who was choking and saved his life. It was incredible."

It's those moments, when I'm certain a patient is lost, and then, all of a sudden, they just . . . breathe. Those moments make me believe in something bigger than all of us.

"That is incredible. Have you ever saved someone?" she

asks, stepping closer to me. I want to tell her that yes, I've held a stranger's life in my hands. I'm a hero.

Instead I tell the truth and say, "For now, I watch and help out, but one day, yeah . . . I'd like to. Maybe even be an emergency room doctor."

Drew says that sometimes the truth's not worth telling. Last year he watched the truth destroy his entire family. But I have to disagree with him on that. It's always better to know what's real.

"Check this out," I say, detaching Genie from my set. Stevie smiles, her eyes crinkling at the corners, and her nose twitches like she's about to sneeze. My palms are slick with sweat and I hold Genie tight to stop my hands from shaking. Girls don't talk to me, plain and simple. I mean, they ask me to pass back a pop quiz or borrow a pencil in class. But they don't *talk* to me. I stopped trying in that department after I asked Kayla Michaels to the eighth-grade dance and she laughed, like I was making a joke. I wasn't kidding, but I played it off like I was, laughing right along with her. It sucked and I never told Drew. It's the one thing he doesn't know about me.

"See the resemblance?" I ask, holding Genie up to my face. And Stevie laughs, like I'm funny. But not funny like the butt of someone's joke. For real funny.

"Your twin. Especially the smile," she says, and I pat my stomach, because let's face it, my gut is more like Genie's than my smile. I try to work up the courage to ask Stevie to come to my party, but my stomach is twisting on itself and my mind won't slow down. Her eyes meet mine as I take a deep breath and tell myself to get it together.

"So, listen," I start to say, but Drew walks in, all beat-up boots and ripped jeans. Stevie doesn't listen. She snaps her head to the door and runs her hands through her long hair.

"Hey, Shane," Drew says, heading this way. "Basketball later?"

"I'll be there," I say, watching Stevie watch Drew.

"Hey, Stevie," he says as he reaches us. All of a sudden, I'm invisible.

"Hi," Stevie says, putting her sax case on the floor and squishing my big toe underneath. I wiggle it free. Drew scratches the back of his head, a move he only makes when he's uncomfortable. The band starts to warm up, music filling the room.

"I should get my trumpet," Drew says, shifting his eyes from Stevie to me.

"Drew," Mr. Abella says as he blows into the room, wearing a sweater vest over a white T-shirt. Even in ninety-degree humidity he insists on those sweater vests. "Glad you could make it on time today."

Drew salutes him and says, "My pleasure."

This act with Mr. Abella is getting old. Ever since Drew joined band last year, he parades around like he has somewhere better to be. He doesn't bother bringing his trumpet home and he's hopelessly late. But when no one's looking, he stuffs sheet music in his back pocket, and one time I caught him after class, asking Mr. Abella about voice lessons. Maybe trumpet isn't his thing, but the fact is, Drew loves music as much as I do. For guys like us, music isn't background noise. Because when life gets rough, music's the one constant, the thing that's always there for me. If Drew wasn't so busy staring at Stevie right now, he'd definitely agree.

"I'll see you for basketball this afternoon," I say, standing, my eyes wide, hoping Drew gets the hint.

"Oh." Drew snaps his gaze to me. "Yeah, definitely. See ya, Stevie," he says before heading to the back music room.

I take a deep breath and force a smile, but Stevie doesn't notice. She's still watching Drew.

"So listen," I say, and Stevie focuses her attention my way, finally.

"Okay, people, take your seats," Mr. Abella announces. I grit my teeth and plop down behind the drum set.

"See ya," Stevie says, heading for the sax section. A trombone peters out, the last note dipping like a low, long fart. If that trombone could talk it would say exactly how I feel. That even though that coin landed on tails, I'm still the guy who always loses.

CHAPTER 2

Stevie

By now it should be easy to make friends. I should have honed flawless social skills from the sheer repetition of meeting new people in multiple cities. But no, the friend thing never comes easy or fast. In fact, stepping into a new school with cliques and social hierarchies fills me with dread, my cuticles bearing the brunt of my anxiety. It took three whole months of sitting next to Sarah in the sax section of our band before we became real friends. And we finally did only because Sarah wouldn't stop chattering on about the bass player, Luke Stevens, and I was willing to listen. The people I meet during the first week almost never stick around. I learned that the hard way in seventh grade when the soccer team took me under their wing and invited me to sit at their lunch table, me naïvely thinking I hit the insta-friendship jackpot. Honestly, I don't even remember their names, because after the season started, they got wrapped up in practices and games. I wasn't part of their routine, plain and simple. It's not like they were being mean, I just didn't fit with their crowd. Or maybe it was me, too consumed with leaving to become a part of something. Thank God for Sarah. Without her, I would have been friendless in Seattle, pun intended.

That's why here, at my fifth school, I bet Ray Stone's going to forget about me after the intriguing-new-girl phase wears off. She's the first ever girl kicker for the Mustangs, which is serious high-school-celebrity status. She's not going to want to hang out with a girl in the marching band. Statistically speaking, this isn't going to last.

"Stevie!" Ray yells as she jogs across the parking lot, her blond ponytail swishing like a windshield wiper. I wrap my pointer finger in a Band-Aid and chuck the wrapper in the garbage. Her gray leggings are covered in grass stains and her cleats click against the asphalt like horse's hoofs. I wipe sweat from my hairline and place my sax on the curb as Ray stops short in front of me. Somehow, there's not a drop of perspiration on her, even though she's been punting a football for hours in the August heat.

"How did practice go?" I ask, as Ray glances over the enormous shoulder pads beneath her blue and gold Mustangs jersey. The rest of the team files in from the field, Brent Miller trailing behind, squirting Gatorade into his mouth. I pray he doesn't see me.

"Ray, let's go," he shouts before disappearing into the building. Ray rolls her eyes at him.

"God, he's such a jerk." Ray grabs her ankle and pulls her foot up to her butt, stretching her knee. "I heard you gave him shit the other day for messing with Shane Murphy. Something about his tiny dick?"

Ray raises an eyebrow at me as heat radiates across my cheeks.

"It wasn't a big deal," I say, even though it was such a big deal, the way I spoke without thinking through each word. It was like I caught a glimpse of the girl I want to be, if I ever had the chance to live in one state long enough to find her.

"It's such a big deal. Everyone at this school tiptoes around Brent like he's a bomb about to detonate. But you . . . you, like, lit the match and didn't give a shit about the explosion."

"I didn't light anything," I say. That comment was an outlier, a onetime surge of bravado that will never be repeated.

"Whatever, you're badass." Ray flexes her foot and bends down again, shoving her butt in the air, not caring who's watching. Her confidence magnifies all my insecurities, and ever since I told her about Dad I can't help questioning her motives for talking to me. It wouldn't be the first time someone was nice to me because they think I have connections. Which I do. But still. She flips her head up, her ponytail whipping at her back. "So how was your practice?"

"It was okay. I'm planning to try out for All-State Band." As I say the words Shane Murphy heads out of the main entrance holding two drumsticks.

"Shane got in last year." Ray nods at him as he passes us. He smiles at me but looks away fast. Mr. Abella raved about him during practice, recounting tales of elaborate drum solos and not-so-subtly relying on him to keep the band in time. He even suggested I partner with Shane to practice for auditions.

"Do you know him?"

"Kind of," Ray says. "You should ask him for help. It was a big deal when he got accepted as a freshman."

"I'm hoping All-State can help me get into NYU."

Shane stops at a black Jeep parked at the far end of the lot. He looks around and shakes his head before dropping his backpack on the asphalt. My phone vibrates from inside my bag. I pull it out and check it, sighing at the predictable message.

Running late. Joey's appointment went long. I'll be there as soon as I can. Love you.

"Do not tell me you're thinking about college already. You just got here. Live a little," Ray says, and I smile. But she doesn't get it. She's *lived a little* in Millbrook her whole life. She's had the same friends and I bet she's had a boyfriend or two. I've never had the chance. College will be the first time I get to live in one place for four whole years.

"Come to Dino's Saturday night," Ray says.

"What's a Dino?"

"It's the town diner, where everyone hangs out."

"People hang out in diners?" In Seattle we tried to get into music clubs or hung out in someone's basement. Diners were for eating.

"I know, most boring town ever," Ray says as she starts to jog backwards. "Gotta get to the locker room before Coach gives my spot away. Rumor has it one of the junior varsity guys is gunning for it, even though he can't kick for shit. I'll text you."

Ray heads for the school eyeing Drew Mason as he bursts through the main entrance and into the sunlight. He won't look at her though. Instead he glares at his phone and shoves it in his pocket. Dark hair hangs in his face, like he's hiding from something or someone. A black T-shirt hugs his torso, putting his tanned biceps on display. It's easy to see why Ray stared at him. Why *everyone* stares at him. I heard his dad is Don Mason. *The* Don Mason. I'm sure most people think that's the coolest thing ever, to have a Dad who can deliver the world on a silver platter. But I know better and my heart clenches at the truth. Dads like Don Mason and Caleb Rosenstein don't have time to deliver the world on a silver platter. And kids like me and Drew, we don't even want the world. We only want to have dinner with our dads, to be more than an afterthought.

Drew shakes the hair out of his face, his brown eyes locking with mine. Those eyes are a fortress, hiding away a sadness that begs to crash through. A sadness I know all too well.

"See you tomorrow," he mumbles, shoving his hands in his pockets.

"Wait," I call out to him, but I have nothing to ask or say. I want him to stop and talk to me like he did that first day, when he pulled me up from the curb and helped me find my way to practice. But ever since then he acts like that moment never happened, like we never even met at all.

He turns to me, his gaze traveling from my eyes to my lips. My mind is an open desert, tumbleweeds rolling through.

"Where's your trumpet?" is all I manage to ask.

Drew smiles and says, "Don't feel like practicing."

His eyes shift to Shane, still waiting by the Jeep, and he opens his mouth to say something, but he's cut off by a booming voice from the parking lot.

"Yo, Ringo," yells Brent as he strides over to Shane, looking like a cheesy WrestleMania action figure in a sleeveless Mustangs jersey and sweatpants.

"Fuck," Drew whispers. "Fucking fuck."

Drew walks into the parking lot, but stops halfway, just close enough to hear. I trail behind him. Sweat drips down Brent's temples as he picks up Shane's backpack, letting it dangle from one of his fingers. The stuffed genie's head sticks out of the bag.

"What's this?"

"Give it back," Shane says calmly, reaching for his backpack. But Brent rips open the zipper, pulls the genie out, and cuddles it against his chest.

"Aw, do you need this to go to bed? Does Mommy still tuck you in at night?"

Shane grabs for the genie, losing his cool, but Brent holds it high above his head.

"Do something," I say, but Drew doesn't respond or budge. His hands are balled into tight fists.

"Give it back, Brent," Shane says, this time with a bit more force. Brent laughs, then spits on the ground. Shane grabs for the genie again, but Brent shoves him, his back hitting the Jeep.

"Motherfucker," Drew says, walking fast now, finally stepping in. I follow him until he reaches Brent and grabs his arm hard.

"Enough," Drew growls. Brent shakes free of him and laughs, throwing the genie at Shane.

"What? We were just messing around. Right, Shane?"

Shane stares at the ground.

"Just go," Drew says, glaring at Brent, his eyes almost black. He's breathing hard and fast, like he's doing everything in his power to restrain himself from punching Brent right in his face.

"Drew, man, chill," Brent says before pulling car keys out of his pocket. "We're all good here. I'll see you later." Brent heads to a black Range Rover parked a few spots over, gets in, and speeds out of the lot.

"Asshole," Drew says under his breath. He focuses on Shane. "Are you okay?"

"You shouldn't have done that," Shane says, stuffing the genie back into his bag. He pulls his EMT hat down low. "I had it under control."

"That's not what it looked like."

They glare at each other and maybe I shouldn't be hearing this. But they don't seem to notice me.

"I can take care of myself," Shane says.

"Don't you think I know that?" Drew reaches for Shane's shoulder, but he shrugs him away. "But your dad told me to look after you before he—"

"That was years ago. I'm not a little kid anymore."

I back away because I definitely shouldn't be hearing this.

"Stevie," Shane says, turning to me as he slings his backpack over his shoulder. "Wait up."

"Uh," Drew says, his eyes shifting between us. "I forgot my keys inside. Be back soon."

I could have sworn I saw Drew shove his keys into his pocket, but he heads for the school, quickly glancing at me. The sun sinks lower in the sky, a cool breeze sailing through the air. Still no sign of Mom's car.

"I wish you didn't see that." Shane sits, his back against the Jeep's tire. He takes a deep breath as he taps a drumstick on the pavement, each tap sounding sadder than the last. I plop down next to him, hugging my knees to my chest.

"What's his problem?" I ask, even though I know the answer. Guys like Brent Miller typically don't have a reason for acting the way they do.

"It started in middle school," Shane says, never breaking the cadence, like each tap gives him courage to speak. "It was at the spring talent show. Brent used to play the drums, like me. He went to this fancy music school, had a ton of lessons."

"Did you go there too?" I ask.

"I taught myself," he says, still tapping away.

The breeze picks up and I huddle into myself. Shane's other hand rests on his knee, a white Ace bandage wrapped

around his palm. He must practice for hours, ripping calluses until they bleed. I want to ask him about All-State, but
it can wait.

"Right before the middle school talent show, Brent
jammed his thumb playing flag football. Not like it would
have mattered. He sucked at drums, even with all the fancy
lessons."

"What happened?"

"We were the finale. Two drum solos back to back. Me,
then him, then me, then him again."

"I bet you crushed him," I say, nudging Shane with my
shoulder.

"I annihilated him," Shane says, smiling. "But then the
whole school ripped into him. He was the older kid who got
beat by a seventh grader. He quit drums and picked up football. And that's when it started."

"Same stuff used to happen to me at my old school. At
least you have Drew," I say.

"Drew doesn't need to protect me," Shane says, an edge to
his voice. "I can take care of myself."

"I didn't mean it like that. It seems to me that he sticks up
for you because he cares about you."

"He sticks up for me because my dad asked him to, and
some days I feel like a charity case. Some days I wonder if he
would be friends with me if we weren't neighbors and bound
by some pact he made with my dad." Shane grabs both drumsticks in one hand, cutting off the beat. He pinches the bridge
of his nose and tugs on the brim of his hat. The parking lot is
almost empty now, except for a couple cars and littered garbage. "Sorry. I shouldn't have said that. I've never told anyone
that."

"What happened?" I ask, trying to meet his eyes, but he
stares hard at those drumsticks.

"My dad got sick. The kind of sick where you know you're going to die. I was twelve and I didn't get it because I didn't think anyone *could* die, you know? But Dad knew, and he sat us down together and asked Drew to look after me, like a big brother. My dad loved Drew, probably as much as he loved me. And Drew loved him right back. And after he was gone, we were inseparable. Still are. But some days I wonder if the immensely popular Drew Mason would still be friends with someone like me if he hadn't made a promise all those years ago."

"I'm sorry about your dad," I say, my mouth going dry. Anything else I could say would sound like a cliché. "You're lucky you've had a best friend for so long. And I don't think he sticks up for you because he made a promise. You seem like someone worth sticking up for."

A small smile breaks free on Shane's face as he glances at me from under the brim of his baseball hat. He places the drumsticks on the ground by his feet, his eyes anticipating what I'm about to say next.

"I wish I had someone like that at this school," I say. "It sucks starting over all the time."

"How about . . ." Shane takes off his hat and his hair looks almost blond in the afternoon light. "I can be that person. The one who has your back."

"You don't even know me." I laugh, the kind of breathy laugh that feels forced and lonely. "And besides, in a year or two my dad will get transferred to another team and I'll move away, and you'll forget all about me."

"I wouldn't forget. I *won't* forget," he says with conviction, like he wants me to know how much he means it. Maybe I'm finally making the kind of friend I always dreamed of. The kind that sticks around forever.

Shane rolls his shoulders, which must be so sore from practice, and kicks at the gravel with his sneakers. He scoots closer to me and takes in a deep breath. "Would you, uh, maybe, want to . . ."

I shift away from Shane, hoping the space between us will be enough to stop him from asking me the question I assume he's about to spill. If he asks me out it'll ruin it all, and I need his friendship more than anything right now. The fact is, people like Shane don't come around often. He's so easy to talk to, like he's been in my life all along.

"Would you want to . . . I mean." Shane curls the brim of his hat in his hand before sliding it on his head. I hold my breath.

A car honk blares from Mom's silver Lexus as it slows beside us, the window rolling down.

"Sorry I'm late," she says, her brown hair corkscrewing in every direction. Joey sticks his tongue out at me from the back.

"Stevie, get in," he yells as his feet kick at his car seat.

I stand and say, "Mom, this is Shane Murphy. He plays the drums."

"Nice to meet you. I'm Naomi."

"You too," Shane says, scrambling to his feet. His eyes linger on my face and he opens his mouth but closes it again, a vise clamping shut.

"I should get going," I say. "Talk to you later."

"Okay," Shane says, slinging his backpack over his shoulder, the genie still sticking out of the zipper. Shane has a quiet kind of strength that you might miss if you weren't looking. But I notice and I bet that genie will be back tomorrow.

CHAPTER 3

Shane

Drew rolls a keg through the living room into the kitchen and out to the back patio. I shake a bag of Doritos into a bowl and head outside, a bag of pretzels tucked under my arm. Drew pushes the keg upright and grabs a package of red Solo cups. He tears the plastic open with his teeth as he pumps the keg. He frees a cup and fills it with frothy foam until clear liquid spills from the barrel.

"Want?" Drew extends the cup in my direction. The sun falls to the earth, fading oranges and reds dominating the sky. Perfect time of day, in my opinion, an ending that also feels like a beginning. But tonight I'm kicking myself for fumbling the ball, not that I have any right to use that expression. The only sport I attempt to play is basketball, and only with Drew on his driveway, so it doesn't count. Anyway, I completely blew it with Stevie. What's even more pathetic is I'm still carrying around that penny, like I might actually have a chance.

"Not yet." I wave Drew's cup away, but truthfully, I hate to drink. I can't think straight and when I have one too many falling asleep is even more impossible than when I'm sober.

I know it's not supposed to work like that. Drew passes out after a few too many beers. Me, my mind circles like water going down a drain, and I start to think about Dad and how I wish he were still here. And that's just too much for me to deal with.

Drew sits on the couch propping his boots on the fire pit. I chuck the bag of pretzels on one of the cushions. The fire warms my cheeks as I extend my hands to the flames.

"Remember how we used to make s'mores out here?" he asks, the whites of his eyes lit up by the firelight. "The best damn s'mores in all of New Jersey, your dad would say."

"He insisted we add peanut butter, remember? That man was a genius."

"Total Einstein," Drew says, and then it's quiet again, the memory of Dad filling the space between us. The fire crackles into the air as the sleepy sky slowly fades to black. I can practically taste the marshmallows and chocolate and graham crackers, and of course, the peanut butter.

"Is Stevie coming tonight?" Drew asks, and I sit next to him, letting out a long sigh. "Please tell me you asked her."

"Okay, I asked her." I deadpan, glaring at him.

"You didn't ask her?" Drew taps me on the shin with his boot.

"I didn't get a chance. Brent Miller kind of stole my thunder. Maybe if you hadn't stepped in, I wouldn't have looked like such a complete dork."

Brent Miller steals my thunder once a week on average. It's been that way since middle school and sometimes I think I hate him for it. I should hate him for it. But I can't ignore the rumors that swirl around our small school, the random bandages and bruises he shrugs away as football injuries. I can't hate him. Not completely. A tiny part of me wants to help him, if he would quit being such a jerk and let me.

"You're not a dork."

"Who's not a dork?" Lainey asks as she appears on the patio and throws a bag of cups at me. I miss, and they fall on the ground next to my sneakers.

"No one," Drew and I say in unison as he retrieves the cups and sets them on the table next to the fire pit. Lainey raises an eyebrow then shrugs.

"Thanks for the keg," Drew says, pouring himself another cup. My older sister is cool like that. She's at Rutgers but comes home whenever I need beer for a party. Not that I ever throw real parties. I would need to be friends with way more people for that.

"You're welcome," Lainey says, taking the cup from Drew. A frayed olive messenger bag covered in peace sign and pot leaf patches hangs from one shoulder. Her eyes narrow on Drew. "You look like you haven't showered in a week," she says, taking a sip of beer. He smirks, shaking his head.

"You look like a farmer who came back from a Dead and Co. show," he counters, nodding at my sister's overalls, vintage Grateful Dead concert T-shirt, and tan Birkenstocks. Her hair, which hangs in two long braids, doesn't help.

"*Going* to a Dead and Co. show." Her green eyes come alive. She's the only one in our family who has cool eyes. The rest of us are stuck with this weird in-between color, which is not really green but not really brown. Drew called them puke eyes once when we were little, mad at me for something I can't even remember. "They're at the Garden."

"That show isn't for a couple weeks," I say, stacking Solo cups on the table by the keg, and she laughs.

"Ah, little brother, what is time really?" Lainey's eyelids droop so slightly, I almost don't notice.

"Are you high?"

"Maybe." A Silly Putty smile stretches across her face and she laughs a slow-motion laugh. "I gotta jet. Larry's out front. Be cool around Stevie."

Lainey gives the beer back to Drew and says, "Later."

"Who's Larry?" Drew asks, but she's already heading around the house to the front gate. Drew shifts his eyes to me.

"Some guy from her anthro class." I rip open the bag of pretzels and pour them into a bowl on the table.

Drew shrugs and takes a sip of beer.

"You told her about Stevie?" Drew raises his eyebrows. "Bro, chill."

"I am chill," I say as my phone vibrates inside the pocket of my gym shorts. I pull it out and read the message.

Any chance you can help me with All-State? It's Stevie, by the way.

"What?" Drew asks, grabbing for my phone. "Who's texting you?"

I flip the phone in his direction. Drew shakes the hair out of his eyes and reads the text.

"Ask her to come tonight."

"What if she says no?"

"What if she says yes?" Drew grabs my phone and starts tapping at the keys. He smiles and hands the phone back to me.

Me

Having a party tonight at my house. Wanna come by?

My pulse escalates at the invitation. She's going to say no. I smack Drew in the arm and he smacks me back, causing my phone to slip from my hands and drop to the paving stones beneath our feet.

"That better not be broken," I say, picking up the phone and reading the screen, which is thankfully still intact.

Stevie

Can't. I told Ray I'd meet her at Dino's

"Told you she'd say no," I say, showing Drew the text.

His eyebrows furrow, the screen's glow casting shadows on his features. His eyes flick up from my phone.

"She's friends with Ray?"

"Apparently," I say. "Since when do you care about Ray?"

"I don't." Drew's full of it but I don't press him on the issue. Ray shattered him last year and he refuses to talk about it. Can't say I blame him. Drew grabs my phone again and taps out a text.

"I am perfectly capable of writing my own text messages."

"You sure about that?" Drew's still tapping away at the keys, not bothering to look at me. "Even though I wish it was me Stevie's texting, it's you. And if it has to be you, don't throw away your shot." He smiles again, like he just finished painting a masterpiece. I grab the phone from him and read the text, which he hasn't sent.

Me

Too bad. But I can still help with All-State. Wednesday after school?

"What if she says no?" I ask again, still staring at the screen.

"Dude, she's the one who asked *you* for help. It's just a text message." Drew grabs for my phone, but if I want to get to know Stevie *I* have to make it happen, not Drew. Maybe I've spent my entire life in my best friend's shadow because I let him watch out for me. I guess part of me wanted to honor Dad's wish so badly that I always defaulted to Drew. But not this time.

I grab my phone and erase Drew's message because it doesn't sound like me. I rewrite the text, my finger hovering over the send button.

Me

Have a great time at Dino's. And yes, I can help you with All-State. How's Wednesday after school?

I read it and reread it, and reread it again.

"We're not getting any younger," Drew sings at me, leaning back on the couch and taking another sip of beer.

"Shut it," I say, reading the text again. I take a deep breath and press send. "Okay, sent."

Drew stands and peers over my shoulder at the three little dots dancing on my phone.

Stevie

Wednesday is great! Thanks, Shane. Sorry to miss the party.

"Congratulations, you have officially asked out a girl," Drew says, patting me on the back.

"It's not exactly a date," I say, shoving the phone in my pocket, stuffing down a small smile.

"But it's a start."

CHAPTER 4

Stevie

A neon sign that reads *Diner* perches on top of a low building, casting pink-and-blue light on the sidewalk. I prop my feet on the dashboard as Mom puts the car in park, her curly hair up in a messy bun. She glances at Joey, his little legs scissor kicking in his car seat. My stomach fizzes and churns, and my pointer finger throbs. A frayed cuticle hangs from my nail, begging to be torn off, but I force my hand into a fist.

"We're here." Mom states the obvious, but I don't budge. "You planning on going inside? I have to get Joey home and to bed."

"Is this a party?" Joey's tiny voice squeaks from the back seat.

"Nah," I say, glancing at his chubby cheeks. "Just some friends hanging out."

Not yet friends. More like the glimmer of friendship, the possibility. I check my phone and reread Sarah's last text.

Sarah

Just go out and have fun.

Me

I might puke.

Sarah

You got this. Walk inside and be the
girl I know and love. They'll all love you
too.

Me

I miss you.

Sarah

Stop texting me and walk inside.

If only Sarah was inside the diner, maybe then I could walk in with ease. But instead she's across the country, too far away to pump me up and make me forget about my nerves.

"You're great at making friends," Mom says, placing her hand over mine. "Go inside and have fun."

I'm the worst at making friends, but I smile through every move and tell Mom I'm fine. But I'm not fine. This time, this town, is different. Moving across the country in high school sucks so much more than being the new girl in fourth grade or middle school. No one cares about making new friends by the time they reach high school. That door has closed, and I have to find a way to pry it open instead of walking through. At least Ray seems cool, possessing the kind of self-assuredness that reminds me of Sarah. Sarah would have physically forced me out of this car by now, yammering in my ear about a new band I *had* to listen to, distracting me from myself.

Mom unlocks the door and says, "Dad'll be here at eleven to pick you up."

"I can Uber it home," I say. Less mortifying than Dad pulling up outside the diner.

"You haven't seen him much all week," Mom says, which is true. He's been working extra-long hours to impress the team. Same story, new season. "He will be here."

I reach for the door handle as Mom leans to me and kisses my forehead.

"Just be yourself. And remember to have fun," she says as I open the door.

"Love my Stevie," Joey yells from the back seat.

"Love you too, buddy," I say before heading for the diner, the front door displaying the word *Dino's,* the *n* partially faded. I catch a glimpse of Joey's hand waving furiously from inside the car as Mom honks once and drives out of the lot. I take a deep breath and push the door open, a strand of metal bells clanging against the glass. The black-and-white checkerboard floor throws me off balance. I scan the restaurant for Ray, but the fluorescent lights knife into my eyes and all I can see are rows of powder blue booths, all of them full. The smell of french fry grease floats through the air, mixed with something sweet like milkshakes or maybe the ornate cakes lining the front display case. I pick at my thumb as my eyes frantically search each table. I shouldn't have come here.

"They're back there," says an older man sporting a graying beard and mustache. A full head of white hair sticks up from his head and a stained apron hangs from his neck. A small nametag on the front of his shirt reads *Dino.* "They're always back there."

He nods at a group of booths in the back of the restaurant. Ray stands on the bench and waves her arms at me like an airport tarmac worker.

"The booths are for sitting only, Ray," shouts Dino as he wipes his hands on the front of his apron.

"Sorry, Dino!" Ray waves me over and plops back down. I ball my hands into fists to stop picking and take a deep breath. When I reach the booths, Ray slides over and pulls me next to her. I sink into the vinyl.

"Guys, this is Stevie," Ray says, and it's déjà vu, the same scene from all my past schools. The one where I'm on display, new eyes staring at me, like I'm an exhibit at the zoo. I run my hand through my hair and tug at the bottom of my ripped jean shorts. "This is Tom Walker, Jenna Reed, and I think you've already met Brent Miller."

My stomach shoots into my throat as Brent eyes me from across the booth. He bites off the end of a french fry and smiles, his light brown hair so shiny with gel it almost looks wet. A small Band-Aid covers a patch of skin above his right eye.

"You have anything else you want to say to me, new girl?" Brent's still smiling, like he's messing with me, but not in the way that he messes with Shane. It's like he's amused by me, like I'm a cute wind-up toy from the drug store. He laughs to himself and wipes his mouth with the back of his hand, missing a small drop of ketchup on his chin.

I break eye contact and gather the courage to say, "No, I'm good."

"Fuck off, Brent," Ray says, as she chucks a french fry at him, hitting him in the chest. "PS, there's ketchup on your chin."

"Seriously, man, don't be a dick," Tom says, flashing me bleach-white teeth.

"The quarterback has spoken, ladies and gentlemen," Brent says, smirking as he rubs his chin with a napkin. He actually has the nerve to wink at me. "Don't worry, I'll play nice."

"Wait, is she the one you were telling us about?" Tom asks, leaning across the table and eyeing me, his Under Armour T-shirt hugging his defined muscles. "Is your dad Caleb Rosenstein?"

I nod, silently willing this conversation to end quickly, to get swallowed up by the din of the restaurant.

"So cool," he says. "What's he saying about the season?"

"Who cares," Brent pipes in, talking through a mouth full of fries. "Jets suck anyway."

Jenna leans her head on Tom's shoulder and rolls her eyes like she's had to endure sports talk one too many times. I feel her pain and the truth is I have no idea what Dad's saying about the season because I've never asked. I couldn't care less.

"You suck," Ray says. Brent blows the wrapper off a straw straight at Ray. She catches it midair, rolls it up, and puts it in her mouth. She then stuffs the wet paper ball in the end of her straw and spits it back at him, the tiny spitball landing in his hair. Normally I would think this is gross, but it's cool how Ray isn't intimidated by them, how she can be one of the guys.

"Gross," Jenna says as she applies gloss to her full lips without looking in a mirror. I never understood how girls pull off this trick. If I ever tried something like that, I'd get gloss on my chin and cheeks—everywhere but my lips. Brent laughs and flicks the spitball out of his hair, almost hitting a waitress walking by our table.

"My dad doesn't tell me anything," I say. "I don't really like football."

It's true. I hate football. But I say this now in the hopes that people won't harass me for stats and strategies. I'd rather not walk the halls listening to a stranger's idea of what plays Dad should run.

"What!" they all say in unison, their heads snapping in my direction.

"Seriously?" Ray asks.

"It's America's pastime," says Jenna, her blue eyes wide.

"I'm pretty sure that's baseball," I say, and she laughs, pushing her auburn hair off her shoulders.

"Whatever, same difference."

Not really, but I let it go.

"I guess growing up with football all the time, I kind of rebelled and went for music instead." I try my best to sound cool, like someone they would want to hang out with. But in reality, I know this thing with Ray and her crowd won't last. It's only a matter of time before they realize I can't get them into the luxury box at MetLife Stadium, before they realize I'm a plain girl who's lived in a lot of places but has actually experienced very little.

"Stevie plays sax," Ray says.

"No way," Tom says. "That's cool as hell."

"She's in the band with Ray's boy," Brent says before taking a long sip of soda. Ray glares at him.

"He's *not* my boy," she says. "Not anymore at least."

Ray stirs the straw in her Diet Coke, a tiny whirlpool swirling inside the cup. She studies the swishing liquid and I know without asking that her boy is, or rather was, Drew Mason. I know it in the same way I know we're about to move, even before my parents make the announcement. Something shifts in the air and although Drew's practically a stranger, it's obvious he's the type of guy who makes girls stare into a fizzy glass of soda, missing something they can't get back.

"I'm sure you met him this week," Ray says, looking up from her soda. "Drew Mason?"

"Oh, yeah," I say, like he's a guy I know from band, a guy I barely noticed. But the truth is, I've been desperate to talk to Drew again, to know if the incessant pounding in my chest means something more than a physical reaction to his soulful eyes and couldn't-care-less hair. But now, knowing what I know, I squash the memory of placing my hand in Drew's, him helping me up from the curb and making me feel a little less alone. Instead I remind myself that he's barely glanced at me since that first day and that it was all in my head. That none of it meant anything. "What happened?"

"We were together last year," Ray sighs. "For a while at least. Until his dad moved out and things got, I don't know . . . weird."

I read about Don Mason's infidelity in the tabloids and even though I'm desperate for more information, I don't ask. It's not my place.

"I'm sorry," I say as everyone at the table leans in, an audience I'm not sure Ray wants, but she keeps talking anyway.

"He was so angry, you know? And I didn't know how to help him."

Brent rolls his eyes and starts talking football with Tom as Jenna feigns interest. Ray pulls her phone out of her oversize bag and sighs, flipping the screen in my direction. It displays an unanswered text to Drew.

Ray

I need to talk to you

"He hasn't texted me back," Ray whispers as she folds a paper napkin into a small square, her eyes glancing at the others to make sure they're not paying attention. "Do you think you can find out what's going on with him? Maybe ask Shane?"

"Sure, I'll try," I say, each word solidifying the death of my crush on Drew Mason.

"You're obsessed with him," Jenna says, nudging Tom in his side and snapping him out of his conversation with Brent. "You talk about him all the time, don't try to hide it. Right, Tom?"

"None of my business," Tom says. "All I know is Drew's a good guy. It was cool when you guys were together. I'm sorry about what went down." He holds out his fist and Ray taps it with her knuckles, nodding at him. He nods back and kisses Jenna on the forehead. She pulls off his navy beanie and kisses him on the lips, a real kiss.

"Get a room," Ray yells, throwing her napkin at them. I glance at my phone and jump up when I see it's eleven p.m., remembering Mom's instructions to meet Dad.

"I have to go, guys," I say, eyeing the door, wishing I could stay.

"Already?" Ray pouts. I don't tell her about my embarrassing curfew or that Dad's likely outside, impatiently tapping his fingers on the steering wheel. In fact, Dad's probably been out there for the past ten minutes.

"Yeah, I'm babysitting my little brother in the morning," I say, which isn't technically a lie. Mom hasn't officially asked me or anything, but I bet she'll want to work on that piece she's been painting of a girl and a yellow balloon. She'll ask me to watch Joey for a half hour and a half hour will stretch into two hours. It's just how it goes. "See you guys at school."

"Later, Stevie," they say one by one, each goodbye dancing in my ears, the possibility of a maybe friend.

It's still warm when I get outside, a humid breeze making the air wet, like one big sauna. I hop down the steps, not bothering to look for Dad's black Maserati, but when I reach the curb, I stop short. He's not here. No one's here. I check my phone and it's ten past eleven. And then a text pops up on the screen.

> Dad
>
> **Sorry, Stevie girl. Practice ran long.**
> **I'll be there as soon as I can.**

All at once I'm furious, my stomach boiling over at every moment in my life Dad has ruined. Every time he's forced me out of my comfort zone away from my friends into a completely new school. Every time he's been late for dinner or gone for weeks at a time at away games. All the thoughtless people who give me hell when Dad's team loses. All the opportunists who beg me for tickets and pump me for inside football information during the season. Never knowing who wants to be my friend for real, all because of Dad's job. And now, making me leave early, like a loser, when he's not even here to pick me up.

I sit on the curb, my throat closing up as I will myself not to cry. I search for the north star, because no matter where I live the sky is always the same, and that star somehow makes me feel like I'm part of something. But tonight, the sky is cloudy, all the stars in hiding. I'm about to head back inside when the bells clang against the door to Dino's. I quickly push wet tears off my cheek, black mascara inking my fingers.

"Stevie, what are you still doing here?" Ray asks, plopping down next to me and stretching her legs out on the pavement. I avoid her eyes.

"My dad's late."

"Need a ride? My Uber's coming in five."

"Nah, he's on his way," I say, kicking the gravel with my flip-flop. "But thanks."

"You okay?" she asks, turning to me. Concern settles in the corner of her mouth as she eyes my runny mascara. "You're not okay."

"He does this a lot," I say. "I mean . . . I don't see him a lot. And I barely even know where I am. I wouldn't even know how to get home, and I don't know anyone, you know?"

"You're at a suburban diner in Millbrook, New Jersey. And you know me."

"I just met you," I correct her, because Ray doesn't get what it's like having to start over, never trusting fledgling friendships until they become solid.

"I'm obsessed with football and soccer and kicking balls in general." She smirks. "My name's short for Rachel, I suck at math, have an addiction to those true crime podcasts, and I used to have a rescue dog named Toast, but he just died, which sucked. Parents are still together but it's obvious they hate each other. I'm the youngest of three girls which means my bathroom is always a mess and two of us are always in a fight. Oh and as you witnessed inside, I'm still hung up on Drew Mason, even though we stopped speaking six months ago."

"I'm sorry about your parents and Toast and Drew," I say.

"Thanks for trying to find out more for me," she says. "Just don't mention it was me who asked."

"I'll be discreet," I say, holding up my hand like a Girl Scout.

"So what about you?" Ray asks, the streetlight catching on the stack of beaded bracelets that hangs from her wrist. "What's your deal?"

"I don't have a deal. I've moved around a lot. So I don't have any close friends, except Sarah, who was my best friend in Seattle. But I haven't heard from her much lately. I guess out of sight, out of mind," I say, an emptiness tugging at my chest. "And I've never had a boyfriend or whatever. All that stuff's hard for me."

"How is that possible?" Ray asks. "I mean, look at you."

At the risk of sounding like a conceited jerk, and I would never, ever say this out loud, I know I'm pretty. I see it in the way guys look at me, eyes lingering on my face for a beat too long. Guys like Drew and Shane, and even Brent. It's the same way guys look at Ray. And I'm not going to sit here and play aw shucks like I don't own it and celebrate it. Because girls have done that for way too long and frankly, it's tiring. The thing is, the way I look on the outside has nothing to do with the way I feel on the inside, like a little kid stuck on one of those tilt-a-whirl rides going around and around, desperately wanting to stop and stay in one spot.

"I would kill for your lips," Ray says. "And your eyebrows. I bet you don't even have to tweeze."

"I grow them myself," I raise my brows at her, and she laughs as a black sedan pulls up to the curb, stopping in front of us. Ray stands as the window rolls down.

"Can you wait a bit? I can't leave my friend out here alone. Her ride's not here," she tells the driver. He mumbles something back. "Yeah, I'll pay extra."

"You don't have to do that," I say as she sits back down next to me.

"I know," she says, pulling her knees to her chest. We sit side by side, the humid air shining our cheeks. She waits with me for the next ten minutes, making me laugh and helping me forget why I was so upset. All my anger at Dad flows out of me, straight up to the night sky as the clouds slowly shift, revealing the winking north star.

CHAPTER 5

Shane

SEPTEMBER

Stevie's in my house, in my studio. No one has ever been in-side this room besides my family and Drew. And now a girl is crouching down and tracing the letters of my initials on the surface of the bass drum. Stevie's slender pointer finger follows the curves of the *S,* my heart hammering against my chest, betraying my mind's instructions to stay cool. Stevie stands and picks up one of my drawings off the mixing board. Her eyes roam the charcoal strokes and colors that pour out of me and onto the page, my feelings on display. I push my hands into the pockets of my gym shorts and my pinky grazes a coin. The Coin. All at once I see Drew throwing that fateful penny high into the air. I shake the thought off. It's not a lie. Not technically.

"What's this?" Stevie gestures at the Dark Carnival poster in her hand, a drawing of a carousel horse shooting fireballs from his laughing mouth.

"Drew's band," I say as she puts it back on the pile. "I do the posters for them."

"It's great," she says, her perfect lips stretching into a smile as she picks up another one, a drawing of a Ferris wheel with guitars and drums as seats. "This says they're having a show Saturday night, after the first game?"

"It's at Old Silver Tavern. I'm actually filling in for their drummer," I say. I should invite Stevie. That would be the natural thing to do. Instead my heart thrashes in my chest like a Metallica drum solo. Just say the words. Three simple words. "Want to come?" I blurt out before I lose my nerve.

"Sure," she says, so fast and simple, like it's no big deal I invited her. Probably because I'm in my usual place, the friend zone. They have a table here reserved in the back just for me. "What's this one?" Stevie pulls a piece of paper from the bottom of the pile and I freeze, my drum-solo heart seizing in my chest. A boy swims high in a cloudless midnight sky littered with a mess of silver stars. He's swimming to a girl, dancing in the grass below. A girl with long, dark hair, almost as dark as the night sky. She could be any girl really. But she's not.

"Oh it's . . ." I step back, my clumsy feet kicking a bin over, endless drumsticks rolling onto the rug. I scramble to pick them up, Stevie helping me. I can't look at her.

Once we get all the sticks back into the bin, I take the drawing from her.

"Sometimes I have trouble sleeping at night," I say, which is easier than explaining what this sketch really means.

Stevie's eyes soften as she sits on the rug, motioning for me to join her. She pretzels her legs and leans to me, like she's about to tell me a secret.

"Me too," she says, her eyes intent on holding my gaze. "I can't fall asleep, like ever. It started before our last move and it's gotten worse since I came to New Jersey. I don't even try to fall asleep anymore. It's exhausting, you know?"

"When my dad died, I kept thinking any minute he would walk through the front door, so I started waiting up. I know that's completely unrealistic, but in a weird way it helped, hoping for the impossible. And now, it's like my body forgot how to sleep. There is one thing that helps though."

"Anything, please. The bags under my eyes are exceeding the airline weight limit."

I laugh, but she's wrong. Those eyes are the reason Van Morrison wrote "Brown Eyed Girl." I take a deep breath, my heart finally slowing to a normal tempo. Maybe it's because I'm about to tell Stevie about the lists that always calm my mind.

"I make these lists in my head. Top five songs, top five musicians, top five anything, really. Thinking up lists helps me fall asleep."

I grab a drumstick and start tapping the carpet, anything to make me feel like myself. Because sitting here across from Stevie, her eyes anticipating some miracle insomnia cure, feels anything but normal. A tiny voice whispers at me from the recesses of my mind. *You only got here because of a coin toss. This isn't real.*

"Okay, so best drummers of all time," Stevie says, grabbing another drumstick and twirling it between her fingers.

"John Bonham," I say, but I'm not thinking about Zeppelin. Drew says the coin toss isn't technically a lie, so this is totally okay. But then again, Drew is never, ever right. About anything.

"Good call," she says, nodding.

"Keith Moon." I'm still tapping at the carpet. "He's a required idol if you're a drummer."

Stevie opens her mouth to say something, but I keep going.

"Do you listen to Rush?"

"Not my thing."

"Okay, okay." I laugh. "Neil Peart was the man."

Stevie asks me to send her some Rush songs even though it's not her thing and I don't know if I can do this. Hang out with her and know I have a secret.

"Oh, and of course Matt Cameron," I say.

"Pearl Jam's drummer?" she asks.

"And used to be Soundgarden's drummer. Their songs are always in unconventional time signatures and Cameron kills it," I say.

"I heard Pearl Jam's playing a show at the Garden."

"Tough ticket," I say, and it's true. I struck out with fan club seats and then got shut out by Ticketmaster. "Show of a lifetime though."

"Seriously," Stevie says with this faraway look in her eyes, like she's picturing herself in the crowd losing herself in the music, and it's clear she's as big of a fan as I am. For me, the beat is the first thing to draw me into a song, but it's the musicians who have something to say that keep me listening.

"Okay, back to the list. Number five is Buddy Rich."

"Who?"

"Buddy Rich. Jazz. He's pretty much the godfather of drumming."

"I've never heard of him," she says, her eyes shifting to the rug.

"We have to change that, Stevie," I say. She has stellar taste in music, and I bet she would love the groundbreakers, the guys who started it all—Gene Krupa, Tony Williams, Bernard Purdie—the ones who built the foundation, the ones every drummer behind a kit tries to emulate. "What are you thinking about?"

"Drummers?"

"You're *not* thinking about whatever it is your mind obsesses over when you're trying to fall asleep," I say, even though at this exact moment I *am* obsessing, guilt settling in my bones over a tiny penny that never should have been tossed in the first place. Who does that? This is different than flipping over which movie to see or who gets to eat the last slice of pizza. I can't sit here and look into Stevie's eyes and know she's here because that coin landed on tails. Let's be real. If that coin landed on heads, she'd be out with Drew somewhere much cooler than my basement. In fact, she'd probably be Drew's girlfriend by now. Who am I kidding, thinking she could be interested in a guy like me? But I can't tell her. A small part of me clings to the notion that maybe the feeling I have in the pit of my stomach isn't one-sided. If I tell her, my words won't come out right and I'll never know if she feels it too. But I can't *not* tell her.

"Thanks, Shane. I think this might work. It's really cool of you to try and help me," she says, but it's not cool. None of this is cool. Sweat breaks out on my forehead and I grab hold of the drumstick to steady my hands. "Can I ask you something?"

She knows. I don't know how she knows, but she knows. The drumstick shakes in my hand, so I drop it on the rug. My gut churns, like someone kneading raw dough.

"Sure," I say, but it comes out like a whisper. I can't look at her.

"Is Drew seeing anyone?"

All at once my nerves disappear, replaced by a pounding in my head. It's the same feeling I got when Dad watched me and Drew play basketball, Drew sinking every shot and me missing the hoop.

She doesn't know about the coin toss. She's into Drew. *Of*

course, she's into him. This is how it always starts. I sigh as disappointment crashes over me. Like I said, the coin toss doesn't matter. She's going to fall for Drew anyway.

"Not right now," I say, the only words I can manage to squeeze out of my throat.

"What's he like?"

"He's . . ." For a second, desperation takes over and I think of badmouthing him. But that's not my style. "He doesn't care about all the annoying cliques at school. He's really into science fiction, and his band, and he can really sing. And no matter what, he's always been there for me. He even lets me win at basketball even though he's much better than me. He's my best friend."

Stevie nods and gazes to the side, like she's picturing Drew.

"Why do you ask?" I regret my question instantly. If she's hung up on Drew, I don't want to hear about it.

"No reason," she says. "Curious, I guess."

Stevie shouldn't be here. She's only here because Drew and I messed with the natural course of the universe. If we didn't flip that coin, Stevie wouldn't be wondering why Drew, the guy she actually has a crush on, is ignoring her. She wouldn't be pumping me for information about him and she certainly wouldn't be hanging out here, with me. We never should have flipped that coin. It's not right. It's wronger than wrong on so many levels and I can't sit here anymore with a girl who literally takes my breath away knowing that if she knew the truth, she'd hate me. God, I don't want her to hate me.

"I can't help you," I say fast and resolved, because I'm backed into a corner of my own creation. I'm not thinking clearly, terrified to do the right thing and beyond ashamed to do the wrong thing. So I do nothing.

"What?" Stevie snaps her gaze to me, confusion settling

on her face. Her nose twitches and her full lips drop toward her chin.

"I just . . ." I stammer. "I can't. I'm sorry."

"Shane, are you okay?" Stevie reaches for my hand, but I pull away like she's a hot stove. If she touches me, I'm done for and I won't be able to put an end to this.

"I'm fine." I stand, throwing the drumstick into the bin and pacing around the studio, pretending to clean up. "Honestly, I don't even know how I got into All-State last year. Pure luck, I guess. I wouldn't know the first thing about helping you."

"Slow down." Stevie's brown hair falls past her shoulders and I want so badly to reach out and brush it out of her face. "What's wrong? You're practically shaking."

"I'm just tired," I say, pulling away from her and walking up the basement steps. She trails behind me, saying nothing. "Seriously. I really am sorry. I'll see you at the Dark Carnival show."

I reach the top of the steps and lead Stevie to the front door, even opening it and gesturing for her to leave. Stevie hugs me, and she smells like vanilla ice cream. I don't want to let her go.

"Are you sure you're okay?" she says in my ear. I nod and she releases her embrace, looking at me like she doesn't believe me. She shouldn't. I don't have the guts to tell her everything she needs to know.

CHAPTER 6

Stevie

"When does the show get going?" I ask, eyeing a makeshift stage in the front of Old Silver Tavern. Shane's drum set rests under a spotlight, waiting to be played, and a microphone stands tall at the edge of the riser. Amps and speakers line the side, wires snaking along the floor. The restaurant itself is ski-lodge cozy, all wood paneling and white Christmas lights hanging from the ceiling. Booths flank the walls and high-top tables are placed haphazardly around the room making it look more like a night club than a burger joint. Although it's my first time here, I like the place immediately. Sarah would love it too, but she hasn't returned my last text. Even though I have the urge to take a photo and message her, I keep my phone tucked neatly in my bag.

"I don't know," Ray says. A crowd builds around us, everyone buzzing about the show. Old Silver, as Ray keeps calling it, is even more packed than this afternoon's football game. The rest of the team isn't here though. *Not their scene* according to Ray. She gestures at an office door by the kitchen, right behind the stage. "The guys usually hang out back there. Want to check it out?"

"You sure Drew would be okay with it?" I ask, not wanting to disturb the band if they're getting ready for the show.

"That depends," Ray says, her hazel eyes searching my face. "Did you ask Shane about him?"

"I couldn't find out much, but he did say that Drew's not seeing anyone right now."

Ray claps her hands together, a small squeal escaping her lips. I don't mention what went down that afternoon with Shane. One minute, he was the shy drummer from band trying to help me fall asleep. But then, out of nowhere, he acted like he needed to get away from me, his eyes darting around his studio. Maybe my nosy fingers shouldn't have gone through his drawings. That's the moment I keep replaying—me picking up that sketch and the color draining out of Shane's face.

"We are so going back there, c'mon!" Ray grabs my hand and leads me through the crowd. When we reach the door, she pushes it open slightly, revealing a couple guys in skinny jeans perched on a radiator, messing around with guitars.

"That's Gabe and Kevin, guitar and bass," Ray says in my ear. Drew sits at a desk covered in receipts, checking his phone, and Shane's on the floor drumming on the tile. Ray's about to push her way into the office when Drew throws his phone clear across the room, smashing it against the wall. Ray's hand freezes on the doorknob and her eyes go wide.

"Dude, what the hell?" Kevin says, his hand flat on the front of his bass. Shane stands and walks to Drew.

"He's not coming," Drew says, staring hard at the receipts.

"He's talking about his dad," Ray whispers.

"How do you know?"

"I just do," she says putting her finger to her lips.

"We should go," I say, taking a step back, but Ray doesn't move.

"I'm sure he got tied up with something," Shane says, putting his hand on Drew's shoulder. Drew shrugs him off. "I bet he really wanted to be here."

"Forget him, man," Gabe says, shaking blond hair out of his face. But Drew doesn't look at him. Instead he glances at Shane.

"If he wanted to be here, he would be here," Drew says, with an edge to his voice, like they've had this conversation before. "You *know* that."

"Don't let this ruin your night," Shane says, shoving his drumsticks in his back pocket. "Don isn't perfect, but he's not the evil guy you make him out to be."

"You don't know him like I do." Drew stands, his voice rising, dark hair hanging in his eyes. "He's not your dad."

"You're right, he's *yours*." Shane gets in Drew's face, his usual quiet demeanor replaced by pure anger. And I don't blame him. Even though my dad's never around, he's still alive like Drew's dad. My heart aches for Shane and everything he lost. If I were him, Drew's insensitive comment would throw me into a rage, but he somehow keeps his cool.

"And you know what?" Shane says. "I'd kill for my dad to bail on this show. To get one more second with him, even if I was pissed at him. You don't get it, Drew. Even if your dad's not here right now, even if he messed up, he's *here*. You don't know how lucky you are."

"Your dad never would have bailed." Drew towers over Shane. "He'd be out there right now, first row, right in front of the stage. Fuck, he'd be an hour early, psyched to see you play. Yeah, my dad's physically on the planet but you don't know what it's like to be disappointed over and over again by the one person you want to trust most."

Drew and Shane stare at each other, years of their shared history passing between their eyes.

"We should really go," I whisper, tugging on Ray's sleeve.

"Okay," she says, quietly letting go of the doorknob. Her eyes are watery, but she blinks it away. "I need to talk to him after the show," she says as we head back to the crowd.

We pass the girls' bathroom and I nod at the crooked sign, asking, "Gotta pee?"

I need a minute without the din of Old Silver ringing in my head—a few moments of quiet, a reset. Is everyone like this? At parties or even small hangouts, sometimes it becomes too much, like the volume's turned up too high.

"Nah, meet you out there," Ray says, and part of me is relieved to be completely alone, a mini break from trying, always trying. Trying to impress, trying to fit in.

Once I'm inside the bathroom, I take a deep breath and run my fingers through my hair. That scene back there was all too familiar. Last year, Dad promised to make it home to Seattle for my band's winter concert. I had the solo, a sax break during "My Funny Valentine." I practiced it for hours, perfecting the notes, imagining Dad cheering me on from the audience, so pumped that he would actually be there. But on the night of the show, the plush red seat next to Mom and Joey remained empty, Mom constantly checking her phone. I eyed the back door to the auditorium, certain Dad was about to rush through at any moment. By the time my solo came around, my nerves morphed into nausea, that empty seat like an open mouth laughing at my naïvety. I stood to play my part, my knees buckling beneath me. The whole audience stared at me, the not-important-enough girl, the girl who always comes in second to football. I butchered the entire thing, each note more sour than the last, heat rushing to my cheeks. And now I feel it all again, this time for Drew.

After a quick check in the mirror and one more deep breath, I push open the bathroom door and smack right into him. I jump, my stomach twisting as if he heard my thoughts through the walls.

"Sorry," Drew mutters, still clearly pissed. He tugs at a ratty T-shirt that hangs over ripped jeans. He's about to walk past me but I reach out and touch his elbow.

"Are you okay?" My words are small, tentative, like maybe I shouldn't be saying them. After all, I barely know Drew. He turns, raking his left hand through his hair, his dark eyes finding mine. Ropes and leather cuffs cover his wrist and maybe a small tattoo, but it's too dark to tell.

"Yeah," he says softly, then hesitates, his eyes lingering on my face. "Well, no. Not really. My dad . . . he just bailed. I shouldn't be surprised, but somehow . . . every time . . ."

"I'm sorry. I know what it's like, if that helps at all. I know how it feels, at least."

"Sucks." He takes a step closer to me, then hesitates, taking two steps back.

"Try to think about the people who show up, you know? The ones who are here." I can't help thinking of Ray and my promise to help her. "You have Shane, and Ray's so excited to see the show tonight."

"She is?" Hope springs in Drew's eyes as he scans the crowd.

"Hey, man," Shane says, appearing at Drew's side, holding his baseball hat and drumsticks. His eyebrows knit together as he looks at me, then at Drew, then back at me. Maybe I shouldn't have come here. Shane doesn't exactly look happy to see me. "We start in five."

Drew shifts his gaze from Shane to me. "Thanks for saying all that." He shoves his hands in his pockets and heads back to the band.

"Listen, Stevie," Shane says, his eyes bouncing all over Old Silver, like he's scared to look at me. I need to apologize for whatever set him off the other day.

"I ... um ..." I start to say, but I have no idea what I'm about to apologize for.

"Thanks for coming tonight," he says, clenching his drumsticks, and I am officially very confused.

"Shane, come on!" someone yells from the back office.

"Sorry," Shane says, putting the baseball hat on his head. He shoves the drumsticks in his back pocket. "I should go."

A quiet cheer grows louder and louder, like a train barreling into a station, as I squeeze next to Ray in front of the stage. She straightens her black miniskirt and shifts on her sandals.

"That was intense," she yells above the crowd.

"Is Drew always like that?" I ask. "Intense, I mean."

"He can be. But he's so many other things. It's hard to explain, but I miss him. Can't stop thinking about him," she says in my ear.

"So talk to him and apologize for the way everything went down last year," I say, thinking about the excitement that took over Drew's eyes when I told him Ray was in the audience. Ray nods, and I can almost see her formulating the plan in her head. "I hope Shane's okay."

"He'll be fine," she says, eyeing the office door. "They

fight like that all the time and the next second, they're inseparable. Drew would literally lay down in traffic for Shane. He
worships him."

"Really?" I would think it's the other way around. Drew's
the kind of person who can command a room, who makes
everyone look up and take notice.

"Drew wishes he had Shane's talent and smarts, and he
thinks Shane is the most stand-up guy, you know? Which
he is, by the way."

"He was kind of weird the other night," I say carefully,
hoping Ray knows the reason Shane acted the way he did
and why he's acting so strange now. "Said he wouldn't help
me with All-State and then asked me to leave."

"Did he say why?" Ray's eyebrows furrow, a tiny crease
forming in the center.

"Just said he doesn't know why he got into All-State and
wouldn't know how to help me."

"He's being modest. Go back over there next week. Tell
him he has to help you."

"Like, just show up?" I've never done anything like that
in my life.

"You want this All-State thing, right?" Ray's eyes are still
on the office door, but she quickly glances at me, raising an
eyebrow. "If you want something, go after it. Nothing's going to happen if you sit around and wait."

Ray's right. She wouldn't take no for an answer. That's
why she's the star kicker of our football team and that's why
she's here right now, trying to make everything okay with
Drew.

All of a sudden, the crowd goes wild as Gabe and Kevin
hop on the stage, guitars slung over their backs. Shane walks
on next and heads for his set, drumsticks in hand. He catches

my eye and smiles, like he didn't just get into the biggest fight with his best friend, like whatever happened between us back there wasn't excruciatingly awkward.

Then I see Drew.

He's changed into a faded black T-shirt that hangs off his tall frame like he couldn't care less about singing in front of the whole school. But when I look closer, I see the tiniest bit of uncertainty as he grips the microphone and scans the room. His eyes land on me, then shift to Ray.

His whole body relaxes, his shoulders falling as a slow smile stretches across his face. He nods and they look at each other for a couple beats longer, having an entire conversation with their eyes. It's easy to see how important they once were to each other.

"Hey." Drew's voice bounces through the restaurant and everyone screams. "We're Dark Carnival." His nostrils flare slightly, and his knuckles get white as he grips the microphone even tighter. Shane taps his drumsticks together four times, counting the band into the first song, a Struts cover. His drumming is like a heartbeat, breathing life into the entire band. Shane's precise and controlled when he needs to be and lets loose for the fills. As he steps up the tempo, the other guys keep up, the entire band becoming one unified sound.

When Drew starts singing, I swear the entire room collectively gasps. His rich tenor sounds raw and dangerous, and seriously pissed. An impromptu mosh pit forms by the stage.

"Come on!" Ray grabs my hand and pulls me closer to the stage, and in that moment, I realize I'm not trying. I'm laughing and weaving through the crowd, Shane's drumbeat vibrating in my chest. Maybe Ray's for real, the kind of friendship that won't disappear after a week. When we reach the stage, Ray pulls me next to her, the curve of her hips swaying back and forth to the beat.

Drew screams into the microphone as he stomps his boot haphazardly. He's not trying to be a front man or steal the spotlight, but it doesn't matter. He's completely lost in the music, oblivious to the fact that my entire high school is slowly falling even more in love with him.

My eyes skim over Drew's shoulder and land on Shane, the guy no one's watching. His sandy-colored hair is all over the place, thrashing around his head as he heads into a solo. Gabe and Kevin quiet their instruments as Drew wails into the microphone. Then all at once the music goes silent, Shane's cue to rip that drum set to shreds. He starts off slow on the snare, and even though it's a quiet kind of tapping, the time he's keeping is expert-level stuff. But then he adds the kick of the bass and a cymbal crash, layers of beats building on each other. His drumsticks are moving fast now, blurred lines instead of two defined pieces of wood. The crowd claps as he goes faster, the rush of beats filling Old Silver. He looks up for a moment, locking eyes with Drew and nodding as the high hat claps in sync with the audience. Drew nods at the rest of the guys as Shane ends the solo and easily slips back into the beat of the song, the guitar and bass joining him. My mouth hangs open.

"Not bad, huh?" Ray says in my ear. I don't care what it takes or how I need to convince him, but Shane is helping me with All-State. And it's not only about All-State. I can't deny the flicker of curiosity that began in my chest during Shane's solo, the way my eyes lingered on him, not Drew.

"Thanks, guys," Drew mumbles into the microphone at the end of the show, his sweaty T-shirt clinging to his body. The crowd swarms Gabe and Kevin as they jump off the stage. Shane walks over to Drew, putting one hand on his shoulder. Drew shakes his head before raking his hair out of his face.

"C'mon," Ray says, pulling me on the stage to join them. "Distract Shane while I talk to Drew, okay?"

"Great show," Ray says once we reach Drew and Shane. I step back, giving them room to talk.

I smile at Shane, who steps back too, tugging at the bottom of his polo then stuffing his hands in his pockets. Sweat beads down his temple.

"Hey," I say.

"Hey," he says, and we stand there looking everywhere around the room but at each other. Words bubble up my throat until I can't stand the awkwardness a moment longer.

"I'm sorry if I was too nosy the other day, poking around your sketches."

Shane wipes his forehead with the bottom of his polo, flashing me his soft stomach. "You weren't nosy. I'm the one who should be sorry. And I am . . . sorry . . . for the way I acted at the end."

Maybe the way Shane acted had nothing to do with me, and suddenly I realize that I hardly know him. But I want to. I want to know what set him off the other day and how he got so good on the drums and what made him want to become an EMT. I want to know *him*.

"So, what did you think of the show?" he asks like he's desperate to change the subject, shoving his hands back in his pockets.

"I think you can really play," I say, and a dimple I've never noticed before appears in his left cheek. On stage, instead of the marching band drummer who can't seem to form complete sentences, Shane was so in control. In fact, he was magnetic, the kind of guy you can't tear your eyes from.

"So did it work?" Shane asks, as a waiter throws him a bottle of water. He unscrews the cap and takes a long sip.

"Did what work?"

"The lists. Did you fall asleep?"

"I actually did." When I got home from Shane's house that night, my mind was on overdrive, obsessing over what I possibly could have done wrong. Finally, I got up and sat at my yellow desk, penning a list of my top five favorite singers. And when I crawled back into bed at close to three a.m., I thought about that list. I heard Shane's soothing voice helping me count off a top five and miraculously I fell right to sleep. "Thank you."

Shane sits on the side of the stage, taking another sip of water. I'm not sure if he wants me to join him, but Ray is deep in conversation with Drew. So I sit, my legs dangling over the edge of the stage, as Old Silver clears out, only busboys left scraping dirty dishes off tables.

"Why did you act the way you acted?" I ask, because something's still not right. Even though Shane apologized, he's distant, distracted. He snaps his head to me. "Did I do something? To make you not want to help me. I know I can be kind of awkward sometimes and I'm not the best with new people and I'm sure I was talking too much or whatever . . ."

"Stevie, no," Shane says, angling his body toward me, his eyes grabbing hold of mine. "Don't ever think that."

"So, then why won't you help me?"

Shane peels the wrapper off the water bottle, ripping it into little pieces.

"I need to tell you something," he says, staring at the scraps of water bottle wrapper that litter his lap. He turns to me with unsure eyes as he flips the water bottle over in his shaking hands. But then his eyebrows rise and his jaw drops, as he stares over my head.

Drew's arms wrap around Ray's waist and her hands run through his sweaty hair. He's kissing her and she's kissing him and I sure as hell have never been kissed like that.

Ray pulls away and says, "I'm so sorry. I miss you."

"I'm sorry too. And I'm sorry about Toast. Sorry about everything, really," Drew says, leaning in to kiss Ray again.

They catch us staring and Ray holds her hand to her mouth, dragging Drew over to the front of the stage.

"Thank you," she whispers in my ear.

Ray is a go-for-it kind of girl. The kind who gets what she wants, because she's not afraid to ask for it. The kind of girl I want to be. The kind of girl I maybe *can* be. I don't know what Shane's deal is, but I'm going to show up at his house on Wednesday. I'm going to make him see that he's the most talented musician I've ever met and that he deserved that All-State spot. And then I'm going to learn everything I can from him.

"Let's get going," Drew says, pulling car keys out of his pocket. "I can take all of us home."

Shane and I stand, and I realize he never finished his sentence.

"Hey, Shane, what did you have to tell me?"

Drew glances at me and then at Shane, communicating with him like he did on stage, with only a look. Except this time it's not about changing up a beat or transitioning into a new song. Drew's face is cryptic as Shane bites down on his lip and turns his attention back to me.

"It was nothing," Shane says. It's obvious it's not nothing. But whatever it is, I'm all in to find out.

CHAPTER 7

Shane

"For the hundredth time, you *cannot* tell her," Drew says, taking a big bite of Mom's lasagna, a gooey cheese string hanging from his mouth. He pinches it between his fingers and stuffs it in. "Shit, this is good."

"I can bring more over. She froze a whole tray last night," I say, sitting next to him at the massive island in the middle of his kitchen. He forks another bite and holds one thumb up. The sun makes its way to the horizon, the light slowly seeping out of the room. Drew stands and flicks the hanging fixture on, tiny rainbows projecting on the ceiling. "And I have to tell her. I'm a nervous mess around her."

Drew sits down and cuts another piece of lasagna. He's probably starving, but he would never complain. He swallows a bite then looks at me.

"We flipped that coin to decide which one of us would ask her out," Drew says. "You do realize you haven't even *asked* her out. Everything that happened, would have happened anyway. Thus, the flipping of the coin is null and void."

"That makes no sense," I say, and Drew smiles his know-it-all-smile, all cheeks and a shoulder shrug.

"It makes perfect sense. You never asked her out. I'm back with Ray. It's like the coin toss never happened."

"But it *did* happen," I huff. "Let's say you won that coin toss and *you* asked her out, because let's face it—you wouldn't have wasted time like me, fumbling all over yourself. You would have asked her out the minute that coin landed on heads. And if you did, she'd be your girlfriend, not Ray."

"You don't know that," Drew says, through a mouthful of lasagna. "Maybe she would've said no. She barely talks to me."

"That's because *you* ignore her," I say.

"None of it matters," Drew says, flinging his hand in the air, dismissing the entire notion of a parallel universe. "Like I said, I'm back with Ray and it's cool."

Drew pushes a noodle around in circles with his fork and fidgets on the stool. Ray's been hanging with us lately, like last year. It's funny how you can slip back into an old routine so easily. Me and Drew shooting hoops after school and Ray sitting at the edge of the driveway messing around on her phone. It's obvious she holds herself back, respecting our afternoon tradition, until she can't help herself and jumps up, stealing the ball from Drew and sinking a basket. And then it's two on one. I didn't mind last year, and I don't mind now. It's fun having Ray on my side because she kills it on the court, and that usually means we beat Drew. Plus, Drew loves it. He cheers her on, especially when she dunks on him. But something's off now, something I can't quite put my finger on. Maybe it's the way Drew hugs her after she wins, like it's an obligation. And Ray, she hesitates before she high fives him. It's like they're out of sync, a record scratch skipping over the best part of a song.

"*Is* it cool?" I ask.

"Sure," he says, but he doesn't sound sure. He tucks his

hair behind his ears, and I stay quiet. If I keep my mouth shut long enough, he'll come clean. "It's like this," he finally says, meeting my eyes. "You think you know someone so well. But then life gets in the way and maybe you don't speak for a while. And then life throws you back together, when the timing is finally right again, but it's not the same. You want it so badly to be the same, but too much has changed. It doesn't mean you care about the person any less, it's just off."

"Is *off* enough for you?" I ask. Drew's not himself around her, instead going through the motions, like he's playing a part.

"I don't know." Drew laughs his nervous laugh, more air than laugh. "Ray's great, right? She's great."

"I mean, yeah, she's Ray Stone. Any guy at school would jump at the chance to be with her," I say. "But it sounds like you're trying to convince yourself."

Drew doesn't respond, instead pushing that noodle around with his fork. He's not saying anything else on this topic and I know better than to press him. But his words swarm around my head, the idea that you could grow so far apart from someone that you can't find your way back to them.

"That would never happen with us, right?" I ask. "The whole life getting in the way thing."

"Never." Drew's eyes are serious. "No way, I got your back. Always, no matter what life throws at us."

"Same," I say. Drew's a constant, always has been, always will be. "So what do I do about Stevie?"

"Forget about the coin toss and just hang out with her. Aren't you supposed to help her with All-State or something?"

"I messed that up too, remember?" I'm still reeling from last week's spectacular failure.

"So un-mess it up," Drew says, digging into his pocket. "Actually, I have something that might help."

He produces two small rectangular pieces of paper and

holds them up to my face. My eyes go wide as I read the print. *Pearl Jam, Friday, October 10th, Madison Square Garden.*

"Are those real?" I say, reaching out to touch the tickets. "How in the world?"

"You told me how much she likes them," Drew says, his voice sincere. "My dad pulled a few strings. After bailing on the Old Silver show, he owed me."

"These seats are right at the side of the stage," I say. "You're coming, right? This show is going to be unreal."

"Nah, can't stomach it, knowing the tickets are from my dad. Plus, you know that's not my kind of music. I got these tickets so you can ask Stevie." Drew smirks and polishes off the last bite of lasagna, pushing the plate across the marble countertop.

"I thought I wasn't technically 'asking her out.'" I make air quotes with my fingers.

"You're not. These tickets are a gift from me. I'm asking her out for you, '*technically.*'" Drew makes air quotes back, a smirk still plastered across his face. He stuffs the tickets in my pocket and stands.

"Don't you have somewhere to be?" he asks, grabbing his keys off the island.

"Huh?"

"It's Wednesday, All-State practice day." Drew heads for the front door.

"I told Stevie I can't help her," I say, following him. He glances out the window and turns to me.

"Then why is she walking up your driveway?"

I run out of Drew's house and cut Stevie off as she heads up my front porch. She jumps when she sees me, almost dropping her sax case. Her hair is in a ponytail, pieces falling around her face, and there's some sort of gloss on her lips, making them shine in the setting sun. Okay. I have two choices here. One, I can continue acting like a fumbling amateur and tell her to go home, which would be an epic fail. Or two, I can bury the memory of that coin toss deep in the recesses of my brain and invite her inside. Maybe Drew's right. He's back with Ray now and the terms of the coin toss don't necessarily apply anymore. It might as well have never happened.

I open my mouth to invite Stevie inside, but she speaks first.

"You're helping me," she says, serious. "You're the best drummer I've ever met. The best musician I've ever met. So, yeah, you're helping me."

Her dark eyes widen anticipating my response, but I'm speechless. No one has ever said that to me, not even Mom.

"I'm not that talented," I say, because being the best is a lot to live up to.

"Yes, you are. You're fantastic," Stevie says, her shimmering lips telling me everything I've ever wanted to hear. "So come on, let's go inside."

She reaches for the door handle like she lives here, but the door swings wide open before she grabs hold. Mom stands in the entryway, her short hair pinned away from her face. Heat rushes to my cheeks like a radiator clicking on. Mom claps her hands together and brings them to her chin.

"You must be Stevie!"

Forget about the radiator. My face is a five-alarm fire, flames shooting out of my eyes, nostrils, and mouth. Mom ushers Stevie inside, oblivious to the fact that her only son is melting in a pool of boiling liquid like Schwarzenegger in *Terminator 2*.

"I'm Kathy, Shane's mom," she says, decked head to toe in the Lululemon workout gear she wears even when she has no plans to go to Zumba. She kisses me on the cheek and says, "Did Drew like the lasagna?"

I nod and say, "We're actually going to head to the studio. Stevie's trying out for All-State in December and we're going to work on her audition piece."

"Sax, right?" Mom asks her and I terminate right here in the middle of our foyer. I silently vow to never ever tell Mom anything again. "I'm sorry I wasn't home last week when you were here. I got stuck at school. The beginning of the year is always crazy."

"Yep, sax," Stevie says, smiling. "It's so nice to meet you."

"Are you hungry?" Mom asks, and I groan.

"We really need to get to work," I say, inching closer to the basement door, which is mercifully right off the foyer.

"Take some cookies for the road," Mom says, scurrying off to the kitchen then reappearing with a zip-lock bag of freshly baked chocolate chip cookies. She hands them to Stevie and smiles like she's the first girl to ever set foot in our house. Well, Stevie *is* the first girl to ever step foot in our house, but whatever.

"Thanks, Mrs. Murphy," Stevie says as I open the door and flick on the basement lights.

"Call me Kathy!" Mom yells to us as we make our way down the stairs.

When I reach the studio, I turn to Stevie. A cookie is half in her mouth as she puts her sax case down and bites through the middle.

"So good," she says through a mouthful of cookie. "This is better than something I would get at a bakery."

I stuff my hand in the bag and grab one because Mom's cookies are legendary, as Dad would always say. We sit on the rug as Stevie unfastens her sax case. She takes the brass pieces out, fitting them together one by one.

"Want to hear what I've been working on?" she asks, as she licks the reed and slips it on the mouthpiece. I'm staring at the tiny divot in her upper lip and the way her lower lip curves and I can't think straight.

"Huh?"

"The piece I've been working on. It's Coltrane." Stevie stands and clips the sax to her red neck strap. It's cool that she has a red one instead of the standard black everyone else in the band wears. I know she wishes she didn't have to start over here in Millbrook, to seamlessly blend in. But I love the way she stands out, just like that strap.

"Definitely," I say, leaning back on my palms.

Stevie launches into a song I don't know. It's jazz and the notes are all in the right place, brassy and raw. Stevie's fingers expertly fly up and down the keys, fluttering notes flying around my studio. No doubt about it, she's good. And this piece, it's technically perfect, but something's missing. It's like she's playing to get it right, to get an A on some test that doesn't exist. But that's not what music's about. Music isn't like scoring points in a basketball game or knowing all the answers to a pop quiz. It's pouring all your emotions into an instrument and letting that instrument express every inch of you. That's real music—the stuff that makes you feel something. Stevie closes out the song and looks at me, waiting for a grade.

"Do you like Coltrane?" I ask instead.

"Huh?"

"Do you like him?"

"Everyone likes him."

"But do *you*?"

Her eyes shift to the side, like she's considering my question. When she looks back at me, uncertainty settles on her face.

"I guess not," she says, a small laugh escaping her mouth. "I don't really like jazz."

I stand and walk to her, unclipping the sax from her neck strap and setting it on the case.

"So who do you like? Actually, forget that. Who do you love?" I ask, already knowing the answer. I just want to hear her say it. "What music do you listen to when you need to work something out in your head? What album do you play over and over?"

"Pearl Jam," she says quietly. "I know it's old-people music, but *Ten* is the album I can't live without."

"It's not old-people music," I say, as my hand digs into my pocket grazing the tickets. It's better than anything on the radio now. "Hold on."

I head for my computer and scroll through my playlists, landing on Pearl Jam. I turn on every speaker in the room and click a few more buttons. Stevie sits in a chair, crossing one leg over the other, eyeing me. I press play and "Alive" fills the room, all kick-ass drums, raging guitar, and of course Eddie's distinct don't-mess-with-me vocals. The music is powerful, the kind of song that fills you up when you feel empty inside. Stevie's eyes lock with mine and I know she feels it too. The song trails off and I pick up Stevie's sax, clipping it back to her neck strap.

"You need to feel like that when you play," I say. "Pick another song."

Stevie's eyes shift to the ceiling and then back to me.

"Springsteen," she says. "I'll need to start from scratch though."

"Then we start from the beginning. We have three months until the audition."

"So you'll help me?" Stevie's eyes are wide. "For real?"

"Top five reasons I should help you." I'm messing with her and she knows it. She folds her arms over her sax, smirking.

"One, I'm really good at eating your mom's chocolate chip cookies," she says, grabbing another one from the bag and taking a bite.

"They are the stuff of legends," I say, taking the other half.

"Two, I'm a quick study and I promise to practice every day."

"If it's the right song, it won't feel like practice."

Stevie smiles at this and eyes the pile of sketches on the mixing board.

"Three, I won't snoop through your stuff anymore."

"You weren't snooping," I say. I don't tell her that I want her to snoop. I want her to ask me everything. To know everything about me. Everything except the coin toss which I vow never to think of again.

"Four, I have great taste in music."

It's true, she does. I shove my hand in my pocket again, touching the tickets, the question dancing on my tongue. But my heart begins to pound in my chest, making it hard to get the words out.

"And five . . . you're the only one who can help me. The only one who hears music the way I do and who understands why I want this so badly."

"Audition with 'Born to Run,'" I say, the double meaning not lost on me. Stevie's been running her whole life, even if it hasn't been her choice. It dawns on me that maybe she's never had the chance to really know someone, and that maybe that's what she really wants. To stand still in one town and make the kind of friend who never leaves. I wouldn't leave, even if she does. But I don't tell her any of that. "Killer sax solo."

"Good call," she says, her hand grabbing hold of her red

neck strap as she unclips her sax. "I guess I should get going for tonight. My mom needs me to watch Joey so she can paint."

"Do you watch him a lot?" I ask. I wonder if Stevie ever comes first in her family. Dad always made me feel like I was the most important person in the room, and Mom, well, she flat out tells me I'm the love of her life. It's beyond smothering, but it would suck the other way around.

"Joey's the best," Stevie says, not answering my question. "Come over to my house next Wednesday so you can meet him."

"How is it? Being in a new house and all?" I've lived in my house my entire life. Dad's firm built it right before I was born, and I can't imagine living anywhere else. I think that's why Mom hasn't sold it yet, even though it's way too big for the two of us.

"You know, no one's ever asked me that," Stevie says. She picks at a cuticle on her thumb. "In all the towns I've lived in, no one's ever thought to ask me what it's like, the newness of it all."

"Is it weird?"

"Beyond," she says, sighing as she opens her sax case. She takes the instrument apart, fitting each piece in its corresponding felt compartment. "And it gets weirder in each house, like I leave a little bit of myself behind with every move. Our house now might as well be a hotel."

"That can't be true," I say. "You might not realize it, but you take it with you, you have to."

"But all my old friends, my old favorite places, they're all gone." She snaps the case shut.

"It's like this," I say. "When my dad died, it felt like this big gaping hole in my life, like I lost something I would never get back. And in some ways, that's the truth of it all. He's physically gone and not coming back. When I graduate in a few years there'll be an empty seat where he would've sat and no big congratulations hug. But on the other hand, he's still here. He's in the cathedral ceiling he designed in our entryway. And I swear I can still hear him cheering when I finish a drum solo. It's why I tried out for All-State last year and why I'm trying out this year and every year—because I can feel him watching me when I perform. And sometimes when I look in the mirror, I see my dad's smile in the reflection."

"You look like him?" she asks quietly.

"His twin," I say. "Just remember, all that stuff from your past happened. And all those friends and favorite places, they're with you, even if you're not physically with them. They make you who you are. And that's everything."

"But what if I want everything to stay the same?"

"Nothing ever stays the same. It's about living in what's happening right now. *Really* living. Not wishing for the past or worrying about when things are about to change."

"That's pretty smart," Stevie says, picking up her sax case and heading for the stairs.

"You're pretty..." I say as I flick off the lights to the basement, the words unexpectedly falling out of my mouth, shocking me. They were in my head just now, and let's be honest, in my head the entire time Stevie was here. But now they're out of me, let loose into the universe. Stevie freezes on the bottom step and we both stand here in the dark, motionless, those two tiny words stopping time.

"I mean smart..." I stutter, my brain short circuiting, sweat lining my palms. "I mean ... you're both ... pretty and smart."

"You think I'm pretty?" Stevie asks quietly, her back to me. Of course, I think she's pretty. Pretty doesn't even cover it. But now I can't catch my breath and I don't know what to say, because she might not *want* me to feel the way I feel. Worse, she might laugh. I'm friend zone. I've always been friend zone.

"You're pretty enough," I say, making light of it. And Stevie does laugh, turning to me, the curve of her smile barely visible in the dark.

"So are you." She punches me in the arm.

Stevie starts up the steps again and then stops abruptly, turning to me.

"I'm really sorry about your dad." She steps closer to me. "It's cool how you handle it, how you see the world. And, um . . ." She fidgets with the handle of her sax and switches it to her other hand. She stares at the case. "Thanks for saying I'm pretty and smart. I mean, I like that you think that."

For the first time in my life I don't think. Every organ leaps around my body and I'm not letting this moment slip away. I grab the tickets from my pocket and hold them in the air between us. My heart is in my ears.

"Want to go?" is all I manage to get out.

Stevie squints in the dark, her eyes focusing on the tickets, and then her mouth drops open.

"No way you got those tickets."

"Yes way."

"How?"

I laugh and she laughs, grabbing the tickets from my hand.

"Drew's dad hooked him up and Drew didn't want them," I say. "So do you want to go?"

"Are you kidding me?" Stevie throws one arm around my neck, her sax case crashing into the back of my knees.

"Is that a yes?" I say in her ear.

"One hundred percent yes!"

She pulls away from me, her eyes still inches from mine,

her mouth so close I could kiss her, but I don't. Because my mind hasn't caught up to my body and I need to process what just happened. Because for the first time in my life, I might not be in the friend zone after all.

CHAPTER 8

Stevie

OCTOBER

Shane and I walk out of Penn Station and we're carried through the street on a never-ending current of chaos. Urgent horns shout from taxis and people scurry past us. I've never been to the city without my parents and a small flutter makes its way from my stomach up through my throat. I take a deep breath of exhaust-filled air. We get to the curb and garbage-can stench smacks me in the face. Shane grabs my hand, his eyes searching for the entrance to the Garden. His fingers lace with mine, tiny shivers dancing their way up my arm. We've been rehearsing for the All-State audition every Wednesday, but we've also been hanging out on Tuesdays and Thursdays. Sometimes we even hang out with Drew and Ray. Ray is convinced Shane's into me, clutching her hands to her chest and swaying dramatically every time his name comes up. I usually roll my eyes, because Shane's never tried to kiss me. But what I haven't admitted to Ray, or even to myself, is that maybe I want him to.

"C'mon," Shane says, leading me through the crowd.

Once we're safely at the entrance, Shane drops my hand, the cold air wrapping around my fingers. Maybe I'm imagining it all, the way we can talk for hours and the way he looks at me, his eyes lingering on my face like he's trying to memorize my features. I glance at the bright electronic sign flashing *Pearl Jam Tonight*. Shane stares at it too and then gestures for me to follow him.

We snake our way through the crowd, arriving at the turnstile, the last barrier between us and the show.

"My first show was here," Shane says once we're inside. "Green Day."

"My first concert was the Wiggles with my parents."

"You saw the Wiggles . . . live?" Shane hands our tickets to the usher who shines a flashlight on them. "Why would you do that?"

"Great seats," the usher says, as we make our way down the aisle, closer to the stage.

"I was four!"

"Please don't ever tell anyone that again."

I shove Shane's side playfully and he shoves me back as we shimmy into our row. The show is packed. We're in a VIP area, a few feet from the stage. Roadies walk on and off the risers, tuning guitars, taking a whack at the drum set, and testing the mics.

"The show should get going soon," Shane says as he inhales deeply and raises his eyebrows at me. Lighters flick on and off a couple seats down from us, smoke wafting through the air.

"Is this allowed?" I whisper.

"This isn't the Wiggles." Shane smirks. "Anything's allowed."

The lights dim and the crowd screams, the whole place coming alive. My heart pounds with anticipation. I mouth *oh my God,* Shane points to the stage, and there he is, right in front of me. Eddie Vedder.

He grips the microphone, and even though he's older now, the joy of playing music, of being on that stage explodes from his eyes. He barely acknowledges the audience before the band launches into "Rearviewmirror," one of our top five Pearl Jam songs. Madison Square Garden fills with sound, chords, and drumbeats circling through every seat and soaring up to the rafters. Eddie stands perfectly still except for his right foot tapping the stage as he screams into the microphone. The deep growl I've listened to for hours in my bedroom pierces through the music. I'm statue still, my five senses attempting to process the magnitude of it all. I glance at Shane, expecting him to be air drumming, but he's watching me instead, like I'm the most captivating sight in the arena. He smiles and leans to my ear.

"I couldn't miss your reaction," Shane says, his cool breath sending goose bumps down my back. Something hitches in my stomach, my lungs tight, holding in air. Shane's shoulder brushes mine and when I turn to him our lips are so close, the smell of his mint gum curling into my nose. Music swells around us, the stage lights illuminating the question in his eyes. The agonizing space between us is pure energy, anticipation. An unsure smile breaks free on Shane's face as he turns to the stage, taking in the band in all their glory. I refocus on the music to still the quiet shaking in my body. But then the floor shifts beneath me, and for a split second it feels like an earthquake.

"Shane?" He's mesmerized, soaking in each note, and I understand why he wanted to watch me. Witnessing Shane in his element is a window into the truest part of him. Right now, Shane is all feeling, absolute awe beaming from his face. He stands on his toes to get a better look as Matt Cameron goes to town on the drums.

"Shane?" I say in his ear when the floor actually moves. "The floor's shaking."

"I know," he says, gesturing to the crowd jumping in sync with the music. His eyes get wide and he jumps too, fist in the air. I can't help joining him, completely losing myself in the guitar chords.

Somewhere in the middle of the set, right when they play "Oceans," Shane takes my hand again. But this time, it's not to help me through the street. Even when Shane claps, he holds on, clapping both of our hands with his free hand. Shane's hand fits with mine, like it was made especially for me. We stand like this for the next hour. He doesn't let go, but he doesn't look at me either. In the dark, while Shane's thumb strokes the outside of my hand, I know this is happening and I'm not imagining it. He wants to kiss me, and I can no longer deny it—I *want* him to kiss me.

They close out the set with "Elderly" into "Free World," the music swelling with Eddie's voice. I squeeze Shane's hand and he finally looks at me, his dimple taking over his cheek. Even his ears smile. I laugh, and he laughs too. As the house lights come on, we're still laughing until he pulls me close and says in my ear, "That was . . ."

"I know," I say.

"Unreal."

We spill out of the arena with the rest of the crowd, and head for the train. When we board, we find seats in the back section. Shane lets me take the window of a two-seater, and when he sits, I rest my head on his shoulder.

"Top five songs of the night," I say.

"'Rearview,' 'Go,' 'Elderly,' 'Corduroy,' and 'Do the Evolution,'" Shane says matter-of-factly. "You?"

"Definitely 'Rearview,' 'Why Go,' 'Black,' 'Corduroy,' and I gotta say . . . 'Footsteps.'"

"Interesting choice with 'Footsteps.' Great song but not an obvious pick."

"Maybe it's not about the obvious choice," I say, closing my eyes, my heart beginning to speed.

"What is it for you, then?" he says, his voice raw from all the singing. I'm not sure what we're talking about anymore, but I answer anyway.

"A song that makes you feel something and maybe understand yourself a little better."

Shane taps the top of my head and I look at him.

"You know that song is about a murderer."

I smack him in the stomach without taking my head off his shoulder and he laughs.

"You know what I mean, Shane."

"I do. I know exactly what you mean."

We're quiet for a moment as Shane rests his head on top of mine, his hair smelling like the rain.

"Why is it that when I'm playing my sax or listening to music it feels so, I don't know . . ." I say.

"Right?" Shane whispers in my ear.

"Yeah," I say. "Why does it feel so right?"

"Because you're living," he says, like it's the simplest thing in the world. "I feel the same way when I'm playing drums, like it's just me and the set, like time stretches on to infinity."

It's not only playing my sax and listening to music. It's also being here with Shane on this dingy New Jersey Transit train. It's knowing for the first time since I moved that *this* is exactly where I'm supposed to be.

"So you liked the show?" he asks, but he already knows the answer.

"I loved it," I say. I want to live inside that concert. I know that sounds weird, but I want this feeling with Shane. I want to live inside this feeling forever.

CHAPTER 9

Shane

I'm the first one on the bleachers and it's just as well. I need to clear my head. The stuffed *Aladdin* genie grins at me from on top of my drum set.

"How about you tell me how to make a move," I say to Genie, but he keeps on grinning, his eyes big and mischievous. The sun is high and bright, and soon the stands will be filled with fans eager to see who will be crowned homecoming king and queen. My bet is on Tom Walker and Jenna Reed, although I know Stevie voted for Ray. Genie stares at me and it's almost like he's saying, *You'd better tell her.* Tell Stevie I'm falling for her or tell her about the coin toss? Because now, we're not just friends. The stakes are way higher, and I can't push that coin toss out of my mind anymore. I can't kiss her until she knows, and God, do I want to kiss her. My eyes squint at Genie, but he doesn't answer.

I grab my drumsticks and take a whack at the snare. The skin vibrates, shooting out a lonely beat. No one's around so I do it again, and again. I hit the cymbals, then the bass, then back to the snare. Around and around until I'm going faster, speeding through the beats. With each hit my head clears, until it's completely blank.

I'm so lost in every beat, this solo slowing my mind, that I barely notice when a hand grabs my cymbal, silencing the crash.

"Who are you pissed at?" Drew says, sitting next to me. I'm pissed at myself for not having the guts to make a move. I'm pissed at myself for participating in that careless coin toss. But I'm most pissed at myself for not telling Stevie about it.

"No one," I say.

"Whatever, man. You don't play like that unless you're pissed and we both know it."

"Are you still pissed?" I ask him. "At your dad?"

"I'm fine," Drew says, his tone clipped. I know he's lying. His eyes shift to the blue sky as he fidgets with his jacket sleeve. "He's talking about spending Thanksgiving with us."

Sometimes I think Drew would be better off if Don left him alone. Each new disappointment piles higher and higher, like a precarious Jenga tower. Drew pretends like it doesn't get to him, but one day it's all going to crash down.

"So how was the Pearl Jam show?"

"Mind-blowing," I say, and Drew smiles.

"*How* mind-blowing?"

"Not *that* mind-blowing," I say, still cursing myself for not making a move on the train last night.

"It's been almost two months. What are you waiting for?"

"I think I have to tell her."

"We've been over this. Do *not* tell her," Drew says, putting on his marching band hat, backwards as usual. "Trust me." He hops down to his section as the rest of the band files into the bleachers. Stevie sits with the saxophones, and the sight of her makes me fumble the drumsticks.

I have to tell her. Genie stares at me, daring me to tell her.

"Hey, Stevie," I yell.

She pulls her hair out of her red neck strap and places her sax in its case. Sweat beads along my back and under my arms. I twist against my uniform. I stand. I sit. My brain pounds against my skull. She heads up the bleachers, taking off her marching band hat.

"What's up?" she asks, sitting next to me. As soon as her brown eyes connect with mine, my throat goes dry. I can't tell her. I have to tell her. Genie smiles at me, taunting me.

I detach Genie from the drums and shove him at her.

"Say thank you to Genie for his services," I say, and she laughs. At least she laughs.

"Thank you, kind genie," she says, playing along, which I appreciate. "We still have a few games left though."

"Stitching's coming loose." I point to a small rip by Genie's shoulder. "Any chance you can sew?" I can't look at Genie's wide smile any longer. He knows all my secrets.

"I have some sewing skills." Stevie takes Genie and stuffs him in her backpack.

"What are you doing later?" I ask. Maybe once I'm out of this marching band uniform I'll have the guts to tell her. "Can I come by after my shift?"

"You better."

I know two things. I'm falling hard for Stevie Rosenstein, and after tonight she may never speak to me again. Tonight, I'm telling her about the coin toss. I can't keep hanging out with her and looking into those trusting brown eyes. She shouldn't trust me. I'm keeping this awful secret and none of this is real until she knows.

I walk up the front steps and smile at four pumpkins

arranged in a semicircle next to the front door. The largest wears a Jets jersey and has a mess of ribbon attached to the stem, which I guess is supposed to look like her dad's curly hair. The next largest one must be for her mom. A mini smock hangs across the front and a paint brush is glued to its side. The two small pumpkins make me laugh. Stevie's pumpkin wears sunglasses and has long straw hair, and Joey's pumpkin sports a Jets hat and balances on top of a skateboard.

As soon as I ring the bell, feet pound the floor and within seconds the front door swings open.

"My man," I say, as Joey crashes into me, hugging my waist hard. He pulls up his track pants, which are too long and hang over his socks. The house smells like tomato sauce.

"Stevie's upstairs," he says, nodding up the wooden staircase.

"Shane!" Naomi appears in the foyer and hugs me hello.

"How did the art show go?" I ask. She's smiling so wide I bet she has good news.

"I sold a painting," she says, her voice overflowing with excitement. She steps around a large box that's labeled *living room*. They still haven't fully unpacked, like they don't believe this is their permanent home.

"Congratulations," I say, but her attention turns to Joey, who has climbed on the banister and hangs backwards off the railing.

"Shane!" Joey flips off the railing and lands at my feet. "Wait!" He takes off running as Naomi shrugs and shakes her head. Joey reappears holding the two drumsticks I gave him. He plops down on the floor, grinning, a gap where his right bottom tooth used to be. It fell out last week and I drew a pretty convincing tooth fairy on the congratulations letter Stevie and Naomi wrote. Part Tinker Bell, part butterfly. They stuffed the letter and a five-dollar bill under his pillow. I think he bought it.

Joey plops down on the floor by my feet and I kneel down next to him.

"Not on the hardwood," Naomi says as Joey starts to tap the drumsticks on the floor. He scoots to the gray and white rug by the entryway and motions for me to follow.

"Watch," Joey says, as he pounds out an almost flawless beat to "We Will Rock You" on the rug. We worked on it for a solid hour right after he lost that tooth, and I'm impressed by how quickly he picked it up. Naomi looks on, pride spilling from her eyes.

"You got it!" I say.

"Another one," Joey says, handing me the sticks. "Show me?"

I place the sticks back in his small hands and guide them, tapping out a simple rhythm. One tap, one tap, two taps, and repeat. Joey plays it back, grinning the whole time.

"Another?" Joey's blue eyes blink up at me. This kid is impossible to say no to.

"Joey, I think Shane came here to see Stevie," Naomi says, smiling at me as she takes the drumsticks from his hands. "C'mon, it's time for bed."

"To be continued," I say, holding up my palm. "In the meantime, practice what I taught you."

"Thanks, Shane," Joey says as he jumps up and high fives me. Such a cool little dude.

I head upstairs and rap on the door three times. One knock, pause, then two quick knocks, so Stevie knows it's me.

"It's open," Stevie yells. When I walk into the room Stevie smiles. She's sitting on her bed and leaning against the yellow headboard. All at once my heart flies out of my chest and sinks to the floor.

I have to tell her. I shouldn't tell her.

I kick off my sneakers and take my place across from her, leaning back on an oversize pillow against the wall.

"All fixed." Stevie holds up Genie. I want to kiss her so badly, but Genie's evil smile taunts me. I have to tell her. I should *not* tell her. "Are you going to Tom's homecoming party?" she asks, her eyes wide and a deeper brown than I've ever seen.

"Nah, I'm wiped from my shift. Plus, I'd rather not be in the same room with Brent," I say. I try to avoid Brent and his crowd whenever possible. "You going?"

"Maybe later." She gazes out the window and pulls on the sleeve of her sweatshirt. "I want to practice a little more tonight. The piece still isn't working."

"We need to practice the middle part," I say. Stevie's right, the piece still needs work and I hope it'll be ready by December. We haven't been practicing as much as we should. Every afternoon starts out with good intentions, Stevie running through the song once and me pounding out a solo on my set. But then, we start talking about some band or some album we love. The other night we spent a whole hour analyzing the lyrics to *Dark Side of the Moon,* riffing on life and what it all means. At first it was life according to Waters and Gilmour, but then it was more about what we think, what we want. Stevie laid on her back, her chestnut hair spilling into a halo on the rug. She said she couldn't wait for college, to be in one place. But then she propped her head on her hand, her hair falling around her neck and said, *Scratch that. I just wanna be here, with you.* All I could do was nod because I couldn't speak. And then she said, *When I'm with you, I don't worry about moving.*

And now I know I'm not just falling for her. It's more than that excited feeling I had when we first started hanging out.

It's finishing each other's sentences and knowing she's going to love a song before she's even heard it. It's being her last call every night before bed, and not being able to fall asleep without hearing her voice. It's not falling. It's landing, finally landing where I want to be. It's all the more reason that I know I *have* to tell her.

"I wanted to bring you this," I say as I dig into my backpack and pull out a plastic container. Stevie grabs it, her eyes igniting.

"You said it was your favorite," I say, handing her a fork. She pops open the container and forks a big bite of cheesecake, rolling backwards.

"So good," she says, even though her mouth is full. When she sits back up, she cuts another piece and holds it out to me. I take a bite and little fireworks go off in my mouth.

"Really effing good."

"Told you Dino's cheesecake is the best," she says as her brown hair falls in front of her eyes. She pushes it back and gets cake in her hair. I bite back a smile.

"What?"

"Cheesecake . . . in your hair," I say, touching the crumbs with my finger.

But instead of taking my hand away, I keep it intertwined with the strands of her hair. Stevie freezes mid-bite and swallows, staring at me. She puts the fork down in the container. My heart bangs relentlessly against my chest, stomping all over my lungs, ribs, and stomach. I swallow again. I need to tell her. I can't *not* tell her.

Stevie looks right at me, anticipation beaming from her eyes. It dawns on me, like a huge neon light flashing the words in my face. She wants me to kiss her. I've never kissed a girl. I don't even know how this works. Sweat collects in my palms, but she takes hold of them anyway, her hands small and soft, not all callused like mine.

A small smile curls her mouth. I have to tell her. I can't kiss her before I tell her. My mouth falls open, but nothing comes out. Instead, I inch my way toward her and my heart jackhammers up my throat and into my skull. I *have* to tell her. But instead, she kisses me, and once we connect I can't stop kissing her, and my heart won't stop pounding, and for a second I stop breathing.

"Hi," she says when we pull apart, like she's just met me. She looks at me differently too, like I'm an entirely new person.

"Hey," I say.

"This is . . ." she starts to say, but before she can finish, I kiss her again, the room tilting as we go.

"Unexpected," she says between kisses. She leans her head on my shoulder, still holding my hand. "You're really unexpected."

"You're not. Unexpected, I mean," I say. "You must have known."

She smiles again, leaning into me, and saying, "What did I know?"

"Come on. I've liked you since the day I met you." I confess because for the first time in my life, I got the girl. And not just any girl—Stevie. It's like I can say anything, like I'm invincible.

"Well . . ." She looks at me through her lashes and raises an eyebrow in the cutest way. "Maybe I knew."

I want so badly to kiss her again, but before I do, an image flashes through my mind. That tiny penny flying through the air and Drew's boot lifting to reveal tails. My stomach twists on itself, like a wet shirt being rung out to dry. I saw the way she looked at Drew at the beginning of the year. I need to know that this is real, that Stevie wants to be here with me, and only me. Not to mention the fact that we never should have flipped that coin. It wasn't right.

"Listen, Stevie?"

"Yeah?" She looks at me, cheeks flushed. I almost chicken out, my pulse beating in my skull, but I take a deep breath and say it fast.

"Back on that first day. Something happened."

"What do you mean?" Her smile falls. I can't catch my breath and sweat breaks out by my hairline. I tug at the bottom of my shirt and clear my throat.

"The first day we met . . ."

"Are you okay?" She reaches out and touches my arm and everything melts around me. Her bed, her yellow dresser, the whole room starts to morph. My stomach burns but I swallow my nerves.

"We flipped a coin. Drew and me. To decide who would get to ask you out."

Stevie stares at me, her face completely blank.

"What?" she whispers. Her features scrunch together as she computes what I told her. She bites her lower lip. I swallow again but my mouth is bone dry.

"We both wanted to ask you out, so we flipped a coin."

"Like a bet." Stevie glances at the floor and shifts away from me. When her eyes finally meet mine, they're like two tiny puddles after a rainstorm. She tucks a strand of hair behind her ear.

"It wasn't like that, I swear." I shift back to her, the bed creaking, but she moves farther away. She closes the plastic cake container, then chucks it in the ceramic garbage can by her desk. My mind shifts into overdrive. She doesn't understand. I need her to understand. "No, really, it's this thing we always do. Drew and me, and—"

"I think you should go." She won't look at me. She's done looking at me.

"Listen, please . . ."

"Leave." Her voice shakes and she wipes her cheek with her sweatshirt sleeve. I get up and shove my feet in my sneakers. I ruined this. Stevie hugs her knees to her chest, burying her face in them. Her hair spills over her knees.

"Stevie?"

"Go." Her voice is muffled and serious, her face still buried in her knees. That kiss was like getting to the top of a rollercoaster only to come crashing down. Why did I have to open my mouth? Maybe Drew was right. Drew and his ridiculous coin toss. Maybe that penny changed everything, because if it didn't exist, and she'd chosen me on her own, I wouldn't have had to tell her, and she'd still be kissing me right now. Then again, without the penny, maybe she would have chosen Drew.

I know two things for certain. I have completely fallen for Stevie Rosenstein, and she's never going to speak to me again.

CHAPTER 10

Stevie

I pick my head up and loosen my grip on my knees. My eyes shift to a yellow piggy bank on my desk, my name displayed in bubble letters on the front. Hundreds of coins collected since I was five years old. Hundreds of wishes for all the things I was saving for, like a bike, and an iPad, and of course all my music. Those coins always represented hard work and dreams. Not a bet. I'm not someone's game. I don't buy Shane's excuses.

I press my lips together, and my heart soars and sinks all at once. That kiss, my first ever real-life kiss, was like trying on a pair of jeans that at first, didn't look right on the rack. But in the dressing room, they glided on perfectly. That kiss fit. It was like I've been kissing Shane my entire life, like I already knew that his mouth would be soft, and his hands would slide around my back, and that when he peeked at me, his eyes would be like fresh honey.

I squeeze my lids shut, the tears creeping up again. Drew and Shane masterminded these last two months, like I'm a pawn in their chess game. I'm sick of not being in control.

From above my bed, the hanging yellow duck grins at me. I grab hold of its foot and yank it down with all my strength, tiny nails popping out of the wall and raining over me. I reach for my phone and punch out a text to Sarah.

> **Me**
> I need to talk to you.

I stare at the screen, willing an answer to appear, but it stays blank. I stuff the duck into the back of my closet and tap out another text, this time to Ray.

> **Me**
> Hey

> **Ray**
> Don't mind me. Just over here wallowing in my pathetic homecoming fail.

> **Me**
> I'm so sorry about homecoming queen. I know you wanted it.

Ray smiled through the whole ceremony, like it was no big deal, even when Jenna's name was announced instead of her own. But I can't think about all that now. I can't think straight at all.

> **Ray**
> Thanks. There's always next year.
> Listen I'm heading to Tom's in a bit with Drew. You coming?

Me

I need to talk to you about
something.

As soon as I type the words, I think better of it. Telling Ray about the coin toss could mess everything up for her too. But at the same time, she deserves to know. I start typing, trying to explain what I still don't understand, when another text comes through.

Ray

So sorry Drew just got here. Let's talk
at the party, okay? I'll see you there!

Me

Okay. See you soon.

I can't talk to Ray until I know exactly what happened at the beginning of the year. There's only one person who can tell me the truth about what went down when that coin flipped high in the air, and I need to talk to him, now.

"I'll walk," I yell to my mom, who's standing on our front steps, dangling car keys from her fingers.

"You sure you're okay? You seem upset and it's dark." She apprehensively looks at the quiet sky.

"I'm fine. And it's around the corner." I'm already half-way down our driveway, leaves and acorns crunching under my boots. "I'll be home by curfew."

"Do you have your Mace?" she asks, as if we live in a city, not a nothing-ever-happens New Jersey suburb. I can't help smiling at her concern.

"Yes, Mom," I groan. "Night!" I wave and pick up my pace. Once I near the end of the block I peek over my shoulder and she waves one last time. I wave back and round the corner, unsure if my heart is racing from my walk-run, my nerves, or from the anger boiling in my gut. My boots stomp against the concrete, dead leaves rustling as I go. Was I a joke to them? A clueless new girl they could take advantage of? A game they played out of boredom? Drew and Shane flipped for me like I'm a nameless, faceless object who had no say whatsoever. But Shane seemed like he was for real. My throat catches when I think about him on the back of the train leaning his head on mine. It all happened, but what if it meant nothing? Tom's house pulses at the end of the block and I pick up my pace.

I step inside, and the air is thick with sweat and beer. Nerves bubble up inside me as I squish through a group of guys jumping around to relentless beats pounding from the speakers. Brent thrashes into me, spilling some of his beer down my tank top.

"My bad, party foul," he says, laughing. My shirt sticks to my back as I glare at him, too preoccupied to care about his antics. Brent chugs his beer and crushes it between his hands. I don't belong here. I belong back in my room with Shane making our lists. But screw Shane and his lists and his coin toss. And screw Drew too.

I shimmy past the beer pong table as Tom sinks a ball in a red Solo cup, the football team cheering around him as he chugs. Jenna plants a kiss on his cheek, the homecoming crown still resting on top of her head. My eyes dart around the party as she runs up to me.

"Who are you looking for?" Jenna asks as Tom pitches another ping-pong ball across the table.

I'm tempted to tell Jenna everything. To have someone hear me and assure me it's all going to be okay. But the only person I want to tell, the only person I *ever* want to tell anything to, is Shane.

"Is Drew around?" I ask.

"Back there." Jenna gestures at the patio and I quickly thank her, determined to get answers.

I pull open the screen door and step on the wooden deck. Drew's leaning on the railing, a beer in his right hand. I'm surprised he's out here alone, and he looks just as surprised to see me.

"Hey," he says, taking a sip of beer. "Aren't you supposed to be with Shane?"

My insides are burning lava, tiny embers flicking my bones at the mention of Shane's name. I glare at Drew, thousands of words flying through my mind at once. Liar. Fake. Full of it.

Dick. Player. Asshole.

"Stevie, are you okay?" He steps to me. "You're shaking. Is everything okay with Shane? Where is he?" His eyes shift to the door, as if Shane might be behind me.

"You flipped a coin for me," I say evenly.

Drew's face turns to stone and he steps back, setting his beer down on the patio table. His eyes shift to the side like he's thinking really hard, and his mouth falls open. He doesn't move until he tucks his hair behind his ears.

"What did he tell you?" he asks, still not looking at me. He knows the answer, I don't have to say it. Drew pulls on the sleeve of his military jacket and sits on the railing, his knee poking through a rip in his jeans.

"It wasn't like that," he says, and I swear if I hear those words one more time I'll scream. I'll move. I'll beg my dad to get another coaching gig. I'll pack up all my things in a way only I know how and move to another town, another state where no one knows me. I'll start over like I always do.

"Tell me, Drew. What exactly was it like?" I cross my arms over my chest and jut one foot out. I'm not buying this for a second.

"That first day, when we all met. When I saw you . . ." He scratches the back of his head, charcoal hair grazing his cheeks. "I just . . . I just liked you. Okay?"

I stare at his sincere dark eyes in disbelief.

"Anyway, Shane's my best friend, and we both wanted to ask you out. We were fighting about it. And Shane and I, well, we do this thing where we flip a coin so we don't fight. God, that sounds childish. But you should know, it was my asinine idea to flip that coin. Not Shane's. Shane wanted no part in it."

"I'm not talking to him right now," I say. "If you're telling the truth, why did you leave it up to chance?"

Drew pulls his sleeve down again and hops off the railing, taking a step closer to me. He raises his eyebrows.

"Because I thought it would be me who got to ask you out."

His hair falls around his face as his dark eyes take hold of me and don't let go. I take a deep breath and ask the question swirling around my mind.

"And what if it was you?"

"I don't know," he says, never breaking his gaze, my insides turning to liquid. "Would you have . . . I mean . . . did you . . ."

"I would have," I say. I know I would have. It's not the thought I want to be having or the words I want to be saying, but it's the truth.

"And now? Now that you know?"

I should walk away, but I'm too mad at Shane for lying to me and I'm too curious to find out what Drew's going to say next.

"I just wanted to know you," Drew says, his face so close to mine that I can smell beer on his lips.

"I did too," I say. "But everything changed after we met on that first day. And now . . ."

"I know," he says.

For a brief flash I see a version of us. A version where Drew's driving his Jeep faster than he should and I'm laughing, my hair flying around my face. A version where he makes me stretch beyond the person I am until I become someone else. But in that version, I'm the person I always was, and I don't need to stretch or bend. I see me. I see me choosing Shane even if in that version a penny chooses Drew.

"Maybe it would have been different," Drew says. "But maybe not. The bottom line is Shane and I never should have flipped a coin to decide who gets to ask you out. It wasn't cool."

"You what?"

Drew and I snap our heads to the doorway. Ray stands there holding two beer bottles, staring hard at Drew.

"Shit," Drew says, starting for her. "Ray, it's not what it . . ."

"You wanted to ask her out? You *liked* her?" Ray's voice breaks. She drops both bottles, the glass shattering all over the deck, beer seeping through the wooden panels.

"It was before," Drew says, reaching for her, but she pulls away.

"Forget it. I'm done." Her hazel eyes turn green with hurt as they shift to me. "Stevie, did you know about this? When we texted earlier did you know?"

"I—" My words stammer up my throat. "I was going to tell you tonight."

"How could you not tell me the second you found out? Stevie, how?"

"This isn't her fault," Drew says, stepping between us, reaching for Ray's hand.

Ray glares at him, her shoulders rising and falling fast with her breath. She turns back to me, tears lining her eyes. I shouldn't have come here and confronted Drew like this. Ray's right, I should have told her first. She pushes the tears off her face and then looks at Drew with all the contempt in the world. "Leave me alone. For good, this time."

Ray storms back into the house, and Drew runs after her. I'm left outside in the cold, still shaking, wishing I could take it all back. My phone vibrates in my bag, demanding my attention.

Sarah
You okay? What's going on?

When I don't respond, a FaceTime call from Sarah comes through and I pick it up. She blinks her ocean eyes as her image comes into focus. And seeing her, that silver streak of hair still framing her face, makes tears fall fast down my cheeks.

"Jesus, Stevie, what happened?" Sarah's voice gives me strength and I realize how much I missed her.

"Drew and Shane flipped a coin for me. Well, to decide who would get to ask me out. It was Drew's idea," I say, still not entirely believing the words as they fall from my mouth. I sit on a lawn chair, my elbows on my knees, staring into my phone and waiting for Sarah's reaction. Her eyes remain calm but a slight twitch tugs at the corner of her mouth.

"Sarah?" I need her to get it. To be outraged like I am. "They don't view me as a girl. They view me as a *thing*. Doesn't that bother you?"

"Of course it bothers me. I would be livid if I were in your situation." Her eyebrows furrow but then slowly relax. "But I can't help seeing it in another way. Two guys were fighting over you. I would kill for two guys to fight over me."

"They weren't *fighting*. It's not like they got into a cheesy teen movie brawl over me. They made a *deal*."

"Well, when you put it that way it does sound kinda gross." Sarah wrinkles her nose. "But not unforgivable."

"It's like this," I say, desperate for Sarah to understand. "I thought this whole thing with Shane happened because I wanted it to happen and because *he* wanted it to happen."

"He *did* want it to happen."

"But he left it all up to chance and that's what makes me sick to my stomach—that he could look at me like a prize instead of an actual person."

"But I thought you said it was Drew's idea."

"It was. But Shane went along with it. He could've said no."

"But—" Sarah starts to say, but I cut her off.

"He was helping me rehearse for All-State tryouts. Did I tell you that?"

Trying out now seems like the worst idea in the universe. I don't know what made me think I could possibly get in.

"You didn't tell me. That's amazing." Sarah stops talking and squints at me as my eyes shift away from the phone. "Oh, do not pull this crap, Stevie. You'd better try out."

"What makes you think I'm bailing on it?"

"Promise me you'll still try out," Sarah says. I don't respond. A "poor connection" message flashes on my phone. I can no longer see Sarah, but I can still hear her.

"Stevie Rosenstein. Promise me."

The screen flashes to black, the connection lost completely. It's just as well. I've already lost it all.

CHAPTER 11

Shane

NOVEMBER

I leave Stevie another voice mail, number twenty. One a day since my confession. No texting because I want her to hear my voice, to know how sorry I am. She hasn't picked up yet, but I won't stop trying. The other day I caught her looking at me during band class. It's unclear if her gaze was directed at me or the clock, but I'm going to count it. Plus, at the Thanksgiving game this afternoon, she made actual eye contact with me, her deep eyes lingering on mine, my heart rate spiking. I almost had the balls to hop down the bleachers and apologize again in person. But then she snapped her attention to the field as Ray completely missed the final field goal, losing our last game of the season. The crowd hissed and booed, and Ray ripped her helmet off, throwing it on the grass. It's like my confession caused this ripple effect, not only screwing up my life and Stevie's life, but messing with Ray and Drew. Last I heard, Ray unfollowed Drew on Instagram and deleted all their photos together. It's like last year all over again, except this time Drew's barely talking to me. When he asked me to meet him at Dino's a few hours after Mom, Lainey, and I polished off the last of the turkey, I immediately replied yes. And now I'm here, heading up the diner's steps, a cold breeze cutting through my jacket to my skin and straight to my bones. I hate Dino's but I'll do anything to stop the ripple, to maybe even reverse it.

"Wait up," calls Drew. He slams the door to his Jeep. I head down the steps and meet him on the sidewalk. He blows into his hands, his breath making a small cloud in the night air. "Fucking freezing outside," he says as he reaches me. He's freezing because he's in a leather jacket layered over a hoodie. I zip my North Face up to my chest and bury my hands in the pockets.

"Hey," I say, unsure if Drew's gonna rip me a new one, but he doesn't say anything. I step closer to him as he stares at the concrete, his face pale and his hair a mess. "Are you okay?"

"My dad," Drew says, his eyes shifting to the side, glassy. The wind picks up, stinging my face as a panic settles over me.

"Is he okay?"

"Of course he's okay," Drew says, meeting my eyes. He tucks his hair behind his ears and glances up at the dark sky, shaking his head, like he's pissed at the world. "He bailed on Thanksgiving. Last minute as usual. I just..." Drew's voice cracks and I put my hand on his shoulder, like I used to when we were little. One time, Drew's dad missed his basketball league tournament, and his game-winning slam dunk. I sat with Drew after the final buzzer and even though he tried his hardest not to cry, it all fell out of him. We were little and I didn't know what to do so I put my hand on his shoulder, just like I'm doing now.

Drew pulls me in for a hug, but he doesn't cry. I haven't seen him cry since that day after basketball.

"You're the only one I can talk to about this stuff," he says, releasing me. He pinches the bridge of his nose and inhales.

"I'm sorry about your dad," I say. "I don't have any excuses left for him. I wish I did though."

"Tell me about it."

"And I'm sorry about—"

"You don't have to say it again. I get why you told," Drew says, as the wind blows his hair back. He pulls his leather jacket tight around his body and rubs his hands together.

"But you and Ray. You were finally . . ."

"I'm not sure it was right with me and Ray, you know? I mean it was fun, but I'm not sure if it was right."

"So we're all good?" I ask. He holds out his fist and I tap his knuckles with mine.

"All good. Always. Even when we're not talking and I'm annoyed as hell, I still can't stay mad at you." He shakes his head, pushing me. I push him back and he laughs. "Is Stevie still pissed?"

"Seems that way," I say. "She won't pick up my calls."

"You kissed her, didn't you?"

I smile, thinking back to that kiss and how everything in the world seemed right for once.

"I knew it. Let's go inside," Drew says, putting his arm around me. "I overheard her saying she was heading here after the game. Maybe face-to-face it'll be different. Plus, how can she resist your charm?"

I hope Drew's right. We head for the door, the warmth of Dino's wrapping around me as we step inside.

CHAPTER 12

Stevie

Ray promised to meet me here after the game, texting me apologies I'm not sure I deserve. Guilt rains over me for keeping the coin toss from her, my restless hands playing with the zipper on my coat as I wait. At least Dino's beats sitting in my bedroom alone wishing my family was together on Thanksgiving. Joey's already asleep and Mom's holed up in her art studio. Forget about Dad. The Jets are down big time and he's never around. They'll probably let him go next year. I hope I get accepted into All-State before I'm forced to move again. Not that I've practiced. I can't seem to bring myself to play without Shane's encouraging eyes watching me.

I lean against the dessert case, right by the strawberry cheesecake, a knot forming in my throat as I picture Shane taking a bite from my fork, seconds before his lips met mine.

"I personally would go for the rainbow cookies," Ray says, leaning against the glass. She's wearing a stained Mustangs jersey and leggings, reminiscent of the day I met her. But her eyes are tired, defeated.

"Sorry about the game," I say, because I know she must

be beating herself up, replaying that kick, trying to figure out where it all went wrong. The thing is, sometimes you miss the mark.

"Should've made that goal," she says, more to herself than to me, her foot tapping at the dessert display. Her eyes shift to meet mine. "I'm sorry I've been distant. It wasn't your fault, what happened."

"I should have told you," I say. Ray takes down her ponytail and shakes out her golden waves, the smell of cut grass wafting through the air. I need to make this right, because I don't want to let go of this, to be the one who walks away. "The second I found out, I should have told you. I'm so sorry."

Ray regards me, taking me in with her contemplative eyes. Both hands fly to her hips and she huffs out a breath of air. Then she flings her arms around me for a tight hug and quickly releases me, her face serious.

"From now on, we tell each other everything, okay?" Ray says. "No secrets."

"Deal," I say, but a small pang of worry still gnaws at my gut. It was me who broke Ray and Drew. I was the catalyst. This won't feel right unless they can get back on track. "Do you think you can work it out with Drew?"

"This whole thing is Drew's fault," Ray says, annoyance dripping from her voice, and all at once it dawns on me that maybe it wasn't me who broke them. Maybe they were already falling apart. "Always is. He never takes responsibility for anything that happens to him. Always blames everything on his dad. But everyone has something they're dealing with, you know?"

I nod even though I don't see Drew that way. And Shane definitely doesn't see him that way. If anything, Drew's lost, kind of like me.

"Have you talked to Shane yet?" Ray asks, leaning on the display case.

"No," I say quietly. But I've listened to every one of his messages. I've saved them too. I almost picked up the other night, because I'm starting to realize I wasn't a bet or a game, that they flipped a coin as a way to make a decision. Maybe they didn't want to fight about it, about me. But mostly I almost picked up because I miss him so much I can't stand it.

"You girls want anything?" Dino says from behind the dessert counter.

"Still deciding," I say, scanning the desserts, my eyes bouncing back to the cheesecake.

"I've seen them flip a coin for the aisle seat at the movies and which Final Four game to watch on TV, stuff like that. But this was different. I get why you're pissed. I'm pissed too. It's plain wrong. At least it made me realize that Drew wasn't thinking about me the way I was thinking about him. If he was, he never would've flipped that coin in the first place," Ray says, hurt settling in her eyes. Deep down I know that's true and I know this is the end for them. "But listen to me . . . Shane, he's one of the good ones, you know?"

Ray points to the rainbow cookie. "I'll take that one," she tells Dino. "And the cheesecake Stevie's been eyeing for the past five minutes."

He wraps the cookie in parchment paper and places the cheesecake in a small box, handing both to Ray.

As we settle into a booth, Drew and Shane walk into the diner. My breath catches as I lock eyes with Shane, longing to talk to him, to hang out in his studio for hours, to feel his hand wrapped around mine. I open the cheesecake box, but I'm not hungry. Shane's only a few feet away but it feels like miles are between us.

"Just forgive him already," Ray says. "I would've forgiven

Drew if he had called me every day. All I got was one weak apology, like he wasn't sure he wanted us back together. But Shane, he's the real deal."

"I know," I say, as Shane peels off his jacket and throws it on the back of a chair.

"So go over there." Ray nudges my arm. "What are you waiting for?"

I stand, about to head over to Shane, as Brent and the rest of the football team walk inside, defeat and exhaustion displayed on their faces.

"Smooth moves out there today, Ray," Brent yells, popping a handful of nuts into his mouth.

"Go fuck yourself, Miller," Ray yells back, giving him the finger.

They take over a booth close to ours, but Brent doesn't sit. He spots Shane and narrows his eyes, chewing the nuts like a cow out to pasture. Drew steps in front of Shane but this time it doesn't stop Brent.

"Hey, Ringoooo," Brent says, drawing out the *o* on purpose. I can smell beer on him as he breezes by our table.

Shane steps in front of Drew and says, "My name's Shane."

Brent laughs like he's heard the funniest thing in the world, shoving another handful of nuts in his face. When he talks tiny pieces fly out of his mouth.

"Oh I'm sorry, *Ringoooo*."

"Brent, chill," Drew says, but Brent ignores him.

"That's not . . . my name," Shane says, his voice dropping low. Brent steps to him, a maniacal smile creeping up to his cheeks. Tom closes in on them as a hush falls over the diner, the whole school hoping for a fight.

"Sorry, *Ringo*."

"Fuck you," Shane says under his breath. Everyone's mouths drop open, even Tom's. Drew stares at Shane in disbelief.

"What did you just say to me?" Brent's eyes narrow.

"Shane, please," I say, holding out my hand, trying to stop whatever is about to happen.

Shane's features soften, his hand reaching for mine, but then Brent laughs again, this time at me. Shane's hand drops to his side and he takes a deep breath, his eyes going dark.

"I said . . . fuck you," he repeats, louder, angrier. My heart is out of control, slamming against my chest.

Brent throws another handful of nuts into his mouth and charges Shane, pushing him hard into a booth. Dino rips off his apron and runs full speed through the diner, waving both hands in the air.

"Enough," Dino yells. Shane steadies himself and pushes Brent back with all his strength. Brent falls against a chair and crashes to the ground, his head jerking backward.

"Oh, shit," Tom says.

"Oh my God," Ray says, suddenly standing right next to me. Brent gasps for air and grabs at his throat.

"Is he . . ." I say.

"He's choking," Tom yells as the entire football team surrounds him. But no one does anything. They all stand there gawking as Brent claws at his throat, his face turning blood red.

"Someone do something," Tom says, helpless. Brent drops the bag of nuts as Dino calls 9-1-1 on his phone.

"Get out of the way," Shane yells, pushing through the crowd. He puts his hands on Brent's shoulders and looks him straight in the eyes. Brent's frantic, gasping for air, fighting to breathe.

"I'm going to get behind you," Shane says, never breaking eye contact with Brent. "You're going to feel me push on your chest, hard. Don't fight me." His voice is steady and sure. Everyone stops talking as Shane gets behind Brent, wraps his arms around his waist, and pushes his fists into his abdomen. Brent's turning purple, fear pouring from his bloodshot eyes.

"Come on," Shane says through his teeth. "Breathe."

He squeezes Brent with all his strength, the veins popping in his neck. And then all at once the nuts shoot out of Brent's mouth, and he pukes all over the floor. He's gasping for breath, his back heaving up and down fast.

"You're okay," Shane says, his hand on Brent's shoulder steadying him. "You're okay."

Brent looks at Shane, his eyes wide, still coughing and struggling to catch his breath. Shane stands and holds out his hand. Brent grabs hold and Shane pulls him to his feet. They stare at each other, both of them drenched in sweat.

"Thanks, man," Brent says, his voice hoarse and humbled. "That was . . . well, thanks."

"Welcome," Shane says, running his fingers through his hair. Shane heads for the door as the crowd swarms Brent. A busboy appears with a mop and cleans up the mess.

"Why aren't you following him?" Ray asks Drew as he joins us.

"I think he needs a minute," Drew says, but I don't listen. Instead I book it for the door, bursting out of Dino's to find Shane sitting on the top step, shivering. It's cold out here, the dark sky littered with clouds. I sit next to Shane, pulling on my purple wool hat and gloves. We don't say anything as Shane blows warm air into his shaking hands.

"Holy shit," he whispers, letting out a long breath. "He's okay, right?"

I wish I could unsee it. Brent's eyes with so much terror in them, knowing he was teetering on that thin tightrope between life and death. But Shane, I wish I could watch Shane over and over. Shane with his steady hands and determined eyes. Shane, saving the life of the one person he hates most in this world. His hair is matted with sweat, sticking to his forehead. I reach out and take hold of his hand. As soon as our fingers connect, warmth spreads from his hand to mine.

"He's okay," I say. "You saved his life."

"I'm sorry, Stevie," he whispers.

"You don't have to—"

"Yes, I do." Shane turns to me, his eyes serious. "You weren't a bet. You have to know that. God, Stevie, you're . . . the girl I put on a pedestal, high above anyone else. I know that's a lot of pressure, but it's the only way to describe this feeling. Does that make sense?"

"I can handle the pressure." I smile, and I've already forgiven him, because I see him that way too.

"It's not only the way you look. I mean, that's what it was that first day. But then after . . . I can talk to you about anything. And when something happens—even if it's small—"

"I have to tell you," I say, finishing his sentence. "These past couple weeks . . . It's the weirdest feeling, to miss someone when they're right next to you. Every time I would pass you in the hall or see you in class, but everything was so messed up, it just—"

"Sucked," Shane says, squeezing my hand and scooting closer to me. "I missed you too."

He brushes the hair out of my face, his hand lingering by my chin. His honey eyes are the warmest, safest hug.

"You're not a bet. You're not a coin toss. Being with you shouldn't have been left up to chance." Shane tugs on a strand of my hair as his eyes reach into mine.

Shane kisses me, and I melt into him, soaking in this unfamiliar feeling, finally understanding where I belong.

CHAPTER 13

Shane

DECEMBER

I know two things. One, I am absolutely one hundred percent in love with my first-ever girlfriend, Stevie Rosenstein. Two, I am sort of, kind of, *maybe* sure she loves me back. I haven't told her yet, but it's getting harder and harder to hold the words back. Her legs scissor between mine as we sink deeper into her bed, my favorite place in the world. That duck is finally gone. Stevie ripped him down the other day and stuffed him in her closet. I was kind of sad to see that yellow guy go. But when we tacked up a Pearl Jam poster in his place, Stevie gestured at the band, excitement brimming from her eyes, and said, "See! Much better."

And now, the poster presides over us, which I have to admit is better than the duck, especially as Stevie traces her fingers down the slope of my neck, each hair standing at attention as she goes. I kiss her, and she kisses me, and she smells like fresh strawberries straight from a garden. "Fields of Gold," one of her favorites, floats through the room. Her hands are down my back and I'm through her hair. My whole body surges forward and I don't have any control. I don't want to be in control. She pulls me closer, and I almost say it.

I reach for her, my breath heavy, and say, "Is this okay?"

She says yes and giggles, her deep eyes magnetic.

"Stop talking," she whispers, and I love her. I can't hold the words in, with her body wrapped around mine, a jigsaw puzzle of arms and legs.

"Stevie, Dad's home!" her mom yells from downstairs.

Stevie jumps up from her bed, straightening out her shirt and wiping her mouth with the back of her hand.

"He's home early," she says, giddy like a kid about to open Christmas presents, or in Stevie's case, Chanukah presents. "C'mon!"

I've met Caleb Rosenstein a couple times in passing, either on his way out to a flight or as he walks in from practice, bone tired. It's always the same firm handshake and the same I've-got-my-eye-on-you look. But I've never actually talked to him other than the requisite nice-to-see-you platitudes.

As we reach the living room, Caleb has a giggling Joey in a bear hug and Naomi's preparing her sold art piece for shipment. The painting depicts a yellow balloon tugging a girl high off the ground. Caleb traces his finger along the lines of the balloon and kisses Naomi. It's beautifully intricate, and I can't take my eyes off it, kind of like Stevie herself.

"Dad!" Stevie says, running to him. He puts Joey down and envelops her in a hug. I can't deny the pang of jealousy that runs through me. An undercurrent of grief is momentarily brought to the surface, a stubborn lump forming in my throat. I sit in front of the TV on a leather chair, which must be Caleb's, and long for my own dad, to feel his arms wrapped tightly around me.

"Hi, Shane," Caleb says as they sit on the couch. Naomi props her painting against the wall and sits next to Caleb, her hand resting on his knee like Mom used to do with Dad. "What are you guys up to today?"

Stevie and I exchange a look. I'm not sure if she's told her parents that we're together, that we're more than friends. I told Mom the minute Stevie forgave me. She got so excited she practically launched into a Zumba routine right there in the kitchen.

"We're getting ready for the All-State auditions tomorrow," I say. "Me on drums and Stevie on sax."

Caleb hasn't yet heard Stevie play and she refuses to put herself out there, to ask him to listen. They don't get it. Just like Drew's dad doesn't get it. They have each other and they're messing it all up.

Joey hops up from the couch and announces, "I'm gonna go play trains."

"Go for it, buddy," Caleb says, refocusing on Stevie. "You guys hungry?"

But Stevie sighs and I want to shake her, so she sees what's right in front of her.

"Stevie's really talented," I say in an effort to help them, to bridge the gap between them.

"Of course she is," Caleb says, uncertainty settling around his eyes.

"Dad." Stevie folds her arms across her chest and meets his gaze. "You haven't heard me play in years."

"That's not true."

"Oh yeah? What's my audition piece?"

Caleb stares at her and says, "I don't . . . I mean . . ."

"Springsteen," she says. "'Born to Run.' Actually, we need to rehearse it one more time before tomorrow."

My eyes are on Caleb, Jedi-mind-tricking him into asking to hear Stevie play. One simple question so she knows he cares. To me, it's so obvious he cares.

Stevie picks at her cuticle. "I'm sure you're busy. You just got home, and I bet you have to unpack," she says staring at the rug.

"Can I hear it?" Caleb asks, and Stevie snaps her head to him.

"Do you really want to?" For a flash I see Stevie at five, staring up at her dad, idolizing him with awe.

"Absolutely," Caleb says, settling into the couch, eagerly waiting.

The next thing I know, Stevie's standing in the living room, her sax clipped to her red neck strap, and she's wailing through "Born to Run." Chills prick up on my arm as she flies through the solo. Even Joey runs in, three trains in each hand, and starts shaking his hips to the music. Through the entire piece Stevie focuses on me, like I'm giving her the strength to play. As the song trails off Stevie finally shifts her gaze to her dad, anticipation spilling from her brown eyes.

Caleb's hand covers his mouth and I swear tears line the bottom of his eyes. He takes his hand away and a huge smile shoots across his face.

"Wow," he says. "Just wow."

"For real?" Stevie asks, unhooking her sax and propping it next to Naomi's painting.

"You're fantastic, Stevie girl." Caleb shakes his head. "I'm sorry I'm not around to . . . I mean . . . I'm sorry I haven't heard you."

"Well, now you have." A triumphant smile erupts on Stevie's face as she takes my hand in hers. Even if she hasn't flat out told them we're together, now it's plain as day. "We have to go finish practicing. Dad, I'm glad you're home, even if it's only for a little while."

"Me too," Caleb says. I would give anything to have that conversation with Dad, anything. And even though this moment may not have fixed it all for Stevie and Caleb, at least they have today.

CHAPTER 14

Stevie

We walk through Rutgers' student union hand in hand, my insides already in a fist fight, my heart racing. Shane is so cute in a button-down and khakis, his drumsticks peeking out of his back pocket. He even attempted to comb and gel his hair, although it still sticks up all over the place. A sign reading *New Jersey All-State Band Auditions* points us up a flight of stairs to a hallway lined with folding chairs. I clench the handle of my sax case as we maneuver past a girl holding a trombone. Shane sits on one of the folding chairs, pulling the drumsticks out of his pocket. He taps out a nervous rhythm on the concrete wall.

"I wish you were first," Shane says. He's about to go in, but then there's over an hour before my audition. At least we can grab lunch after he nails his solo.

"I'm glad you're first," I say. "You can give me the inside scoop. Tell me which judges I need to suck up to."

"They're going to love you," Shane says. I place my sax case on the folding chair next to him and open it up, checking for my sheet music. "Just like I—"

"Oh no!" I stare at the open case, shuffling through the sheet music and checking the pockets. "No. No. No!"

"What?" Shane peers over my shoulder. It's not here. How is this possible? The one thing I need is not here.

"My neck strap," I say, still rummaging through the case, even though I know it's useless. "It's not here."

"You don't need it," Shane says trying to reassure me, but he's wrong. That neck strap is a part of me. Without it, my sax won't hang right. It'll all feel wrong. Shane grabs a spare black neck strap from my case and places it on one of the chairs. "Stevie, look at me."

Shane's confident eyes hold mine as he cups my chin in his hand.

"Top three reasons you don't need that neck strap. And only three because we don't have time for five."

"I'm going to skip the audition," I say, tears pricking my eyes. "I don't know why I thought I could make it as a sophomore. None of this will matter anyway. I'm sure we'll move again in a year or so."

"One," Shane says, never breaking his gaze. "You have practiced this song. You know it. I bet you could play it backwards by now."

"Shane Murphy," a woman announces into the hall. She's holding a clipboard and a pen, scanning the chairs. Shane doesn't even glance in her direction.

"Two, it's just a neck strap. You have a perfectly good spare one. You don't need the red one."

"*You* need to go. They called your name." I gesture at the clipboard woman, but Shane ignores me.

"Three, all you need is you. That's it. You got this," Shane says, kissing me.

"Shane Murphy?"

"Right here," Shane says, then whispers in my ear. "I'll be right back. Wait for me. Do not bail on this."

He heads for the audition room, drumsticks in hand. As Shane disappears behind the double doors, I plop down in a plastic chair and pull the spare black strap over my neck.

CHAPTER 15

Shane

"Shane, so glad to have you back," one of the judges says, but I don't look up to see which one. I pace in front of the drum set, not bothering to sit. "Whenever you're ready."

I'm ordering an Uber on my phone, punching in the student union address and Stevie's home address. The neck strap is there, it has to be. If I leave now, I should have enough time to grab it and get back before her audition. Light pours in from the floor-to-ceiling windows, casting a glare on my phone. I squint at the screen as I press the order button, the car only two minutes away.

"Shane?"

Three judges stare at me, then glance at each other. The woman on the end with cat-eye glasses taps a pencil on the desk. I'm about to give up the chance to jam with the best musicians in the state, to bang out a prestigious solo and feel Dad watching me play.

"I'm sorry, I have to go," I say, backing away from the drum set. The judges eye me, all furrowed brows and confusion. Even though I rationally tell myself to stay, that Stevie can audition with another neck strap, my whole body moves to the door. A frantic and desperate I-can't-let-her-fail feeling surges through me. We practiced over and over, and she finally got it, then finally got me. Stevie needs to know that not everything in her life will disappear, that she can achieve her goals before they are ripped away from her. She needs to know that people will stick around. Because even if she moves next year, in two years, whenever, I'm not going anywhere. The way I feel about her propels me to the door and I push it open, turning to the judges one last time.

"I'm really sorry," I say before taking off, ducking through the players in the hall so Stevie doesn't see me.

"Can you wait?" I plead with the Uber driver as he pulls up to Stevie's house. My heart pounds as I glance at my phone. I have exactly twenty-five minutes to retrieve the neck strap and get back to Rutgers, which is maybe doable if there's no traffic. Maybe. God, what am I doing? A text comes through on my phone and I glance at it.

Stevie

Where are you? You should've been
out a while ago. Everything okay?

Me

It went great! Sorry about lunch.
One of the judges wanted me to
talk to another drummer and I got
caught up. I'll be there soon.

Stevie

I'll wait for you.

Sweat breaks out on my palms as I fumble the phone.

"Can't wait," says my Uber driver, a middle-aged guy in a windbreaker. "Already confirmed another customer. You have to call another car."

"Can you cancel your next customer? I'll pay extra."

"Afraid not," he says, glancing at me in the rearview mirror. "Sorry about that."

"Shit!" rips from my mouth in agitation. "Sorry." I get out of the car, my heart rate spiking as he drives off stranding me in front of Stevie's house. I run up the front steps and ring the bell, but no one answers. The house is still and my whole body deflates as I realize they're not home. I peer at Stevie's window and seriously consider climbing the side of her house Spider-Man style when a splash of red in the grass catches my eye. Twenty-three minutes according to my phone, as I book it through the front lawn. The neck strap is half underneath the bare branches of the willow tree by the driveway. Twenty-two minutes and there's only one person who can help.

Me

I need your help. Can you drive me to Rutgers? I'm standing outside Stevie's house. It's important.

Drew

Be there in two.

Twenty minutes until Stevie's audition, and Drew's Jeep pulls up to the curb. I throw open the passenger side door, hop in, and click my seatbelt in place.

"Dude, you're out of breath," Drew says, raking his hair back. "What's going on?"

"Start driving," I say and Drew jams on the accelerator, the Jeep jolting forward. He's going fifty in a thirty-five and I don't tell him to slow down. "Stevie dropped her neck strap and I have to get it back to her before her audition. We only have twenty minutes."

"It's at least thirty to get to Rutgers," Drew says.

"That's why you need to go fast," I say.

"If I get a ticket, you're paying."

"Deal," I say, clutching the neck strap. "Just drive."

Trees and houses blur past us as Drew weaves around our neighborhood streets, heading for the highway. Snow begins to fall from the sky, dotting the windshield. Drew turns on the wipers but doesn't slow down. Eighteen minutes and pop bubblegum music grates through the speakers. I wipe sweat from my forehead, then rub my hands along my khakis.

"How'd your audition go?" Drew asks, tapping his thumb on the steering wheel in time to the music.

"It didn't," I say. "I bailed."

"What?" Drew turns to me then focuses back on the road, as a thin dusting of snow covers the asphalt.

"I had to get this." I hold up the neck strap.

"I don't think I've done anything like that for anyone in my life."

"Not true," I say. "You've backed me up in front of Brent for years."

"Doesn't count," Drew says. "I was just doing what anyone would do. Plus, now you don't need me anymore."

Ever since the scene at Dino's, Brent's been treating me like a celebrity. Scratch that, a king. He practically bows down to me in the halls and has said thank you more times than I want to hear. All the kids who used to ignore me throw me high fives and fist bumps on the way to class, like I'm a super-hero. It's funny how one moment can change everything.

"Look at what you're doing for me right now. It's a per-fectly good Saturday and you're spending it shuttling me to Rutgers so I can give my girlfriend her neck strap. Pretty selfless if you ask me."

I'll always need Drew, always.

"Just being a friend," Drew says and he's the best kind of friend, the best friend I'll ever have. "Plus, it's easier than watching some moving truck pack all of Dad's stuff and drive it off to his new family."

Drew bites his lip as he turns the radio up. I put my hand on his shoulder and he's quiet, his eyes fixed on the road. No discussion, just plain fact. Don's gone, but part of me knows there's still time to fix what's broken between them. I pull my hand back and just like that, the moment's over.

Fifteen minutes as Drew merges onto the parkway. We're never going to make it but he hits the accelerator hard fly-ing through lanes and passing any cars that slow us down. Green exit signs whiz by us, a few more to go before we reach Rutgers.

"Can you go any faster?" I glance at my phone as a white tractor trailer cuts in front of us.

Drew taps the blinker and sails into the right lane, the speedometer creeping up to eighty, eighty-five. Snow chunks smack at the windshield, obscuring my vision. Drew double-times the wipers. He's almost past the truck when it sud-denly begins veering into our lane. My hand flies to the door and I brace myself. Drew slams his fist on the horn, the Jeep screaming at the truck to get out of the way. And then it's all in slow motion. Drew's hand pounding the horn. The truck's front wheels barreling toward us. Drew flooring it, trying to make it past the truck before we collide.

"Watch it!" I yell, grabbing the wheel and yanking it hard to the right.

"No!" Drew screams, trying to steady the Jeep, but it's too late.

The car flies off the side of the road and we're flipping, tumbling down. I don't know which way is up, but trees snap and the Jeep crunches around me, metal jamming into my leg. Flashes of green fill the car and then everything stops. My leg throbs and when I reach down I don't feel my jeans, only wetness. Something hisses from behind me, and I pray it's not gas. I try to move, but I'm stuck. Everything blurs and waves, and the car is so twisted I can't see Drew. But I hear him. He screams for help over and over, his voice going hoarse. I can't keep my head up and rest it against the door frame. The window's shattered. My breath comes out short and fast. Mom and Lainey sit around a Monopoly board as I clutch the thimble in my fist. Dad watches me in a crowd as I pound out an intricate drum solo. Drew shoves a basketball at me, sweat dripping down his temples and I sink it into the basket. A coin flips high in the air, copper against a blue sky. And Stevie. Stevie on that first day, standing up to Brent Miller, *noticing* me. Stevie dancing to Pearl Jam, leaning her head on my shoulder on the train. Stevie kissing me and me breathing her in. The hissing grows louder. Drew screams for help, but he's fading and then I can't hear him anymore. My breath comes out short and fast. Short and fast. One, two, one, two. Until it slows, slows . . . slows.

PART THREE

HEADS

CHAPTER 1

Stevie

THE FUNERAL

We sit in silence on the church steps, remnants of last weekend's snowstorm beneath our feet. Family left for the gravesite, but we're not family. We have nowhere to go. He squeezes his eyes shut. After a moment he looks at me, his lashes wet. He pinches the bridge of his nose and closes his eyes again. His black suit is wrinkled and I'm sure the thought of ironing it never crossed his mind. I'm in an ugly black dress I bought with Mom at the mall. She plucked it from the rack and said something like *this one is pretty,* but I wasn't paying attention.

He pulls his knees up to his chin, burying his face in them. I haven't talked to him since last week, really talked to him, but I heard what happened. And even as I sit here now, resting my head on his shoulder, part of me hates him, almost as much as I hate myself.

My eyes are so tired it's like they forgot how to stop tears. When I think I have none left it starts all over again, and I'm wiping my cheeks or soaking my pillow in the middle of the night. Everything in me hurts and this is more than sadness. This is unbearable, like wanting to run but being frozen still. Forced to face a truth I wish was a lie. I'm glued to these church steps, because if I get up and go home, this whole sickening day will have actually happened. And I want to erase it all.

Ironically, the day is perfect. A cloudless December sky. The accident feels like a year ago. They were driving to find me, chasing after my liar's text. *Got in an Uber. Not auditioning. Leave me alone.* But I was in the bathroom, nowhere to be found. I allow myself to pick at my cuticle until Drew covers my trembling hand with his.

"Where were you?" he asks quietly, a thin layer of accusation coating his voice. I jerk my head up and pull my hand away. "I texted you nonstop. It took you over an hour to respond. Why?"

I turned my phone off. I was so pissed at them that I needed to silence it all, to get through the audition without all the noise. But now, the idea of them flipping a coin for me seems so trivial. Shane's gone. I can't yell and scream at him. I can't grab him by the shoulders and shake him until he explains himself. Deep down I'm certain he cared about me. I heard the beginning of their conversation and watched the way Shane's face came alive when he said my name, how it crumbled when he noticed me standing there.

I'll never hear him apologize.

"I was angry," I whisper. Now a different anger surges through me, an unstoppable rage burning in my gut—at Drew, at myself, at the whole damn universe. "I turned my phone off."

"I called your house." Drew's eyes are flat, hollow. His dark hair falls over a large bandage on his forehead. "Your mom said you weren't home yet. How is that possible? You left before we did."

I close my eyes, stinging tears seeping through the lids. My breath is caught somewhere between my lungs and my throat. I can't look at him.

"I didn't leave." My voice is a garbled mess. The December air bites at my tear-stained cheeks, but I barely feel it. "I was in the student union bathroom when I texted you."

The realization falls over Drew's face like a cloud shifting in front of the sun. His chest heaves up and down fast and he winces like it hurts to breathe. I bite at my lip as my throat gets tight, my lungs pinched together in agony.

"You never got in an Uber?" Drew's nostrils flare.

"No," I whisper, my face drenched in tears. "I only texted about the Uber so you and Shane would leave. So I could audition with a clear head. I was upset and turned my phone off."

Drew stands and sways a bit before stepping to me, favoring his right leg. He clasps his hands behind his head as his breath forms a ghostly cloud that quickly vanishes in the air. I can feel his eyes on me, but I don't have the strength to look at him, to witness the pain I caused.

"We were chasing after you, Stevie. We were chasing after you, and you weren't even *there*."

I finally shift my eyes to Drew's, and he looks like he's about to get sick. I'm crying so hard my shoulders begin to shake.

"I know," I choke out. "Don't you think I know that?"

This tiny detail, this one small link in a chain of events that led to the worst possible event, will haunt me forever. It'll stay with me. It'll torture me and follow me, and I'll never be able to forgive myself.

"Fuck," he whispers to himself. He breathes in and out fast, like he's about to hyperventilate. "I can't think straight."

"What happened?" I ask because I need the truth, from his lips only. I need to know what went down in the car, on that road, to try and understand what my mind is struggling to unravel.

"I can't do this," Drew says, walking to a row of hedges beside the church, a few tiny flowers still clinging to life in spite of the snow last week. "I can't fucking do this."

"I need to know what happened, please." My heart clenches in my chest as my voice breaks. "You're the only one who can tell me."

Drew takes a deep breath in and pinches the bridge of his nose again, looking at the sky. Tears spill out the corner of his eyes and he pushes them away.

"It was the snow and the damn deer," Drew says, his voice strained, like it hurts to say each word. "Shane took off his seatbelt. Wanted his jacket off, God knows why. A deer jumped out of nowhere. Shane grabbed the wheel and jerked it away from me. He got scared. He was so scared."

He crouches in front of the bushes, his back rising and falling fast. I follow him, putting my hand on his shoulder, but he shrugs me off.

"And I—I couldn't control the car. I lost control," Drew whispers, then turns and gets sick all over the flowers.

We don't talk during the drive home from the funeral. Drew doesn't bother turning on the radio. It's the loudest kind of silence, the kind that makes your head hurt from all the screaming inside. We're in a loaner car, similar to his old one which must be totaled. This Jeep is olive green and filled with that chemical new car smell. No Mardi Gras beads swing from the rearview mirror. Drew drives carefully, waiting an extra beat at stop signs and slowing for yellow lights instead of blazing through them. When he pulls up to my house, I jump out before the Jeep is fully in park.

Drew rolls down the window and yells, "Stevie, wait."

I don't have the energy to turn around, but I stop walking, midway up the path to my front porch. Shane's funeral crashes through me. It settles on my skin and through my body, now a permanent piece of me.

"We didn't mean it," Drew says. He's talking about the coin toss, trying to make one thing right in a world where everything has gone wrong. "Shane and me . . ."

"Shane's dead," I say, my back to Drew. My legs give out and my knees crash to the pavement.

The car door opens, then slams shut again. I expect to hear Drew's boots on the walkway, but then I remember he wore dress shoes for the funeral. When I glance over my shoulder, he's on the hood of his car, like that night at the beach. But he's hunched over, balled into himself. I make my way back to the car and climb up next to him, pulling the hem of my dress over my knees.

"I'm sorry," I say, the cold air sending a shiver across my skin. I apologize for being so blunt. I apologize for being in that bathroom, for lying. I even apologize for Drew's pain, my pain. But an apology will never be enough.

"It's all my fucking fault," he says quietly. His arms wrap around me, enveloping me in his smell—lemons and pine needles. I want to fall into him, let him hold me, and cry into his shoulder. But I can't. Because he was driving the car, and he flipped a coin over me, and because most of all, I wish he were Shane.

TAILS

CHAPTER 2

Stevie

MILLBROOK HOSPITAL

The generic black saxophone strap dangles from my neck as I burst through the hospital doors, the smell of ammonia stinging my nose. I sign the visitor sheet at the hospital entrance, my chicken scratch name barely legible.

When I get to the waiting room, Drew doesn't notice me. He sits on a rust-orange chair, his head bowed in his hands. His knee pokes through a rip in his jeans, jittering up and down like a jackhammer. A white bandage covers most of his right arm and there's a nasty gash on his cheek.

"Drew?" I ask, my stomach turning over. He slowly raises his head at the sound of my voice. His eyes are raw and desperate.

"Stevie." The winter pink on his cheeks and nose drains from his exhausted face, his skin bone white. "I texted you."

"I know." My heart pounds, desperate to know why Shane

isn't sitting beside Drew, to know where Shane is, praying he's still *here*. Back at the audition, I was already panicking. Shane was late to meet me for lunch, and I stopped buying his questionable excuse—that he was helping another drummer. My frantic texts went unanswered and as each minute passed in silence, I tore another cuticle from my nail. Moments before my turn, a message from Drew detailing the car wreck and the hospital address dinged on my phone. Suddenly, the audition didn't matter.

"There was a car accident. Shane." Drew tries to stand but thinks better of it. His hand trembles as he stares at me. He keeps talking, telling me the pieces I already know. I grab hold of the black neck strap, the one Shane gave me, his voice encouraging me, believing in me. A sickness swims in my stomach, threatening to push its way up my throat. Drew takes a deep breath as his nostrils flare and his eyes cloud over with tears. He closes them for a second and starts again.

"He was at your house. He left the audition to look for your red neck strap. He found it and asked me to drive him back to Rutgers, to bring it to you."

He left the audition for me, for a piece of fabric. For a moment my heart expands at Shane's selflessness, but then I notice the blood stain on the bottom of Drew's sweatshirt. My stomach revolts again as pins and needles march across my skin.

"It's pretty bad, Stevie." His voice is completely shot, like he's been screaming.

All at once I can't feel my legs and I lean into the chair next to Drew, my breath coming out fast.

"Is he . . ."

I can't get the words out. My mouth is dry, like I swallowed sandpaper. My ice-cold hands rake at my knees as the room begins to spin.

"He's not awake." Drew's dark eyes swim with sadness. "They're not sure if he's going to wake up."

HEADS

CHAPTER 3

Stevie

AFTER THE FUNERAL

It's been two days since Shane's funeral. When I walk into school for the first time since the accident, I feel sick. Part of me could puke, part of me wants to sleep, and part of me is drained, like someone attached a hose to me and sucked out all the happiness. I don't go to my locker first, and instead walk to the band room.

As I head through the double doors, I'm shocked to see the whole band scattered about the room whispering quietly. Shane's drum set glares at me, silent and waiting to be played. Two drumsticks rest on top, right where he left them. I run my fingers along the edge of the bass drum, willing him to appear, wishing for the impossible.

"Stevie, take a seat," Mr. Abella says like he's coaxing a baby bird out of its nest. The plastic chair is extra hard when I sit, and no matter what I can't get comfortable. I glance at Drew. He stares into space, like his body is here but his mind, spirit, and soul are somewhere else.

"I'm glad you're all back at school." Mr. Abella straightens his glasses, eyeing Drew and me. His voice is unsteady, and his eyes are drawn, like he barely slept. "The principal says you are free to use this space all day if you need to. There will be a counselor here if anyone needs to talk. I'm here to talk too, if you need . . ."

"Fuck this."

The entire band turns to Drew's careless voice.

"Excuse me?" Mr. Abella says, taking a small step forward

"I said." Drew raises his voice. "Fuck. This."

"Drew, I know you're upset . . ." Mr. Abella starts to say something about grief, but Drew interrupts him.

"Upset? Mr. Abella, seriously? Upset? I'd be upset if someone dented my Jeep in the parking lot. My best friend is gone. And it's on me. I don't think there's a word for what I am right now. So yeah. Fuck. This."

"Stop it," I say under my breath.

"Stop what?"

He slumps in his chair, arms folded across his chest, and his hair is in his face. His shirt is sort of tucked in, like he was in the middle of getting dressed and forgot to finish. I don't recognize the look in his eyes, his normal sparkle replaced by an icy stare. It's like I'm looking at a stranger and it's terrifying.

Everyone gapes at us, and a wave of utter sadness washes over me. My eyes blur with tears and I try my best to swallow them back, but it's no use.

"You barely knew him," Drew says, his eyes slicing through me, stinging my flesh.

I *knew* him. Maybe it was only for a little while, but I knew him. And he knew me, better than any friend has before. A once-in-a-lifetime connection that's gone forever, that I'll never get back. I miss him so much that it's hard to exist, to sit in this chair and listen to Drew minimize it, like it was nothing. What I'm about to say will cross a line, but I can't stop myself. The words scream from inside my head, demanding to be let out.

"I wish he won that coin toss."

Drew stands so fast that his chair flies out from underneath him crashing into Shane's drum set. Cymbals spin on the floor and the drumsticks roll down the aisle. The snare wobbles back and forth on its side before it stops completely.

"Drew, maybe you should take five," Mr. Abella suggests, but it's more like an order.

"Fine," Drew says before looking at me. "It wasn't a game, Stevie."

Drew heads for Shane's drum set and quietly puts everything back in place. He grabs his bag and jacket, his bloodshot eyes glancing back at the drums before he heads out of class, slamming the door behind him. A slow murmur flows through the band room, making my head pound. The bell for first period rings, but no one moves.

The day is a blur, and once it's over I sit on the curb, stretching my legs on the concrete. Since the funeral Mom has insisted on picking me up after school, but she's not here yet. The olive-green loaner Jeep is parked in Drew's usual spot. When I look closer, I see he's inside. His head rests on the steering wheel and I'm not sure if he's moving. A panic rises in my chest and I'm about to go check on him when his shoulders jerk up and down. The car shakes as he picks his head up and slams his fists on the steering wheel. He takes a deep breath and looks to his left and then to his right. I keep perfectly still, never taking my eyes off him. His chest heaves, slower now. He wipes his eyes on the inside of his sweatshirt and runs his fingers through his hair. I stand to go to him, to take back those awful words I said, but a black town car pulls up beside the Jeep. An older man gets out wearing a hoodie, jeans, and sneakers. I recognize him from the Netflix documentary and music blogs—Don Mason. He knocks on the window of the Jeep as Drew flings the door open, almost knocking over his dad.

"Fuck you," Drew yells, pushing Don's shoulders. "Go home. You don't live here anymore."

Don says something I can't quite make out and Drew lunges at him again, but this time, Don catches him and wraps his arms around his back. He smooths Drew's hair back, saying something in his ear and then Drew falls into him, sobbing and shaking, right in the middle of the parking lot. A couple of people stare, like I am, but mostly everyone gives them their space.

Don repeats the same string of words into Drew's ear and as I squint, I can read his lips.

I got you.

Drew steps back from his father and wipes his face on the sleeve of his sweatshirt. My eyes lock with his, and he flashes me a half smile, an apology smile. I step off the curb to apologize first, for lying about the bathroom, for the despicable thing I said in class. But Drew looks away and gets into the town car with his dad, leaving me and the Jeep alone in the lot.

TAILS

CHAPTER 4

Stevie

MILLBROOK HOSPITAL

Drew and I navigate a maze of sterile white halls, sickness wafting through the air. We reach Shane's room, and I hesitate at the door, afraid of what's behind it. Drew nudges my arm and we walk inside, my legs weak. The room is all linoleum floors and white bedding, machines and wires. Lainey sits on the edge of a hospital bed, half hidden by a flimsy sea-green curtain. Her stringy hair obscures her face, and her boot shakes against the metal frame.

"Lainey, please," Kathy says from a chair in the corner, her voice broken and tired. Lainey steadies her foot but doesn't respond. Drew and I approach them slowly. I try to take in a breath, but it gets stuck somewhere deep in my lungs.

Once we're on the other side of the curtain, my breath shoots through my mouth, my chest heaving fast. The bed is empty. No Shane. No one speaks or even looks at us. I lose my balance, swaying into Drew who steadies me with his arm.

"Where is he?" Drew asks, his voice shaky.

Kathy and Lainey turn their heads slowly, like it's an effort to acknowledge us.

"CT scan," Lainey says, her voice flat.

Kathy glances at Lainey then turns her attention to Drew, tears filling her eyes. She pushes them off her face and takes a deep breath.

"I'm so sorry, Kathy," Drew says, his voice bending and breaking. "I didn't mean . . . I . . . I'm so sorry."

"It's not your fault." Kathy stands, pulling Drew close for a hug, but he swallows hard, his hair hanging over his eyes. She's right, it's not his fault. It's mine. They were speeding back to the audition to bring me that neck strap. Shane was in that car because of me.

"Oh Stevie," Kathy says as her eyes connect with mine over Drew's shoulder. She releases him and envelops me in a rose-scented hug.

"At least Shane wore his seatbelt," Kathy says as she resumes her spot in the corner chair. "The officer said he wouldn't be alive if he didn't have it on."

I have to sit down. But there are no other chairs, so I lean against the wall with Drew.

"He's in an induced coma," Lainey says, her foot twitching again.

"For how long?" I ask, my eyes shifting from Kathy to Lainey. Lainey shrugs.

"When's he going to wake up?" Drew asks. But no one answers.

HEADS

CHAPTER 5

Stevie

AFTER THE FUNERAL

I turn up the music, pushing my headphones close to my ears in an attempt to block out the world. The day of the accident runs on a loop through my mind, and I hate myself a bit more each time around. I pull my knees to my chest, tears dotting my leggings. Mom and Joey are out on errands and I'm alone on the living room couch, as usual. No word from Sarah all day, our friendship officially a joke.

I think about eating, something I haven't done much of since the funeral. The kitchen is fully stocked but nothing sounds remotely appetizing. I turn the music up even louder, the notes and chords hurting, likely damaging my eardrums. But I only cry harder because for the first time in my life music isn't helping. Nothing is.

A hand touches my shoulder and I jump, my heart flying up to my throat. Dad stands in front of me, then kneels down by my side with a tissue. I pull the headphones off as he blots my face like he used to when I skinned a knee or fell off my bike.

"What are you doing here?" Dad should be in Boston.

"I left as soon as I could."

He sits beside me, dropping a green duffel bag on the rug. His Jets hat is clipped to the strap next to an airline tag. Dark circles shadow his eyes, and the tiny wrinkles around his mouth appear deeper than I remember.

"What do you mean, you left? Isn't the game in a couple days?"

Dad sighs, and a familiar unease settles in my bones. We're leaving again, I know it. On top of everything, I'm going to have to pack up my room, trek somewhere new, and start again. I don't have it in me this time.

"I told them my family needed me." He shifts to me and his eyes go soft in a way I've never seen before. "You're more important than a football game."

My heart swells at the words I've longed to hear my entire life. And then all at once I'm nervous Dad will lose everything. I can't be responsible for one more thing, especially after sneaking around with Drew behind Dad's back. Especially after the accident. I'm not a daughter worth risking everything for.

"Will you lose your job?"

"Probably." I brace myself for the news, but then he smiles like he doesn't have a care in the world. "But I'm thinking I might try for a college gig in the area. I took all the NFL jobs for the money, to provide a comfortable life for you and Joey. But we will be fine if I take a pay cut, and no amount of money is worth being away from my family."

"Wait, what?" I don't deserve this, not now. Not when the one person I want to share this news with is gone. "Why?"

"What happened to Shane . . . I can't ever lose you like

that. It's enough with the traveling and moving." Dad puts his arm around my shoulder, and I lean into him, a lump forming in my throat. "I'm so sorry you lost your friend."

Tears fall down my cheeks again and Dad rocks me, squeezing my shoulder, shushing in my ear like I'm a little kid. I wipe my face with my sweatshirt sleeve and look into Dad's blue eyes.

"Dad," I say, dreading these next words, words that have to come out of my mouth to make everything right. "I was sneaking around with Drew. I'm so sorry I lied."

I expect disappointment to crash over Dad's face, but instead he looks defeated, lost in his own sadness.

"I don't like that you lied, but I also should have been around more. And I should have listened to you more. I want you to know that from now on, I'm listening."

That's all I've ever wanted to hear.

Still, my chest is heavy, the weight of my actions making it hard to breathe.

"I was in the bathroom," I say, my whole body tensing, my breath shallow. "I told them I went home, that I bailed on the audition. That's why they got in the car. To go after me. To convince me to go back inside. But Dad, I was in the bathroom the whole time. I *did* audition. While Shane lay in the middle of the road dying, I was in the middle of a pointless saxophone solo."

I can't catch my breath, but I also can't stop talking, the confession tumbling from my mouth.

"They flipped a coin for me, to decide which one of them would get to ask me out. I was so pissed, Dad. So beyond pissed. So I lied and I hate myself for it. If I didn't lie, then maybe—"

"Stevie, stop." Dad's eyes are on my side, fully and unconditionally. I'm still struggling to breathe as he pulls me in close and rubs circles on my back. "Slow down. Take a deep breath."

Dad counts to ten and I inhale, soaking the shoulder of his polo with tears until my body calms. He slowly releases me and looks me in the eye.

"Those boys did a thoughtless thing flipping a coin, that I won't excuse. You had every right to be upset. You did the best you could."

"But what if—"

"There are no what-ifs." Dad puts both hands on my shoulders. "Only what is. You did not cause that accident. Do you understand me?"

I nod, sniffling, but I can't stop replaying it all in my head, rewinding to the beginning and praying for the chance to start over.

"I love you, Stevie girl, you need to know that." He kisses the top of my head.

"I love you too." I bury my face into his shoulder. "Dad?"

"Yeah?"

"This hurts too much. Why does this hurt so much?"

Dad sighs and smooths hair away from my forehead.

"You really cared about him, didn't you?"

"Yeah," I whisper.

"I wish I could take your pain away. I would take it all from you in a heartbeat if I could," Dad says, his voice breaking. "But the only way out of pain is through, and it might take you a while to get to the other side. But I promise you there's another side waiting for you. And when you feel stuck, I'm here."

A sob escapes my mouth and lands on his shoulder. He pulls me to him, hugging me tight, and says, "From now on, I'm here."

TAILS

CHAPTER 6

Stevie

MILLBROOK HOSPITAL

"Doritos or Cheetos?" Drew asks, holding two snack bags.

"Neither," I say, my eyes fixed on Shane. Kathy and Lainey went home for a shower and a change of clothes. "Not hungry."

The room is dark except for the blinking lights of the machines keeping Shane alive. Tubes and wires stick out of him, and a ventilator controls his breathing, his chest rising with the whoosh of the machine. His eyes are closed, and his arms are still by his side. A hospital blanket is pulled up to his torso, and a huge bandage covers most of his forehead. His leg is raised above the bed in a cast. Drew pulls a chair next to mine and opens both bags, the fiery Dorito cheese stinging my nose.

"You should eat something."

I wave him away. He crunches on a Dorito and I'm struck by what a loud chewer he is. I never would have thought Drew Mason would be a loud chewer.

"He's going to wake up, right?" I ask, my voice barely a whisper. "I mean, once they bring him out of the coma, he's going to be okay, right?"

"If I were the one in that hospital bed and Shane were sitting here, he'd say . . . yes, he'll be okay, I know he will." Drew sighs heavy and slow. "But I'm the one sitting here and he's in that damn bed and I have no fucking clue if he'll wake up."

Drew puts the snack bags on a tray by the bed. "For the record, I'd trade places with him if I could."

I reach out and place my hand in Shane's open palm and run my fingers over the drumming calluses. He's warm and present, like he's here with us.

"Do you think he can hear us?"

"God, I hope not," Drew says. "If he can, he's probably making fun of us in his head right now. Like, stop being so dramatic, guys, it's all good."

I laugh a little. A drop of liquid drips down the IV bag and slides through the tube to Shane's hand.

"Why did this happen?"

"I knew it was a gamble, trying to pass that truck." Drew's voice breaks as he shifts away from me. "He pulled the wheel at the last minute. Probably saved my life . . . again." Drew's empty eyes connect with mine.

"It's my fault," I say, never breaking eye contact. "If I didn't drop that neck strap, if I wasn't so careless, he never would have asked you to bring it to me."

"You weren't the one driving the car."

"*You* weren't the reason he was on the road in the first place."

We stare at each other, then shift our gaze to Shane, his body desperately clinging to life.

"Maybe it's no one's fault," Drew says, sighing.

"Then *why* did this happen?"

"I don't know." Drew hides behind his hair and sniffs in, his nose twitching.

"Drew?"

He clears his throat, looking at me with bloodshot eyes.

"Shitty things just happen. We try to make sense of it to make ourselves feel better. To attach some sort of meaning to the darkness. But sometimes there is no bigger meaning. There's no why. There's only what is. And like I said, this is a shitty thing."

"Shane would say there's always some bigger plan." My finger traces his palm. "He believes in everything."

"I know," Drew says, gazing at his friend. "What do you believe?"

"I don't know." I give Shane's hand a little squeeze. Maybe if he wakes up, I'll have an answer.

CHAPTER 7

Stevie

AFTER THE FUNERAL

"I brought you a surprise," Dad says, standing. I'm still processing the news. We're staying in town. For the first time in my life, I'm *staying*. "Thought you could use some cheering up."

Dad walks to the front door and opens it, saying, "Come on in."

"Shit, this house is big," Sarah says, gazing up at the ceiling. At first the sight of her doesn't seem real. She's in an oversize sweatshirt and black leggings. Her short hair is back in a ponytail except for the silver streaks that hang by her face. She locks eyes with me and cocks her head to the side, her face filled with concern and sympathy.

"Sarah?"

She runs full speed in my direction, throwing her arms around my neck. Her citrus shampoo envelops me and grounds me, a momentary escape from the immense hurt that has set-

tled over my life. For the first time since Shane died, an unexpected smile breaks free on my face.

"My work here is done," Dad says, as he flashes me a
thumbs-up. "I'll be upstairs if you need me," he says over his
shoulder as he disappears from the living room.

"I'm starving," Sarah says as she releases my neck and
marches to the kitchen, rummaging through the cabinets.
She pulls down a bag of chips, salsa, and Mom's secret stash
of chocolate, which she somehow finds easily.

"How did you . . . How are you here?" I ask, sitting
on one of the counter stools and swiveling around to
face her. My throat catches when I notice the black and
gold ponytail holder in her hair. She's still wearing it, like
I am.

"Your dad bought the ticket. But I can only stay the night.
My mom said I can't miss more than one day of school. But I
figured one night is better than none." Sarah scoops a huge
mound of salsa on a chip and pops the whole thing into her
mouth, smiling. "Want?"

"No thanks," I say, my stomach still on strike.

"Please tell me you're eating."

"I'm eating." My voice squeaks out as I shrug. Sarah raises
an eyebrow.

"Gotta bring out the big guns, then," Sarah says, as she
pulls bread, cheese, and butter from the fridge. I know where
she's going with this—her famous grilled cheese. "Where does
your mom keep the pans?"

"That one." I gesture at a bottom cabinet and Sarah retrieves a large frying pan.

"I cook," Sarah says, lighting the stovetop. "You talk."

"There's nothing to say." I sigh. "Everything just . . ."

"Sucks. I know. I'm so sorry."

Sarah doesn't ask me if I'm okay because she knows I'm not and she knows that asking only makes it worse.

"It was my fault," I say, as bread and cheese crackle in the pan. Sarah presses a spatula onto the sandwich as the edges brown.

"How was it your fault?"

I launch into the whole story. I tell her about Drew and Shane and the coin toss that led to me to Drew. I tell her how first I fell for Drew, and then slowly for Shane. I tell her how being with Shane felt like coming home. I tell her about hiding in the bathroom and how Shane was in that accident because of me. And after I'm done telling her all of it, I begin to cry again, wet heavy sobs.

"That's not your fault," Sarah says as she turns off the burner and transfers the grilled cheese to a plate. "That's life."

"That's not life," I say, brushing tears off my face. "That's death and it's unfair and wrong and it makes no sense."

"That's true," Sarah says, sliding the grilled cheese across the counter until it lands under my chin, the smell of grease wafting up my nose. My stomach grumbles but I ignore it. "But it was an accident. Out of your control."

"Do our choices even matter? We all walk around thinking we have control over our lives. But in the end, we bounce around like a pinball in a machine, landing wherever gravity, and whatever other forces we want to believe in, take us."

Sarah grabs half of the sandwich and takes a bite, her eyes shifting to the side. When she's done chewing, she looks straight at me.

"It's both, Stevie. Our choices matter. *Your* choices matter. But you don't have complete control. No one does. This *wasn't* your fault."

Sarah's words are a release, but not a reprieve. Maybe one day I'll believe her. I inhale and try to breathe it all out—the accident, my grief, a loss I may never comprehend.

"*This* you have control over," Sarah says, gesturing at the sandwich. "And you should most definitely choose to eat."

Sarah nudges my shoulder and I grab the grilled cheese from her hand, taking a big bite. As the gooey cheese melts inside my mouth, a sense of calm settles over my tired body. But it's not only the food. After months of wishing Sarah was by my side, she's finally here.

"I made my first grilled cheese in fourth grade when my grandfather passed away," Sarah says, a shadow passing across her pale blue eyes. "Sometimes it's the smallest things, the least expected moments that help."

"How did I not know that?" I ask, my heart breaking for a young Sarah grasping for comfort, searching for a way to mend her broken world.

"You never asked," she says, and she's right. There's a lot I don't know about Sarah because I never asked, never took the time to notice. I always figured I was moving, and the more I knew, the more I would eventually have to leave behind.

"I should have asked," I say. "About a lot of things."

For the first time, I realize it's me. It's been me all along. I worked so hard to shield myself from the pain of leaving friends behind that I never really let them in. Except Shane. He was the one person who got through. Maybe it's not about the moving and leaving. Maybe it's about being in the moment while it's happening and living.

"I'm sorry I haven't been around," Sarah says. "I've been a shitty friend. The time difference is so hard. Every time I try to call you it's either too early or too late, you know? But that's no excuse. The bottom line is I miss you like hell."

"You can't be a shitty friend to someone who doesn't let

you in to begin with." My voice is filled with regret for holding Sarah at arm's length, afraid of losing her. I wasted too much time protecting myself.

"I love you," I say, the words falling from my mouth easily. I've never told Sarah how much her friendship meant and still means to me.

"I know," Sarah says, smirking. "I love you too."

Shane's been gone for two weeks and I'm beginning to forget the sound of his laugh. After the funeral I called his phone and listened to his voice mail greeting, trying to memorize the exact timbre of his voice. But his mom must have canceled his plan, because now instead of Shane's voice there's a generic automated message.

I turn the combination on my locker and yank the door open. It's an absolute mess. Books are vertical and horizontal, and pens are loose in the back. As I grab a notebook a little folded piece of paper falls to the floor. The hall empties out as I pick it up. I slowly unfold it and recognize the handwriting immediately, falling against my locker, my heart pounding.

I'm not sure if I can read it, but I can't *not* read it. As my eyes skim over the first sentence, I can hear Shane's voice clearly, as if he's standing right next to me. My throat catches as the paper shakes in my hands. I miss him so completely, so desperately, like a hole that can never be filled.

Stevie:

I thought about writing you this letter every day this year. I really should have had the courage to tell you in person. I also should have told you sooner. I should have told you the second it happened. But I'm telling you now. That first day we all met . . . Drew and I flipped a coin to decide who would get to ask you out. I promised him I wouldn't say anything, but some promises are made to be broken. The penny landed in Drew's favor and the rest is history, but I thought you should know. You should also know it wasn't a bet or game for either of us—it was real.

But this note isn't about Drew. It's about me and the way I feel about you. I should be thankful really. It's because of that coin toss that we became such great friends. Hanging out with you is the best part of my day. I can't fall asleep without first hearing your voice on the other end of the phone. But, at the same time, I'm tired of pretending. I can't not tell you anymore. Because I think you might feel it too.

If I could turn back time, I would tell Drew to forget his coin toss. I would have told you then what I'm telling you now. I love you.

—Shane

TAILS

CHAPTER 8

Stevie

MILLBROOK HOSPITAL

An incoming text dings on my phone and jostles me from sleep. My neck spasms as I uncurl myself and slowly sit up on the waiting room bench. I'm still in my audition outfit, my white button-down wrinkled and untucked. It's been two days and still no change. My phone dings again and I check the messages.

> Sarah
> **Update?**

> Sarah
> **Any change?**

I pop a piece of gum in my mouth as I write Sarah back. She's been checking in nonstop, our friendship slowly piecing back together. But it's like we're building an entirely new puzzle, the pieces of us changed by time and distance.

Me
Nothing yet.

Sarah
Okay keep me posted. I'm here.

Drew slowly wakes up and wipes the corners of his eyes. He winces as he sits, cradling his bandaged right arm.

"What time is it?" he asks, his voice raw.

"Nine a.m.," I say, the sun streaming through the window, making everything in this waiting room too bright. Drew suddenly laughs and I turn to see Ray barreling toward us, a giant bouquet of blue and gold helium balloons trailing behind her.

"Guys!" she yells when she sees us.

"Shhh!" An older lady presses her finger to her lips and glares at Ray.

"Sorry!" Ray hunches and pulls the balloons through the aisle of chairs to the corner. I spot a couple blue ones that say *Get Well*.

"What are you doing here?" Drew asks, but it sounds more like an accusation than a question, like Ray has no right visiting Shane. They aren't exactly friends, so I get where Drew's coming from, but knowing Ray, she's trying to do what's right.

"She's allowed to be here," I say, standing next to her, raising my eyebrows at Drew. He blows out a breath of air and manages a small smile.

"Sorry, just stressed," Drew says as he stands and hugs Ray. "It's cool you came. What's up with the balloons?"

"They're from the football team," Ray says, struggling to untangle the ribbons. "We also want Shane to have this."

Ray pulls a card from the pocket of her jacket and hands it to me.

"You can read it," she says. "I know you want to."

The card says *Get Well Soon* on the front and the inside is filled with signatures from the team, from people who aren't friends with Shane, but still care about him. My eyes scan the names until they reach the corner of the card. Someone wrote an actual message.

I'm sorry for all of it and you'd better pull through.
—Brent

I flip the card around and point to Brent's message as Drew's eyes skim the handwritten note.

"About time." Drew smirks and shakes his head.

"Thanks for coming," I say to Ray, as she throws her arms around my neck, hugging me. "For being here for Shane."

"I'm here for you too, you know."

Ray's not only here to deliver the balloons and card. She's here for me, and even though she'll probably never admit it, I bet she's here for Drew too. She gazes at him as he scratches the back of his head, obviously uncomfortable. Ray shifts her attention to me and asks how I'm doing. I'm about to tell her that I'm scared, that even though I've left so many people behind with each move, I've never truly lost someone. And the difference between leaving and losing is so clear to me now, a difference I wish I could have understood years ago. But I don't get to tell Ray any of it because a loud beeping fills the hall. Drew snaps his head to the noise, then looks at me.

"Let's go," he says, taking off toward the sound, me right behind him. "Wait here," he shouts back to Ray.

Drew and I round the corner as a team of doctors rushes into Shane's room. Kathy and Lainey are ushered into the hallway.

"Stand back," orders the doctor. Lainey's hands cover her mouth and her eyes are wide, unblinking. Kathy stares at the ceiling, mouthing prayers at the fluorescent light. Drew paces in front of the window, trying to see past the curtain that blocks his view. The beeping grows louder and faster as white lab coats surround Shane.

"They brought him out of the coma and his heart rate . . ." Kathy's voice trails off, her eyes still fixed on the ceiling. The beeping is so fast, a panicked alarm piercing the air.

"Fuck," Drew says under his breath, his eyes wild.

Finally, the beeping slows to a steady pace and my heart slows with it. A procession of lab coats exits the room, nodding at us. Kathy rushes to the lead doctor.

"He's stable. Not out of the woods yet though." The doctor is tall and authoritative, but his words are short and precise. Kathy nods, tears spilling out of the corner of her eyes. Lainey takes hold of her hand.

"How long do we wait?" Lainey asks.

"There's no telling. I'll be back to check on him during my rounds."

The doctor turns, his lab coat trailing behind him. He doesn't hear me say, "But he's going to wake up, right?"

I close my eyes and will Shane to wake up, picturing the dimple forming in his cheek when he smiles. I imagine him sitting up in his hospital bed, forking a piece of cheesecake and rubbing his stomach as he swallows it down. I repeat the same word in my head as I feel Shane's lips on mine, kissing away the fear that consumes my body.

Please.

CHAPTER 9

Stevie

AFTER THE FUNERAL

I don't tell anyone about the note. Not even Drew. And I never will. It's a secret that keeps me close to Shane. I reread it constantly, and it's almost like he's with me.

It's sundown and Mom thinks I'm in my room, but I'm outside under the weeping willow. I'm listening to "Fields of Gold" on my headphones, wondering if Shane is looking down on me. Pinks and oranges cut through the bare branches, bouncing off the grass, and the notepaper almost glows. I read it and reread it, and reread it again.

I picture Shane at the beginning of the year, all sweaty and awkward. I dig my heels into the grass remembering how I longed to stay put in New Jersey, to find my place. How I cared so much about being the *new girl*. I always thought that with each move I was leaving the important things behind. But all the towns, people, and experiences came with me. They made me *me*. It doesn't matter where I live. It's the people who know me, who *really* know me, that matter. I understand it now. Now that it's too late. Divots form where my shoes were, and I shuffle the soil back together, the ground hard and cold.

The branches rustle, startling me, a dusting of snow falling to the earth. I quickly shove the note in my back pocket and take my headphones off. When Drew pokes his head in I scoot backwards. No one has ever been under the willow with me before. He sits, leaning back on his hands.

"Cool spot," he says, looking at the branches.

"How did you know I was here?"

"I saw your shoes poking out when I parked." He taps my foot with his.

Drew's quiet, pulling blades of grass one by one from the ground. His hands move faster, his eyes darkening as he goes.

"I can't feel like this anymore," he says, letting out a long breath. "It's like I'm drowning."

"I know."

Drew reaches for my hand but pulls away fast.

"Sorry," he mutters. "I don't know what I'm doing."

"Everything is upside down," I say. After the accident, Drew and I didn't just lose Shane. We lost each other.

"I can't make sense of it. I replay that whole day, trying to find the part where it all went wrong," Drew says. "Me and the car and that fucking deer. Shane grabbing the wheel. Why did he have to grab the wheel?"

"I don't know."

We sit in silence, the winter air picking up and shaking the willow. I pull my hat over my ears. The chill makes me shudder, and it's like no matter what I do, I'll never be warm again.

"The coin toss . . ."

"Drew, you don't have to . . ."

"I needed to come here and tell you. It wasn't us trying to . . . I mean, we weren't . . . You weren't a bet," he says.

"I'm sorry I said I wished Shane won. That was awful, maybe the worst thing I've ever said."

"I deserved it."

"No," I say, looking him straight in his bloodshot eyes. "You didn't."

"We never should have flipped that coin. Maybe if it landed on the other side . . ." Drew runs his fingers through the grass. He's quiet again, picking at each blade, until a small brown spot of dirt appears between his boots.

"You can't think like that," I say.

"You haven't thought it? If the coin landed on tails, maybe you would have been with Shane. Maybe he wouldn't have been in my car."

Of course I've thought it, and it's maddening. The idea that something so small as a coin toss could change everything makes me sick to my stomach. But Shane was in Drew's car because of me, not because of a coin toss.

"Anyway, Mr. Abella wanted me to bring you this," he says, pulling a white envelope from his back pocket. "It's from All-State."

I reluctantly tear open the envelope, not caring what's inside. A laugh escapes my mouth as I unfold the letter and read it. I throw the paper on the ground.

"I got in," I say, hating the letter because there's only one person I want to celebrate with and he's not here. "If I didn't send you both that text . . . If I didn't audition, Shane would still be here."

Drew stares at me, but his eyes aren't accusatory, they're compassionate, like he understands how it feels to relentlessly beat yourself up for something you can never take back.

"It was my fault," I say, forcing the words from my lips.

"He was in your car because of *me*. Don't blame yourself for this. Don't blame a coin toss. If you're going to blame anyone, blame me."

Drew buries his face in his hands, then pulls his hair back. His eyes are wet.

"Don't say that." He sniffs in, his nose red. "Maybe it's no one's fault. Maybe one random thing leads to another and then another and sometimes it works out how you pictured, but other times . . ."

I inhale the biting winter air and push tears away from my eyes. Maybe it's not one thing that determines the trajectory of our lives. Maybe it's a million decisions and twists and turns that lead us to where we are.

I pick up the acceptance letter and turn it over in my hands. It feels like grief and regret. I chuck it back on the grass.

"I'm declining it. What's the point?"

"Don't do that." Drew picks up the paper, folds it in half, and places it on my lap. "Don't throw away your chances."

"I can't do it without him," I whisper, my throat closing.

Drew's eyes search my face.

"I miss him," I say.

"Was it him all along?" Drew asks, his deep voice strained. "Even in the beginning, before Ray?"

"It was both of you," I say, trying my best to explain it. "With you I kind of got lost, in good ways and bad ways. And sometimes I felt like I couldn't keep up. But with him—"

"It was easy." Drew's eyes shift to the grass again and he lets out a long breath. "It was always so easy to be around him."

The wind pushes Drew's hair off his face and wraps around me, slicing through my jacket. I hug my knees to my chest and blow into my purple gloves.

"I'm staying," I say. "In town. My dad's getting a local job."

"Figures." Drew shakes his head. "I'm going. My dad invited me to live with him through the summer. I think it would be good, you know. To get out of here, to be with him for a little. Shane always told me to give him a chance, to not take him for granted. And Shane was always right, about everything."

Shane was right. He knew it from such a young age when he lost his own father. This life, even this moment, is fleeting. Nothing is permanent no matter how tight you hold on. And that's the whole point, to live the hell out of what you have. It's the reason Shane was so easy to be with, the reason he raced around saving people's lives, and the reason he could pound out the most mind-altering drum solo. He didn't take any of it for granted.

Drew and me, we're only now beginning to understand.

"Are you going to be okay?"

"I don't know," Drew says, his eyes fixed on the grass. "Maybe one day, just not today."

"You can take it with you, you know?" I reach out and hold Drew's hand, because even though it's not right and we don't fit, we're still going to need each other. He glances at me, eyes tired.

"Take what with me?"

"Him," I say. "I moved my whole life and I never got it. Not until now. But wherever you go, you can take all of it with you."

"It's not the same," he says.

"But it's something."

Even though I'm not awake, I know it's a dream.

Shane sprawls out on my bed and I nestle in the crook of his arm. His fingers run through my hair slowly, and I grab his hand. He pulls my hand toward his chest and his heart beats steady, like a perfect rhythm he used to play.

"You tired?" he asks quietly.

"So tired, Shane. I can't sleep." I look into his golden eyes and I miss him so much it actually hurts. "Can you come back?" I squeeze his hand tight and he inches closer to me.

"I'm right here." His smile is warm, like he knows something I don't yet understand.

"But I miss you," I say, a little panicked that I'm going to wake up before I get to tell him. "Come back, okay?"

"I can't."

"Why not?"

"You know why not."

"Shane—" My voice cracks and I'm squeezing his hand so hard now, afraid if I let go, I'll wake up. He's starting to fade, like smoke from a chimney, and I know I have to tell him. "I love you. I think I've always loved you. Please come back. I need you to come back."

"I'm with you," he says, but I can barely see him. His voice softens to an echo and I lean closer.

"Come back to me." My lips graze his, but I can't feel anything. His hand slips from my grasp.

"I'm always with you," he whispers in my ear, and then . . . he's gone.

TAILS

CHAPTER 10

Stevie

MILLBROOK HOSPITAL

The calluses on Shane's hand scratch against my fingers. I squeeze his palm anyway, hoping for any kind of sensation in return, but he doesn't move. Even his pinky lies perfectly still. Everyone's asleep in the waiting room, and Drew left a few minutes ago to join them. The hospital room is quiet except for the machines until the overnight nurse pops in and flashes me a weak smile. She holds the IV bag, squinting at it, before unhooking it and replacing it with a new one. I scrutinize Shane's face, watching for a twitch or jolt, or anything that would mean he's somewhere in there. But, nothing.

"You okay, sweetie?" the nurse asks, washing her hands in the sink. She's young, maybe a few years older than Lainey, with blond hair pulled into a low ponytail. "It's late."

"Is he . . . does he know I'm here?"

"I'd like to think so. But there's no way to know for sure."

"He's going to wake up, right? They said he's stable and he's not technically in a coma anymore. They even took out his breathing tube. That's a good sign, right?" I ask, holding his hand tight and leaning into him, his breath on my cheek. The nurse doesn't answer.

"Get some rest, sweetie," she says before drying her hands on a paper towel and leaving the room.

Shane's chest moves in waves. The moon is high and bright, shining down on us from the corner window. Flowers displayed on the medicine cart cast an eerie shadow on the wall. Lainey had good intentions bringing them this morning, but they remind me of a funeral, and I don't want to think about funerals.

"Come back," I whisper in his ear, then shift my eyes to his face, holding my breath. Still, nothing. "Top three moments I wish I could do over. I'm too tired to think of five," I say, missing him so badly I can barely get the words out.

"One . . . the first day I met you. I barely paid attention to you. I should have paid more attention." My voice cracks and I swallow it back.

"Two . . . when you told me about the coin toss. I should've known it wasn't a bet or game. You're not like that. You're the last person on this planet who would be like that. And I shouldn't have ignored you and stayed mad at you for so long. I wasted too much time being mad." My eyes shift to the heart rate monitor and it peaks and valleys in the same pattern. No change.

"Three . . . I should have just tried out. You were right. I didn't need that red neck strap. I should have listened to you. If I had, you wouldn't be here, and we'd be in my room coming up with a much happier list."

I stop talking and stare at his face, forehead bandaged. He looks asleep, and then I swear an eyelash twitches, but it's dark and I can't be sure.

"I have another one," I say, my voice barely a whisper.

"It's not so much of a do-over as it is a regret. I wish I told you. Okay? I wish I would have told you, so you have to come back because I need to tell you."

His eyes flutter, his lids moving in tiny tremors, and I squeeze the hell out of his hand.

"Shane?"

His lids open slowly, and his eyes roll around, like they're trying to remember how to see.

"Shane?"

"Hey," he croaks out, his honey eyes focusing on me.

"Hi." I breathe in and out fast, and blink to make sure I'm not imagining this. He smiles slowly, his deep dimple appearing in his cheek. I press my lips to his hand and he brushes the side of my face as tears well in my eyes.

"Drew!" I yell into the hallway.

"You okay?" I whisper, and he nods. His eyes aren't scared, they're sure. Drew runs into the room and crouches beside the bed.

"You're awake? Buddy, you okay?" Drew eyes frantically search Shane's face.

"It's all good," Shane says, clearing his throat. Drew lets out a relieved breath. "I'm sorry I grabbed the wheel."

"I'm sorry I wasn't being more careful," Drew says, shaking his head.

"Stupid truck," Shane says. Drew laughs at this, and then Shane laughs too, wincing.

"You scared the crap out of me, Shane. Thank God you're awake." Drew lets out a long breath of air. "I'll go get Kathy and Lainey," he says, before heading for the waiting room.

Shane reaches for my hand and gives it a little squeeze.

"I need . . ." he says, slowly, quietly. ". . . to tell you too."

"To tell me what?" I lean close to him, grazing my lips on his.

"You *know*." He takes in a breath, too weak to kiss me, so I kiss him lightly. He winces again, but smiles. Of course I know. I've known all along and maybe even since the day we met. He squeezes my hand as tears fall to my cheeks, relief washing over me.

And he knows how I feel too, without me even saying the words.

But I tell him anyway because I'm not wasting another second.

And because all I care about is this moment.

The one I'm living in.

Right now.

Epilogue

AUGUST

It takes an instant to change course, to derail an intended destination or to lock into a dream. On that day, back in August, Drew and Shane weren't thinking about all the ways their lives were about to unfold. They were thinking about the chestnut-haired girl who appeared in their town and made them forget about every worry. As Drew flipped a penny into the air, Stevie was all they could see, both of them hoping the coin would land in their favor. At that very moment, Stevie was making her own plans, and playing the cards she was dealt—ones she had no control over. It was impossible to know the outcome, to ensure their own personal happily ever after. But they all tried anyway.

Shane pulled hard on Drew's boot, the penny concealed underneath, but Drew wouldn't budge. Shane squinted at him, shielding the sun with his hand. Rays of light streamed through his fingers and onto his cheeks as a light breeze floated through the air, the hint of a new season peeking around the corner.

"Come on, man, let's have it," Shane said, his voice impatient, silently willing the universe to choose him.

"Hold on." Drew shifted a little, careful to keep the coin hidden. "You're cool either way?"

Shane sighed. "I'm cool. Are you? Either way?"

"Always." Drew shook his hair out of his face.

"So, what are you waiting for?"

Drew slowly lifted his boot off the ground and crouched next to Shane, both of them examining the coin. Their eyes went wide as they stared at the penny and then at each other.

"Holy shit," Shane said.

Some call it fortune, some call it fate. It's neither. Every moment led to this, and this chance would lead to more moments, all stringing together a life. We chase every dream and reach for every imagined finish line. But it's not about the end.

The happily ever after is in the living.

Acknowledgments

First and foremost, this book is for a boy I once knew, a boy who flipped a coin and lost. I only knew him for a short period of time—too short, forever frozen at fifteen. And I always wanted to write him a better ending, the kind of ending he deserved.

So many talented people helped usher this novel into the world. I have immense gratitude for my incredible agent, Alex Rice. Her tenacity, insightful notes, and vision are invaluable. She is the strongest advocate and I am so thankful for her constant support. Thank you to the entire CAA team for championing this story. And many thanks to Dan Bodansky for passing my manuscript to Anthony Mattero at the beginning of this wild ride.

Alex Sehulster is a dream editor. Her notes are impeccable, and our brainstorming sessions are not only fun but inspiring. I adore working with Alex and I am so grateful for her guidance and always spot-on advice. The entire Wednesday Books team worked tirelessly to release this book into the hands of readers. I am so fortunate to work with top-notch design, production, marketing, publicity, audio, and support teams. Thank you from the bottom of my heart: Mara Delgado-Sanchez, Alexis Neuville, Meghan Harrington, Jonathan Bush, Anna Gorovoy, Jeremy Haiting, Melanie Sanders, Emily Dyer, and Amber Cortes.

Throughout the four years it took me to write *Where It All Lands,* so many gifted writers and readers critiqued its pages. Thank you for taking the time to read my words: Katherine Locke, Jennifer Walkup, Beverly Walley, Lauren Barth, Kristyn Friedlich, Rochelle Friedlich, Lynn Vande Stouwe, Cheryl Boxer, Jennifer Kessler, and Olivia Palker.

My Tuesday night writing group, Holly Rizzuto Palker, Sophia Freire, and Karen Jackson, are not only critique partners—they are friends and trusted confidantes, a bright spot in every week. Whether in person or on Zoom, I know I can always count on them for thoughtful notes, laughter, plentiful dark chocolate, and tea.

I met Erinn Salge through our shared love of writing, but now I can't go a day without texting her random thoughts. She is my opposite and yet in so many ways we are kindred spirits. Erinn read this novel through countless iterations. She always tells it like it is and I am so grateful for our friendship.

But it all started with Anne Ellen Geller and the Visual Ink Program, helping me navigate through one of the most challenging times in my life through words. I will never forget what Anne did for me and how working with her helped me heal.

Thank you to my entire family and friends—you know who you are. I am so grateful for your support and encouragement.

Debbie Baron offered to read this story in its infancy and made me believe I could publish it. Quite simply, she is my person. We met at twelve years old and she has been by my side ever since. I love my Jake and our enduring, decades-long, once-in-a-lifetime bond.

Brian Friedlich is my younger sibling, but in a lot of ways I look up to him. He is brilliant and funny, sometimes without realizing it, and his support means the world to me. Oh, and his smartest decision was marrying Kristyn Friedlich—she is the absolute best. I love them both more than words.

My father, Leo Friedlich, is me and I am him. We have always been on the same wavelength, thinking alike and laughing at the same jokes. He instilled in me an endless love of music, introducing me to all the greats, some of which grace the pages of this book. He is the opposite of the fathers in this story—the best listener, most loving, and a present father. I am so lucky he is mine.

My mother, Janet Friedlich, has read and believed in this story from the very beginning. I treasure our relationship and still ask her for advice even now that I have a family of my own. She is not only my mother but my friend, the most loyal person I have ever known. I cherish our daily chats and unwavering love for each other.

Duffy Wexler curled up by my side as I wrote this book, offering much-needed cuddle breaks. And although she doesn't say a word, she is the absolute best writing partner.

My best friend and husband, Adam Wexler, is a constant support of not only my writing, but every endeavor I choose to pursue. He has held me up during my lowest lows and cheered me on during my highest highs. He is the kindest soul and best karaoke partner. He never fails to make me laugh and I love him with all of my heart.

My son, Colin Wexler, is the greatest joy of my life. He is everything that is right with this world and my love for him is endless. Colin, if you're reading this, live for the moment, never lose your zest for adventure, and always pursue your dreams.